LEVIATHAN RISES
©2022 CRAIG MARTELLE

Aethon Books
www.aethonbooks.com

Print and eBook formatting by Steve Beaulieu. Artwork provided by Vivid Covers.

Published by Aethon Books LLC.

Aethon Books is not responsible for websites (or their content) that are not owned by the publisher.

To those who support any author by buying and reading their books, I salute you. I couldn't keep telling these stories if it weren't for you and for the support team surrounding me. No one works alone in this business.

SOCIAL MEDIA

Craig Martelle Social
Website & Newsletter:
https://www.craigmartelle.com

Facebook:
https://www.facebook.com/
AuthorCraigMartelle/

BATTLESHIP: LEVIATHAN TEAM INCLUDES

BETA / EDITOR BOOK

BETA READERS AND PROOFREADERS—WITH MY DEEPEST GRATITUDE!

Micky Cocker
James Caplan
Kelly O'Donnell
John Ashmore

The Main Players Within
Ambassador/Major Declan Payne
Executive Officer/Major Virgil Dank
Mrs. Ambassador/Lieutenant Mary "Dog" Morris/Payne
CEO Tech Inc/Tech Specialist 7 Katello Mateus "Blinky" Andfen
Tech Specialist 6 Laura "Sparky" Walker
Tech Specialist 6 Augry Byle

Tech Specialist 4 Salem "Shaolin" Shao
Tech Specialist 4 Huberta "Joker" Hobbes
Combat Specialist 7 Cointreau "Heckler" Koch
Combat Specialist 5 Marsha "Turbo" Skellig
COO Tech Inc/Combat Specialist 3 Alphonse "Buzz" Periq

To those who support any author by buying and reading their books, I salute you. I couldn't keep telling these stories if it weren't for you and for the support team surrounding me. No one works alone in this business.

[1]

"Sometimes the hardest fight is not in combat." –From the memoirs of Ambassador Declan Payne

"One H-bomb took care of the infestation on PX47 because the Ga'ee don't like water. Their foothold only consisted of the one rocky land mass," Major Declan Payne explained to the Mosquito pilots of Space Fighter Squadron 317, the Tricky Spinsters.

Major Woody Malone, the squadron's commanding officer, ground his teeth. Their job on this deployment was finished. The hangar bay wasn't its usual buzz of activity. Leviathan was getting a human-interfaced clean up following the battle with the Ga'ee.

"But Berantz lost four planets in their entirety and half of their homeworld where they've fought the Ga'ee to a stalemate. With Space Fleet committed to resupply, they should eventually be able to push the Ga'ee back."

"How's that going to work? Resupply, I mean?" Woody asked.

"We have to build a portal into the Berantz system, but it'll be at BD18, Brayalore, because we don't want to commit where the Ga'ee have a toehold in the system." Payne waved that the briefing was over. It had taken less than two minutes. He'd personally talked with each unit and their personnel to make sure everyone got the word.

On ships throughout history, "the word" was a many-headed hydra. Once unleashed, it morphed and changed. Became diabolical and destructive.

"The fight with the Ga'ee has been won for now. The seven races paid a steep price—humanity, the Ebren, the Rang'Kor, and especially the Berantz. They lost the most and are clinging to life by their fingernails. It's not pretty out there."

"You talk like the Ga'ee are coming back. Captain Pel'Rok and the rest of us handed them their asses. They ran away, hurt bad. They probably died halfway back to their home planet."

"Lev has analyzed their trajectory and found there are no planets within a billion light-years. That trail is cold. If they're going that far, they won't be a threat for generations to come, but we think they are going to adjust their course and reestablish themselves. What we saw on the Berantz homeworld was that they can establish a colony and start building ships within a month. They can return to space within a year."

"They have no drones left. They'll have to build more and then expand. It's an immense amount of work." Woody tried to find a reason to believe the Ga'ee would no longer be a threat to friendly space, but he knew the answer. Payne didn't have to articulate it.

The Ga'ee didn't care about the work. They'd do what they needed to do.

Then they'd be back in a new ten-kilometer-long carrier filled with a hundred thousand lethal drones so it could continue seeding the habitable planets.

With no regard for the seven races.

"We have to stop them," Payne stated.

The others hadn't followed his train of thought. Only Woody heard what Payne hadn't said.

"They'll be back," Woody confirmed. "We need to be ready. Better tactics, better missiles—and no mercy."

"The Ga'ee aren't a merciful race." Payne kicked at the deck. "Take some downtime, then polish the ships. Work with Lev to bring the squadron back up to full strength, even if you don't have the pilots. We're going back to Earth and will recruit some more."

Woody looked over his shoulder as his pilots milled about their ships, talking among themselves.

"How long do we have?" Woody asked.

"Straight to the point. A year, more or less. *Leviathan* is ready now, but not really. We need eyes and ears everywhere. A picket for the entirety of friendly space. That's a tall order, but not if we can get them the FTL communication code. That'll help us respond in force. Also, we gotta get those portals built. The one near Earth took a whole year, but it was the first. Our dreadnoughts are going to become construction haulers over the near term to get the builder ships in place."

"Is that the best use of the big boys? They need to train and be ready for the fight."

"That would be my choice, too, but we have limited assets and too much work to do. If they train, then the portals don't get built, and we'll lose whole planets waiting for a counterattack force to arrive. We need all the shipyards to max their production starting right now."

"Listen to you talk like an admiral. If I didn't know better, I'd think I was talking with someone bucking for promotion. Like being a major isn't good enough."

Payne snorted, but he couldn't laugh. The situation weighed

heavily on him. Lev would be the first one to reach Earth. He would help Major Payne tell them what happened.

He was afraid they wouldn't listen. "It'd be nice if I could wave a magic wand and get people to do the right thing, but just convincing Earth's new leadership of the reality of the Ga'ee will be a challenge. At least we have lots of video to draw on. Lev and my team are working on a twenty-second video to shock their consciences, then a follow-up five minutes of more detailed footage to show them what we're up against."

Woody nodded solemnly before shaking Payne's hand. "Go get 'em, Dec. Get me some more pilots. I could use fifteen, make sure we have a few in reserve. Our track record is better than most, but we still suffered fifty percent losses. The Ga'ee aren't like anything we've ever faced before."

"They most definitely are not." Payne headed for where Combat Specialist "Heckler" Koch and his wife, Combat Specialist Marsha "Turbo" Skellig, were animatedly addressing the maintenance team.

"That wriggler smeared silicon snot on my foot while I was trying to stomp the shit out of it. There I was, pinning it with one foot," he mimicked stomping with one foot on the other, "but it wasn't working. I fired my rail cannon. Damn near blasted my foot off, but this was life or death!" He waved his hands like a lunatic before taking aim with a make-believe gun and blasting at his own foot.

The watchers gasped. "This fucker refused to die," Turbo interjected. "It slimed its way up his leg," she pointed out the path in meticulous detail, "until it got to his arm, where it started to eat. The. Fucking. Suit!"

Heckler picked up the narrative without missing a beat. "So, Mars shoots the bastard off my arm like Annie-fucking-Oakley! Pow, pow, pow." He pointed his finger at his arm and stabbed with each verbal shot.

"It flew off, and Heckler stitches it with his railgun. We each grab a side and pull the thing in two. It's still fighting us!" She ripped at the air before her, then tossed her make-believe prize to the deck.

"I blast the insides with my cannon, and now we're seeing progress. The thing is not liking having its guts ripped out. Mars hits the other side, then the Berantz hand me a plasma torch."

Turbo demonstrated activating the torch, complete with hissing sounds as it came to life.

"They can't stand the heat, so they had better stay out of Koch's Kitchen! The two halves of the thing shriveled up. Dead! Finally."

Heckler and Turbo caught Payne choking while trying to listen to their story. "Here's Major Payne." Heckler grabbed Payne by the arm and pulled him close. "We have to go underwater, ten thousand fathoms deep, after one of those drones that got away. This fucker..."

"Major," Payne corrected.

"Major Payne, in their ass, finds a fish that swallowed the ship! So, we hit it. It's dragging the major across the ocean bottom. It swallows one of our people whole! No shit. We were there and seen it with our eyes. Joker starts stabbing it. The major is clinging to the outside, trying to ride it like he's some sort of space cowboy."

Turbo jumped in. "Heckler is stabbing away at the thing's head. No railguns underwater, so we're carrying tridents like King *Fucking* Neptune!"

"We beat the thing into submission, and then we ate it," Payne offered. "You two. You're needed on the bridge." Payne gestured with his chin toward the door.

Heckler gave him the thumbs-up. "Gotta watch yourselves around the wrigglers. They'll kill you ugly. Good luck guys. Bring the Payne!"

The two hurried toward a cart waiting near the door.

"Heckler," Payne called in a normal tone of voice.

The combat specialists stopped when they were close enough to escape if need be.

"Was there anything you told those people that was true?"

"Absotively! The Ga'ee will kill you ugly. That's the bald-faced, bare-assed truth."

Payne chuckled. "I'll give you that. You and Turbo don't get to back-brief anyone ever again."

Heckler closed on the major and hugged him. "Thank you for that. I was worried we'd have to repeat the show, and who's got that kind of energy?"

"You were loving it," Payne replied.

"Not in the least, sir. No love at all. Are we needed on the bridge? We'd rather go to the range."

"No need for you two on the bridge. Go to the range and find me something that'll kill a Ga'ee with one shot."

Turbo pointed at Kal'faxx, the ever-present Ebren warrior. He had been watching from a position in the shadows. "The plasma cannon would have worked, but it got destroyed on the way down."

"If you're not careful, you two knuckleheads will be hauling plasma cannons for a living. Twice the work for half the pay."

"That's downright unneighborly, Major. To think I gave up a career in extreme sports to put up with this kind of abuse," Turbo protested.

Payne looked down his nose at her. "Career. The Vestrall aren't the extreme sports types."

"But we got to do a lot of shooting," Heckler countered. "If you don't mind, Major? We'd love to stand here and chew the fat, but those weapons aren't going to fire themselves. The one we really want hasn't been invented yet, but it will be soon enough. Come on, Lev. We got work to do."

Turbo jumped into the cart first, and Heckler dove in after her, pulling her in for a kiss. They appeared to be punching each other's mid-sections as the cart drove away.

"That is the most screwed-up relationship I've ever seen," Payne muttered to himself.

Kal joined him. "I don't know what they see in each other besides a mirror of themselves."

"That sounds horrible when you put it that way, Kal."

"Truth is stranger than fiction, pardner," the Ebren drawled.

"Lev, can you just update the whole crew at one time and beam my brief into everyone's brain?" The artificial intelligence used telepathy to deal with the flesh-and-blood entities that populated the ship.

"Of course, Declan. I would have suggested it, but you seemed so happy taking on the burden of talking with a thousand people personally."

"It made sense until what I saw from Heckler and Turbo."

"They think briefings are boring," Lev replied.

"That much is obvious, Lev. Their desire to spice things up added no value. 'Annie Oakley.' How many Fleet personnel know who she is?"

Lev didn't reply. He wouldn't have known who she was except for the images in the minds of Heckler and Turbo. Davida Danbury, a human integrated with the ship, hadn't known about trivial things like historical figures. Her role was more technical and mutually supporting for an individual like Leviathan, who needed the company of others to keep him grounded. He hadn't known how much he needed it until he let humanity through the airlock and inside the great ship.

"No matter," Payne continued. "Can you tell me where Mary is and maybe Virgil, too?"

"Mary is on the bridge with Harry and Nyota, and Virgil is with the administration team one level down." Mary Payne had been Mary Morris when she was first foisted on him and his team by Fleet when they returned to Earth during the campaign against the Vestrall. He'd had no choice but to accept her onto the team.

She'd tried to prove she deserved to be there by working harder than anyone else, but her role in the show *Bikinis in Paradise* hadn't prepared her to be a Space Operations Force Teammate, a SOFTie, despite personally working toward that goal.

She kept getting injured and spent a great deal of time in the med lab getting fixed up. Her injury on BD18, Brayalore, had been the last straw. Even though it had been an unlucky friendly fire attack, she'd felt she was holding the team back. Since she was now married to the team leader, she'd decided it would be best if she took on a supporting role. Wearing a massive scar as her badge of honor, she bowed out.

Mary Payne, team logistics. She had been working with Lev, designing and outfitting *Ugly 5,* the team's stealthy insertion craft.

Major Virgil Dank was the executive officer of Team Payne. He should have been working with the team on fitness. Some of the members had been hard-pressed to return from their days as soft civilians, Payne included. Dank was in the administration section. Payne still had not met Virgil's girlfriend. It was okay that the XO took time for himself.

But the lack of fitness had been three months ago. Since then, their universe had been turned upside-down. Getting regular and healthy meals had been beneficial, along with establishing a workout routine.

The team was getting back in fighting shape.

They would be taking on an enemy they still weren't sure how to fight. All they could do was prepare for the last battle since they had no idea what the next would look like.

"Lev, take me to the bridge, please. I need to talk with the admiral."

[2]

"When the time comes, make the time." –From the memoirs of Ambassador Declan Payne

"Payne, my boy," Fleet Admiral Harry Wesson called. Payne strolled onto the bridge. Only half the positions were filled. After the last engagements, and given the relative peace of the moment, the admiral had assigned the crew minimal work hours. A quarter of the crew served for twelve hours at a time. That meant thirty-six hours off between shifts.

It gave the more than one thousand hands on board *Leviathan* time off to rebuild and recharge their bodies. The workout facilities on each deck were occupied, and humans strolled through the gardens with great frequency. The corridors had more people walking rather than riding carts.

With a five-kilometer-long ship and more than forty decks, a thousand people did little to fill the spaces. The emptiness seemed greater since most humans were contained on three sparsely filled decks, but even a few were more than none.

Lev was happy for the company.

"Admiral, Commodore, wife," Payne greeted.

Two of those present snickered while Mary smiled and gave Declan the hairy eyeball. "Asswipe," she replied.

"Marital bliss!" Nyota declared.

Payne softened. It was, but he had the universe to save. If not from the Ga'ee, then from the powers that were misguiding the seven races. He wondered how he had lost that authority, which had been granted solely to him by the Braze Collective and his victory over the Vestrall. The only ones who didn't accept his role were the humans. They were happy to keep him in a subservient position as the ambassador. It sounded impressive, but by keeping him on Vestrall Prime, they had eliminated his ability to influence the Braze Collective or humanity.

"When are we going back to Earth?" Payne asked after wrapping his arm around Mary's waist and hugging her to his side.

"Any time now. I'm not in a big hurry, but we have to go." The admiral looked around, then leaned close to Payne. "You see, I was never reinstated to the military. I usurped this position, and everyone just went along with it. I expect if I return to Earth, I'll be arrested. Me and Nyota both."

Payne chuckled before shaking his head. "Changes nothing. We have to go back and report what happened here and rally support for building the ships we need to counter the next Ga'ee invasion."

The admiral nodded solemnly.

"And," Payne said, "as long as you stay on board *Leviathan*, Earth can't touch you. Lev will protect you. This is sovereign Godilkinmore territory. You wouldn't let us paint a big Fleet flag on the side, would you, Lev?"

"No flags," the AI confirmed.

"There you have it. One big *fungu* to those who won't accept you as our Fleet admiral." Payne's mind raced. He wouldn't tolerate politicians being hostile to Admiral Wesson.

11

The admiral shrugged. "Nyota and I will remain on the ship. That is the least confrontational solution, but someone is going to have to convince humanity to build ships. That will be you two."

Mary pointed at herself. "Why me?"

The admiral and the commodore looked at each other in confusion, then faced the Paynes once more.

"Because you two have the look humanity appreciates. They'll listen to you."

Mary raised an eyebrow.

"Show them your scar," Payne urged.

"No." Mary glared at him.

He laughed in reply. "We'll wow them together. We better practice our shtick." Payne stared into the distance while flexing. "Got a dollar to save humanity? Give it to us."

"Exactly like that, Major Payne, except completely different. You better get to work since we'll be there soon."

"Do we want to fold directly into Earth's space?" Lev asked.

The admiral looked around. "We have a bunch of fighters in case Earth is miffed about our last departure. But yes. We'll transmit the report of our engagement with the Ga'ee. We'll end with the carrier ship transitioning to FTL while on fire."

"Hurt but not dead. An injured animal that may see itself backed into a corner. I'd like to think there was another way, but there wasn't. The best we could do was drive them off for now. There's no way they're gone for good."

"I concur, Declan. They will reconstitute. As long as there is even one survivor, they can rebuild their species. Each of them contains the sum total of their knowledge. The Godilkinmore were masters of DNA, and they inserted certain coding into humanity's genetic material, but never anything so audacious as all the knowledge," Lev explained. "That was masterful, even though it has been a formula for genocide."

"We will fight them with everything we have to prevent the complete destruction of the seven races. We need portals to each of the Braze Collective's home planets, and we need a fleet of ships that can stand toe to toe with those bastards." Payne pounded a fist into his hand.

Admiral Wesson smiled. "That's the passionate delivery of a message humanity can rally around shoved right down the throats of Earth's leaders."

———

"Stand by to be boarded," a tense voice warned.

The tactical screen showed a cruiser and a frigate, both squawking Blue Earth Protectorate identifiers. Commodore Freeman should have recognized the captain's voice, but she didn't. She'd been gone from the BEP for less than a year and a half. Anyone coming up the ranks would have passed through her office at some point.

She stood tall in her BEP uniform and replied, "You will do no such thing. This is Commodore Freeman, formerly of the BEP. We will not fire on an Earth ship, but you'll not have access to *Leviathan* unless we agree." She waited for a moment before adding, "Period."

"Earth Authority has declared you as possibly hostile. We are ordered to determine your intentions and loyalties," the voice replied. The captain still had not shown himself.

A voice blasted into their minds. *I am* Leviathan *of Godilk-inmore. You have no standing to demand access to me. I and I alone determine who boards this ship. I see in your minds that you fear me. As you should! Stand down, Malcolm. You will wait for three days so you can appreciate your place in the galaxy. You are not at the top of the food chain. Humanity is very far from it. In the interim, prepare to be boarded. The leader of the seven races is coming to you, and he's bringing a contingent that you will receive and to whom you will give your highest honors.*

"Or we could just do that," Payne said. "Way to go, Lev. Give 'em the high, hard one. By the way, when did we agree to leave *Leviathan*? Those squirrely fuckers could arrest us."

"They will not. Their orders were to harass us, nothing more. Well, there was one more thing, but it doesn't really apply."

"Lev, buddy, don't throw that juicy tidbit out there and think we aren't going to pounce on it like two Cabrizi on a beef bone."

"They have arrest warrants for Harry and Nyota, but since they aren't leaving the ship, it is a moot point, is it not?"

"Thanks, Lev," the admiral deadpanned. "Never has there been such a warm welcome."

"We'll clear that up," Payne promised. "Who's going ashore?"

Mary raised her hand and waggled her fingers.

"I'd be mighty proud to ride at your side," Kal drawled. "And my posse, too." He wrestled briefly with the Cabrizi, massive dog-like creatures with vicious fangs that Payne rescued from an Ebren space station. They'd taken a liking to him and Mary before Kal joined them. Cabrizi were the property of the influential and wealthy on Ebren, a status symbol. Kal had never entertained the idea of having them until Payne had beaten him unconscious and then asked him to look after them. They'd bonded with him, too. The Cabrizi ran into the corridor ahead of the Ebren.

"Fuck it. I'm taking the whole team. Lev, have Team Payne join me in the starboard hangar bay. We'll take *Ugly 5*."

"Might I suggest leaving Katello and Alphonse behind? We are still working on decrypting the neural transmissions between the Ga'ee. And if I may be so bold…"

Payne waited, but Lev waited longer.

"Lev, you have never hesitated to be bold, so what's on your mind?"

"They could surreptitiously enter Earth's digital systems and remove unwanted certificates, information, and *warrants*."

"You want them to hack into Earth's records and delete the arrest warrants. That *is* bold, Lev!"

"I can't agree to that," the admiral said. "We understood what we were doing. Should we choose to return to Earth proper, we'll face our punishment."

Payne chuckled. "Good thing you're not in charge. The leader of the seven races requests Lev's assistance in helping Blinky and Buzz kill those ridiculous warrants. While they're at it, they're going to restore the admiral's and the commodore's status as active. End of story."

Declan Payne walked away, waving over his shoulder on his way to the corridor. He held Mary's hand with the other hand. They walked lightly, as if they had not a care in the world.

While the entirety of the human race was counting on them to save humanity from itself.

Kal and the Cabrizi waited in one cart while Mary and Declan jumped in a second. Lev controlled the carts as part of his telepathic link with all flesh-and-blood entities who were on board the ship. He was also able to project a short distance, as evidenced by what he had just done with the BEP cruiser. The other ship's systems were idling while he recharged.

It took three days for the ship to do that after he transferred between two points instantly as if a two-dimensional universe had folded back on itself, warping space-time.

It drained every bit of energy from him before functionality to the ship returned. In between, he was left with bluster and embarked units to defend himself. He generally folded into a spot three days' faster-than-light travel from their ultimate destination in the middle of interstellar space, where there was only a remote possibility of an enemy accidentally stumbling across the great ship.

For Earth, Lev assessed the risk as low to non-existent that *Leviathan* would be threatened. The hostile stance of the BEP had been unexpected.

Lev sent the carts to the hangar bay, where Team Payne waited near their equipment cage.

"Do we get to blast some BEPers?" Heckler asked.

"No preemptive blasting, as much as you might like to. No suits, but arm up. I don't trust these people. All of you are here to protect Mary and me. Don't shoot unless they shoot first or if they try to take us into custody."

"What if they don't call you 'leader of the seven races?' Can we kill them then?" Heckler pushed.

"No killing them unless they try to kill you first."

"Sir, you're confusing me. Are we supposed to protect you or ourselves? The best way to protect me and Mars is to not go over there in the first place. Is that an option?"

Payne blinked quickly as he tried to internalize Heckler's arguments and finally settled for something less confrontational. He pumped his fist and pointed at *Ugly 5*. "All aboard!"

Kal called the Cabrizi to him. Blinky and Buzz waved while backing away.

Payne stabbed a finger at them. "Don't get caught."

"Caught doing what?" Blinky tried to look innocent.

"And don't you forget it." Mary gave them two thumbs-up. She and Payne strolled to the latest version of the stealthy insertion craft. Payne and his team had a tendency to leave wrecked uglymobiles scattered across the galaxy, but each new variant was better than the one before. *Ugly 5* was the biggest one yet, carrying extra armaments as well as a full team's worth of gear as a backup. They wouldn't be without boots should they go in for another hard landing.

Major Dank counted the heads. "Ten on board. Ten ready to go," he reported.

"Take us to the cruiser, Lev," Payne ordered. "Please."

The ship's sides levered down into place to seal the ship, restoring its original egg shape. It lifted into the air and squeezed through the minimal opening of a hangar cutout designed specifically for *Ugly 5*. The ship transitioned to space without a bump or a bounce.

They flew slowly across the intervening distance.

"This is the shuttle carrying his supreme preeminence, the leader of the seven races. Prepare to receive by opening your cargo bay door," Joker announced, using the insertion craft's comm system.

Payne closed his eyes and held a hand over his heart. "You people are going to be the death of me," he muttered.

"You need to fill that role if we're going to leverage these people to take us to Earth."

"An official escort." Payne shrugged. "I mean, I deserve it and all..."

That earned him a sharp elbow in the ribs.

"Shuttle, this is *Ephesus*. The door is open. Welcome."

"It worked. I'll be damned!" Joker exclaimed. "I should have asked for hot cloths to wash off the rigors of the trip. I mean, we were trapped in here for a good fifteen minutes."

Payne gestured for silence. "Once we break this door open, it's all business. I don't trust these people, but I need to win them over to our side. They should be believers by the time we arrive on Earth. Everyone we run into has to know about the threat. If the Ga'ee show up in Earth's space, we'd lose our homeworld."

"That's no joke," Joker added. "We're with you, sir."

17

Turbo and Heckler looked at each other.

Payne fixed them with an unblinking stare. "Don't you reprise your grand storytelling. Stick with the videos."

"And we don't get to kill anyone. Will there be *anything* worth doing on this trip?" Heckler asked, throwing his hands up in surrender.

"Sorry. We're going to have to do the down-and-dirty grind. You know, the usual. Fun won't be had until we return to *Leviathan*. You know Earth doesn't have any weapons worth firing compared to what we have back home."

"Home," Mary murmured.

Heckler and Turbo pulled out their Desert Eagles, forty-five caliber slug-throwers from an earlier time. The rest of the team showed theirs.

"Hand cannons for us enlisted types," Heckler verified.

The ship touched down. They waited until *Ugly 5* verified that the outer air was pressurized and breathable, then both side walls popped and retracted. Declan Payne walked off first, with Mary close behind.

The others followed them off the ship, with Virgil Dank bringing up the rear. Turbo and Heckler fanned out to the sides, so they could see what was in front of them, but it wasn't alarming.

Three officers stood at attention next to a boatswain, who blew a whistle to announce the arrival of the leader of the seven races. At least the tradition of piping the side had continued.

"Bring the Payne," Mary whispered.

[3]

"Act like you belong even if you don't." –From the
memoirs of Ambassador Declan Payne

"Payne" was how he started his introduction. He continued,
"Leader of the seven races," and held out his hand to the ship's
captain.

The captain sneered. "Major Payne."

"Is that the game you want to play?" Payne asked. "You
were a toddler, whatever the fuck your name is, but then you
grew up. I *was* Major Payne at one point, but then I took my
team on the greatest warship ever built, out there," he pointed
toward space, "to save humanity from a threat that would have
overwhelmed us.

"We stopped a war that had been fought for a generation, or
have you forgotten about the battle for Earth? That wasn't even
two years ago. Shame on you. You call yourself a professional
military man?"

The captain recoiled, and his face warped through a series
of emotions. "I supported that battle from Earth."

"How?" Payne asked. The Cabrizi broke free from Kal's grasp and started running.

"Don't make any sudden moves, and they won't bite you," Mary warned with a wink.

The captain shifted nervously, glancing at the Cabrizi before addressing Payne. "By making sure the people serving on those ships were suited for service in the BEP and that their records were up to date."

Payne held his hand up, fingers spread wide to keep his team from commenting or even making faces. "That is one of the things we're here to discuss. We need logistics and personnel support for a battle that is coming, and it could come all the way to Earth. I need you to take us to Earth's leadership. Or just get us close, and we'll take our own ship."

"That is an..." the captain searched for the word, "interesting vessel."

"That design has saved our lives on multiple occasions. You didn't see us coming, did you, even though you painted the space around this ship with the best systems you have?"

The captain shook his head before dropping his eyes to the deck. "I'm new to space, but I have been with the BEP for a long time. The experienced space types have moved on."

"We can talk about that later, but we have to get the machinery turning. We need to focus the world on what happened in Berantz space and what is coming."

"Follow me," the captain directed.

Mary whistled, then yelled at the Cabrizi in Ebren. Kal berated them in his native tongue until, properly cowed, they rejoined the group.

"Stop being buttholes!" Payne growled in English.

"Do they respond to that?" the captain asked.

"Never, but I feel obligated to tell them anyway. They don't speak English, which gives them a reason to ignore me," Payne explained.

The captain smiled, losing his hard-nosed façade. It wasn't a look he could pull off. He was an admin type, not a warship captain used to playing poker with the worst the universe had to offer.

"What's your name, Captain?" Payne asked.

"LeClerc. Yes, that's my real name."

"Captain LeClerc. Nice to meet you." Payne offered his hand, and the two shook. "This is my team, starting with my wife..."

Payne introduced the group. The captain looked at Mary with a faint hint of recognition but shook it off to look up at the Ebren warrior.

"I've never met an Ebren in person before. I'm honored. I see why you are great warriors."

"Y'all are sweet," Kal drawled. "When it comes to the fight, I used to be the champion of all Ebren. Then Declan Payne came along and put a whoopin' on my ass that still stings. He's the champion now."

The captain's eye twitched.

"That's a story for a different day, LeClerc. Until then, let's contact Earth Central and see how we can drop in...to see..." Payne stopped. "I admit that I haven't been on Earth in so long that I don't know who's in charge or where they work."

"President Sinkhaus is headquartered at the United Nations in New York City. Nothing has changed in a long time."

"Sinkhaus? Is that his real name?"

"Her name, and yes. What's the issue?"

Payne didn't explain. He fought to keep from laughing. "Let me introduce the rest of my team. Heckler, Turbo, Joker, Byle, Sparky, Shaolin, and Virgil Dank."

"Now it's my turn. Those are their real names?"

"Heavens, no. That's how they are known. If the bad guys learned their real names, the entirety of civilization might collapse. Now, we have other fish to fry. What is the current status of shipbuilding?"

LeClerc glanced at Team Payne before answering, "The Ceres shipyard is building FTL-capable freighters as fast as possible, last I heard."

Payne sucked a breath through his teeth. "That's probably not going to work for us. We need to build four portals, starting with BD18 in Berantz space. We can't take a year to build them like we did this one. We need to have all four in place and functioning in eleven months or earlier."

"I'm not the one to talk to about that," the captain admitted. "After we get you on a shuttle to Earth, we'll return to our patrol."

"You'll want to stay far away from *Leviathan*. You should advise the other BEP ships in the area. Your intent to arrest Fleet Admiral Wesson and Commodore Freeman is unacceptable and borders on making you an enemy of the greatest warship ever built."

The captain tried to control his expression, but he had no ability to hide his emotions.

"You're thinking, how did we know? You don't get to find out. Just understand that we know what you're trying to hide. Subterfuge doesn't become you, LeClerc. You don't have the temperament for it. Be proud of that *flaw* in your personality."

The captain nodded while staring straight ahead. They reached the bridge in the middle of the ship, which was the best location to improve the survivability of the ship's most experienced hands. Then again, with the promotion of a paper pusher into the captain's chair, the survivorship axiom no longer held true. Highest ranked, yes, but most experienced?

No. Not this time.

Payne wanted to drill into the man to find out how such a thing could happen. How the experienced hands had retired or resigned in droves, leaving the defense of Earth to greenhorns.

"Bring the shuttle to *Ephesus* and leave the rest to us."

"It's already here, attached to the port airlock."

"We'll go there straight away," Payne replied. He hadn't even gone onto the bridge.

Mary stepped up. "Give me a comm link to the surface, to the UN. I'll coordinate the final details of the visit to make sure it is conducted at the appropriate level. And a second link for our communications specialist."

The captain leaned through the hatch to the bridge and snapped his fingers. One of the crew ran to him and handed him two earpieces with boom microphones.

"How quaint," Mary replied when the captain gave one to her. Joker reached out to take the other. Mary wrapped it over her ear. "Testing, testing, one, two, one, two."

"Yes, ma'am, I hear you loud and clear," a voice replied.

"Who do I have the pleasure of talking with?" Mary asked.

"Specialist McGuinness," came the reply. "I just gave you the earpiece."

"How about you connect me with Earth, Specialist? The UN, protocol office." Mary tilted her head sideways and looked at Declan in exasperation.

They had barely started this trip.

"Our patience has grown remarkably short," Payne whispered. "We need to get used to this because it's only going to get worse."

Mary patted his face with one hand. "These are the times that try our souls."

"Ma'am?" the captain wondered.

"We try to keep things light because the life-or-death thing can wear you down. We're playing the long game. No sense in stressing out over little things, am I right?"

"Yes, ma'am."

Mary stood taller, but once connected, she was all business. "Delegation of ten, headed by the leader of the seven races. The team is armed and will remain armed throughout the meeting. The team also has their protective animals for an added layer of safety for the leader. You will accommodate all, two bowls with water and two with meat. Burger or steak is fine, about five pounds each."

Payne listened casually as Mary put the Cabrizi before the humans. Then she detailed the rest of what she wanted to happen to best set up the visit for success. His attention waned as he tried to focus on swaying those who had no interest in what he had to say.

The fate of humanity depended on how persuasive he could be.

———

The shuttle landed on the roof of the new United Nations Headquarters building. The wide, squat edifice filled an entire block and looked nothing like the skyscrapers that surrounded it.

The team disembarked. Kal watched the receiving delegation carefully—young people, good-looking by human standards. Not the leadership.

Mary and Joker hurried ahead of the team. Payne took his time.

The Cabrizi were less than pleased by their arrival on the top of a building. The wind whistled between the surrounding structures, adding to their discomfort. They howled miserably and pulled. Kal maintained his grip, his fingers digging deep into the hair on their necks. Payne took control of one.

"I'm beginning to think we shouldn't have brought them."

Kal vigorously shook his head. "They are part of your entourage as the new Ebren champion. They have been with you through the hardest times, and they are part of your aura as the leader of the seven races."

"As are you, my friend. We'll make it work." Payne leaned down to talk softly to the Cabrizi. The tone of voice was as important as the words. Kal took a knee beside Payne. The team took positions around them, securing the space as the escorts watched.

After scratching behind their ears and calming them, Payne and Kal stood and continued. Heckler and Turbo made room for them to walk through.

"Always trust a person who loves dogs," the head of the reception committee stated. "My name is Paragon Virtue, and yes, that's what my parents named me. If you'll follow us, we have a banquet hall set up for you and your good boys."

Payne nodded. "I'm Declan Payne, and this is my team. They'll go wherever I go, for reference, and they'll remain armed no matter what your rules are."

"You have a waiver. There will be no holdups or efforts to break up your group. If anything happens, it will be wholly unintentional."

Payne stopped. "You can tell a politician is lying because their lips are moving. Your job is to make sure we aren't separated in any way. If that happens, intentional or not, people are going to get hurt, maybe even killed. Here's the clear guidance. Do not separate me from my people. You're to make sure that every individual in this building knows that and knows beyond a shadow of a doubt that were such a situation to happen, it wouldn't last for long. Do I make myself understood?"

"Yes, sir," the aide replied, uncomfortable about using the military designation. Whoever had coached him had probably served. In their parlance, "Sir" was a pejorative. In Payne's, it was a sign of respect for the rank and the position.

"Don't fuck with us," Heckler added. Payne silenced him with a quick look.

"Lead on, Paragon," Payne directed. Mary raised an eyebrow. Declan took her hand with a smile, and they walked through the doors. There were stairs on one side of the entryway and a small elevator on the other. Virtue looked at them. "The answer's easy."

Paragon glanced at the stairs and the elevator.

"We don't split up," Payne reminded him.

"But it's seven stories down."

"We'll never get there if we don't start." Payne gestured at Kal. "We'll get ourselves there."

He strode boldly to the stairs' door and attempted to open it, but it was locked.

"I don't have the key," Virtue admitted. The look on his face suggested he was neck-deep in the dilemma and saw no way out.

"Really? You're going to make me tell you how to do your job? Call some-fucking-body to open the fucking door!" Payne snarled.

Virtue held up his hands.

"Don't tell me. None of you dumbasses have a phone with you." He motioned at Joker.

"Got it." She linked through the shuttle's comm system and called the main information line for the UN building. "I've got Paragon Virtue here. He is attempting to escort the leader of the seven races, and he's locked us on the roof. Can you send someone to unlock the door, please? To the stairs, not the elevator. Our delegation is too large to fit in the elevator. Yes, we know it's seven flights. No, that doesn't bother us. Please hurry. You're driving the leader into a rage. Pretty soon, humanity will have an eighth chair at a table for the seven races, and it will be one hundred percent Paragon Virtue's fault. Yes, I know that's his real name. It's quite the misnomer, don't you think?"

Virtue watched, mortified by the exchange. The two with him had shrunk against the wall and were trying not to look at anyone.

"So, do you meet many delegations on the roof?"

"You're the first," Virtue admitted. "Are all the delegations like this?"

Mary answered, "Assume they are and be ready for all contingencies. Ambassador Payne instructed the UN that he was bringing his entire team. You failed to plan for the contingencies that created."

He nodded. "You look familiar."

"My name is Mary Payne. You can call me Mrs. Ambassador."

Virtue winced. "I'm screwing this up, aren't I?"

"No. Whoever assigned someone inexperienced showed us exactly what they think of our delegation and the leader of the seven races. That's all. It's what we expected, I'm ashamed to say. Do they have food for the Cabrizi? If nothing else, they can get a meal out of it. Don't beat yourself silly over this. You were set up to fail."

He stared at the wall before the lightbulb went off. "*Bikinis in Paradise.*" He smiled in a way that made Payne want to punch him.

"That was a long time ago," Mary replied.

"They play reruns every night. Still popular. I don't know why it took me so long. Do you do any modeling?"

"What?" Payne retorted, but Mary patted his arm.

"I'm the partner of the leader of the seven races, and before you say I married my way to the top, understand that I didn't join Team Payne. I was sent there as a publicity stunt, but Declan Payne put me to work. I spent a lot of time in the hospital recovering. I have a scar that goes from here," she pointed at her breastbone and then drew a line, "around to here where I was almost cut in half by a Berantz bomb. If you persist in this line of questioning, I'll have to beat you senseless."

"You go, girl," Turbo muttered.

Virtue looked from face to face, noting how many women Payne had on his team. "You guys stopped the Vestrall?"

"This lot and two more who are working on a project with *Leviathan*."

The sound of someone running up the steps drew their attention to the still-locked door.

"I understand. On behalf of the United Nations, I apologize for any inconvenience or discomfort that I've caused in your arrival."

The door popped open to reveal an out-of-breath security guard. He held the door. Payne tipped his chin to the man and walked through, with Mary and Kal close behind. The Cabrizi ran through and started down the stairs.

"Hold on!" the guard called when Heckler tried to follow. "No weapons."

"Paragon!" Payne yelled. "You slimy, lying sack of shit."

"*No!* I swear. You have a waiver. This is the delegation of the leader of the seven races," Virtue explained.

"This pack of clowns?" the guard snapped before slapping a hand over his face.

"Get the fuck outta my way." Heckler elbowed him on his way past.

The others glared first at Virtue and then at the guard as they continued past. Dank, the last one through, shoved the guard into the area beyond and closed the door behind him. The group could arrive at the bottom floor via the elevator without those in their charge.

Payne whistled on his way down the stairs.

"Why are you so happy?" Mary wondered.

"I have to say that I like fucking with bureaucrats more than beating other enemies, but that was the warmup. The real challenge is up ahead. Still, we'll take each victory as it comes."

Seven stories to the ground floor. They walked out to find Virtue and the two other escorts waiting. The security guard was nowhere to be seen.

"Did he get fired?" Payne quipped.

"As a matter of fact, he did. No one calls any official delegation a 'pack of clowns.' That's not acceptable."

"Even if it's true?"

Once again, Paragon Virtue was stumped for how to answer.

"*Especially* if it's true," Mary offered. "Although that doesn't apply to us, not as far as you know."

Virtue tried to smile but couldn't pull it off. He had been taken out of his routine and was on his heels. In a boxing match, he'd be down for the count.

"This way," he offered and led the team down a wide hallway and through swinging doors of the type that separated a kitchen from a dining room before turning into a large hall half-filled with people dressed in their best formal attire. Payne looked at his team, which, like him, were wearing their shipboard jumpsuits.

"I didn't quite think this through all the way," Payne whispered.

"We don't have dress clothes," Mary replied.

"We do. You had some made."

"*We*," she emphasized, twirling her finger to take in the whole team.

Understanding dawned on him. "Yes. *We*." He shook the cobwebs from his brain. He kept reverting to the smoke-and-joke version of himself, the personality that had saved his life and sanity through the long war.

He stopped and pulled the group close. The Cabrizi whined at the unfamiliarity and strange smells. "Gametime, people. No comments. Save them for later when we can laugh in peace. Until then, nothing untoward, and that includes me. We need humanity to fire up their shipyard and build Kaiju-class dreadnoughts in addition to helping us construct four new portals. That is our whole goal."

Payne nodded at them, close-lipped. There was nothing else to say.

Paragon Virtue hurried to an individual who seemed to be waiting. After a short conversation, the president of the United Nations headed toward Payne.

[4]

"The pen is mightier than the sword, said nobody with a pen facing somebody with a sword." –From the memoirs of Ambassador Declan Payne

"I'm President Sinkhaus," the older woman said, offering her hand. Payne took it and shook it without squeezing too hard. She had a decent grip, but he could have crushed her hand had he wanted. Restraint with the first step in good diplomacy, he told himself.

"Ambassador Payne. I want to thank you for this kind reception." He gestured toward the banquet tables, where a mini-feast was arrayed. One of the servants carried two dog bowls. He put them down, and Kal turned the Cabrizi loose. They dove in headfirst and cleaned the bowls in a matter of seconds. The first servant backed away carefully. A second appeared with two bowls of water. The Cabrizi caught her as she bent down. They vaulted close and sniffed her face while she froze.

Kal said something in Ebren before switching to his Western movie English. "You can stand up now, ma'am. They won't put a hurt on you."

"You brought your dogs to the UN," Sinkhaus murmured in a dry voice.

"They are Cabrizi and a symbol of royalty on Ebren. I won them in combat. They show my place in Ebren society."

"But you're on Earth now."

Payne closed his eyes and prayed for patience. When he opened them, he found the president staring at him. Payne broke out the few words of Ebren he memorized to deal with the animals. He called them to him and ordered them to sit. They took their positions on either side of him. One of them belched. With their ears perked up, they looked like reincarnations of Anubis from ancient Egypt.

"I'll get right to it." Payne didn't think he had enough patience for the reception in addition to a meeting. "The Ga'ee are a threat to every flesh-and-blood creature in this galaxy. They destroy whole planets and purge the carbon-based life forms. We fought them to a standstill, but they escaped. They will be back, and we have to be ready. I need humanity to build Kaiju-class dreadnoughts, as many as possible, while also helping the former Braze Collective build their portals to give the Fleet instant access anywhere in known space."

"I suppose there's a short timeframe to work this miracle."

"You suppose correctly. We estimate one year."

"'Estimate.' Do you know for sure?"

Payne stared at her. "I told you the answer before you asked the question. I admit that I'm not good at playing politics or gotcha or whatever you're used to. What do you say you dispense with that part of this conversation? I need to convince you of the threat. We've sent the videos of what the Ga'ee are capable of. We can broadcast that to every news outlet on the planet if you'd like to save you time trying to convince humanity to save itself."

"We will take care of that when the time is right."

Payne saw red. He clenched his fists, but Mary caressed the back of his hand until he let her intertwine her fingers with his.

"President Sinkhaus, I'm Mary Payne, the ambassador's wife. What do you need from us to convince you of this threat and our analysis of the timing for the Ga'ee to reappear?"

The president smiled, but not in a warm or friendly way. She looked like a predator about to pounce. "Send us the information, and we'll get back to you when we've had time to analyze it. Simple as that."

"We've already done that," Mary replied with an equally condescending smile. "It shouldn't take more than a day or two. We can schedule to meet again in three days for a more involved conversation regarding the threat and what Earth will do to counter it."

"Three days. We can contact you at that time regarding when we'll be able to meet. The Earth doesn't stop rotating just because Declan Payne shows up."

"It should," Mary replied. "Because he's not here to waste anyone's time with anything that's not critical to the survival of the human race. Don't take this request lightly, President Sinkhaus, because it's not a request. Leaving humanity by itself for refusing to participate in a united operation to protect our mutual interests will not be good for us or the galaxy, just when Earth found traction and the opportunity to lead the alien races... Do not throw away this opportunity over what will look petty in the history books."

"History will judge us all, Mary. Some more harshly than others." She glanced at Declan Payne. "If you'll excuse me, I have work to do. Please enjoy the reception. Follow Paragon's lead to the receiving line, and you'll get to meet the senior leadership of Earth."

Without waiting for a reply, she walked toward a side door.

Payne sighed. "What a jackass."

"She will never be convinced," Mary replied. "But let's see what we can do as part of a receiving line. Everyone will have to pass us to get to the banquet table. You see, no one has eaten yet, and diplomats love to eat."

"I like how you think." He waved to the man named Virtue, who hurried to his side. "Set up the receiving line. Let's get these people to the banquet, shall we?" He leaned close and spoke softly. "I don't know who any of these people are or their level of importance. How does it work?"

"You don't know how the Earth's political system works?"

"We already had a conversation about not being a douchebag, so just explain it. You have one minute."

Paragon smiled. "I'm sorry. You've been off-planet your entire adult life. I'm too used to being here. Maybe I can visit your ship?"

"I think that would be most beneficial for all parties involved. They've never seen a ship like *Leviathan* because humanity has never had such technology. We still don't. Lev only shares certain things, but those are big and are helping us cement our place in the greater universe. Get with Mary to arrange that after we've survived the day."

"The United Nations consists of all one hundred and twenty-four member nations. Each carries a vote equal to their population and their gross domestic product. Heavily populated poor countries have equal say to lightly populated but rich countries. It's a balance, not all one way or the other. What we have in this hall are fifteen of the top twenty in the voting pool."

"That is information I can use. Thank you, Paragon."

"My pleasure, Mr. Ambassador."

Payne nodded at the banquet table. "How will I know who's the most important?" Payne whispered.

"They'll do it for you. The most voting clout will be first

down the line. You see the Ambassador for the Solomon Islands Collective heading toward the back of the line?"

The representatives were casually working their way into order.

Paragon stood behind Payne, with Mary to her husband's right. The aide whispered as the first individual approached. "From the Greater American Coalition. The representative is new, having taken the position after President Sinkhaus moved up."

"Mr. Ambassador, I'm Representative Peter Tollivar. We hope we'll be able to get fifteen minutes of your time before you leave the planet."

"For?" Payne asked undiplomatically. Mary nudged him with her hip.

"A casual conversation. That's all."

Payne bit his tongue. A casual conversation with a politician. Then it dawned on him. "Mr. Swiss wants off *Leviathan* and is afraid to ask me himself."

"I assure you, Tamony Swiss is secondary. However, he has contacted me and asked for a favor."

Payne smiled. "I look forward to it. I need your help, too. We all need to talk about the Ga'ee, but later, after we've enjoyed the UN's hospitality."

The two shook hands, and the next in line moved up.

"The European Union has a single rep, but also they have individual representatives," Virtue whispered.

"Double your pleasure, double your fun," Payne quipped.

"Representative Heinz Machmuller of Germany, also representing the EU today." He bowed his head in greeting.

"Nice to meet you, Heinz. Declan Payne. The EU has their own space program separate from the UN-operated program, doesn't it?"

He remembered hearing that while talking with the admiral

and commodore over a meal. The BEP was able to recruit members from both places, giving it access to a broader swath of potential trainees.

"We do. Most astute. Point-seven percent of our people are veterans of Fleet and BEP service. We are proud to supply the greatest per-capita percentage of personnel in support of Earth's space aspirations."

"Your country's sacrifices are greatly appreciated. We fight as one, no matter where we come from." Payne turned somber. "But, I'm afraid I'm going to be asking for more."

The two shared a moment before the representative moved on. That was how the conversations continued for the next thirteen representatives.

Mary kissed him on the cheek after the last walked by, and they joined the queue to browse the banquet table.

"What's that for?"

"You might someday make a great diplomat. All you need is a little practice."

"I'd rather tell people my sister works in a whorehouse than admit to being a diplomat. I'm not, by the way. We need those portals and the ships to fly through them. That's all. I just need to make sure they understand the urgency."

"Which takes diplomacy. Just telling the truth and then giving an ultimatum isn't how humanity will get what it needs. You should send a fruit basket to the president. I'll take care of sending that, along with your heartfelt words regarding her hospitality."

Payne's eye twitched anew. He couldn't reconcile the world of politicians with the greater universe of fighting humanity's enemies. "You know that chaps my ass."

Mary shrugged. "As you say, take it like a man. Stiff upper lip. Smile and be cordial. Ask them about their countries. At this point, all you have to do is be nice. Following this, we'll retire to a briefing room, where we'll show some videos. We included suit captures from your time on Brayalore. Up close and personal with the Ga'ee."

"I don't want to relive that, but that'll show them what we're up against. They don't want the Ga'ee tearing up their backyards. Just one, and we risk losing the entire planet."

"That's the message. With tact, Declan."

"I'd like to say I'm always tactful, but that would be a lie." They smiled at each other. Payne waved at his team. "Grab some chow."

Citrus permeated the air at the front of the line, owing to spiral-sliced oranges.

The staff had brought two thick blankets for the Cabrizi. They curled up behind the table in their comfortable beds after eating too much, freeing Kal to join the line in front of Payne.

The representatives moved farther away from the table while the armed crew prepared their plates.

"Maybe I shouldn't eat. Just stroll around and talk with people," Payne suggested.

Mary nodded. "But grab yourself a drink first. They'll be more receptive if you don't have your hands free. It looks like they have a barista."

Payne stared. "Is that what he is? I haven't had designer coffee in...damn, I can't remember. Maybe we can take some samples back for Lev to analyze and add to his repertoire."

"You talked with the Colombian rep. Maybe follow up by asking for a sample of the coffees from his country?"

"We will never go without again!" Payne declared, hopping out of line and heading straight for the barista and his coffee-making station.

Kal put his plate down and followed, forcing Mary and Declan to stop.

"Get something to eat," Payne told him.

CRAIG MARTELLE

"No can do, boss man," Kal rumbled. "I am where you are."

Payne was only torn for a moment. Then he turned around to get back in line. He picked up Kal's plate. "Tell me what you want, and I'll load it up for you."

"You shouldn't be doing that," Kal replied without the drawl. He glanced nervously at the representatives.

Payne took a second plate and added bits and pieces he thought Mary might like. Kal wouldn't point to anything, so Payne haphazardly filled it with what he thought were the worst samples of human food.

At the end, he found Heckler holding out his empty plate. "More, sir?"

"You're going to walk funny with that plate shoved up your ass," Payne shot back. "And, hands are full." He held up the two plates.

Mary relieved him of one, and Kal took the other.

"Now eat it, you goofy bastard."

"Y'all gotta say such hurtful words," Kal drawled, but he inhaled a crepe filled with something black. "Food from the gods!"

"That was kinda nasty," Turbo mumbled.

"First day watching him eat?" Heckler replied, earning him an elbow aimed for his ribs. He danced out of the way and returned to the banquet table.

Payne motioned for Mary and Kal to follow him to where two of the representatives were in line for the barista.

"Aren't you from Colombia? Are you assessing how the coffee is here in the extreme north?"

"Indeed!" The man beamed. "I have some special blends in my office. I'd be honored to give you some."

"I'll be honored to receive them," Payne replied. He shook the man's hand.

Mary winked at her husband.

Kal ate quickly and finished off his plate. He didn't want to leave to drop it off with the staff. Mary grabbed it from him and took it to the waitstaff. When she returned, she made eye contact with Declan.

"What?"

"When did I become the mother to your mighty band of miscreants?"

"You're one of us, Dog." Payne didn't think that would be the end of it, so he continued. "Not like a mother, more a stepmother."

She gave him her best hairy eyeball.

"Stepmonster," Virgil interjected, scanning the area while he waited in line for his own coffee. Kal stood to the side.

"I get it!" Kal declared with a hearty chuckle.

"I don't. How did I become the butt of your jokes?" Mary jammed her fists into her hips before composing herself and smiling pleasantly.

Dank opened his mouth, but Payne stopped him from speaking by pointing and staring wide-eyed.

"Because we love you. If we didn't, we wouldn't give you shit, and you would know you weren't welcome here."

"I know," she conceded. "We all have our part to play in this grand circus of life, the greatest challenge with the loudest ring-master calling from the hallowed halls of the UN. Still, someone must energize the crowd with more than words. The performers must go on, and then they have to delight the crowd. You're not the ringmaster, Declan Payne. You are the headlining act. You play your part, and we'll play ours."

"Damn, Stepmonster's going deep with the philosophy. But I get you." Dank tapped a finger to his brow in salute. He stepped out of the line and directed the team to better positions around the leader of the seven races. Virgil moved back to Payne. "It's all you, Dec. Show them what they're up against. If they give us what we need, they'll never have to see firsthand what the Ga'ee can do to them."

Payne nodded. "I don't deserve you guys. Any of you, but I'm glad that you're here. Let's get back to work. Well, as soon as my coffee is ready."

[5]

"The end of days won't come with fireworks and grand speeches. It'll come at the end of a decline orchestrated by failure after political failure." –From the memoirs of Ambassador Declan Payne

The shuttle lifted off the roof of the United Nations building. Paragon Virtue waved at the team while huffing and puffing from the climb Team Payne had made quickly, knowing the discomfort it would cause their escorts. No one waved back as the ship accelerated into the sky.

"I think it went well," Mary said. "It could have gone better if you had been on your game with the president, but you won over the other fifteen."

"She rubbed me the wrong way." Payne scowled while leaning sideways to get a better view of the front screen, which showed space.

"I'm sure she rubs everyone the wrong way, but she has power—the power of an entire planet." Mary wasn't sure how Declan could reach her. This battle was being fought under

41

different rules. She knew some of them, but not the ones the president played by. That was a whole different level.

"Can't wait to get back to *Leviathan*," Payne muttered. "There's something about the warm embrace of millions of tons of metal."

"And his touch in your mind," Mary added.

"It used to bug me that he was always reading my thoughts until I realized that he only used the information to help us." Payne hopped out of his seat and looked at the team. "Heckler, what kind of new weapons do you have for us?"

"None, but we're thinking long and hard on it." He pointed at Turbo. "We need something that fires thermite because once thermite is burning, it keeps burning, unlike plasma. It needs to have energy applied to keep it liquid."

"It doesn't have to be long-range. How far away do you think we'll be shooting at a juvenile Ga'ee?"

"Ten meters, maybe. That helps, Major. Thanks."

"*Ugly 5* outfitting. Is there any jerky on hand?" Payne wondered.

Mary shook her head. "We load up fresh stuff usually, but our departure for *Ephesus* was rather abrupt."

"Keep stock on board and ask Lev to rotate it weekly, along with anything else stored on board that could remotely be considered perishable. Even a trip to Earth might have a need for supplies."

"Like now? You're hungry, aren't you?"

Payne held his hands up in surrender. "You know me so well."

"We can grab something on the cruiser. I think Captain LeClerc is expecting us to stay on board while we're negotiating with the UN."

Payne made a face. "I like my own bed."

"Don't be an old woman."

"Speaking from firsthand experience?" Payne quipped.

Mary crossed her arms and refused to look at him.

Crap. Lev, save me! Payne called from his mind, but they were too far away, and the AI couldn't hear him.

"Even saying I'm sorry won't get me out of this one, will it?" he asked softly.

"Shh. Stepmonster is mad at you," she shot back before smiling at him. "Gotcha."

"Holy crap, Dog. You had me shaking in my seat."

Dank waved to get Declan's attention. "Are we going to get Kaiju-class ships and four portals? I couldn't follow anything that was going on."

"That takes the president. We have fifteen advocates, I think. It takes her to bring it to a vote, which is the ultimate vote. If she doesn't bring it to the floor, we'll get nothing."

"Can we do it with just the four races?" Virgil wondered.

"*Five* races. We can bring the Vestrall on board since I'm the leader of that mob. We can expedite the construction of the portals with their help. We can do without Earth, but we need the dreadnoughts if we're going to mass firepower against a Ga'ee carrier."

"Maybe we just make weapons platforms. A Kaiju has a crew of a couple thousand. That's a big ask," Heckler said.

"Explain." Payne leaned close. The rest of the team did too.

"Lev has all kinds of plans for ships. How about something that's more automated and less *manned*. Something with a crew of a couple hundred and firepower that's on par with a battle-ship. We could staff ten of those rather than one Kaiju. Lev could build them if we had the raw materials. Two weeks to ten battleships."

"Then why are we asking Earth?" Payne asked.

"We need raw materials for ten battleships, but the limiting factor is crews. That'll take some cooperation," Major Dank interjected. "The gathering of raw materials will interrupt their shipbuilding for a certain amount of time, but nowhere near what it would take if they were to do all the building themselves. Then getting experienced personnel who can be trained quickly. When we get back to the Fleet forces in forward locations, we'll probably get more volunteers than we can handle. Until then, raw materials and people."

"We ask for a one-month interruption, or we return to Vestrall space and undertake the shipbuilding there, then bring our new fleet through the portal to Earth," Payne offered.

"Or that." Virgil inclined his head.

The team leaned back and disappeared into their own thoughts. They were relieved to know that they didn't have to rely on Earth's politicians to save the planet, but they hoped the UN would do the right thing. Payne wanted to believe. Although his team gave grief to the political class, they wanted to believe, too.

The shuttle continued to *Ephesus*, where it docked at the airlock it had departed from ten hours earlier.

"I feel like I've been beat with an ugly stick," Turbo remarked.

Heckler clamped his mouth shut and stared at the bulkhead. Byle, Joker, Sparky, and Shaolin nodded. Dank blurted, "Me, too!"

Payne looked at Mary's knee because he knew if she caught him looking, he'd start laughing. She nudged him with her elbow.

"Don't," he pleaded. "There's no men-against-the-women on this team."

"It was pretty funny," Mary whispered.

Payne leaned his head against the shuttle's bulkhead and closed his eyes. "From the dark days of old, when a casual word could get one mauled, we have evolved to a better place, where words matter less than actions. I find myself peering into the abyss, a slave to my words, restrained from action until such time as I'm compelled... No, until such time as I am able to act, *with prejudice*, against a relentless foe. We're out here. Not the talkers. It'll never be the talkers."

"Why you gotta be such a buzzkill, sir?" Joker asked in a small voice.

"The weight of the universe is on my shoulders, but not just mine." He gestured at everyone in the shuttle. "All of ours."

The airlock popped. Payne winked and stood. The others joined him and stepped through the airlock into the cruiser. "Permission to come aboard," Payne asked, which he'd forgotten to do earlier at their frosty reception.

"Permission granted," LeClerc replied. "Your quarters are this way."

Payne hesitated. "We have three days before we need to go back to Earth, so if we could, please take us back to our ship."

"My orders are to accommodate you," the captain replied.

"And you will...by taking us to our ship."

The captain didn't move, and the tension increased beyond simple discomfort.

"I don't care what Earth's leadership told you. Take us to our ship." He looked at his team until he saw who he wanted. "Joker, contact *Leviathan* and request a tactical assist from the Spinsters. Looks like we'll need an escort home. Launch immediately."

"Hold on. You don't need to launch anything," the captain replied. "There are two fugitives onboard *Leviathan*. I've been directed to leverage you to get them."

Payne stepped close. The captain tried to back up, but Payne pinned him against the wall. Kal, Heckler, and Turbo faced off against the ship's security personnel accompanying the captain. Team Payne outmatched them from the word go.

LeClerc was torn.

"Listen. The people onboard *Leviathan* have traveled the galaxy fighting for all humanity. Who are you fighting for?"

"Humanity. If we don't maintain a civilization based on good order and discipline, then what are we saving?"

"I'd try to conjure a yawn for rebuttal, but I'm too tired of dealing with self-aggrandizement. Those ordering you to maintain good order and discipline are only in support of their version of it when they're in charge. You need to recognize the difference, Captain. Don't make us shoot our way through your ship.

"Now you see why it was important for the leader of the seven races to maintain a well-armed and well-trained security detail? In the Solar System, dealing with humans, I have to threaten to use force to keep from being held hostage. You're pathetic. Take us to our ship."

Payne mouthed the names Blinky and Buzz.

Mary shook her head. They had ten hours to expunge the crusade against the admiral and the commodore.

The Cabrizi were anxious. The corridor was small, and they were restrained. They growled to share their discomfort with everyone within hearing.

"Are you sure there's legal actions against anyone on *Leviathan*?" Payne asked, looking for confirmation. He had confidence that Blinky, Buzz, and Lev could break into any human system.

"I was ordered. I have my orders."

"Are they legal orders?" Payne pressed. "We'll stop by the bridge on the way. You can check."

Payne stepped away. The captain reluctantly followed. Payne strode boldly. He took a left, and the captain stopped.

"What?" Payne asked.

"It's this way." LeClerc pointed in the other direction.

Payne looked skeptical until Dank covered his hand gesture directing them in the way LeClerc wanted to go.

"Just testing you. You've passed."

Payne, Mary, Kal, and Turbo entered the bridge with the captain. The others remained in the corridor.

"Verify the detention order on Fleet Admiral Harry Wesson and Commodore Nyota Freeman," Payne stated. The captain nodded his approval to a crewman at a position with a wrap-around screen.

After much tapping, gesturing, and confusion, he turned back to the captain. "Sir, they are both registered in good standing."

"Following an illegal order makes you complicit," Payne reminded him softly.

"The order came directly from the head of the BEP!"

"No one is above the law, LeClerc. No one!" Payne pounded a fist into his hand while fixing the captain with his best steely-eyed killer gaze.

"Absolutely. My sincere apologies. Crewman, please register a complaint with the inspector general about the order received from command authority that is counter to the data you just accessed. Something is wrong, and it's their job to get to the bottom of it."

"Now we'll retire to *Leviathan* until we're needed back on Earth."

The captain hurried into the corridor, waved off his security, and walked quickly to the cargo bay. *Ugly* 5 had been chained to the deck.

"Really?" Payne asked.

The captain personally attacked the lever on a manual load binder, releasing the tension and ratcheting it loose. Byle and Shaolin unlatched the other two. Kal flipped the chain off the top of the insertion craft and let it bang on the deck on the far side.

Once clear, the captain bowed his head and continued to mutter apologies until Payne stopped him.

"Captain LeClerc, you're in charge of the most powerful ship in the BEP fleet." Payne guessed that was true because the BEP had been virtually obliterated in the fight to protect Earth from the Ebren's and the Rang'Kor's attacks. "Walk with confidence because you're sure you're doing the right thing. You always have to ask yourself if what you're doing makes humanity better. A civilization worth saving and a life worth living."

Payne offered his hand, and reluctantly, the captain took it.

"Those are words the president should be saying," LeClerc suggested.

"But they're just words. What are people doing? That's the question you have to answer. If all they're doing is protecting their power, they are not doing right by the people." Payne pointed at the cargo bay door. "Lev is doing more for humanity than we're doing for ourselves. He doesn't *have* to say a word, but when he does, we should all listen.

"Words from those who have put their lives on the line for the security of humanity are worthy. What they do matters. Next time, please, believe the words of those whose actions speak for them."

The captain came to attention and saluted. "I will."

Ugly 5 disengaged its side doors and levered them upward. The team climbed aboard. Mary and Declan waved as the doors closed. The captain left the cargo bay, secured it, and opened the cruiser's outer door.

The insertion craft accelerated into space. The tactical screen appeared, showing *Leviathan* a long way away. "What happened?"

"Remember the part where we boarded the cruiser, and it flew to Earth?" Mary asked.

Payne groaned. "Damn BEP!" He dropped his head toward his knees. "Everybody make yourself comfortable. It'll be a couple hours. Can we get any more speed from this thing?"

Sparky laughed. "As the team's engineer, I have to answer. This thing is shaped like an egg with internal engines to limit its profile, and a load limit to provide additional signature reduction, but even so, we're probably lighting up their screens. So, no. This is it. We're cooking at top speed, and everyone can see us while we're doing it."

Payne looked at his wife. "Maybe you can work with Lev to make this thing faster when we want it but still stealthy the rest of the time."

"No." Mary crossed her arms and closed her eyes. "This is the biggest design that maintains the stealth capabilities. Any bigger, and we'll block out the stars."

Payne smiled. "That's only because you're still thinking inside the box."

Mary opened one eye for a moment before returning to her sleeping pose.

"A bathroom would be good while you're working on it," Payne added.

"I second the bathroom." Turbo gave a thumbs-up.

"I could get behind that proposal," Virgil added. The rest of the team offered their support.

"See? Outside the box, Dog. It's where all the best ideas are found."

Mary kept her eyes closed and ignored her husband.

"Sparky, join the design team. Rotate the jerky, so we don't have to suffer like we are now with nothing to eat."

Byle reached into the panel behind her and pulled out an emergency ration bar. She tossed it to Payne.

He looked at it before deciding against it. He tossed the bar back. "I've had enough of these over the past two months to last me a lifetime."

"I guess you're not that hungry, sir." She tucked it back into the storage panel. "Food at the banquet was good, except that nasty crepe thing Kal seemed to love."

"Hey! Y'all are mean as snakes. Here I was, minding my own business, keeping the pups calm, and bam! Attacked out of nowhere. Mean as snakes, I tell you," the Ebren drawled. "Those things were good. I took one for Lev to replicate."

Dank patted his pocket since Kal'faxx didn't have any. Virgil also carried the coffee samples the Colombian representative had shared.

Payne settled for a thumbs-up, then relaxed and closed his eyes. His stomach growled. He didn't bother thinking about a future engagement with the president of the UN. He expected that he wouldn't return to the hallowed halls of Earth's political elite. He had more important things to do and could make a better investment with his time.

[6]

"When you're hungry, eat. When you're tired, sleep. When you can't do either of those things, you'll remember the last time you did and the opportunity you didn't take." –From the memoirs of Ambassador Declan Payne

Payne climbed out of the uglymobile and reached back to help Mary. "You have your orders. Now, go away, and don't do anything productive for the next twelve hours. Right here, tomorrow, oh-eight-hundred local time. No, make that ten hundred hours. Be ready to work. I need to pummel something, but only after an obscenely long shower. I have to wash the UN off my body."

The team chuckled while heading to the carts. The Cabrizi didn't bother. They had energy to release, so they ran to the far end of the hangar bay and back, then into the corridor as the first cart traveled out and disappeared.

After the others had gone, Declan pulled Mary into a long hug. "I can't do this without you," he admitted. "I know, me being all soft and squishy is abnormal, but it's how I feel. I can't just beat some sense into people. They have no fear of things they should be afraid of. I find that frustrating."

Mary nuzzled his neck. "You'll never be able to convince all of them. The president will never come on board because you're in a higher position. I expect she covets the title of leader of the seven races, but there can only be one person with that. It's not going to be her because that person has to earn the respect of the Ebren by fighting their champion. She doesn't strike me as the physical sort." Mary pushed away and flexed her biceps, but the effect was lost under her jumpsuit.

"Lev, take us to the bridge. I want to debrief with the admiral."

"Then you don't want to go to the bridge since he's not there."

Payne snorted. "Word games for a hundred, Lev. Please take us to wherever the admiral is. Unless he's naked. Then we'll wait."

"I'm sure he's not naked. Climb aboard. The last train to Clarksville is leaving."

"Lev! Studying more ridiculously old pop culture?"

Mary looked at Declan, confused. "Shit! I understood your reference. You dated me as old, you bastard. I'm going to get you back."

"You have never once in all our time together gotten me back. You should give up while you're behind."

They climbed into the cart and held each other as it maneuvered easily away from the team's equipment cage. They weren't in a hurry, and Lev knew it. The cart accelerated down the corridor and up one ramp, then backtracked to a conference room on a mostly unused deck.

"I could still use a shower. I have the slime of politicians on me," Payne grumbled. "But we don't want to keep the admiral waiting."

The Paynes kissed in a way that promised much more.

Until someone cleared his throat.

Loudly.

"Damn! How'd we get here?" Payne asked while looking around. "Hey, Admiral. We've been to Earth, and I don't recommend it, but we hear you've been reinstated as the Fleet admiral. The commodore, too."

"That'll only remain until they figure out their system has been compromised." He led the way into the conference room. Nyota was sitting next to the admiral's chair.

The Paynes sat across the table from the admiral. Declan rolled his chair back to put his feet up on the seat to one side while leaning against Mary on the other.

"I hate those people," he started.

"Nothing new there. I'm also not a fan, but let's move past that to something a little more substantive."

"They'll get back with us in three days, but I think that's when they'll ask to schedule the follow-up meeting. I see zero sense of urgency from the president."

The admiral sat with his hands clasped before him, seemingly insulated from reacting emotionally to the bad news. "The images of the destruction should have been enough without you going in person."

Payne shook his head.

"Many of the big voters seemed to be swayed, but they all said they could do nothing without the president. She decides at her sole discretion whether to bring an issue to the floor. The president wields all the power. Nothing comes to the floor that she doesn't support, and I suspect she won't bring something if she doesn't already have the votes to get it passed. Only her bills get passed."

"How do we get her to bring it to a vote?" the commodore asked.

"We don't. We take Lev to the Vestrall system, where there is a robust shipbuilding capability that was idled when we took over the leadership of Vestrall Prime. We turn the shipyard back on and build what we need there. Then we portal to Earth, and *Leviathan* jumps ahead to help build portals in the other Braze systems."

The admiral winced. "We need Earth..." He didn't take the thought further.

"We need humanity," Payne clarified. "What do you think, Lev?"

"I think your defense of me was admirable. What if I don't want to build ten battleships?"

"Then we go with Plan C. We beg the other races to do it since they are more invested. Especially the Rang'Kor, and since I'm the undisputed champion of Ebren, we can bring them on board. The Berantz have seen the threat up close and personal, but they have almost no resources to draw on. We need you, Lev. This isn't a time to equivocate."

"I know, Declan. I was just joshing you."

"Joshing?"

"I am doing my best to stay on my linguistic toes, so to speak. Restoring the shipbuilding in Vestrall space is the lowest risk, but the ships will come without crews. We will still need those."

"Easy enough, Lev. Don't we have about a thousand people on board who aren't doing a whole lot besides *not* being on Earth?"

"I shall canvass their skill sets and make recommendations. Bravo, Declan."

"Battleship design. Once you have enough power, build at least one bridge simulator, and we'll get the crews a little practice before they take the helms," Payne directed.

"I'll do that once I'm up to speed. Will you continue to

engage with the president?" Lev asked. "I would like you to succeed in this task."

Payne twisted his mouth sideways while scowling. "What Lev isn't telling you is that I feel like a failure because I couldn't convince the leadership of Earth that the threat is real. I was too ham-handed. I like it when things are cut and dried. United Nations politics. Ack! You can't just tell them something. Two points apply to every statement. One, that you'll be believed, and two, that they'll do something about it."

"You're not a failure," Mary countered.

"I know, but I should have been more persuasive. We got blown off with a capital B." Payne made a fist. "If I could have punched her in her smug face just once, enough to splatter her nose, I think I could have made my point about the danger of ignoring the leader of the seven races."

"The *dangers*," the admiral stated. "The danger is ignoring the Ga'ee threat or wasting time instead of preparing. Alas, Declan, you are simply a messenger, no matter your title. You both look tired. Go and do what newlyweds do."

Declan and Mary stood. "Lev, can you show me what you have for battleship plans?"

"Of course. I have a number of designs. The Vestrall weapons platforms hold promise to penetrate the Ga'ee's shields. They are battleship-sized, and I can modify them to be battleships, complete with defensive systems. That will change them from being expendable drones to operate with a minimal crew as a complete combat package."

Payne bent to sit down. The admiral waved at him. "What are you doing?"

"I was hoping I could, you know..." Payne pointed at the holographic image of a Vestrall weapons platform, ready to be modified to become a battlewagon.

"When the time is right. Not today, and definitely not right now. Go. You're off-duty, leader of the seven races. Rest up, power up, and we'll see you tomorrow."

Mary smiled. "That's the exact same order he gave the team."

"See! Smart people thinking alike and all that. Be on your way." The admiral jabbed his thumb over his shoulder.

Payne surrendered and headed out. In the corridor, the cart waited. They climbed aboard for a high-speed trip to their quarters. They had to cling to the cart for all they were worth. Lev apparently wasn't going to give them a chance to change their minds.

"Chow, Lev!" Payne cried as the cart raced through the team's quarters area. It stopped, and they climbed out. The cart zoomed away. "Lev used to love me."

Another cart approached. Payne waved at it to get the riders' attention, but no one was there. In the seat, they found trays of a variety of their favorite foods, steaming hot.

"By eating here, you can't get distracted," Mary told him.

"Did you conspire with Lev?"

"I didn't, but had I thought of it, I would have." They retreated into their quarters. The door closed securely behind them. Plates and utensils awaited them.

"It's not the man but the quality of his friends. Thanks, Lev."

"You are welcome. We have a lot of work to do, but it'll get done, Declan."

Mary prepared a plate while Declan paced. "So much work to do, but it's mostly you, Lev."

"Fear not, Declan. I will rise to this challenge. The Ga'ee cannot be allowed within ten thousand light-years of here. I will fight them with everything I have."

"You are a better friend to humanity than that festering cesspool on Earth. It will happily tell everyone that they are the answer to all humanity's ills, the ones people like them have created and will extend in perpetuity."

Payne waited for an answer. Mary dropped her jumpsuit to the floor and continued eating naked.

Her scar raged an ugly purple.

"That's one sexy scar," he commented.

"Only you would think that. But then again, I guess it doesn't matter since you'll be the only one who sees it. My bikini days have come to an end. That's not right either. They came to an end when I joined the Fleet. No, wait..." She smiled in a way that told Payne it didn't matter.

"Mrs. Ambassador, how many times do I have to say it? It's not what we look like that matters. It's what we do." He stuffed his mouth and chewed quickly while trying to undress. He trapped one leg before it was out and bounced around until he lost his balance and fell.

———

"*Leviathan*, this is the office of the president with a message for Ambassador Payne. She has him scheduled for a week from Tuesday and would like him to confirm."

Payne fumed despite it being what he expected. He counseled himself to deliver a measured response.

"Office of the president, I won't be here a week from Tuesday, but two weeks from Tuesday, I would be happy to meet with the president. I need to discuss the threat to friendly space with our allies. When I return, you'll know it. Please confirm, two weeks from Tuesday."

"The president has two weeks from Wednesday, available with the same time slot, eleven to eleven thirty."

"Consider it confirmed, office of the president." Payne drew his finger across his throat to cut the signal, but Lev had already taken care of it. "You know what we need to do next, Lev. Spin up the portal and take us to Vestrall."

Leviathan accelerated toward the Solar System's gas giant, where the Vestrall-designed portal was located. Physically, the portal appeared as a shiny reflection. It was an empty ring until the energy arced across it, flashing and snapping until it settled into a shimmering pool.

"Lev, buddy, maybe we should take it easy, make sure it's stabilized before crashing into the event horizon like a bunch of idiots heading over a waterfall in a barrel. Lev!"

Leviathan accelerated through the portal and into the space of Vestrall Prime. Lev angled onto a trajectory that took the ship away from the home planet and toward the shipyard. By using the portal, Lev was completely functional. He didn't have to wait three days to start the construction process. He transitioned briefly into faster-than-light speed to further condense the timeline.

When they reached the idled shipyard, Lev had his hangar bay doors open, and the construction bots were preparing themselves to deploy. He had reconfigured them for the task of building drone-style battleships, not drones, in case the Ga'ee tried to take over their ships like the Vestrall had tried.

Lev slowed to a stop, and his repair bots flooded into the void to start dismantling one section of the massive shipyard. "Saves us from having to smelt four battleships' worth of high-density materials," Lev had explained.

"Do we want to do that?" Admiral Wesson asked. "The shipyard can continue building battleships after we leave. I think ten is a good start, nothing more."

"I'm leaving a construction capability behind, capable of turning out a battleship a week if the raw materials can be mined and delivered. When Declan sent the drone fleet into the sun, it did not include the mining and supply ships supporting the shipyard. I'm updating them and sending them back to the moon of Vestrall Two, where the mines will be reestablished."

"You think of everything, Lev," Harry remarked.

The rest of the ship's company was separated into crews to run the new ships. Lev immediately began building two simulators. That allowed the leadership team to build a schedule of twenty-four two-hour training blocks for hands-on engagement. The rest of the time was allocated to classroom-based instruction.

The first battleship would be ready in a day, with an additional day to stock the ship with biomass, water, and air and bring the interior to a standard human-acceptable temperature.

After their arrival at the Vestrall shipyard, construction and training began in earnest.

Leviathan's corridors were oddly empty. It reminded Payne of when they had been the only ones on board. An empty ship, but they were never alone.

The activity left Team Payne with nothing but time.

"Workouts, two hours in the morning and two hours in the afternoon, with tactical training in between," Payne told them in the corridor outside the bridge.

"Did anyone notify the Vestrall that we're back and what we're doing?" Major Dank asked.

Payne frowned. "No, but I guess I better do it. I'll join you at the gym." He returned to the bridge. Mary joined him. "This won't take long. I'll catch up."

She shrugged. "I'm a civilian now," she replied, flicking her hair over her shoulder.

"Upstart! Maybe we should find Tamony Swiss and have him help you with logistics. He's a civilian, too."

"Is he still on board? I haven't seen him in months."

Payne shrugged. "Lev keeps him away from us. And I'm kidding. I don't want that tool anywhere near our logistics."

"I figured," Mary replied. The bridge was empty except for the admiral and the commodore.

"This is a different look but familiar," Payne stated.

"More peaceful for an entity like *Leviathan*. And me, too. Everything we need is handled at the speed of thought. Crew interactions interfere and slow the pace." The admiral smiled at his own statement. "There was a time when humanity made us great. It enabled us to fight off the entirety of the Braze Collective."

"We would have succumbed to the Ga'ee had they invaded human space first," Payne suggested. "Every human in the Solar System would have been killed. We can't let them take another planet. It's our time to live free. Lev is giving us the ability to fight back. With fifty battleships sporting the single-shot energy weapon, we can mass our fire and deliver a knockout punch to a Ga'ee carrier. Make it too expensive to colonize our part of the galaxy."

"And then send every bit and piece of their ship, along with all the drones, directly into the nearest star unless we have a shipyard nearby where we can use Ga'ee scrap to build new ships for ourselves," the admiral replied.

"That's the plan. Lev, can you connect me to the Mryasmalite council chambers, please?"

"Of course." Lev made the connection, and Payne made his announcement.

"Lesser Mryasmalites. This is your regent, Declan Payne. We are co-opting the shipyard to build battleships to fight the Ga'ee, an invasive silicon-based species that has attempted to invade our galaxy. We will forward videos of their attacks for your viewing pleasure. That is all. We'll take questions when next we are in the council chambers together."

Payne walked away.

"I thought you said you were going to talk with them?

Talking at them doesn't count." Mary looked at Declan sideways.

"There are fewer arguments this way, and any misunderstanding can go unresolved since I don't care if they understand or not. We need to do this to protect them as much as to protect the other six races."

"Sounds like the president of the UN."

Payne stopped. "Does it?"

"She gave you no chance to talk. It was a one-way conversation," Mary explained. "Her issues were more important than yours."

"The Vestrall have no issues that need me or the shipyard. You saw it when we arrived. It was idle. The mining operation was idle. We are taking over what they didn't have access to. I didn't need to tell them anything."

"When does that stop?"

"It's already stopped since I told them what we were doing, even though it didn't affect anything they were doing. Unlike Earth. The Ga'ee will greatly affect what humanity is doing."

Mary shook her head. "You won't always be right."

Payne took a long time to blow out a single breath. "I know that. But in this case, I *am* right. We agreed, even though this is the bubble of our existence on *Leviathan*. Lev wouldn't allow me to cross the line, and neither would you. Those people killed most of Virgil's team, and they almost killed Kal, too. They tried to stymy all of humanity. We've already shown mercy by allowing them to live."

"After a year of living in Leeyaness, you still have anger and disdain for them. When will you forgive them?"

"That's a tough question." Payne ran a hand through his hair and resumed walking toward the cart waiting in the corridor. "I don't know. Means I will probably need to step down so we can begin with a clean slate. Hey, Lev, what do you say we go looking for the Godilkinmore? Once we're finished with the Ga'ee, that is."

"Where did that come from?" Mary wondered.

"If I'm too big for my head, then I need to go someplace where I am sure to be a nobody. The Vestrall turned out to be a bunch of punks. The Godilkinmore, if Lev is an example, will be something that we can aspire to. It would be nice to know. I hope they are well."

I do, too, Lev said into their minds, softly but with power.

"We'll talk about it once the Ga'ee are toast." Payne started to pace. They had not yet made it into the corridor. "Lev, if your projections are correct, we should know in about eleven months. Hey! Can we build some of the pieces for the portal here and carry them with us? Maybe get the Berantz portal up quickly to use as a base. Two-week travel from there beats the hell out of the alternatives."

"We can build sections sized for the hangar bays. The biggest challenge is in the software to align the portal with the others in the system. It took three months to get humanity's active," Lev replied.

"The Vestrall have to get better with each one. We'll pick up the crew running the portal near Jupiter and take them to the soon-to-be new one in Berantz space."

"What if they don't want to go?" Mary asked.

Payne stared into the distance for an abnormally long time. "I hadn't contemplated that."

"You'll come up with something to compel them, but think like a negotiator and not a dictator."

"I'm a benevolent dictator," Payne replied.

"Are you two ever going to leave? We were hoping we could make out for a while." The admiral made eyes at the commodore.

"Aren't you too old for that?" Payne asked. "Not that I'm judging, but I am judging."

"How old do you think you have to be before you don't wish to kiss that beautiful wife of yours?" the admiral asked as if Mary weren't standing there. "Go on now. You have things you need to do. It's not just eleven months of waiting. We have to be ready to fight. We need insertion teams with full-powered armor ready to exterminate an infestation. The enemy cannot be allowed even the slightest toehold."

"Weapons. Besides the Vestrall's energy weapon. Did Lev use his when finally engaged?" Payne wondered

"No, because it overloaded my systems. I need to completely reconfigure a power grid, which means taking the ship offline for two days."

"Then do that. We need that weapon." Payne walked back and forth with his hands clasped behind his back.

"We can't do that. All the systems means Davida. I won't do it."

"Can't we provide temporary power to her? A portable generator or something?"

"No. She's tied into the entire ship. She cannot be disconnected. It's all I can do to keep her supplied for the first few minutes following folding space."

"I didn't know," Payne admitted. "I don't think anyone did."

Payne turned around but couldn't take a step because Mary held his arm and pointed toward the corridor.

"That was not for anyone to know. The others don't see a healthy relationship like you do. They do not approve."

"Sometimes, reading minds has to suck."

"The alternative is a step backward if you ask me. At least I don't have to deal with lies. Only when people try to lie to themselves."

"I wish you could have been in on the UN meeting. The

subterfuge probably would have melted your circuits. But next time, if we use the portal, you can hang out in the sky above. Give me some intel to help me influence those we need influenced. Those will be the professional liars."

"I understand. We will see what can be done when next we travel to Earth." Lev committed to nothing. He didn't usually share what he saw in the minds of others.

Mary waved at the admiral and the commodore. "We're leaving."

Payne followed her into the corridor. Mary secured the hatch once they were out. They found Kal waiting for them. He threw a ball down the corridor, and the Cabrizi ran after it.

"Maybe we can get our quarters expanded, like, double the size. Especially if the crew is going to move to the battleships," Payne mused.

"Is that how your mind works? I'm sure I'll never get used to that."

"What? Those topics were done. Now it's on to other things like bigger quarters. Especially if we're going to be here for the duration."

"I wasn't a fan of Vestrall food," Mary replied softly. "I like it here."

"We all do, Dog. What do you say we hit the gym and get super buff?"

"From one workout?" Mary quipped.

"Super buff starts now. With the right exercise program, we can look like Kal." Payne pounded his fist against his chest.

"I don't want to look like Kal."

"High reps for you, then. I need to build my power back to the old Ebren days. That was, like, a million years ago."

"Less than two years, Dec."

"Infinity in universe time. Wait, maybe that goes the other

way. An instant on the grand scale. Still, I need a title, and what better than His Beefy Supremeness, Declan Payne?"

"No." Mary crossed her arms and blocked the cart.

"We gonna duke it out right here, and the winner gets called His Beefy Supremeness?"

"We are not, Mr. Ambassador."

"Fairly stated, Mrs. Ambassador. Shall we? Those weights aren't going to lift themselves. And while we're there, Lev, can you do something with our quarters? You see what I have in mind. A study with bookshelves and a full bathroom with a walk-in shower for two."

"The waste of space is counter to my programming," Lev deadpanned.

"There's room for a hundred thousand on board, and pretty soon, we'll be down to a couple hundred at the most. It's shameless decadence, but you have to concede that humanity is populated almost exclusively by selfish bitches."

"I don't think I'll concede that," Lev replied.

Mary climbed into the cart and motioned for Payne to come aboard.

"Gym, Kal. See you there." Payne waved. Kal jogged to a second cart and jumped in. He fought the Cabrizi off, making them run alongside.

The carts raced down the corridor and up one level to the deck dedicated to Payne and his team. There was a great deal of space on the ship if one wanted to disappear into their own thoughts or be alone when there were a thousand other bodies around.

"I want to lift weights and think," Payne stated. "I need to see what's ahead. What aren't we doing that we should?"

"More people are thinking about that question than you realize..."

"Everything we do is measured in time." –From the
memoirs of Ambassador Declan Payne

Major Woody Malone strolled onto the bridge with his new
executive officer, Lieutenant "Biggy" Fries.

"I'm sure you wondered why I called you here," the admiral
began.

Woody shook his head. "Truth be told, Admiral, I haven't.
We're busy as all get out. Training, preparing, and mostly,
staying out of the way of Lev's construction fleet."

"I'm Biggy Fries." The lieutenant offered his hand.

"You pilots and your ridiculous names. Don't be offended if
I don't call you Biggy." He assessed the pilot, who was skinnier
than a teenager.

"Not at all, Admiral. I'll be happy if you can pick me out of
a lineup with more than one person in it."

The admiral blinked. "Why would you be in a lineup? Is
Earth onto you, too?"

"Me, *too*? No. What? Who else?" the lieutenant stuttered.

The admiral casually turned his attention to the commanding officer of Space Fighter Squadron 317, the Tricky Spinsters. "You and your squadron will remain assigned to *Leviathan*. We will do our best to embark more firepower, three more squadrons of Mosquitoes, or possibly a new fighter. Lev has a few designs. Work with him to see if it might be worth our while to take raw materials on board to build new ships as opposed to bringing older fighters with us. New equipment. New blood."

"How many Mosquitoes are left in the Fleet's inventory?" Woody asked.

"Lev, did you get that information when you were near Earth?" the admiral asked.

"I did. There are no operable space fighters in the Solar System. On the border with the former Braze, scattered across fifteen hundred light-years, Fleet believes there are one hundred and seven."

"We don't need them out there," the admiral started to say.

The commodore shook her head. "Pre-positioned in case of another Ga'ee attack," she suggested. "Where exactly are they, Lev?"

"Four squadrons are in Ebren space, and two squadrons are deployed in interstellar space along the border with the Arn."

"I wish I could ask Arthir why he deployed them like this, but Ebren... A portal is currently being built in Ebren space, is it not?" the admiral asked.

"It was delayed to expedite Earth's portal," Lev explained.

"How long is it from being finished?" the admiral wondered.

"Eight months, according to the old timeline, but that is pending a restart of construction. *That* is pending someone providing the materiel and equipment to do the work."

"Looks like we're going to have to return to Ebren space to

restart work on that portal. We'll contact our forces while there and relieve them of three of their squadrons. They'll join us, with your permission, Lev."

The commodore interjected, "We'll need the construction team from Earth, if they agree to come. And we'll need three more teams of Vestrall engineers."

"How do we entice them to leave Vestrall Prime?" the admiral asked.

"Payne will have to make the pitch. He's the regent," the commodore replied. "But he just left. You can talk to him later. Let him work out for his mental health if nothing else."

"Mental health? What are you talking about? Besides our mutual loathing of the pencil-pushing asswipes on Earth, he's every bit as tuned in as I am."

"Lev, is Payne okay?" the commodore asked.

"I prefer not to comment on what I see in other people's minds, so I'll decline to answer at this time. If it becomes an issue, I'll bring my concerns to you."

"See? Even Lev thinks he's fine."

"How did you come to that conclusion?"

"If his mental health becomes an issue, Lev will tell us. Pretty straightforward that it's not an issue since he's not telling us anything," the admiral explained.

"I think you're reading a lot into Lev's answer, but I'll let it go *for now*."

Woody shifted from foot to foot after a quick glance at the lieutenant. The admiral tried to look confident. "I called you here to talk about training whoever will join us as well as designing the next generation of fighters with Lev. The two efforts go hand in hand."

Woody leaned in. "Any requirements we think we need to fight the Ga'ee?"

"The Ga'ee is the enemy we'll use these against," the admiral confirmed.

"Are you sure they'll be coming back? I mean, they got their asses kicked last time they were here. Royally. They fled without any of their drones, and their ship was on fire, with her back broken."

"Judging from the ship they were building on the Berantz homeworld, eleven months. The planets here are conducive to the expansion of their species. They don't have to look any farther for planets to colonize. They only need to be a little bit stronger than us, and they'll have free rein in our part of the galaxy." The admiral assumed his executive position, hands behind his back while fighting to keep from pacing so he wouldn't look like Payne.

Woody chewed the inside of his lip. He would follow the admiral's orders regardless, but he felt he had a say. With a good conversation, he could buy into the mission. "We'll be ready, Admiral. We'll take the new old squadrons on board, and then we'll see what we can do with building a test bird or three. I like that we can build a ship in a day as long as we have the metals and other minerals on board. That blows my mind."

"As soon as we have the battlewagons online and the crews boarded, we'll build a sample of each fighter you design with Lev. Better get to it, gentlemen."

"Lev, you better be at the top of your game since we're bringing it. The most exotic fighters in the existence of the universe are about to make an appearance." Woody beamed with pride.

"You pronounced 'functional' wrong. Go on, now. I have work to do, and so do you." The admiral tipped his head to the pilots.

The two junior officers saluted and hurried off the bridge.

"What do you have to do?" Nyota asked after they'd gone.

"Nothing. It sounded profound, though, and it encouraged them to leave. I need to do that with Payne."

"Payne is an ally just like everyone on *Leviathan*. You're surrounded by good people."

"Including you, Nyota. Without Arthir, I need your counsel."

"No one is an island, Harry. Not even *Leviathan*."

The two faced the tactical board, where the construction status of ten battlewagons was displayed as simple thermometers going from zero to one hundred. The first ship was at fifty percent and the second at thirty. The third through the tenth had moved forward at least five percent. Lev was overlapping construction to maximize the available equipment. Nothing sat idle. In nine days, ten brand-new battlewagons would be powered up and running their crews through space trials.

"Show us the view outside the ship, Lev, if you would be so kind. I'd like to watch the magic as it's happening."

"Not magic, Harry. Process refined with zero inefficiencies."

The shipyard was being torn apart by small bots cutting or unbolting the structures, whichever was deemed to be the quickest. The superstructure and supporting hubs were separated into basic parts by the next series of robotic assemblies. Those delivered the high-tech parts to the hangar bay, where they were repurposed into new circuit boards, processors, relays, and more.

The heavy metal was smelted into a three-dimensional printer that shaped and built the ship from the inside out. As sections were completed, the inner workings were delivered from *Leviathan* and installed by an army of small multi-armed bots. In the time it took to transfer a piece from one to the other, it was installed and the next delivered.

Modular systems within, a single structure without—and a

weapon integrated into the hull to deliver power in a way even the Ga'ee couldn't defend against.

The first ship advanced to fifty-two percent after they watched for less than five minutes.

"Simply amazing. I'm glad we didn't waste too much time with Earth."

"We still need them, Harry," Nyota countered. "We need humanity standing shoulder to shoulder with the Braze."

"If only they see it that way. It won't take anything to convince the Ebren to go to war. Or the Rang'Kor, or the Berantz. The Zuloon and the Arn will come on board when they see that they might be next."

"The Zuloon Partnership is closest to where we last saw the Ga'ee."

"Arthir took the armada to talk with them. That should have happened weeks ago. It'll be nice to talk with her and see where we stand. When will we meet up with *Cleophas* and the armada?"

Lev replied. "Unknown. They are too far away for me to see their energy vibrations now and even when we were in Earth's Solar System."

"Then we need beacons. Faster-than-light-capable ships that can relay messages through their engine signatures," the admiral suggested.

"That would be one way to make it work. The other involves smaller ships that can transit the portals back and forth to relay messages," Lev replied.

"A primary and a backup. The Ga'ee took out space stations that hadn't attacked them. I suspect they'll do the same thing to a portal. We still need a faster-than-light comm."

"A poor man's long-range system," Nyota added.

The admiral nodded slowly. "Nothing poor about any of it, but it works. Thanks to Arthir."

"What's next?"

"See the ship construction through to completion, and as soon as possible after the last ship is ready, we return to Earth. Payne has an appointment."

"You should go with him," Nyota suggested.

"I don't look good in stripes or behind bars. When you put those two things together? I'm going to have to say 'no.'" The admiral gave his most emphatic look.

"You mean yes, and you know it."

His look hadn't been enough. Nyota was right. He was going with Declan Payne to see the president and convince her of the work Earth needed to do. It was worth the risk because Nyota was right about something else, too. Humanity needed to stand side by side with the other races and fight off the Ga'ee together.

————

"Mryasmalites, this is the regent. I need your help." Payne rolled his eyes and bit his tongue.

"What?" was the curt reply from a member of the former ruling council.

"I need four engineering construction teams for a year to manage the building of portals in Braze Collective space. I assume we'll be able to transfer the team that is on Earth since the Jupiter portal has been completed."

"That's all? You only want our leading scientists and engineers to spend a full year off Vestrall Prime?"

"Yep," Payne replied. "That's all. I'll need them in nine days. Put together a list of volunteers, and I'll review it."

"No." The former Mryasmalites were less than accommodating when it came to Payne asking for anything. He usually ended up making it an order, then leaning heavily on anyone who opposed his edicts.

"Okay. I'll consolidate the list and order those on it to the spaceport. I'll take double the numbers to be sure I get the minimum number I need. They'll be paid double-time for their efforts."

"What does double-time mean?"

"Twice the normal pay. They'll earn it." Payne was sure they would, even though he didn't have any credits or money to pay them. He assumed he'd figure it out over the next year.

"We don't use such an economic system. That means nothing to us. You lived here for a year, and still, you know nothing about us."

"That about it sums it up," Payne replied. "But it doesn't. Your economics are meaningless in the rest of the universe. If your people are going to live and work out here, they need to understand what it takes not only to survive but to thrive under humanity's economic system."

"Maybe the rest of the universe should follow our model," the voice retorted.

"Or you could learn to deal with reality the way it is right now and not some fantasy version. Your ideal didn't work, and that left me in charge of the Vestrall. I know how fucked up that sounds. It does to me, too.

"Until you guys figure out how to play nice with others, you have to deal with me being in charge. Four teams of engineers to manage the construction of four portals. It's not a hard task. It would be easier if your boy on the space station hadn't murdered all of your people, so maybe it *is* better that I'm in charge. You people are too violent for your own good."

"The Vestrall are not violent. We left that to the Braze Collective."

Payne groaned. "That doesn't make it sound any better.

Please understand that you killed millions of humans through your proxies. I'm going to continue being shitty to you until you show a little fucking remorse. Get me those teams. I'll be back in touch tomorrow so we can bring them aboard *Leviathan*."

Payne closed the connection.

He smiled at his wife. "That's taken care of. What's next?"

[8]

*"Being powerful is like being virtuous. If you have to tell
people you are, you aren't."* –From the memoirs of
Ambassador Declan Payne

"They should have names," Mary stated. "Just having a number
is so..." She struggled for the word before settling on "Sterile.
Loyalty to their ship starts with a name they can embrace."

"If we let the crews give them names, it'll take longer than
the time we have," the admiral replied.

The four stared at the tactical screen. The new
battlewagons were running through their paces by blasting
designated asteroids with undesirable metal content. The main
weapons were as devastating as the four remembered.

"Names," Payne said. "Damn, Dog. You're making things
hard. These things usually take committees and votes and years.
You're not giving us that kind of time, are you?"

"Five minutes," she replied.

"Which suggests you already have the answer. Spill it."

The admiral looked confused. "You call your wife 'Dog?'"

Payne waved him off. "Don't give her an escape. Names, *Dog*."

"BW-1 should be called the *Sinkhaus*."

Payne grabbed his head to keep it from exploding. "You have got to be shitting me. That toad? That asswipe of a human being. Detritus from the bottom of the cesspool..." He stomped his feet and stormed around the bridge.

"Hear me out," Mary called.

"I see now why he didn't win her over on his first trip. Confirms it. I'll be joining him for Round Two."

Payne stopped ranting. "Sir?"

"I'm going with you," the admiral told him matter-of-factly. "Assuming your team's work in restoring me to Fleet admiral is still in place, of course."

Payne looked at Mary for support. She pointed at the screen. "*Sinkhaus*. One hundred percent about swaying her opinion."

"Won't it look that way? Can't we just call it *President*?"

"He has a point," the admiral interjected.

"You see where I was going. The names will give our people something to be loyal to while bringing the politicians to your side." Mary smiled with the revelation.

"The rest will be called America, Europe, Lesser China, Australia, Lemuria, and so on?" Payne guessed.

"Cheesy but sound. We numbered them in order of their designated- and self-importance. If we make fifty more, then we go down the list of voting importance. It's not controversial," Mary replied. "And your bureaucrat buddies would look for any reason to complain."

"I'm thinking the numbers make more sense. Earth gov. Not my idea of those we want to name ships after," Payne countered. "No, you're right. With the admiral's concurrence, tell our fleet of battlewagons what their names are."

"Send it, Lev." The admiral pointed at the screen, and the ships' names were added to the designations. BW-01 became BW-01 *The President*.

"I feel like I need to take a shower," Payne grumbled.

Mary backhanded his upper arm. "Deal with it, you big baby."

Payne forced a yawn. "Bored."

"We'll be returning to Earth soon," the admiral inserted. "Better get dressed."

"Unlike last time, when I could have done better." Payne made a face. "I don't know what medals I have for my dress uniform."

"Put on a row of gold stars and top it with a solar flare," the admiral advised.

"I didn't get the solar flare. I would have remembered that." The solar flare was the highest decoration in the Fleet, usually awarded posthumously.

"You earned it. We stopped doing paperwork on that stuff when we realized it didn't matter. We brought warfighters, not paper pushers, on Operation Stranglehold."

"Or Brass 'Nads," Payne added. "That was a good operation."

"Solar Flare. At least one. And a whole row of gold stars. Wear them with pride, Declan."

Payne nodded. He and Mary headed out into the corridor to the waiting cart, where they found Kal and the Cabrizi waiting.

"You can join us on the bridge," Payne suggested as the five bodies squeezed into the single cart. Mary and Declan each had a Cabrizi filling their laps.

"I'll give you your privacy. Plus, it's a might boring in there when y'all get to talking strategery like you do," Kal drawled. "It makes me want to take a long walk off a short pier."

"You have to keep the Cabrizi entertained, too, or they'll

wreak havoc," Mary suggested. "Let's go back to the room and see what there is to see."

"Sounds like an invitation for snuggle time. I'm jiggy." Payne flicked his eyebrows.

Mary gave him her best bored expression. Turnabout and all that.

The cart departed and continued up the ramp and into the corridor where the team's rooms were located. It stopped near the main corridor, not the outboard hull.

"We've been assigned new quarters." Mary opened the door to reveal a massive suite with multiple rooms like a condominium on Earth.

"Lev, buddy!" Payne didn't know what else to say.

"If this is going to be our home, we might as well make it a home and not a bunk on a warship. Everyone on the team is getting the same thing. Six individual cabins become a single suite, and it doesn't affect Lev's capacity. We can still board a hundred thousand refugees and move them to a new planet if needed."

"Home. Still feels weird, Dog, but I'm comfortable here."

"I am too, Dog," Mary replied.

"I'm sure it doesn't work that way. We can't both be Dog."

"Have it your way, Snickerdoodle," Mary replied.

Payne blinked rapidly. She was four moves into the chess match before he realized they were playing. It was his move.

"I'm thinking 'Champion,' or maybe 'Stud Muffin.' Something that people imagine when they think of me."

"Pudding Pop? Snuggle Bunny?" Mary smiled. He had made his move like an amateur.

The board cleared, and his countermove became obvious. "How about we tour the mansion instead, Mary, my love?"

She hugged him and kissed his cheek. They walked from room to room. A study with multiple screens on the walls. A walk-in bathroom with a shower for two and a tub with air jets. A living room with a couch. A bedroom with an oversized bed, big enough for both of them and the Cabrizi on the odd days they didn't stay with Kal.

"A home we don't deserve. Thanks, Lev." Payne opened the closet to find a Fleet dress uniform with the medals already attached. "More stuff I don't deserve. Everyone on the team should be wearing the same thing. None of us made it on our own."

"You fought the Ebren champion by yourself."

"With Lev's help in juicing me, so I was every bit the engineered combatant Kal was."

Mary shrugged. "A level playing field. That's all it was. You still had to fight, and if I remember correctly, you were beat to hell and could barely stand for a week afterward."

Payne tsk-tsked. "It was three days at the most."

"That was the turning point in the war. And it was just you."

Payne didn't reply. He didn't feel right about taking credit. "But it wasn't. It was ten billion souls on Earth counting on me to be strong. It was my team wanting me to come back. And it was you. I wasn't going to fail you." His eyes glistened, but only for a moment. "Lev, when do we need to be dressed?"

"You have three hours. The admiral has asked the Payne-class battlewagons for two more maneuvers to make sure they can fire together, coordinated to deliver the single most powerful strike possible should the Ga'ee materialize before we're ready."

"Payne-class? That hurts my head. But if they all fire at the same time, they'll all be down at the same time, too."

Payne looked at the inviting bed. He wanted to break it in properly, but his duty to the Fleet took precedence. "Why don't you wait here? I won't be long."

"The only way you won't be long is if I come with you." Mary was in the corridor, where a cart waited. It was as if Lev had known they would have to return to the bridge.

Payne tapped his foot like an impatient teenager as the cart accelerated down the main corridor.

"How many years did you not have me as a distraction?" Mary asked.

"Enough to know that I have a lot of time to make up for!"

Mary snorted. "Not the answer I was looking for, but fair enough. I don't have a witty retort. You have played the trump card. Well done, Mr. Payne."

"My pleasure, Mrs. Payne. We'll be here for no more than an hour," Payne declared. "You hear me, Lev!" Payne shook his fist at the overhead. "An hour and we're leaving. We have business to take care of."

"Your definition of business is nonstandard, Declan, but it seems that Mary shares your, shall we say, desire?"

"Lev! I never took you for a prude." The two laughed as the cart slowed.

"Heaven forbid! Compared to what I hear from Marsha and Cointreau, you two are missionaries from a different era."

"*Lev! Don't tell us that,*" Payne shouted. He winced before continuing. "I won't be able to look at them. I already can't look at them.

"Your team has needs, Declan. Some are taken care of, but others warrant some consideration."

Payne lost his humor in a sudden pang of guilt about having Mary by his side. She gripped his hand. "Not your fault."

"But it's mine to fix. What can we do for Virgil or any of the others? I should have asked before we transferred everyone to other ships."

"Not everyone, Declan. Annaliese is now a member of the SFS-317, along with Federico, Alex, Wysteria, and Digitus."

"I feel like I should know those names, but I don't. You'll need to help me, Lev."

Mary leaned close as if Lev were speaking aloud. They only perceived it that way, but Lev spoke directly into both their minds.

Annaliese is who Virgil has been trying to keep secret from you since she's still a new recruit. Federico, Alex, and Wysteria have been dating Laura, Augry, and Huberta. And Digitus has been trying to woo Alphonse away from his computer. It appears to be working, much to Katello's dismay.

Payne stared at the wall. "My whole team is dating, and I didn't know it."

Salem is taking her study of the Shaolin way seriously, which doesn't allow for romantic relationships. Katello is happy as he is.

"Sparky, Byle, Joker, and Buzz all have girlfriends and boyfriends in the Tricky Spinsters. Shipboard romances don't usually turn out well, Lev. Mary and I are an exception to that rule. We can't have those relationships turn sour, Lev. Otherwise, it'll be hell for everyone."

I have selected the most compatible souls, arranged the introductions, and encouraged the right behaviors.

Payne's eyes shot wide. "You're a matchmaker and played with their minds to put them into happy relationships? Lev, buddy, that's a bit of a stretch."

The admiral cheered from the bridge.

Payne wanted to continue the conversation with Lev, but only for a moment. "Dammit, Lev! You've known all this time, and you waited until we're in the final tests of the new ships, along with on our way back to Earth. That's when you choose to deliver this nuclear depth bomb! You suck."

Payne stormed onto the bridge. "Pudding Pop, arriving."

The admiral and commodore stared at him.

"What was the yelling about, and who is Pudding Pop?"

"Sir, there seems to be a difference of opinion on optimal times to break news to people. I owe Lev a sound ass-kicking."

"How do you propose to accomplish such a feat when Lev has no ass?"

Payne crossed his arms and lifted his head. "I'm adding it to a long list of injustices perpetrated unto me by his lordship, Lev of the Void."

"I like that," Lev replied via the overhead.

The admiral shrugged the madness off him like a dog shaking water from its coat. "Massed strikes should overwhelm Ga'ee defenses."

"Five and five, so we're not completely defenseless in between. And who named them Payne-class?"

"Aren't you full of piss and vinegar today? That doesn't have anything to do with your impending meeting at the UN, does it?" The admiral waited, but Payne didn't reply. "With a forty-second recharge time, we're going to have gaps."

"If we fire one at a time, the gaps are only four seconds. During that time, the Ga'ee can launch thousands of drones. Lev's analysis suggests we need five simultaneous attacks on a single point of the Ga'ee ship to guarantee they'll overwhelm the energy shield and penetrate the interior. Twenty seconds later, we can do it again."

"Twenty seconds is an awful long time in space combat. Too many bad things can happen in that window, especially if our ships can't defend themselves."

"That's why the strikes need to be precise. We have to hit them at a range of less than fifty thousand kilometers. And the battlewagons aren't exactly helpless. Two completely separate and distinct power sources. The main weapon has its own supply. Everything else is on a separate grid, nearly as powerful. So, these ships can shoot while moving, unlike their predecessors."

"I almost can't wait for the Ga'ee to return, but for us to array our Fleet against them, but they'll have to have already done some damage to one of the seven races. I don't want to see that. I just want to make sure the Ga'ee never return to our space."

The admiral pointed at the tactical display. The last five battlewagons were lining up to take their shots. Each maneuvered aggressively, as if dodging incoming fire before turning their bows at the last instant and aligning them toward a single asteroid. They fired as one, and five massive energy waves slammed into a rock twenty kilometers across. The waves obliterated the asteroid, turning it into nothing more than space dust.

"That was impressive." Payne stared at the point in space where the hefty asteroid used to be. "Time to go to Earth?"

"After a quick debrief, but you don't need to be in on that. Lev tells me you had something else to take care of before meeting the president."

"We do. I mean, I do. We'll meet you at *Ugly 5* when it's time to go ashore."

"This time, your transit will be a little different. Lev is going to the UN. He'll represent himself." The admiral and the commodore looked pleased with themselves.

"See you in a bit. We'll be dressed for the occasion."

Declan and Mary strolled out to find Kal waiting for them. "Did you get new quarters, too?" Payne asked.

"I did, and would you believe it, the one I'm supposed to be watching out for abandons me, left for the vultures to gnaw my bones."

"We're on board *Leviathan*. He won't let anything happen to us. Lev is in everyone's mind and knows if somebody has ill intent."

"Easy for you to say. Next thing you know, a rattlesnake will be two fangs into your calf," Kal drawled.

"I'm pretty sure there are no rattlesnakes on board. But we're going to the UN. If you have a dress uniform of some sort, let Lev know, and he'll fix you up."

"You fought me in my dress uniform," Kal deadpanned.

Payne threw his hands up. "You have to wear clothes, Kal. You can't be shaking your dangling dino at the president."

"Have it your way, Declan. Me. Unwanted, unloved, and dressed in rags."

Payne climbed into the waiting cart. "None of the above. Take a load off and find something fancy-schmancy to stuff yourself into."

Kal yelled at the Cabrizi in Ebren so he could usher them into Payne's cart. Once they were settled, he tipped his head to the humans. "I'll be taking a walk to clear my mind. If you can watch the boys for a bit, I'd be obliged."

Payne's mouth fell open. He and Mary held onto the beasts as the cart took them back to their quarters. They opened the door, and the Cabrizi ran inside.

"This is Lev's doing. He's punishing me."

Mary pulled herself tightly against him. "If you want to get dressed, you need to get undressed first."

"Now you're talking!"

The alarm started softly and grew more insistent the longer Payne tried to ignore it. "What now? Lev, you could have just told us."

"You were in the middle of something," Lev replied.

"Lev! We haven't even started yet. Just tell me."

"The Ga'ee have dropped out of FTL. They are in the Vestrall home system."

[9]

"There comes a time in everyone's life when they have to stop what they're doing and focus on the one thing that will save their existence." –From the memoirs of Ambassador Declan Payne

Payne took off running. Mary and the Cabrizi caught up. They piled into the cart unceremoniously, clinging to each other as the cart accelerated away.

"What the hell?" Payne snarled. "At least we're armed and ready. Two weeks ago, the Ga'ee could have annihilated Vestrall Prime. Two hours from now, they could have done the same thing."

Mary nodded. The timing seemed odd and fantastically lucky. Payne had shown her that luck was nothing more than working hard at the right things, but that had nothing to do with *Leviathan* being in the Vestrall system for ten total days.

And that was when the Ga'ee showed up. When the cart arrived at the bridge, Declan and Mary ran inside.

"Have they communicated why they're here?" Payne wondered.

The admiral shook his head. The battlewagons arrayed themselves to engage the Ga'ee carrier the second it was close enough.

"They are here for a reason. There is zero chance they showed up randomly while we're here. What do they want, Lev?"

"I shall attempt to talk with them."

Blinky and Buzz burst onto the bridge, rushed to a communications station, and plugged in to bring up the latest. The digital team was in place and ready to go.

Lev spoke at the speed of light using binary. No human could follow it. They waited until he was done.

The Ga'ee ship slowed to a stop in the orbit of the fifth planet, an outer planet that was on the far side of the Vestrall star.

"They are here to discuss terms for our surrender," Lev reported. "This ship doesn't have our language files. It has not learned the lesson of the other."

"When we have an optimal solution, be ready to fire," the admiral said softly.

"Wait. *Please.*" Payne watched the tactical screen for any indication that the Ga'ee carrier was either launching drones or continuing deeper into the system. "Whenever they spoke before, they said the opposite of what they meant. Are they looking to surrender?"

"I will clarify," Lev offered. "I'll ask them to turn around and face out of the system if they intend to surrender."

After a brief conversation between Lev and the Ga'ee, the carrier ship turned around. Its side doors remained closed.

"We need to board that ship before we do anything," Payne said. "Admiral, with your permission, I'll take Team Payne to the Ga'ee ship. Have them open the doors for us."

Payne waited. Mary shifted from foot to foot.

"Lev, give them their instructions, including our language files. They're to open a single outer door to allow *Ugly 5* to land. It doesn't matter if they have heat or atmosphere, but we'd appreciate it if they did." The admiral looked at Payne. "Team Payne is a go."

Declan took Mary by the shoulders. "Look after the Cabrizi while we're gone."

Mary nodded tightly. It had been her choice to leave the team. Now came the hard part. She had to watch them leave without her.

Let the waiting begin.

Like spouses of old, she said what had been said a billion times before by voices across the galaxy. "You better bring your ass home, and not in a body bag, either!"

"New quarters that we have yet to break in? You know I'll be back." He kissed her fiercely but quickly and ran for the corridor.

Mary caught the Cabrizi and struggled to hold them as they tried to join Declan and Kal. "Lev, secure the hatch and fire up the captain's chair. I don't need to know Godilkinmore anymore, but I do need to speak Ebren."

"Please take a seat. This will only take a moment," Lev replied.

———

Payne vaulted into the cart. Kal jumped in beside him, squeezing him half-out. The vehicle launched forward. It was a straight run to the hangar, up three ramps with no turns except at the end. Payne clung to the seat and Kal's arm with all the strength in his fingers.

The cart hovered except when cornering, where the wheels provided the necessary friction for tighter turns. It also had to slow to drop low enough for the wheels to engage. On a straight run, it didn't need to do that.

In all his days aboard *Leviathan*, this was the fastest he'd ever gone. He felt like he was riding in his old skimmer, *Glamorous Glennis.*

They reached the hangar bay in record time. No one else had yet arrived.

"Lev, update," Payne requested.

"No change in their orientation or posture, Declan," the AI replied. "They are waiting for you."

Payne stripped off his clothes and stepped into his powered combat armor. During the sealing process, Heckler and Turbo arrived. Payne carried his helmet.

"Are we going to blow up a Ga'ee ship?" Heckler asked, tearing off his clothes as he walked. In twenty seconds, he was securing his suit. Turbo was ready moments later.

"That's not the primary plan, but bring enough explosives in case the plan changes and we need to take out a deck or three. Do we have any weapons to deal with these things yet?"

Heckler blew out a breath between clenched teeth. He shook his head.

"I didn't think so but had to ask. Kal, bring the plasma cannon. And you two, bring a second cannon. It's the best we can muster for this fight—if there is a fight."

Dank ran in from the corridor with a young woman close behind him.

"Team area only," Payne told her. She slowed to a stop and stared at Major Dank.

"I'm Annaliese," she explained softly.

As much as Payne felt time was racing against him, he took a moment to do what he felt needed to be done.

He held out an armored hand. "Declan Payne. You're here to see Virgil off. That's good. We know what we're fighting for, but that reminder, the last sight of our loved ones, isn't a bad thing. I just left Mary on the bridge. You should go there and talk with her as soon as we're out the door. I need to go, but we can all talk later when we have time."

She nodded but kept her mouth closed. The others arrived in two carts and dismounted as if it were a military movement. They headed straight for the cage and started undressing.

Payne returned to the team area. "Explosives, and for want of anything better, railguns. We'll have two plasma cannons for the team in case we need to secure a hostile egress."

"That usually does it," Sparky mused.

Three others arrived and joined Annaliese. It put Payne on edge.

Then Mary showed up with the Cabrizi. She yelled at them in fluent Ebren.

Kal bounced and nodded approvingly.

"Get on the ship," he ordered his team while he walked the other way.

He scanned the faces of those who looked far too young to serve in the Fleet, but serve they did. They'd been surreptitiously transferred to Woody's squadron to keep them on board *Leviathan*. Payne had a hard time reconciling himself with that. He'd kept them on Vestrall Prime for over a year with no other humans.

He was happy for them and glad that no one had asked for his approval. He wouldn't have given it.

Accept the decisions that are in the best interest of your people, Payne told himself. *And in your best interest.*

He cleared his throat before speaking. "I'm Declan Payne. This job is hard. It's a sacrifice." He toed the non-skid coating on the hangar deck. "I'm glad that you came to see us off, but we need to go. I will do everything humanly possible to bring everyone home, something I've been able to accomplish in every mission we've undertaken. We've trained hard to get here, and we have something to come back to. All of us. If I can ask one thing of you, it's this. Please don't hurt any of my people. They can stand toe to toe with any alien and fight through the blood and pain, but we're not good at dealing with our emotions." He locked eyes with Mary. "My wife will talk to you after we've gone. She'll help you understand what we do and how we do it. Help you to help us."

They continued to watch him as if expecting him to say more. He put his helmet over his head and locked it into place, then walked away. This wasn't a distraction he needed, but he understood they all needed it.

He boarded, and the doors dropped into place, sealing *Ugly 5*. It immediately lifted off the deck and angled toward the hangar opening.

The Ga'ee ship hung in space, a monument to danger and fear.

The team avoided looking at Payne.

"I'm sure Lev put them up to it, you knuckleheads!" Payne pointed an accusing finger at each of them. "And it's okay. It's about time you people had something to do in your off-time besides get in trouble."

Joker leaned next to Sparky. "I don't remember getting in trouble when I was off. Do you?"

"He's projecting. The only one in trouble was him." Sparky nodded at Payne, who was two seats away.

"I'm not sure I got in trouble," Payne said over his speakers. He was the only one wearing his helmet, which reminded him. "Get your helmets on in case the Ga'ee pull a fast one. We need to be ready for anything."

The team quickly snapped their helmets into place.

Payne dialed up a P2P channel, point to point, with Major

Dank. "Keep them on their toes, Virgil. Don't let their friends distract them from the mission."

"Or us, Dec. Brief us on what to expect. The details for this mission were scant, to say the least."

"I was fixing to do that very thing." Payne switched to the team channel. "About twenty minutes ago, a Ga'ee carrier ship entered the Vestrall home system. They didn't have our language files, so they probably aren't associated with the other Ga'ee ship. Also, judging by the distances, they would have had to get underway about the same time as the other ship. Did they ship 'colonists' out across a broad swath of the Milky Way?"

Payne's brief became an analysis of the situation.

"But they offered to surrender, which is a very un-Ga'ee-like behavior," Virgil suggested.

"That's what we're going to find out. We're about to board the Ga'ee carrier. Blinky and Buzz, I need you guys at the top of your game. If they are truly offering to surrender, the first thing I'll ask for is access to their database. I need you in there and finding what there is to find even if they don't give us access."

"We'll be undertaking some major digital spelunking," Blinky replied. "We have our link with Lev, but I don't expect that to be sustainable. We'll be on our own in there."

"That's not bringing me joy, Blinky. I want to feel the love. I want to feel like we're in charge."

Blinky's helmet rocked back and forth. "We'll do our best. We'll collect more data about their neural network, regardless."

"And if we don't make it out alive?" Sparky asked.

"Enough of the negative energy, Sparky." Payne raised his armored hands for calm. "We're going in there to accept their surrender. If they try to play fuck-fuck games with us, we're going to kick some ass and take names. We'll be at their mercy for a short period, but keep those plasma cannons on hand and ready to deploy. Railguns to suppress, but our leverage point is our explosives. We'll crack that ship in half if we need to."

"Place them during ingress?" Dank asked.

Payne wanted to say yes, but he couldn't. The art of diplomacy twisted his insides.

"We have to give them the benefit of the doubt. Until we know for sure whether we have a shot at getting them to stand down, we have to wait. But be ready."

The team grumbled, and Payne let them. This enemy had been merciless toward anyone and everyone in the space of the six races. Now they were in the seventh race's system, and there was no reason to believe anything had changed.

Except for their non-confrontational posture. That was different, and it warranted a unique approach.

One with less violence and destruction.

The only reason he considered meeting with the Ga'ee was that he also stood ready to inflict the maximum amount of damage to them and their ship. Never negotiate without a plan to destroy the enemy.

It bolstered one's confidence.

Payne nodded but not enough for his helmet to move. No one saw.

"Heckler, on point with Turbo. Don't be trigger-happy, but don't let the wrigglers get on you."

"How about we ask that they meet us in the hangar bay?" Virgil asked.

"I'd go with that as long as Blinky and Buzz can intercept a signal and get into their database. I doubt we'll come to an agreement on this trip, but I want their data. I want everything there is to know about them from their perspective. I want to know where they come from. I want to know how they communicate. Most importantly, I want to know what their intentions regarding this part of the galaxy are."

"We'll need their database to be certain," Virgil replied.

"I'm going to ask them up front, too. See if they are willing to obfuscate like they've done to us before."

"They can masticate a cauldron of Richards!" Joker blurted.

"You used to be the quiet one," Payne replied. "But I like the new you."

"A year on Vestrall Prime will make you weird," Joker said and held up one thumb. The other team members gave the thumbs-ups in solidarity.

"It's okay if I never step foot on Vestrall Prime again," Payne suggested. "I think the Vestrall are good with us not coming down there either, but in the interim, I'm not good with the Ga'ee being in this system. We'll land and see what the wrigglers have in mind. Then we'll do the right thing for all humanity, as well as the Braze Collective."

"What if they're willing to leave the rest of us alone if we give them Vestrall Prime?" Heckler asked.

"I'd be inclined to give it to them if Vestrall Prime were mine to give. Despite my awesome title and position of Mryasmalite regent, I can't give away what isn't mine."

"It was just a thought. People who thought nothing of the rest of us being able to sacrifice themselves for the rest of us. Turnabout is indeed fair play when it comes to the Vestrall." Dank exaggerated his nod to make sure his helmet moved for the others to see.

The tactical screen showed the Ga'ee ship getting bigger. A small door was inset into the cantilevered sides of the flying shoebox, designated as *Count Boxenstabby* by Admiral Wesson. They flew toward the small door, but the larger doors remained closed.

"That's a good sign, at the very least, for *Leviathan* and our battlewagons."

The ships maneuvered into acceptable firing positions while

the Ga'ee sat with the ship's backside turned toward them. It would make for an easier escape, but ten massed energy weapons would obliterate the ship.

Payne was confident that the Ga'ee wouldn't leave the system alive.

Ugly 5 approached the outer door and passed through the small opening. Every member of the team leaned close to the screens in the doors to look at the contents of the hangar bays. Where they expected to find tens of thousands of drones, they saw only empty space stretching far into the distance. The hangar bay wasn't lit except for *Ugly 5's* lights.

"That's different." Payne said what they were all thinking. "Maybe they *are* for real."

Ugly 5 continued across the hangar bay on a vector the Ga'ee had provided. The insertion craft approached a supply door that led into the ship and toward the backbone. Other access points were no more than half a meter high.

The Ga'ee weren't very tall.

"Lev, do we still have you?" Payne asked.

"I am here, and I have a clear signal," the AI confirmed.

"What do you make of this?" Payne wondered.

"A suspicious individual might look at this as a decoy. The Ga'ee thrive with the hive mind approach, so it's disconcerting that I can't scan the ship to see if there are any life forms aboard. To be fully functional, the ship should be filled with Ga'ee."

"Blinky and Buzz, get to it. Find a way in and steal their data. Do it fast because I'm not liking what I see. Would the Ga'ee sacrifice one of their carriers to kill Team Payne?"

"At the faster-than-light speeds the Ga'ee carrier showed, had they sent this ship from PX47 space the instant the other ship arrived, it would still need another month to get here. Berantz space is even farther away. Only Ebren and Rang'Kor space are closer. This ship should have no knowledge of Team

Payne. They only spoke binary, not Rang'Kor or Standard like the other Ga'ee ship, which had received language files during their first encounter."

Payne had a decision to make, and he didn't like it.

"We're going to leave *Ugly 5* and continue on foot into the ship. Keep your line with us active. Set up an alarm so if our signal gets cut, we can take immediate action."

"I am adding that kernel to your suit communications systems." Moments later, Lev confirmed, "An alarm will sound if you lose contact with me."

"They shouldn't be here," Buzz mumbled while hammering on his computer.

"Blinky and Buzz, where are you two better served, with us or on the uglymobile?" Payne asked.

"Here," Buzz replied instantly.

Blinky shook his head. "We're getting the same signals we've had little luck tapping. We need to access a hardline so we can isolate the data. It doesn't look any different than static in the airwaves."

Payne gestured for them to stow the equipment they had just taken out.

Ugly 5 settled to the deck nearly two kilometers into the hangar bay. Close by, an oversized hatch started to swing open. Payne waited inside the buttoned-up insertion craft for the movement to stop.

"Maneuver us so we can see inside, Lev."

The ship lifted slightly off the deck and turned to shine a light down a long and empty corridor. The shadows of connecting passageways appeared at set intervals to the far end. Lev dialed a narrow, high-intensity light to show the hatch there.

Dank commented, "Looks like the drone delivery system for both the port and starboard hangars."

"I agree," Lev confirmed.

"Open the doors. Let's see if we're going to have an escort."

"Is it just me, or is this spooky as fuck?" Sparky wondered.

"It's not just you," Joker replied.

"Changing up the formation. Kal on point with the plasma cannon. Heckler next to him, with Sparky providing railgun support. Then Turbo with the tripod for Heckler's cannon, I'll be next, and the rest are behind me. Virgil, bring up the rear, and don't hesitate to boobytrap those passages as we pass. Byle and Shaolin, if we make it to the halfway point without changing direction, I'll need you two to run ahead and open that far hatch. See if they're hiding anything in that port hangar."

"I'll stick a motion detector in each connecting passage at the least," Virgil stated.

The sides of *Ugly 5* levered upward to allow the team to exit the ship nearly simultaneously.

The team members ran off and established a perimeter around the insertion craft. If they hadn't been in their suits, they would have taken a knee to limit the profile they presented to a watching enemy. In their suits, they activated their sensors with the extended range that being upright gave them.

No threats.

"Looks like a dead ship, Dec, except that they opened the doors for us, whoever *they* are." Dank hurried from one SOFTie to another as a final double-check on position and operational status. Each suit carried a health indicator on the upper chest plate. The data on his heads-up display, his HUD, matched what showed on the indicator.

Checking it on the ship was one thing, but operational status was best verified once deployed.

Even if it was on a hangar deck.

Payne verified the ambient temperature: minus seventy Celsius with an oxygen-nitrogen atmosphere.

"Almost like it was meant to make us feel welcome. Almost. Keep your helmets on, people. A little brisk out there, even though they only seeded planets that were warm with breathable air. Might be an indicator that they don't have any of their people on board."

Payne couldn't figure out the enigma that was the Ga'ee.

"I agree with you, Dec. I don't think there are any Ga'ee on board," Virgil replied. "Could be an AI running the ship, just like Lev."

"Are we dialed in to find the silicon life forms, Blinky, Buzz?" Payne asked.

"As much as possible," Blinky replied. "It's part of your ground materials scan inside your HUD. Should be top right on your screen."

"Right where it was last time we had to deal with these bastards. Nothing there. No sign of a silicon life form," Payne said. He pumped his fist and pointed with his arm at the open hatch. "Move out, people. And Lev, if anything weird happens, I'd appreciate it if you came and got us. Cut this tin can open, and we'll meet you outside."

Dank opened a P2P channel. "Where did that come from?"

"I got a bad feeling about this, Virge. If there are no Ga'ee on board, what the hell is the ship doing here?"

"That's what we need to find out," Virgil replied.

"And that's why we're headed inside instead of taking the easy path, which is leaving and blowing this thing to kingdom come as a technology demonstrator of our new battlewagons."

"That would give me a warm and fuzzy, but roger on your bad feeling, Dec. I think we all have it."

Payne returned to the team channel as Kal and Heckler moved into the lead, barely able to fit side by side since Kal was nearly doubled over.

"Stay frosty, people. We're on a mission to find out what

makes this thing tick. Fighting Ga'ee wasn't on my dance card for today, so I'm already pissed off. They better not give me any reason to get angrier."

The team moved into the tunnel. Payne could see nothing besides the backs of the suits in front of him. Behind him were more suits filling the space. He studied the metal walls of the supply tunnel through which they passed. If the Ga'ee tried to flood the tunnel with drones, the team had two plasma cannons, but they would be boxed in.

"Spread out," Payne ordered. "Virgil, remain at that hatch. Keep it open, even if you have to blow it."

The team confirmed their orders and spread out. Dank walked backward the few steps it took to block the hatch with his body.

"Temperature is rising," Kal reported. He wore a mask with a tank, but his fibrous body was exposed to the elements. He sensed the change more quickly than those who watched a hundred numbers scrolling by on their HUDs. He wasn't overwhelmed with information.

Disorientation swept over them quickly, then was gone. An alarm sounded within the team's suits.

"Lev?" Payne asked, but he knew he wouldn't get a reply.

The Ga'ee ship had transitioned to FTL speed.

[10]

"Your problem is only a problem when you have the wrong attitude." –From the memoirs of Ambassador Declan Payne

"Those bastards," the admiral mumbled. The Ga'ee ship was gone. They had the heading and little more. "Lev, order the battlewagons to Earth. Commander Josephs will relay our sitrep and follow through on our meetings. They'll move in five-ship hunter/killer squadrons to Berantz space to protect the portal construction and to Arn space for their portal. Transfer the Vestrall off this ship right now."

"We don't have the lift assets to move the Vestrall," Lev reported.

"Drop them on the remaining section of the space station," the commodore suggested.

"And make it quick," the admiral added. Lev adjusted his orientation and used faster-than-light speed to deliver *Leviathan* to a position barely a hundred meters from the station.

The admiral and commodore recoiled when the station filled the main screen.

"Damn, Lev. You should warn us before a maneuver like that."

"You said quickly." Lev brought *Leviathan* into a position where an arm of the shipyard reached into the environmentally controlled hangar. "The Vestrall are on their way to the hangar for immediate transfer to the shipyard."

"Since we have a minute or two, get me Commander Josephs."

A moment later, Commander Josephs appeared on the screen. "We saw it, Admiral," he said by way of greeting.

"We're going after them. I need you to take the battleships to Earth and then to Arn and Berantz space. Five each. Don't split them up any farther."

"Yes, Admiral. If the Ga'ee found us out here, I have to believe they know where Earth is."

"That is a sound supposition," Lev noted. "But we have no confirmation that they have the ability to communicate extreme distances by either folding space or detection of FTL signatures through interstellar vibrations."

"The fact that they sent a ship to us and kidnapped Team Payne tells me we better assume they have the capability. That means Earth is at risk. Commander Josephs, new orders. Leave five battlewagons to protect Earth, and make sure you train future crews. Even if humanity won't help, we can get volunteers from the Fleet to crew the Payne-class ships before we can source volunteers from the forward-deployed ships."

"I will make it my sole purpose in life to recruit and train the assets we need to protect humanity and all members of the seven races." The commander saluted.

"Build those portals so we can move among the Braze systems easily and quickly. We need to stop the Ga'ee before we lose any more planets. Pick up the Vestrall engineers on the shipyard station and take them where they need to go to help us build those portals."

"I understand, Admiral."

Harry Wesson saluted. The commodore snapped to attention and saluted as well. Commander Josephs returned their salutes. "I won't let you down."

He disappeared from the main screen.

Leviathan moved away from the shipyard, adjusted heading, and transitioned to FTL speed.

"Can you see the Ga'ee ship?" the admiral asked.

"I cannot. It's like they learned the lessons of the first Ga'ee ship and adjusted their output accordingly."

"That's disconcerting." The admiral scowled. "Keep trying. Well, you already knew that."

Mary Payne rushed through the bridge access and stood there. The Cabrizi raced in after her. With a couple sharp Ebren words, they sat next to her, vibrating with energy, ready to leap into action.

"You already know," the admiral greeted.

"The Ga'ee took Team Payne." She stated what she knew. "I should be on that ship."

"No, you shouldn't, and that was your choice." The admiral moved close. "It's part of the deal. I have to send good Fleet personnel like Declan Payne into danger, and we both have to watch them go."

"He's supposed to be the leader of the seven races," Mary replied softly. She focused on scratching the Cabrizi behind their ears.

"After this, he might be the leader of the eight races. We're going after him. We'll be there when he forces the Ga'ee to their knees. We're something like five minutes behind them."

"Six minutes, eleven seconds," Lev corrected. What the AI didn't say was that if the Ga'ee dropped into normal space, reoriented, and re-engaged faster-than-light speed, he would lose them. He would continue racing into the void until they realized they were lost. He invested his and Davida's power in solving the mystery of why they couldn't track the Ga'ee ship by their energy disruptions rippling across the fabric of space.

The admiral and the commodore sat at stations on the bridge and watched the screen, never feeling more helpless. "I wonder if we should have gone to Earth instead?"

"Don't second-guess yourself. We are committed." They glanced at each other, but neither had words of support. They were as empty of hope as the void.

———

Commander Jimmy Josephs stood on the bridge, eschewing his seat to help him feel more in touch with the fleet. And instantly, there was a war with an unknown enemy.

And now he was in command of a fleet of ten powerful warships. He expected when he arrived through Earth's portal with such firepower, he would be replaced, and all ten ships would be commandeered by the BEP.

"The Vestrall engineers are embarked, two on this ship and two on the *Levant*," his executive officer, Lieutenant Barry Cummins, reported.

He nodded at the XO.

"I need to protect the fleet," he mused. "I have my orders. The question is, how do we carry them out?"

"I don't understand, sir," Cummins replied.

"Battlewagons Six through Ten, designated Hunter-Killer Squadron 02, the instant we clear the Jupiter portal, you are to transition to faster-than-light speed to BD18, Brayalore. You have your two Vestrall engineer teams. Turn them loose, and let's get that portal built. Drum up all the support you need. If you run across any Fleet ships en route, tell them what we're doing to counter the Ga'ee."

"Commander Yeldon, *Levant*. What I hear you saying is we're on our own to get that portal built. We'll coordinate with the Berantz once we're in-system. Nav tells me the trip will take nearly a month."

"You'll be under the gun to build that portal. Target is six months."

"Can't be done. Impossible," the commander quipped. "We'll shoot for five." He gave the thumbs-up, having no idea if it was possible. "Yeldon out."

Josephs smiled while shaking his head. He would have his hands full, trying to convince Earth to participate—a challenge he hadn't contemplated until ten minutes ago. He didn't have to worry about the other five battlewagons getting conscripted into Earth's service.

If the first five Payne-class ships were allocated for Earth's defense, the commander would have no more authority than a regular ship's captain. His choice would be limited to following the orders he received.

"Get me the other four ships in the first flight," he requested.

The communication officer tapped a couple icons on his screen. "Line is open."

"Josephs here from Hunter-Killer Squadron One. When we embarked on *Leviathan* months ago, we were happy to leave behind the authorities who had lost sight of what the Fleet was meant to accomplish. They were trying to create the BEP 2.0, a force that would have failed had it not been for Fleet assets carrying the war hundreds of light-years away from Earth. That Fleet is scattered across thousands of light-years. To consolidate them, we need to build the Vestrall portals. That is our primary job.

"These five ships will be pulled in ten different directions. BW Zero One will establish a secure channel that we will use to maintain our integrity as Fleet Admiral Wesson's chosen leadership. We have to keep our eye on the ball. Otherwise, we risk watering down our combined firepower and losing our punch if and when the Ga'ee show up.

"Earth has no clue. They are enjoying the peace dividend bought and paid for by Fleet blood. Once we transit that portal, our job gets harder. We no longer have to fight just the Ga'ee. We have to fight bureaucracy, something we can't fight with missiles, plasma fire, or our main energy weapon.

"Keep your wits about you and keep this channel secret. We don't need the BEP listening in. They won't understand because they can't understand. Admiral Wesson has been right all along. He deserves our loyalty. We will continue to carry out his orders. We will defend Earth with our lives, no matter what they order us to do."

The other ships' captains, three commanders and one lieutenant commander, agreed. With crews of one hundred and twenty-five each, they could have filled a frigate, but the ships' smart systems, not quite AIs, were enough to run the ships without human interaction.

Battlewagons, nearly as powerful as a Kaiju-class, with more punch than a Whale-class battleship. Captained by the committed. Crewed by the loyal.

"Give me the Fleet," the commander ordered. With a gesture from his comm officer, he delivered the order. "Form up and transit the portal. Hunter-Killer Squadron Two, after you. Orient and engage your FTL the instant the fifth ship is through. Squadron One will follow, in trace, through the portal and continue to Earth orbit. Nav, activate the portal to Earth."

It took a minute before the portal connected, creating a hole in space. From their viewpoint, the portal created a black spot over the gas giant, showing space within the Solar System half a galaxy away.

Yeldon moved *Levant* into position and slowed while the other four ships of Hunter-Killer Squadron Two formed up behind him. The portal was big enough to easily accommodate one at a time. By flying keel to keel, they could have squeezed two through at once, but they didn't go to that extreme. One after another, with barely a kilometer between them, the ships accelerated through and exited on the other side, no longer in Vestrall space. They changed direction and winked out as they transitioned to faster-than-light speed after the last ship of Hunter-Killer Squadron 02 passed through.

"Helm, set us up."

The pilot of *The President* moved into the same position *Levant* had occupied. The others adjusted their courses and fell in behind the lead ship.

The commander took a deep breath. He should have been proud to lead these five ships, but dread hung over his head. "We're here to fight the Ga'ee. Keep them from colonizing our sector of space by destroying them. Take us through."

It was over within fifteen seconds. They arrived to a barrage of communications from the Blue Earth Protectorate, demanding that the first five ships return.

Commander Josephs gestured at the comm station. "Let me talk with them."

"This is Commander Jimmy Josephs, captain of the Vestrall battleship, *The President*. We are here on the orders of the leader of the seven races to assist in the defense of Earth. We do not answer to the BEP, but we must work together for the most effective defense of Earth's space."

He referenced a chain of command outside the BEP and Earth to give himself maneuverability.

It took the BEP three seconds to call him on it.

"You're human. You answer to Earth. Move your ships to Lunar Station Sierra Seven," the less than amused voice began. Josephs drew a line across his throat, and the comm officer cut the link. He closed his eyes and tried to take a deep breath, but it was as if the air had been sucked out of the bridge. "Grant me the patience to deal with these assholes. Payne was willing to get kidnapped by the Ga'ee instead of coming back here. Payne is wise. Listen to Payne."

"They want to talk with you, sir," the comm officer interrupted.

"Put them on, please." He assumed his best plastic smile. "Commander Josephs, how can I be of assistance?"

"Prepare to be boarded," the voice replied.

Admiral Wesson had debriefed the series of events that had taken place the last time *Leviathan* had entered Earth's system.

"Stand by," Josephs said and muted the signal. "Get the chief Vestrall engineer up here."

He ignored the incessant beeping. The BEP wanted immediate compliance.

"Would Captain LeClerc be available?" Josephs asked to kill time until the Vestrall appeared.

"He is on Earth at present, conducting a liaison mission with Fleet leadership."

"Sounds important, but it should, considering he's the captain of *Ephesus*. Stand by." Josephs cut off the other's response when the Vestrall walked through the hatch. The commander turned his back to the screen to talk to the Vestrall engineer, Loresh.

Both voices relayed through the bridge's speakers since neither spoke the other's language.

"I need you to tell the idiot on that screen that this ship is Vestrall property, and as such, he has no authority to board us."

"I don't care if he comes aboard or not," Loresh replied. "I thought we were here to build a portal? There's already a portal in human space."

"There is. We'll transfer you to Ebren space as soon as possible to complete work on that portal before moving to Arn space. The other engineers will build the portals in Berantz and Zuloon space. We can't do that if the people on that screen behind me think they can say what these ships do."

"Fine. I'll lie."

"Is it a lie?" Josephs pressed. He needed the Vestrall engineer to be convincing. "Did we not build this ship with materiel from the shipyard in Vestrall space, a shipyard built by and for the Vestrall?"

The Vestrall waited for the translation to finish. He leaned around the commander to look at the individuals on the screen. Three were in view, and all of them had their arms crossed. They vibrated from their incessant toe-tapping.

"That is logical. I will tell them they cannot board the Vestrall ships. We are allies, after all, are we not?"

"Now you're talking, Loresh. Thank you." The commander turned around and smiled at the comm station. The link went live for both audio and video.

The Vestrall stepped forward. "My name is Loresh, Chief Engineer of the Vestrall Portal Project. These ships are Vestrall in origin. You will not board them. We will transfer to Ebren space to finish building their portal before moving to Arn and Zuloon. Do you have any questions?"

"How are Vestrall in charge of a ship squawking an Earth Fleet code?"

"Because we are all on the same side," Loresh replied smoothly. "Aren't we?"

The face on the screen blinked rapidly. "I need to coordinate with my superiors. Commander Josephs, prepare to transfer to the runabout *Jefferson* for delivery to the *Ephesus*."

Commander Jimmy Josephs wasn't sure what to do. He had no team of railgun-armed warriors ready to destroy a ship from the inside to ensure he wasn't detained.

"You seem to have a one-play playbook, and it makes Earth look like a bunch of assholes. No. I'm not going to transfer to a BEP ship. I'm Fleet. We'll take *The President* to the UN to meet the president.

"I'm acting under the orders of Fleet Admiral Wesson and the leader of the seven races, Ambassador Payne. We're no threat to you. Quite the opposite. It's just us girls, so what is with the tough-guy act? You don't need to do that. How about a please and thank you? You know what they say. You catch more flies with honey than vinegar."

"Please come to *Ephesus*. We will dispatch a runabout with champagne and chocolates to welcome you," the face on the screen replied with a fake smile.

"There you go! That wasn't so hard, was it? Alas, I won't be able to take you up on your far-too-kind offer. If my chronometer is correct, the meeting with the president is scheduled for tomorrow. We will be in touch with our flight profile to the UN before then. Josephs out."

The bridge crew laughed until the commander shook his head and held his hands up for quiet.

"I fear that I've made us Public Enemy Number One. Barry. If I don't return from the UN, you're to take these ships to the Jupiter portal. You'll need to find transportation to take the Vestrall to Ebren."

"An inauspicious start, Commander," Lieutenant Cummins drawled. "But they gave you no choice. And for the record, since I'm a Texas boy, you catch the most flies with bullshit."

The commander snorted. "They seem to only understand brute force. Be that as it may, prepare to move the ship if you think my return is questionable or an unreasonable amount of time has passed. Don't fire on Earth vessels, no matter what. Just run if it gets that tense.

"Make sure the squadron has their noses pointed at Ebren for immediate transition to FTL. These BEP are peacetime soldiers, trying to show the Fleet that they're every bit as tough. They might be, but trying to put us in our place isn't the way to prove it. We'll end up showing them they don't have a clue about how real space battles are fought.

"They're trying to be the big dog, peeing highest on the fence post. If we start shooting, they'll run for cover. If the Ga'ee show up, they'll instantly be all for us being between them and the enemy.

"We can counter their bluster, but the second one of us fires, we risk humans killing humans. That would be a civil war, Mister Cummins. Don't be the one to start it. We don't want to be the ones to end it, either. We don't want to participate in any intramural firefights. We're more than happy to save our weapons for the Ga'ee.

"Once you're away from Earth, say in the asteroid belt. Work on the squadron's volley fire. Show humanity what we have at our command."

The lieutenant saluted, and Jimmy Josephs waved in reply. "I'll be in my quarters, researching what I'm supposed to know and building my presentation to the president."

"Go forth, slideshow warrior," the lieutenant joked.

The commander stopped and hung his head. "I miss the old days when I could just do my job and fix the ship if it broke. Now I know why Ambassador Payne and Admiral Wesson lean so heavily on each other, and even more importantly, why they have their wives with them."

"I don't understand," the lieutenant replied. "Is that what 'better half' is supposed to mean?"

"Not at all, Barry. Trusted advisors who keep them from going insane. They keep them going in the same direction."

The lieutenant's eyes grew starry as he stared at the image of space on the main screen. "And a bikini babe..."

"Shut it!" the commander growled. "I won't have that kind of talk on my ship. Mrs. Ambassador. That's the only way you refer to her. Do you understand me?"

"Yes, sir," the cowed lieutenant replied.

"Don't be like them." Josephs pointed in the direction of Earth. "We're better than that. Humanity is more like us than them, and we're worth saving."

The commander clapped Cummins on the shoulder.

"Stay true to what we are—the good guys." The commander strolled off the bridge and two doors down the corridor to his quarters. The admiral had made sure the crew quarters were close to where they worked. The corridor leading to the bridge, centrally located in the battlewagon for maximum survivability, was lined with quarters for the bridge crew. With a small crew and a large ship, everyone had quarters to themselves. It made duty on a starship far more congenial.

Morale was good at the moment, and Josephs needed to keep it that way.

In his quarters, he accessed the comm system. "Lieutenant Cummins, report to my quarters, please."

In fifteen seconds, there was a knock on the door.

"Enter," the commander stated. It was the first time he was able to do that as the ship's captain. The door opened slowly. The lieutenant jumped inside and locked his body in the position of attention.

"I'm really sorry about that quip, Commander..." the lieutenant started.

"Stop. At ease, Lieutenant. That other issue is dead and gone since I'm sure you'll not say anything like that again. This is completely different. I need you to run damage control drills as we continue our transit to Earth. General quarters and damage control.

"This crew has been together for a grand total of seven days. They need to learn to work together. I was pleased with what I saw for the movement to the portal and our arrival here. Simple as that was, they made it look effortless.

"I want that same level of execution in case we get damaged. More so. They need to be able to react without thinking, and no one is familiar with this ship. Arrange for my inspection at eighteen hundred today. I'll tour the ship's main spaces."

"Consider it done, Commander." The lieutenant saluted and hurried out.

"You can't put it off any longer," Jimmy Josephs told himself. He opened his system and accessed the knowledge that Lev had uploaded to each battlewagon. It was the sum total of everything Earth knew, along with select information that Lev decided humanity needed and could handle.

Over the ship-wide internal comm system, projecting into every room and every space, a voice announced, "This is a drill, this is a drill. All hands to battle stations. I say again, all hands to battle stations. This is a drill." The message repeated.

The commander fumbled with the unfamiliar systems in his room to turn down the volume of the broadcast. When he finally found the correct screen and made the adjustment, he cheered to himself.

"If everything were that easy. Stop goofing off!" he berated himself. "President Sinkhaus, on behalf of the Vestrall and the Braze Collective, I bid you greetings."

He looked at the screen. "Maybe the Ga'ee will show up in the next day, and I won't have to do this," he mused to no avail. "At least you're not Payne, racing toward the galaxy's nether regions."

[11]

"Sometimes you have to hump the enemy's leg to show them who's in charge." –From the memoirs of Ambassador Declan Payne

"Turbo, Heckler, Byle, and Shaolin. Check out that far hatch. Sparky, Joker, and Kal, with me. Virge, keep your eye on our tech geniuses. I feel that if we're going to make chicken salad out of this pile of chicken shit, they'll be the ones to do it. Let's see what hand we've been dealt," Payne explained.

Virgil replied, "When you're back, I'll check supplies on *Ugly 5*. See how long we can go if need be."

"We'll blow the FTL before we turn Donner party and hope that Lev or one of the battlewagons is following us." Payne took one step down a side corridor, adjusting his lights to maximize how far ahead he could see. The long, empty corridor had doorways at regular intervals. Doorways without doors, like those that fed into the main corridor.

"You know, Lev wasn't able to track the Ga'ee ship. He never saw it coming into the Vestrall Prime system," Blinky sent over the team channel.

"I wonder why I didn't bring that up, Sunshine?" Payne shot back. "Lev will figure it out. He's right behind us. I have no doubt about that. As long as we don't drop out of FTL, we'll remain on the same vector we had when we entered faster-than-light. To help our friend track us, we'll be messing with the drive system to warble or do something we know Lev can see.

"That's our new objective, people, once we determine that we're alone on this ship. Blinky and Buzz, how about you two get into the Ga'ee computer system and find me a diagram of this vessel? I need to know where I'm going. Ten kilometers is a lot of ground to cover if we're playing hide and seek."

"I don't want to play hide and seek," Blinky admitted. "We have the previous scans showing the power generation systems within. We can build a map as we go with our suits' systems. Ship scans are more informative when done from this side of the energy shield."

"And get the heat turned up while you're at it. Minus anything C isn't going to do it for me. This blip is nothing more than the heat we're generating from the warmth of our personalities," Payne replied.

"We haven't even broken in yet." Blinky and Buzz sat down where they were and went to work. "As a reminder, we spent a couple weeks on BD18 and never made any progress accessing the Ga'ee neural network."

"You weren't properly motivated." Payne followed his statement with a dry chuckle. "If you don't get into the system on this ship, we'll probably die. We need you in there and driving this boat. Otherwise, I fear the Ga'ee will have something special waiting for us if we find ourselves in their space."

"Who's the ray of sunshine now?" Blinky grumbled.

"Get on it, people. It's not getting any warmer, and I expect we're getting farther from known space with each passing minute. The clock is running, and time is not in our favor."

Payne thought for a moment. "Time is never in our favor. I don't think I'm ever obligated to say that again. Get to it, people."

He activated a P2P channel with Kal, Sparky, and Joker. "Joker, take point. Sparky, bring up the rear. Let's see what's in this direction. Looking at going no more than a kilometer."

Joker squeezed past to get in front. She held her railgun before her and moved ahead quickly, using her active sensors to build a schematic of what lay before them that the systems could penetrate. She forwarded the feed to Blinky and Buzz to allow them to build a consolidated map of the Ga'ee ship. It would serve them now and in the future, should the need arise.

If they were able to send it to their people before they died.

Payne scowled. He let his railgun slip under his arm so he could use both hands to flip a double bird at the ship. He cranked his external speakers to maximum. "We are going to be the worst guests ever."

"Sir," Sparky started, "are you okay?"

"Sometimes, you just have to shout at the cloud in the sky," Payne replied. "Carry on."

Joker reached the first T-intersection and checked left, then right. She pointed to the right and went that way. Payne stepped into the intersection to cover the other two directions, left and straight ahead. Kal was almost too big to move through the confined space.

"Big room with equipment," Joker reported. "Movement."

Payne turned and ran toward her, with Kal scrambling after him. Payne brought his railgun up.

Sparky rushed forward to secure the intersection.

"Looks like maintenance bots," Joker reported. "I'm going in."

Payne was right behind her, ready to move into the open when space allowed.

"Hey, little fella," she said as a bot raced toward her, then two more. The first one activated a torch and put it against the leg of her suit. "Hey! They're bitey. Off you go, you pesky little bastard."

Joker booted the thing halfway across the unlit space. The next two activated their torches and approached.

Payne moved so he had a clear line of fire. "Cover your ears." He leaned on his railgun and fired well-aimed three-round bursts, pouring accelerated ions into one, blasting it apart, and then the other until they were both destroyed. It was almost as gratifying as the older railgun models that sent tiny magnetic slugs.

A reticulated tentacle dropped from the ceiling and slapped Payne's armor. He snapped his attention to it. "The fuck?"

He grabbed the metal arm in his armored fist and used the suit's power to squeeze the device until it separated beneath his fingers. He tossed the torn-off end away. Kal opened up with the plasma cannon, firing slowly and methodically across the large space.

Payne stooped to scan the remains of the closest wreckage, looking for signs of a silicon life form. There weren't any. "Just stupid bots," Payne announced while studying the data scrolling across his HUD.

"Watch yourself," Joker said, taking aim at a growing mass of self-propelled machines moving toward them. She fired her railgun, blasting from left to right. Payne joined her in hosing down the area, deciding it was best to remove anything that could be a threat rather than retreat and leave active bots behind.

Kal stopped hunching and took a knee, watching for extraneous movement of anything bigger than bots no larger than a meter on their longest side.

"Like fish in a barrel. Woohoo!" Payne shouted. The bots

were no match for the railguns, and soon enough, debris littered the deck. "You go left. I'll go right."

Scans showed a space that was two hundred by four hundred meters. The machines secured to the deck were cold, not having run in a long time. This was a starship without living creatures, and that meant there was no dust. There was no way to tell how long the equipment had been idle except that it had reached the ambient temperature of seventy degrees below freezing.

But it wasn't minus seventy anymore. It was up to minus sixty-five. It had shown warmth earlier, but that was the main corridor. Payne had discounted the warmth as nothing more than what they generated from their suits.

"Joker, Sparky, check your suits. What temp are you showing?"

"Minus sixty-two," Sparky replied from the corridor.

"Sixty-five below," Joker noted. "Looks like the ship is heating up from the central axis out."

Payne brought up the team channel while studying a tube-shaped machine with curved forms on a conveyor-like belt. "Blinky, are you guys into the system yet?"

"Sir, you gotta have some patience. We just got set up. You've been gone, like, two minutes."

Payne checked his chronometer. "Ten," he corrected. "Why is the ship warming up?"

"They want us to feel welcome?" Blinky guessed.

"Keep doing what you're doing. We need control of this ship sooner rather than later. The automated systems have activated and attempted to drive us off. At least this production space won't be producing drones anytime soon."

"Portside hangar bay is empty," Heckler reported.

"Return via the corridor and take the first longitudinal corridor heading aft. I assume it's a mirror image of this one. I suspect this ship is perfectly symmetrical. Head into the first space outboard and see if it's a manufacturing area. If it is, you'll have company soon. Construction and maintenance equipment are sufficiently juiced to come after you. Destroy them while taking it easy on the ammunition. I'm pretty sure we won't be getting a resupply before we're done with the Ga'ee ship. By the way, watch for ceiling tentacles."

Payne gestured to tell Joker it was time to leave.

"Ceiling tentacles, aye. Now I won't be able to look anywhere else since I gotta see one of those things," Heckler replied. "Conserve ammo. That almost goes without saying, just like the time thing. We have no time and not enough ammo. Welcome to Team Payne."

"And Blinky and Buzz will save our butts through master manipulation of the digital universe," Buzz added.

"Touché," Blinky commented.

"You guys. I'm thinking you're not into the system yet, but you have enough time to jaw-jack with us?"

"Be cool, warrior leader. Less stress, not more."

Payne made faces inside his helmet while trying to process his tech professionals, who deserved a lot of the credit for keeping Team Payne alive and humanity safe. They could have left Team Payne and started their own company on Earth, but they hadn't. Payne didn't need to coddle them, but they liked their props.

"And you will save us once more, tech gods of penultimate godliness. As soon as we find their main computer systems, we'll let you know so you can skip the digital handshake and virtual chin tickle and tap directly in."

"That would help immensely," Blinky agreed.

"Then we'll stop talking and start doing. I'll continue heading aft. The first manufacturing space is cleared. Our goal is to find the computer hardware. It may have limited access where only Ga'ee can get to it. That would be a pisser."

Heckler dove into the tactical side of the conversation. "Heading aft now. Seeing a cross-corridor. Have you checked yours out?"

Sparky shined her light down the transverse corridor. Heckler shone his light back at her. The walls were smooth between them. Sparky suggested, "Looks like a way to move drones between the manufacturing areas, from port to starboard and vice versa."

"Map is updated," Blinky reported.

Payne checked his HUD. The layout they had captured so far was the epitome of simplicity, but there was a great deal of dead space. "What's in the space from here back to the main corridor?" Payne asked about the section that went from his group to Heckler's team and back to the corridor where Dank waited with Blinky and Buzz. One hundred and fifty meters by one hundred meters.

"There are two corridors on this side. Two entrances between the longitudinal shafts that seem to head to the forward and aft ends of the ship," Blinky stated.

"I thought we were heading aft?" Payne asked.

"Heading forward." Sparky pointed down the longitudinal corridor in the direction they intended to go.

"I had the ship turn around and face away from Vestrall Prime, and we came in on the starboard side," Payne remembered. "Dammit. Just like a boot lieutenant."

"Leave it to me, sir," Heckler stated confidently.

"If I remember correctly, I said to go aft when I meant forward, and you went the same way as me. I have to ask, leave *what* to you?" Payne wondered. He had intended to go aft to find the power plant driving the engines and do what he had to to drop the ship back into normal space. "Are you saying you land-nav better than me?"

"After the little fore-aft debacle we just witnessed, I'm inclined to say yes, sir. Instead of the truth setting me free, I feel like it might get me in trouble."

"Conserve your ammunition but clear that space. I'm returning to the main corridor to make a circuit of this space and see if there's a hidden doorway. If not, we'll do it the hard way."

"Roger," Heckler replied. He had a space to clear.

"Sparky, find me a way into that area. I can't believe it's solid."

Payne and Kal stayed back and let their engineer figure it out. With her sensors at maximum power, she kicked the wall before her and "listened" for the resonance. "No, sir, not solid. Not empty either. Vibrations suggest this wall is at least ten centimeters thick, a veritable bulkhead."

"How do we breach a bulkhead?" Payne wondered.

"Through an airlock or a bulkhead-heavy door."

"Find me one of those, Sparky. Otherwise, it's the hard way." Payne punched a fist at the wall.

"You keep saying the hard way, but what I hear is that you have explosives burning a hole in your pouch, and you really want to use them." Sparky walked away slowly, scanning up and down for a seam or any other indication of a way to access the space.

"If we need to. I'll go with brute force if there's no other way." Payne wanted to blow a hole in the Ga'ee ship. Everyone knew it, but they were traveling at faster-than-light speed. Too many bad things could happen when transitioning to normal space, like if *Ugly 5* launched from the hangar bay and passed through the FTL bubble. The rigors of getting caught by normal space would destroy the insertion craft. The stresses were so great that even the big ship could suffer catastrophic failure, like stepping out of a moving car and into a brick wall.

Payne's idea of pulling the plug was more complex than that. It involved incrementally reducing power until the safeties kicked in and took the ship out of FTL before it didn't have sufficient power to manage the transition.

Payne strolled casually while Kal had to walk hunched over. "The Ga'ee suck," the Ebren remarked, imitating Payne's voice.

"Couldn't have said it better myself." Payne held a thumbs-up over his shoulder for Kal to see.

Joker remained in the intersection so she could keep an eye on Heckler and his group as well as Payne and his people.

Payne would take two steps and stop to keep from bumping into Sparky, who examined the wall at as close to a microscopic level as possible.

The sounds of railgun fire echoed down the corridors. Payne stopped to listen since no one was firing on full auto. Those were well-aimed shots to conserve ammunition.

A great number of shots.

When the firing stopped, Heckler announced, "Clear. Searching the area."

"Scan for silicon life forms," Payne reminded him.

"No intelligent life in here. Not even the machines were smart," Heckler replied.

Sparky reached the main logistics corridor and took a hard right. She stepped over Blinky's and Buzz's legs where they were sprawled on the deck, focused on their computers. Various communication devices like dishes, center-fed dipoles, and log periodics were scattered around them as they continued their search for the signal that connected the Ga'ee.

Payne stopped and loomed over them. "What if there are no Ga'ee on board and there's no signal to find?"

"Sir, you have an evil streak that belies your status as the leader of the seven races. Do you torture puppies and kitties in your off-time?"

"What?" Payne continued to loom.

"You seem to like it too much. Is it because we're smart?"

Payne leaned against the wall and crossed his arms to look casual. "You're not wrong. It's because I don't understand what you do or how you do what you do. You make hard things look easy and impossible things possible. I appreciate what you do. If I didn't give you shit...well, you know the rest."

"We already figured there probably isn't a signal, and we're playing video games until you guys find the physical access."

"Really?" Payne wondered.

"No." Blinky and Buzz continued to tap. Payne couldn't see the expressions on their faces. He decided that was for the best.

He didn't bother telling them to keep on keeping on.

Sparky pulled out a multitool and scraped a big X on the bulkhead before continuing her examination.

Payne turned to Kal, who shrugged.

They followed at a snail's pace.

"Orders?" Heckler requested.

Payne thought for a couple moments. "Continue forward to the next space. Keep your eyes peeled. Cross to the other side of the ship and see if the spaces are still mirrored. I believe we'll find what we're looking for along the centerline of the ship. It won't be a symmetrical space, but unique, like where the power-plants are located. Mind-meld, people. Give me your thoughts on this ship and the way forward."

"I've been thinking the same thing," Major Dank noted. "Everything that matters on this ship will be on the central axis."

"Sparky?" Payne asked.

"The more I see from this, the more it supports the center-line-slash-central axis premise." She pointed at the mark she'd made on the wall. "If we can't find a way in, that wall is half the thickness of everywhere else."

"Does that mean they've sealed their important stuff inside the safest location on the ship because they don't need access to it?" Payne postulated.

"We'll see," Sparky replied.

Payne knew the answers he needed would be found centrally located, in the location of highest survivability. It suggested the Ga'ee had learned as humanity had learned—by fighting. Space combat was unforgiving. You adapted, or your race would fall.

The Ga'ee hadn't fallen. They had become powerful, so much so that on their first foray into the space of the seven races, they had nearly won. The carbon-based races were closer to extinction than they dared allow themselves to think.

Now the Ga'ee had found *Leviathan* and Team Payne in the Vestrall home system.

That wasn't a coincidence, so Payne needed to find out how they had known.

[12]

"In the give and take of life, most of the time, it's better to give, especially when you're in close-quarters combat."
–From the memoirs of Ambassador Declan Payne

Sparky continued her inspection of the wall that secured a substantial interior space within the Ga'ee carrier. She went around the corner into the longitudinal corridor. The mirror image construction confirmed what she had thought. The thinner panel was the emergency access to the sealed compartment. They would need a torch to cut through it.

Payne watched his HUD and followed Heckler's group as it moved forward. The map gained detail as the team's sensors scanned ahead. He conducted his own map study, looking for more inaccessible spaces along the ship's centerline. There were plenty.

Sparky reported her findings.

"Heckler. If you find another construction area, secure a bot with a plasma torch and bring it to us. I'd prefer that to using the plasma cannon to bash our way inside. I suspect that wouldn't be best if we want the equipment to still be operational after we get inside."

"We might be able to recover equipment from that first space we cleared. We mainly went with headshots. There was a contest, and it *seems to me* that I'm up four on my lovely bride."

"Bullshit!" Turbo replied. "Shooting baby-sized bots that were harmless wasted ammo. You should be docked for doing that. We're even at the worst. I think I'm ahead."

"You two can duke it out later when you're destroying your next planet. In the interim, get me a plasma torch."

Dank returned from his inventory of *Ugly 5* and activated a P2P channel. "Your bride did us proud, Dec. We have enough food for a month, and that includes a little jerky each day to take the edge off the rations. With the two weeks in our suits, that gives us time. We can recharge the suits using *Ugly 5's* power, but we'll have to do it while wearing them."

"I'm anxious to see what's inside here. There's no chance to go where the Ga'ee would have worked because wriggler corridors are only ten centimeters high. I would think their spaces are equally compressed. How do you keep the other sentient races from playing with your toys? Be a completely different size. The only access we have is through the drone-processing corridors and whatever mainframes we can find."

"We know where the powerplants are located," Virgil offered.

"Direct power. We'd have to make sure we could regulate the delivery. Blowing out a suit wouldn't be optimal right now. I'm not seeing any clothes or blankets we could use to keep someone warm."

"There's some of that in *Ugly 5*. It is stuffed with survival gear. But to keep someone from dying when it's minus sixty? That's completely different."

Payne checked the temperature. His suit showed that it was sixty-three degrees below zero. "It's not getting any warmer."

"Reinforces your point about getting inside that space, Declan. Let me take Joker into the space you cleared. I'll see if I can jury rig a torch out of what's left."

"We may have had a little too much fun blasting the metal," Payne replied.

"I like that. Maybe I'll play some Banging Stones while we're digging through the piles."

"Those guys are trash, but as long as I don't have to listen to your sordid taste in music, do what you need to do, Virge." Payne waited, but Dank was moving down the corridor on his way to the manufacturing space. "Do you like her?"

"Her? You mean Anneliese? Yeah, Dec. I like her a lot."

"Then let's get control of this ship so we can go home to *Leviathan*. We all have someone to go back to, thanks to Lev's matchmaking."

"You think that's what it was?" Virgil wondered.

"He's in everyone's mind. Who better to line up a date?"

"He shouldn't be doing that. I found Anneliese on Earth."

"What about our people, Virge? We're human and not meant to be alone. How do the rest of us find someone? I appreciate Lev caring about us enough to make the introductions."

"You found Mary on Earth," Virgil noted.

"No. She was foisted on me by a leadership that wanted to put a face on the successful Team Payne that could be exploited for their recruiting efforts. I was given no choice. They said I had one, but I didn't.

"Like you and your teams. Take what you get. Gotta keep the propaganda machine churning, and that cost lives because these people weren't properly trained. We all paid for the interference of the ground-pounders into our business. I would not have chosen Mary if I had a choice, but it would be ridiculous of me to claim that I'm not happy with how things turned out."

"I see your point. Doing the wrong thing for the right reasons to get the right result. I'll think more on it, but for now, let me play the role of a maniacal supervillain and see if I can turn this scrap heap into a functioning plasma torch."

"Rock on, Virge. And thanks. I'm glad you're on the team."

"If for no other reason than to watch the romantic comedy that is the Heckler and Turbo show. Dank out."

Payne dialed up the team channel. "I have good news and bad news, followed by more good news, so I'm going to deliver a good sandwich." He waited, but no one had a witty comeback. They were working on what they needed to be doing at that point in time. "Good news is that we have enough rations for roughly six weeks, and that includes the ability to recharge the suits using *Ugly 5*. The bad news is that it's still too cold to get out of the suits. I don't want to say that you might have to wear them for six weeks straight since that would be pretty gross, but we might be in these things long-term if we can't find a way to heat at least one space. The good news is that we think we have a place to look for access to the systems. We need a plasma torch. Major Dank and Joker are trying to fabricate one from the refuse we left behind."

"Twenty credits says we can build one faster," Heckler interrupted.

"You're on," Payne replied. He didn't have high hopes for Virgil and Joker since they hadn't left much, unlike Heckler's claim of headshots only. "I'll wait with Blinky and Buzz since they love having me watch them."

Payne returned to the main corridor. He chose a spot away from the two specialists and slid down the wall to sit. It looked uncomfortable, but it wasn't. It took a load off overtaxed legs, although the tubes to collect waste created lumps where there normally wouldn't be.

Over the years, those who wore suits had gotten used to the connections and worked around them.

"Far too cold," Payne muttered to himself. He settled in to watch the HUD, checking his sensors and his team monitors. Each member's pulse was no more than seventy. They were as relaxed as they needed to be. Suits were functioning at one hundred percent. Payne had burned more power than anyone else, and he'd only used four percent.

At fifty percent, he'd start cycling team members through *Ugly 5* to recharge.

"We need to find the engines. However they're propelling this monstrosity, we need to clip their wings and change whatever they were doing to make the ship invisible." Payne suspected harmonics of some sort that blended the energy vibrations into the background radiation.

He guessed there was more to it than that. The team's engineers and technogurus would figure it out once they could look at the internals.

All Payne had to do was keep them safe.

"Once we have access to that space and see our next steps, we'll begin moving aft. We need to address the engines since how they're working now is invisible to Lev. We need to change that."

"Roger," Major Dank replied. No one else engaged in the conversation. Payne wasn't telling them anything they didn't know.

They had a great deal to do and little time to do it.

Payne accessed his P2P. "What do you think, Kal?"

"I think I'm hungry, and I didn't bring any jerky with me. The thought of it makes my mouth water."

Payne worked his way to his feet. "Then let's snag a little for you before it's frozen so hard that you can't chew it."

"It's already too cold for that, but I'll keep it in my mouth and enjoy the flavor for a long time before I swallow it." Kal lumbered down the corridor after Payne.

On the team channel, Payne told everyone where he and Kal were going. No one was supposed to walk off without a plan and a report. Rescues were easier when they knew where they had to go.

They accessed the ship via the smaller forward hatch. Inside, they found it was a degree above freezing. Payne took off his helmet to enjoy a moment of freedom. Kal dropped his helmet and backpack. He helped himself to the ship's storage area, carefully removing two pieces of jerky before resecuring the locker.

He took a small bite from the first and chewed slowly with his eyes closed.

"Kernel of Lev running *Ugly 5*," Payne started, "how long can you provide power and heat?"

"The insertion craft can operate for thirty days at current power consumption. Beyond twenty-five days, *Ugly 5* will not be able to fly into space."

"You should have better prepared me for the good news, bad news scenario. We have twenty-odd days within which to work before we have to make decisions and trade-offs. If we can't get off this crate by then, we have to heat it up. No matter what, we have enough food and water for six weeks as long as the recycling systems in the suits remain functional, which depends on *Ugly 5* having enough power to recharge us." Payne spoke in a stream of consciousness.

Everything related to the team's existence was interconnected. One thing affected the next, which affected the next. They had to take over the Ga'ee ship.

He had known that before they landed.

"Can we recharge *Ugly 5* using power from the Ga'ee ship?"

"Depends what kind of power and in what quantity," the voice answered.

"I'm going to assume we can do it since the alternative is less than savory. In the interim, keep the temperature like this, one degree C, and we'll figure it out so we can survive."

"How long do you think we'll be here?" Kal asked after shifting his jerky to one side of his mouth.

"Plan the worst. Hope for the best. We'll plan for six weeks and hope for a few days."

"What if it's longer than six weeks?" Kal asked pointedly, not using his Western drawl during the private conversation.

"Anything after six weeks, and we'll learn how long we can go without food and with only recycled water. I don't want to know that answer, Kal, so if it gets to that, we'll hit the power plant with explosives until it takes us all into oblivion."

Kal held Payne's look. "I want to go on record as saying that I am not in favor of your alternate plan. I'm supposed to protect you. I can't do that if you do us all in."

"Me neither, but I'm not going to watch us starve to death while the Ga'ee take us on a death ride to nowhere. We need our smart people to figure out how this ship works and then how to take control of it. If anyone can do it, they can."

Payne contemplated why the Ga'ee would commit an entire carrier for the purpose of collecting Team Payne. He put on his helmet.

"Virgil, join me and Kal in *Ugly 5*, please."

"Just when I was winning the plasma torch construction challenge, too. Be right there. Joker, why don't you join Heckler on the port side? There's nothing we can work with over here. Scorched Earth Payne has come and gone."

Payne chuckled while taking his helmet off. Kal took

another bite and chewed slowly. Three minutes later, the hatch popped, and Major Dank hurried inside.

Virgil popped his helmet off and took a seat, reclining with his legs up on the opposite seat. "Whatcha thinking about, Dec?"

"There's no way this was random. The Ga'ee can talk across vast distances. They must have a fold drive or the equivalent, even if it's only for communications. They sent this ship to collect us based on our actions at BD18. We tried to board. They knew it was too enticing for us to turn down. Somehow, they figured out that we were important, even though they almost killed us. Almost. They didn't kill us. And *Leviathan*. By snagging us, they gain two for the price of one."

"By us, you mean you, the leader of the seven races. And two for the price of one means you think the Ga'ee knew *Leviathan* would follow when at BD18, Lev did not."

"But Lev and Team Payne showed up at the Berantz home-world together. They can talk long-distance. Did they drop comm buoys with extreme-range capability?"

"Even Lev can't do that," Virgil countered. "Then again, the Ga'ee were able to fend off Lev's world-killers. I wonder if this crate has that energy shield? If we can acquire that information, we'll be much more ready for the next engagement. Assumes we can stop the ship and get off, though."

"Everything assumes we can get off. I don't think there's any Ga'ee on board. This is an automated ship with a single purpose. The Ga'ee have one design, so it cost them however long it took to build this thing to use as a cheap tool to kidnap Team Payne."

Virgil grunted as if he had been punched. "If the Ga'ee knew enough to come to Vestrall Prime, they have to know where Earth is. They have to know where everything is. They didn't attack those space stations and ships just to destroy them.

They took their databases with the sum total of all their knowledge, the Rang'Kor and the Berantz and maybe even human and Ebren."

Payne propped his elbows on his suit's knees. "That's sobering, Virgil. We need as many plasma cutters as we can make. We need to start cutting this ship apart until we find whatever can help us."

Virgil started to put his helmet on but stopped. Kal offered the last bit of his jerky. Virgil took it. "Thanks, buddy. This will hit the spot."

Payne helped himself to one he'd had in his suit pouch, folding it and stuffing it all in his mouth at once before putting his helmet on.

"Team Payne. Your orders are to build every plasma torch we can make. We're going to cut this ship apart until we find what we're looking for, starting with the space off the main corridor.

"Heckler and Turbo, find me a way to the engines. Everyone else is on plasma torch fabrication. We'll rally in the portside drone manufacturing facility. That means you, too, Blinky and Buzz. We'll find you a direct line to tap into. No sense wasting your time with a signal that isn't there."

The team rogered the orders and turned to.

[13]

"Even verbal jousting can leave scars." –From the memoirs of Ambassador Declan Payne

Jimmy Josephs rocketed out of the battlewagon using an escape pod. He decelerated during his descent to land on the roof of the UN. Total travel time, forty-eight seconds. *The President* hovered over the building while fighter aircraft burned holes in the sky around it.

They couldn't hurt the ship, even if they resorted to nuclear weapons, which wouldn't do the city below any favors.

The new battlewagon was safe.

Commander Josephs had warned the XO not to scratch the paint on their new ride while he was gone. The lieutenant hadn't seen the humor in it.

Jimmy Josephs used humor to allay his concerns about the upcoming meeting. According to the information packet the admiral had sent, he thought he would be met by an individual called Paragon Virtue. The commander had a hard time taking anyone seriously who had such a name and worked for someone called Sinkhaus. That was the equivalent of the military's

CINC House, or commander in chief of the home, usually the military member's spouse.

Josephs pushed his skepticism down. These people had authority over all humanity. That made it more than a bad joke.

When he popped the hatch on the escape pod and climbed out, he found three individuals waiting for him. A youthful man in a modern cut suit approached. "I'm Paragon Virtue, and I'll escort you to your meeting with the president."

"Commander Jimmy Josephs of the battlewagon *The President*, named in honor of the leader of the UN."

"Exceptional testament to humanity," Virtue replied smoothly. "I'm sure President Sinkhaus will be most pleased by the honor. Who named this ship?"

"Leader of the seven races Ambassador Payne. The other ships are named after the leading nations of the free world."

"Another honor. Bravo!" The young man clapped softly while looking at the ship looming above. "I don't recognize the design."

"Payne-class battlewagon. They operate best in hunter-killer squadrons of at least five vessels to deliver maximum firepower calculated to destroy a Ga'ee carrier."

"Payne-class. Did the ambassador name the class, too?"

"Fleet Admiral Wesson named the class. Ambassador Payne was, shall we say, resistant to the idea."

The young man nodded. An elevator appeared, and the four climbed in. Josephs sized up the other two, knowing them to be security. Virtue hadn't bothered introducing them.

No one spoke as the elevator descended. Josephs didn't watch to see which floor it was on. His discomfort increased with each step closer to the president's office. They arrived, and Paragon ushered the commander out into the hallway. The president's office suite beckoned from the far end. Etched glass proclaiming the burdens of those serving within, doing the business of all humanity.

Josephs took a deep breath and nodded. Virtue walked toward the doors with the confidence of one who had made this trip hundreds, if not thousands, of times before. Josephs tried to buck up his confidence by marching as a proud member of the Fleet. With head held high, he strode through the door Virtue held open into the outer office.

He took three more steps and stopped since it was no longer obvious which way he needed to go.

Paragon smiled at the commander's confusion. "This way." The young man continued guiding the commander until they stood outside an open door. The president was having a low conversation with the vice president. She acknowledged that she saw the entourage but didn't beckon them to enter.

"You came alone. Last time, we had a small army join us from *Leviathan*." Paragon motioned toward a drink cart that had a variety of beverages available.

The commander shook his head. "Ambassador Payne is far more important than me and has more people available to him. On Oh-One, we have barely over one hundred humans. We have twenty-four Vestrall embarked as well to manage the completion of the Ebren portal, along with the construction of new portals in both Arn and Zuloon space."

"Sounds like you have your hands full," Virtue replied noncommittally. He glanced into the office, and the president waved them in. "President Sinkhaus will see you now."

"Thank you," Josephs replied stiffly. The vice president remained inside. Virtue closed the door after the commander entered, leaving him alone with the career politicians.

"I was expecting Ambassador Payne," the president said as warmly as if it weren't a trap.

The commander was instantly on guard. "He wasn't available because he is currently engaged with the Ga'ee in Vestrall space, attempting a negotiation." Josephs prayed that was still true despite the ship's departure from Vestrall space. "I'm Commander Jimmy Josephs of the battlewagon *The President*, leading Hunter-Killer Squadron One."

"Negotiate with the Ga'ee? I was told there was no negotiating with them. That could change our entire approach. Do we need to do that?"

The commander thought back to his academy days and his philosophy professor, an old war dog who spoke in sarcasm-laced riddles. "We should always attempt negotiation while preparing for the failure of those negotiations. It's easier to negotiate when one has the upper hand militarily."

"Is that what you think?" the president grilled the commander. He understood why Payne and Admiral Wesson weren't fans.

"What I think is irrelevant, President Sinkhaus. It's what you think that matters." He attempted to turn the conversation around.

"I think I listen to my military commanders, so your position is not irrelevant."

Then why didn't you listen to Payne the last time he was here? The commander bit his tongue and schooled his expression to keep from showing his disdain. "We need to build portals for rapid movement of combat power between the systems of the seven races to counter an imminent Ga'ee threat.

"That means we need to bolster our combat power. The Payne-class battlewagons are only one element of that power. We need all the races to support us with more ships and crews."

"Straightforward. I like that." Her fake smile suggested she didn't. "You said Payne is attempting to negotiate with the Ga'ee. Does that mean they reappeared?"

"They did. A Ga'ee carrier arrived in the Vestrall Prime

system thirty-six hours ago. *Leviathan* engaged with them when they did not attack. Team Payne is currently on board the Ga'ee ship."

"Then what are *you* doing here?"

The commander had never intended to tell anything but the truth. "The Ga'ee ship departed on a heading toward uncharted space shortly after Team Payne boarded. *Leviathan* followed the Ga'ee as they transitioned to faster-than-light speed."

The president finally made a face. She tipped her head down to look incredulously at the commander. "The Ga'ee kidnapped Ambassador Payne and his team?" she asked. "And they've lured *Leviathan* away from its primary duty of protecting the space of the known races? Do you wonder why I'm hesitant to take your advice, Commander Josephs?"

Jimmy clenched his hands into fists. The president glanced down, and he followed her eyes to his white knuckles. He forced his hands open and took a step back. "The ambassador and his team put their lives on the line to give us a chance to deal with an enemy who could overwhelm us. Leviathan doesn't answer to anyone except himself.

"It is an amazing feat that Ambassador Payne was able to convince Leviathan to help us and the other six races. They headed toward what we assume is Ga'ee space to engage the enemy in the same way that they engaged the Vestrall to end the war on humanity. Please don't forget their substantial and continuing contributions to the sanctity of Earth."

The president strolled to the other side of her desk and sat down. She didn't give any indication that the commander was to sit, but he wouldn't have been comfortable. He was better off standing.

"President Sinkhaus. The Fleet is ready to give their lives for the safety of their fellow humans. We don't want any of those lives to be wasted. We also don't want to leave humanity unprotected. The five battlewagons that are here have one mission, and that's to defend Earth from the Ga'ee."

Josephs didn't know why he'd added that information. The president was well aware of the oath Fleet personnel took and what it meant. Maybe she needed to be reminded, though. There hadn't been any Fleet personnel in her inner circle. None of the people he'd seen had served. He could tell. Their bearing would have been different. The advice would have been better.

"I see," the president said, followed by another fake smile.

The door opened, and Virtue rushed in. President Sinkhaus glared at him for the interruption.

"Madame President, a box-like ship has dropped out of FTL at the outer reaches of the heliosphere. The ship is headed toward the Jupiter portal."

"I have to get back to my ship." Josephs bolted from the room without waiting for permission.

The Ga'ee had arrived.

Jimmy sprinted to the end of the hallway and hammered at the call button. When the elevator arrived, he found Paragon Virtue next to him. They entered the elevator together and headed up.

"I'll be joining you at the president's request." Virtue met the commander's questioning eyes. Josephs settled for a simple nod.

When they reached the roof, they stepped out to find that the battlewagon was gone.

"That was the right decision," the commander muttered. "The ships have to get into the fight as soon as possible. There's only one course of action, and that is to destroy the Ga'ee ship before the drones can destroy us." He looked at the sky before turning to his escort. "I need to talk with the BEP and any military on Earth. If the Ga'ee made it this far, we have to kill them before they can get a foothold on Earth." He took the young man by the lapels and stared into his eyes. "They will kill us all without hesitation."

"I believe you," Virtue replied, shrugging the commander's hands off his suit.

They took the elevator to the basement where the communication center was located. Inside, they went to a small area dedicated to monitoring Earth's defensive systems. The five battlewagons had reformed into a single squadron and were racing to intercept the newcomer.

They winked into FTL in an attempt to beat the Ga'ee to the portal.

The Ga'ee carrier blinked out as it also accelerated to faster-than-light speed.

"That's not good, is it?" Paragon asked.

"It means we're relegated to sitting and watching the fight over the portal." He didn't add that a new lieutenant was leading the fight for Earth's space. "It also means we'll want to rally anything that can fly and get them into the sky. If the Ga'ee attempt to send any of their drones to Earth's surface, they'll have to be incinerated. No ifs, ands, or buts."

———

Lieutenant Barry Cummins stood in front of the captain's seat. He didn't feel comfortable in the big chair, even though the fight was coming. He'd tried to contact the commander, but failing that, he had taken *The President* into space to rally the other four battlewagons to confront the Ga'ee.

"They aren't supposed to be here!" the sensor systems operator blurted.

Cummins saw an opportunity to lead. "The only thing that matters is that they *are* here. We have been given one mission by the Fleet admiral: protect Earth by destroying the Ga'ee as quickly as possible. That's why we're here without the commander. We had no choice but to follow orders, and now, we'll do as we trained. We'll line up the five ships for a clear shot, and we'll hit the Ga'ee with an energy weapon salvo that should obliterate them. What will send a stronger message to them than that?"

"Nothing, sir!" the sensor operated shouted in response to the lieutenant's rhetorical question.

"Just do your jobs as you trained to do them. The ship will take care of the hard stuff. We'll handle the coordination, and then we'll party like it's nineteen ninety-nine. You hear me?" The lieutenant shook his fist at the screen. Somewhere in the darkness of the outer reaches of the Solar System, the Ga'ee carrier flew toward them.

The crew was watching him. He lowered his fist and smiled. "As you were. Today is as good a day as any to show what we're capable of." He backed into the captain's chair and sat down. He leaned forward to study the screen, but in FTL, nothing changed. It was the last image before they transitioned. A countdown clock showed eighteen seconds remaining until they dropped into normal space.

"Defensive weapons, prepare to fire. Bring the main weapon online."

"Primary is one hundred percent," the weapons station reported. "Defensive systems are on automatic and ready to fire."

All eyes focused on the main screen's clock.

Cummins' jaw clenched tighter with each passing second. He almost stood but knew that he needed to project calmness. He leaned back into the chair.

The clock hit zero, and the quick wave of nausea passed over the crew. The screen populated immediately.

The Ga'ee carrier hung in the sky, with clouds of drones leaving its hangar bays.

"Fire!" the lieutenant blurted.

The main weapon launched a focused energy beam at the Ga'ee ship. Like a comet, it flared through space.

All alone.

The lieutenant gasped at his mistake. The other ships followed suit, but it wasn't the salvo they had been trained to deliver. Cummins had a hard time taking a breath. When he could finally speak, he said what he was thinking.

"I've killed us all."

The beam hammered into the Ga'ee energy shield. It made it flicker and flash with the intensity of the power.

Two more energy beams flashed from Battlewagons Two and Five. They slammed into the remnants of the energy shield and took it down.

The drones powered through the attack and away from the Ga'ee carrier. Tens of thousands of them separated toward six unique targets—the portal and the five battlewagons.

The BEP cruiser *Ephesus* headed away from the fight at its fastest speed.

The last two energy weapons headed toward the unprotected Ga'ee ship. It was too close to maneuver away from the attack. It accelerated, but not before the fourth weapon hit the ship, tearing off a substantial section and sending it into a spin. The last round kissed the side of the ship on its way past.

"Recharge and prepare to fire. Helm, all astern, spin to five o'clock high. Evasive maneuvers as far from the Ga'ee as possible for all five ships. Coordinate the new salvo attack time to coincide with Battlewagon Number Four. They'll be the last to come online."

The five ships changed their courses and accelerated. The drones came after them.

"FTL, now, now, now!" Cummins ordered.

The ship transitioned away. The other four ships were seconds behind.

The clouds of drones followed for another second before changing direction and consolidating. As one massive sun-blocking cloud, they accelerated toward the Jupiter portal.

After ten seconds outboard, the five ships returned to normal space and reoriented one hundred and eighty degrees before transitioning to FTL.

"Expect the drones to be waiting for us. Prepare to flush all defensive batteries upon return to normal space. Wait to fire the main weapon until we can salvo with the other four ships," Cummins ordered.

What had he learned from the first shots?

No time to think. Ten seconds passed in the blink of an eye, and *The President* returned to normal space. The drone cloud was on a final trajectory to the portal. The first impacts showed as flashes of light. The lieutenant resisted the urge to puke.

The other four battlewagons appeared in normal space. They maneuvered to gain an optimal firing angle.

Cummins didn't have to repeat his order. When Number Four was ready, the five ships fired. Five different angles. Five unique shots.

The portal was taking a beating. The ring started coming apart as the drones cut through the ring from inside to outside in a thousand impacts from the tri-spear-tipped vehicles.

The energy weapons hit the Ga'ee carrier within half a second of each other. The damaged ship had reconstituted part of its shield. A massive green-yellow flash enveloped the ship before the shield collapsed anew, bringing with it the full energy of the Vestrall weapons.

The carrier bowed and twisted before a power plant went critical and exploded, then another, and another. A hundred secondary explosions tore the ship apart.

"Protect the portal. Accelerate into the cloud and fire all weapons," the lieutenant calmly ordered. The drones assumed ballistic trajectories, having lost guidance from their mothership.

They still needed to be destroyed. The five battlewagons waded in and started shooting.

Vestrall Chief Engineer Loresh appeared on the bridge. "We can fix that," he announced. "But we'll need the materials from the Ga'ee ship and its drones."

"Inform Hunter-Killer Squadron One that we will gather the debris from the Ga'ee ship and they are to continue destroying the drones. Once they are finished, they are to sweep the area to collect the debris for repurposing, to rebuild what they've damaged."

Barry Cummins leaned back in his chair. No humans had died in the engagement, and the portal was salvageable. They'd also learned a valuable lesson: even an uncoordinated attack could pay dividends. It had taken three shots to blow through a fully operational shield. It had taken five to kill the ship, but ten shots had made it nice and dead.

[14]

*"Regroup, rearm, reload, and reengage, all while under attack. That separates those who do from those who don't." –*From the memoirs of Ambassador Declan Payne

"Lev, any progress?" the admiral asked. He was slouching heavily in a bridge chair. Even Nyota Freeman had a limit on how many hours she was willing to camp out on the bridge while nothing changed.

"We are still unable to see the Ga'ee ship's vibrations. We continue to search for an answer."

"Is the insertion craft squawking or sending any signal?"

"The six-minute lead time is enough that any signal has dissipated. We need to be closer. Should the Ga'ee ship return to normal space, we will fly through the signal, and then we'll know. Since we have flown through no such signal, I am confident that the Ga'ee ship continues on its original heading and we are behind them."

"By six minutes," the admiral reiterated. "What do you think Payne is doing?"

Lev turned it around. "What have you known Declan not to do?"

"That is a valid point, my friend. Payne will do everything humanly possible to rip a new one into that ship. We didn't see any silicon life forms, so what was the ship doing?"

"I have discussed this at length with Davida. If we assume the Ga'ee came here on purpose, we have to validate other assumptions, such as that they can communicate beyond the limitations of light speed and FTL travel. They have an extensive presence somewhere in the universe and probably even within the Milky Way galaxy. They know what there is to know about us, despite their appearance as only knowing binary."

"I came to that same conclusion, Lev. Which also means they know about Earth and where it is."

Lev had seen that realization in Harry's mind. "You sent ten ships that are more than capable of destroying a Ga'ee carrier to protect Earth and Berantz space. Over the next month, five more will transit the portal and head to Ebren space."

"We're doing what we can, but those new ships will need crews, even minimal manning. We have to count on Josephs to convince Earth to support us and build more long-range cargo haulers if they won't build some Kaiju-class ships for us."

"I doubt Earth will build more warships once they see the Payne-class vessels."

"Bring the Payne," the admiral murmured. "I'm sure you're right, Lev. Do we need anyone to build warships if we can build them in Vestrall space?"

"Who's left to defend Vestrall space if the Ga'ee arrive in a second ship?"

"That is a distracting thought, Lev. What can we do if they slip in behind us? Don't answer that. I know. We lose Vestrall Prime, and we lose the shipyard. If we turn you into the sole source of ship construction, we lose your ability to deploy and fight. And how would we know? We're not just flying through the void. We're in the black hole of information. Outside of this ship, we have no idea what's going on."

"I can track the Payne-class battlewagons once they are energized and moving, at least for a while longer before we move out of range."

"You can see the first one that's finished, using just shipyard construction techniques?"

"When it moves from the construction zone to the staging area."

"Let me know when that happens, Lev."

"Of course, Harry. The instant the ship fires its engines."

The admiral straightened in his seat. "Until then, we'll follow Team Payne into the middle of nowhere, also known as, Ga'ee space."

"The odds favor this direction being closer to Ga'ee space than where we started."

"That is a noncommittal answer, Lev. Are the Ga'ee this way or not?" The admiral jumped to his feet and walked toward the front screen.

"The Ga'ee are somewhere in this direction, but it would be folly to believe the Ga'ee chose a direction that led straight to Ga'ee space."

The admiral shook his head. "I don't think the Ga'ee are intimidated by us. We haven't shown them we can stand toe to toe with them. I doubt they're worried we'll invade their space."

"Your insight is valuable. Logic drives their actions, but it doesn't. Why kidnap Team Payne?"

"Because Team Payne survived when they shouldn't have? Are the Ga'ee scientists without ethics or souls? They take over planets with lesser species for the propagation of their own race. Now they have something worth studying, maybe to improve how they can eliminate such creatures in future engagements."

"You paint a bleak picture, Harry. I have talked extensively with the Ga'ee, but they reveal little about themselves. They are calculating, but they don't understand carbon-based life forms."

The admiral chuckled softly. He leaned against a console while watching the main screen. "They kidnapped Team Payne to help them better understand humanity? I think their calculations might be off."

Lev hesitated. "I think Team Payne is an excellent cross-section of humanity. They are vibrant and selfless and all that humans hold dear."

"That's probably best. Imagine if they kidnapped a bunch of politicians? They'd be calling for the extermination of our race, and I wouldn't blame them."

"Harry!" Lev ejaculated. "It seems the Fleet has a universally poor opinion of the civilian leadership. Why do you still serve if those who you serve are such foul creatures?"

The admiral bowed his head to the AI. "My compliments on the excellent usage of our language to convey your thoughts. For me, I'm in a position where I can shield those below me and help them understand their higher purpose. I get to remove the civilians from the equation. The Fleet only sees me. We have very little to do with Earth except to recruit and bring the new Fleet personnel into our fold, where we look out for each other.

"Team Payne is the embodiment of all that I've tried to accomplish. They stay true to the mission. They are loyal to each other. They are the best that humanity has to offer."

A snuffle jerked the admiral's attention to the hatch, where Mary Payne stood with her eyes closed.

"We'll get them back, or rather, they'll return. They'll probably be driving that Ga'ee carrier."

Mary nodded while focusing on her breathing. "I want to believe that."

"Don't ever stop believing that they'll find their way home.

And don't doubt that we will do everything we can to help them." The admiral pointed at the screen. "Lev, show the star chart of Vestrall Prime and where we are now. Can you guesstimate a destination?"

The lights on the bridge dimmed, and the walls, ceiling, and floor became a starfield. A dot appeared near the captain's chair, where Vestrall Prime was shown oversized. A line appeared and traced across the deck a short way before becoming a dashed line. It continued to the front and up to eye level, where it disappeared into the void.

"We will eventually have to change course. This vector leads to the great void between galaxies. A hundred thousand light-years of darkness."

"What if there's something there? It can't be completely empty," the admiral wondered.

"I will only state that it is dark, not that it lacks substance."

"The moon is made of blue cheese and the void of black pudding." The admiral stared at the line. "We have to know when they drop out of FTL, and then we need to see them change course, Lev. I'm not sure I can express that there's anything more important than that."

"I'm doing all I can, Harry. We need Team Payne to make that ship visible."

"If only we could show them we're right behind them," the admiral mused.

Mary leaned against the admiral. "Help us, Lev." She turned to the man next to her. "I'll be on the firing range, picking up where Heckler and Turbo left off. We need a better weapon to deal with Ga'ee infestations, and we don't have it yet."

"Focus on that. We'll catch up to them, and there will be hell to pay for the Ga'ee. We'll make them sorry they ever set foot in our sector of space." The admiral made a fist and held it against his chest. "I promise."

Mary nodded and headed for the corridor. She had work to do if humanity was going to fight back. She was convinced of two things. That the Ga'ee were coming to take over the habitable planets of the seven races, and that Team Payne was the best example of humanity.

And maybe a third. Declan Payne would do what he had to to keep that ship from returning to Ga'ee space.

————

Payne tried not to watch the glacially slow progress of using a jerry-rigged plasma torch to cut an access into the sealed space.

He decided on something to keep him busy.

"Virgil and Turbo, run the portside hangar bay. Scan everything as far forward and as far aft as you can get. Kal and I will take the starboard side. If you get any hits on Ga'ee, let us all know. Heckler, Byle, Joker, you're the emergency response team. Drop the cannon and keep to railguns unless otherwise requested."

"First one back gets a cookie?" Major Dank asked.

"Better. First one back with full scans gets bragging rights. I'm looking for an elevator or a shaft that leads to other decks. The entrance to these centerline spaces could be from above or below."

"Bragging rights?" Turbo asked. "I had my hopes up for a cookie. How about twenty minutes of private time with my man?"

"Ew!" Payne grunted. "I hope everyone has as healthy a relationship as you two. Thank you for not blowing up Vestrall Prime. While we're at it, don't blow up this ship either, not until we want it blown up."

"You know they just do that to get a rise out of you." Dank edged down the corridor to get a head start.

"I know." Payne took off running. Kal struggled to keep up since he was hunched over. Payne ran with his head ducked to keep it from bouncing off the ceiling. Once they covered the three hundred meters to the massive hangar bay, Kal was able to stand up straight. "Are you okay?"

Kal nodded. "I much prefer running upright. I guess I'm spoiled like that."

"We're ruining you, Kal. You're starting to sound like us when you're not sounding like a Western television star."

"Y'all are too kind with your perfumey words and slick manners," Kal drawled.

Payne chose to go aft first. He started to run, assuming an easy pace for the first five steps, then accelerated to fifty kilometers per hour. Kal kept up for a short time but started to fall back quickly. Even though he could tolerate the cold, his muscles weren't performing at peak efficiency. Payne slowed to forty, then thirty to let Kal catch up.

They completed the last kilometer of the run together.

"The hangar bay is eight kilometers long," Payne reported. "A little more to it than I thought, but that accounts for most of the ship, at least on these levels. If we could only access other parts, like the engines."

Kal took his time catching his breath while Payne moved along the forward bulkhead, scanning through the metal as far as the system would reach. He couldn't see spaces beyond fifty meters. That left over nine hundred meters of unmapped ship. He continued to the longitudinal bulkhead. The metal was thinner by a fraction, but the space beyond was mostly open, separated into subdecks.

"Looks like ten decks for them and one for us. Nothing we can get into here." Payne pointed while staring at his HUD. He sidestepped his way down the wall. Five hundred meters down, he found an access. The signature of a pulsing power center lay beyond.

The door blended into the wall. Payne didn't expect to find a handle or some other human-sized actuator. He took a knee, then lay prone to look at the bottom of the door. To the right, a centimeter off the deck, was a small indent. He removed the multitool that all the SOFTies carried.

"Kal, can you open the screwdriver for me?"

The two struggled to get the multitool open. They had to use a second tool to help them with the first.

Payne poked the indent with the tip of the screwdriver, and the door retracted straight back into the wall for ten centimeters before slipping sideways. Payne popped to his feet and hurried through. Kal moved in behind him. Payne watched the door expectantly, but it remained open.

"Stay," he coaxed it before turning around and sizing up the space. "This is much bigger than the central corridor."

Kal stood to his full height. "I like this space better."

There were no intersecting corridors. Only one way to go: straight to the power plant.

"Keep an eye out, Kal. I'm head down into the pit of despair." Payne ambled forward, barely watching where he was going. There was nothing to run into. Kal took the lead. "It's a modular system. Plug and play. Pull out the old power plant, put in the new."

"Do their power plants need replacing with such frequency that they need a plug-and-play system?" Major Dank asked. "Why was there a manual access to the door when the Ga'ee use their brain link for everything?"

Payne checked to find he had been on the team channel the entire time.

"I think it's a backup. They probably opened it with their

combined thoughts. As to changing out the plant quickly and why? Unknown. It would make construction easier. There's no need to build a ship around the engines like we do."

"Higher survivability with plug and play?" Dank accessed the power plant from the far side, having gone aft first, the same as Payne. "Thanks for showing us the way in."

On the central axis, the power plant was the same height and width as the corridor, but the device was much longer. It had been moved in, then rotated within a circular space to align along the ship's length. Payne leaned down to study the foundation.

"A platen. They move the plant in, and the support base rotates like a lazy Susan."

"It's almost like they're really good engineers," Dank remarked. "Standard stuff, but it's not. Making something that is complex look simple takes a higher level of understanding."

Payne scanned the plant. He studied the information that fed into his HUD. "I don't know what I'm getting. Sparky, can you hear me?"

"I'm here. Let me pass off the cutting duties to Shaolin." Swearing funneled into the silence. "We're good. What do you have?"

"Take a look at these scans. What is this thing, and how does it work?"

"Give me a few. This thing is kinda complex. Keep streaming the info. I want to see it cycle."

Payne stood still, letting his suit do the work. Dank and Turbo walked around the device.

"If this is a power plant or an engine, how does it feed the ship's systems?" Turbo asked.

Payne pointed at himself. "I hope you don't expect me to know the answer to that."

"I got this," Virgil replied. He leaned down while scanning.

"Energy surging through an access in the plate. It hooks up manually, although there's a residual in the air. I think they have a certain amount of wireless electricity to power their systems, too. Just not enough to drive a big gear like the engine. I think the engines are direct drive with the power generated here, and the conversion to motion is done in the sealed aft section of the ship."

Turbo nodded. She backed away from the platen upon which the power plant rested to lean against the wall with her arms crossed. The suit made the stance look less comfortable than it was.

"I think I know what's going on," Sparky said after she finished her preliminary examination of the data. "It's a hydrogen fusion reactor, just like our sun. They swap out the reactor when the fuel runs low, maybe once every six months to a year. *Ugly 5's* scans confirmed what we learned from the drone scan back in Berantz space. There are six identical reactors on this tug."

"How many do they really need?" Payne wondered.

"This one is a backup to the engine plant," Sparky replied.

"How did you come up with that?" Payne stepped back from the machine.

"It's the second one, and it's not operating at capacity. Your scans are showing the aft-most power plant running at one hundred percent, as one would expect from the engine driving a ten-kilometer-long ship at FTL speed," Sparky explained.

Payne jammed his hand into the bottom of his faceplate as if he wanted to rub his chin in thought. He knew what they had to do. "These things are plug and play, which means there has to be access to the engine's power with a corridor that we can use. Spread out and find it."

Kal waited for Payne. Dank and Turbo retreated down the corridor to the port hangar bay. Payne led the way to the starboard hangar bay. He walked aft, retracing his steps and the search he'd done before.

"If you do the same thing, you get the same result," Kal commented.

"And I am. What do you suggest?"

Kal waved the plasma cannon, which he carried as easily as Payne carried his railgun. "Where's the thinnest point?"

Payne scanned anew, looking solely for the weak point. He found a panel that reminded him of the one his team was trying to cut through along the centerline. Payne scratched an outline and drew an X in the middle of it. He jogged around Kal to get out of the line of fire and blast debris.

Kal took aim and gently squeezed off the first round. Payne's sensors lit up as the thrum of the vibration echoed through the chambers beyond.

"Hold up, Kal." Payne studied the space beyond the thin panel. "Hit it from this angle. When you blast through, you shouldn't hit anything important."

"'Shouldn't,'" Kal repeated.

"You're one of us, Kal. You wield the appropriate level of sarcasm to deliver rounds on target every time." Kal had only been with Payne for a year and a half, but he continued to evolve as an individual, becoming as human as any other member of the team. Payne wasn't sure if that was a good or bad thing, but he appreciated Kal's efforts to blend in.

The Ebren adjusted his position and aiming point and blasted the panel, following the outline Payne had drawn. He strode forward and kicked at the hanging pieces to clear the access.

"I got it, Kal. Don't cut yourself on the sharp bits." Payne stepped in to expand the ruptured metal to create an opening they could easily walk through.

"A lot warmer in here, boss," Kal drawled.

Payne checked his sensors for radiation, but the reading was normal for interstellar space. "Ten C, Kal. Downright balmy. Let's see where this goes."

The suit lights showed a corridor going off toward the ship's central axis at a thirty-degree angle from where they stood at the aft end of the starboard hangar bay.

At the end, they found that there wasn't one but two power plants supplying the engines.

"Come to the starboard hangar. You'll find an access leading to the power plants that feed the drives," Payne announced. "Now that we're here, what do we do about these things?"

"See if we can access them," Sparky suggested. "I'll be right there, and I'll bring Blinky and Buzz."

"Hang on," Blinky interrupted. "We're almost done cutting into this space."

"*We* means *me*." Byle grunted. "Be done in a minute."

"Carry on." Payne wanted to take over the Ga'ee ship, but he didn't know how to go about it. He wanted to take it out of FTL. He wanted to know where it was going, and he didn't want to wait. He smiled within the privacy of his helmet. He could feel their fortunes changing.

At the fusion reactors, the ambient temperature was twenty degrees Celsius. An oxygen-nitrogen atmosphere surrounded them. Payne removed his helmet and took a deep breath.

"That's nice," he said. "Maybe a little too warm. We could get time without our suits in here. Decrease the charging time."

Kal took off his helmet and put it on the deck. "If there's breathable air, I can do without that thing," he noted. "Even if it's cold."

"We'll chuck your gear in *Ugly 5* so we have it when we leave."

"I'm through," Byle announced.

Payne held his helmet close and spoke into it. "Heckler and

Shaolin, clear the space. Blinky and Buzz, see if it's what you think it is."

Virgil and Turbo showed up.

"Isn't this something?" Dank noted. "Looks like the other one times two."

"The real question is, how do we take it down so we drop out of FTL without disintegrating the ship? Looks like the engines are sealed farther aft."

"Are they?" Virgil pointed forward. "I think they're right through there."

Payne hurriedly put his helmet back on. "What are you seeing that I'm not seeing?"

"An FTL drive." Dank forwarded the consolidated data.

Payne saw the overlapping scans: ultraviolet, infrared, millimeter wave, and sonic resonance. None individually showed the outline of a massive machine that was much different from the boxy reactor units.

Payne kept his helmet on as he tapped his way around the wall. He couldn't find an access point like they had for other spaces along the central axis.

"That looks like a huge space. What if the access is from the end of the backup reactor? Go take a look, Virge. I'm going to start pulling plugs and see if we can upset this apple cart."

"I'm sorry, you're going to do what?" Virgil stared.

"I'm going to wait for Blinky and Buzz. Why? What did you think I said?"

[15]

"Technology can be your friend unless it's your enemy's." –From the memoirs of Ambassador Declan Payne

Blinky and Buzz waited for Heckler and Shaolin to finish clearing the space.

When Heckler returned to the newly cut doorway, he gestured at the techies. "Looks like a playground for your ilk."

"'Ilk?'" Buzz questioned. "If you mean the stud muffins who'll save your troglodyte ass, then yes. Our *ilk*."

Heckler wanted to punch him if only to reinforce his point. "As you wish, Fetus."

"Hey!" With his arms full of their gear, Blinky stepped through first.

Heckler blocked Buzz. "Still the new guy." He moved out of the way after he made his point. "And yeah. Save our asses since this ship is getting on my nerves. Get in there and tell it what to do with itself."

Buzz's hands were full of gear too, so he held out his elbow.

Heckler bumped it with his elbow. After Buzz was in, Shaolin removed herself from the space.

"Did you see anything?" Heckler asked.

"Modules and gear and not a single connection anywhere. It's like stuff plugged into a circuit board. You don't get to see the plugs. Judging by what the others have seen with the aft power systems, that's how this ship is built. That scares me."

"How so?"

"As you get better at manufacturing something, you streamline the construction process. This ship is pretty streamlined."

"I hate it when things make sense," Heckler grumbled. "You better share that with the major, although I suspect he already knows."

Shaolin accessed the team channel and shared her thoughts.

"Makes a lot of sense," Payne replied. "Blinky and Buzz, bring this ship out of FTL. The sooner, the better. I have a bad feeling about what the Ga'ee are doing. It might not have just been Vestrall space they sent a ship to. What if they sent ships to all the habitable planets' systems?"

"And we're out here incapable of doing anything about it, and I bet we have Lev right behind us. Remove the greatest warship in the galaxy from the space you intend to invade. That is worth the cost of sending a full-size carrier. It wasn't us they were after. It was *Leviathan*, but we were the ready and willing bait. Last time, Lev left us behind."

Virgil chimed in. "Last time, Lev didn't know we were still alive."

"How did the Ga'ee find that out?"

"Maybe their link works for more than sharing information between the Ga'ee. The Progenitors figured out telepathy and built a system to use it. The Ga'ee are as advanced as those who built *Leviathan*, although in a different way. We have every right to be afraid since they are two steps ahead of us, almost. I think they underestimated Team Payne's ingenuity, though. Why didn't they just kill us once we got here?"

"Maybe they want to study us, Virge, because we defeated them. They might not have experienced that before. Now they have the team who took out their colony on BD18 and the ship that coordinated the beat-down of a carrier and the destruction of over a hundred thousand drones." Payne spoke over the team channel with grim determination. "But they grossly underestimated Team Payne. Blinky, Buzz, make them sorry for crossing us."

"On it. We need the torch in here to cut open a couple of these panels."

Four and a half kilometers from where Blinky and Buzz were attempting to break into the computer systems running the Ga'ee carrier, Payne continued his study of the fusion reactors that drove the engines. He was planning where to put the explosives in case his computer technicians failed, and the Ga'ee succeeded in getting Team Payne to their home space.

"Wire the reactors," Payne ordered. "If we drop out of FTL to change course, we'll blow them. We probably won't have much time, maybe only a few seconds. I need multiple people to be able to light 'em up just in case. Me, Virge, Turbo..." Payne hesitated. "Hell, make sure every single one of us can detonate the charges, but not individually. Two have to pull the trigger, and that'll blow them. That means we need to blow the secondary reactor too. Come on, Kal. We'll take care of the backup."

"Got you, Dec. There won't be anything left of these two when we're done with them."

Payne locked his helmet into place and jogged down the angled corridor with Kal beside him. The Ebren hadn't bothered with his helmet and tank, but he carried them just in case. Being separated from one's source of air was never a good idea when they didn't know what the next moment might bring.

In the systems space half a ship away, Blinky and Buzz needed to make their digital magic happen. Team Payne's other choices went from unsavory to downright horrible.

———

"This is Lieutenant Barry Cummins, acting captain of the battlewagon *The President*, requesting to speak to Commander Jimmy Josephs, last known to be at the UN."

It took a few seconds for the signal to get back to the battlewagon. "Wait one."

"Really?" the impatient lieutenant asked with his comm unit off. He scanned the faces on the bridge to find each person looking at him.

He was in charge, and they were looking to him, a leadership lesson he had heard of but never experienced before. Everything he said and did would be viewed under that microscope.

"No kidding. They have to go to the nearest restaurant, where he'll be eating the good stuff!" Barry quipped to mild snickers before he turned serious. "Thank you for saving me from my jerked-off first order to fire. We didn't coordinate, and we almost lost the portal.

"But we didn't. When we recycled for the second round, we sent those bastards straight to hell, and the battlewagon's defensive firepower eliminated the tens of thousands of drones polluting the void. With these ships, we have the means to protect Earth. We have the ability to protect all the space occupied by the seven races, which means we have the responsibility.

"Prepare to be deployed until we can be certain the Ga'ee

threat has been eliminated. When we talk to the commander, we'll see about improving the quality of rations available and maybe bring some beer and champagne on board, too. We are going to be our only port of call until this war is over."

A sobering thought, but the crew deserved the truth.

For now, Earth space was safe.

"Commander Josephs. Tell me you didn't scratch my ship, Barry," a voice crackled through the bridge speakers.

"No scratches, sir, but we've painted the silhouette of one Ga'ee carrier on the prow. Request permission to pick you up."

"Not yet, Lieutenant. I still have to meet with the president and the council. The Ga'ee's arrival has changed the dynamic, and further conversations are called for. Most importantly, the hunter-killer squadron has proven the concept. We'll need roughly five thousand personnel to crew the rest of the battlewagons in production, so lots of work to do. Lev's not here to help us with the simulators, so we'll have to train them the old-fashioned way."

"We didn't have time to cross-deck the equipment," Cummins lamented.

"Adapt and overcome, Lieutenant. Put together the training package based on what Lev gave us. You'll need to start training new hands immediately. The delivery of BW11 is in a week, with a new ship every week thereafter. Turn to, Lieutenant Cummins."

"Aye aye, sir." The lieutenant snapped to attention and saluted. The bridge crew snickered, and the commander raised one eyebrow.

"As you were." The commander cut the link.

Cummins' cheeks flushed. "Ha-ha. Have your laugh. Just showing a little respect for the boss man."

The navigator raised a hand like she was in elementary school. Cummins tipped his chin at the young woman.

"He hasn't fought the Ga'ee, but you have."

The lieutenant smiled. "*We* have, and I fucked it up. Now, no one knows better than me what *not* to do." He stepped away from the captain's chair. "Training. You heard the commander. Check the procedures for each of your positions and be ready to deliver that to the new blood. Hopefully, they'll have served in the Fleet, but if not, have patience.

"But they only get a week, no more, to figure it out. We had ten days total from when we started training until we were engaged with the Ga'ee. That is the training standard. XO, pass the word to the rest of the crew!" Cummins jumped forward and turned to face where he'd just been. He saluted smartly. "Share the plan of the day. Aye aye, sir!"

Cummins ran from the bridge, only to return five seconds later to use the communications built into the captain's chair. He winked at the navigation officer, then activated the ship-wide intercom and repeated what he'd told the bridge crew.

When he closed the connection, the bridge crew clapped. A salty old enlisted member of the Fleet walked up to him. "Lieutenant, a word." Without waiting, the chief specialist headed for the corridor. The lieutenant followed him out like a whipped puppy.

Once the hatch closed, giving them privacy from the crew, the chief started. "That's exactly how you do it, sir. You've come farther and faster than anyone I've ever seen these past fifteen years. I know, I look like I should be retired. It's not the years but the space klicks traveled. I've died twice, did you know that?"

Cummins laughed. "Damn it, Chief. I thought you were going to give me my daily comeuppance."

"Don't you already do that to yourself?"

"Are you a Fleetie or a chaplain?" the lieutenant asked.

"I'd like to think a little of both. We used to have senior

enlisted on these boats. Called them COB, chief of the boat. I think we should have them again. Keep the crew calm and going in the same direction. And before you tell me that's an officer's job, I'll tell you it's not.

"Look at Team Payne. Eight specialists, two officers, and an Ebren warrior. Those two officers carry the same gear and jump into the same fights. Everyone working as one team. The Ga'ee won't know what hit them. Keep doing what you're doing." The chief clapped Cummins on the shoulder.

"I'll talk with Commander Josephs and see if we can make that happen. COBs for all the battlewagons. Small crews. They need to click."

"Exactly. Now, get back to work. The crew needs you."

"Why are you out here fucking off, COB? We got work to do."

"Yes, sir, Skipper." The chief hurried back to the bridge.

With newfound confidence, Barry Cummins headed for the engineering section. He needed them to go the extra kilometer in training the crews. When everything worked, no one needed to do anything, but if there was any damage to the ship, that was when the most would be asked of them. Getting damaged systems online as quickly as possible would be the difference between life and death.

The crew of *The President* had had nine days. Cummins knew they weren't ready, but they would be responsible for training the second generation of crews.

They had to get it right.

The Ga'ee had given them a second chance, but there would be no more. They had to get it right from the outset.

[16]

"When it comes to choices, make sure you have more than one." —From the memoirs of Ambassador Declan Payne

Paragon Virtue held his hand in front of the elevator door to keep it open while Commander Jimmy Josephs strode toward him. They nodded to acknowledge each other.

"Next stop, the president of the UN. Are you ready?"

"More ready than I was last time. Now, we have evidence of the threat. It's not me shouting that the sky is falling."

"But since you've neutralized the threat, what is the urgency? We have nothing but time on our side," Virtue asked casually.

"We stand on the edge of the precipice. We can defeat the enemy as we've shown, or we can rest on our laurels and watch the habitable planets fall, one after the other."

"I'm just prepping you for the hard questions. The answer was good, but the look of disdain won't work on the president. It didn't on me either."

The commander smiled. "It was that obvious, huh?"

"Just a lot." The elevator stopped, and the door opened. Virtue walked off first, and the commander hurried to get beside him.

"Did your parents not like you?" Jimmy asked before they reached the president's office suite.

He sighed before answering the old, tired question. "They liked me just fine, but they were New Age and wanted to tell the world what their son would be. It was just virtue signaling, shall we say."

"You've answered this question before. I'm sorry, Paragon. Let's do this thing. We need crews for the coming battlewagons, and we need them now."

"That's how you need to phrase it. The president's time is at a premium."

They walked through the outer offices and were ushered straight to the president's inner sanctum. She looked up from her computer as they entered and leaned back in her chair, clasping her hands across her stomach.

Paragon waited until the commander was inside before he stepped back, closing the door to leave the commander alone with the president.

"I need to thank Ambassador Payne," the president said. "He wanted us to build ships, but there was no way we could build them in time. He managed better, delivering firepower when we needed it. His foresight saved Earth." She paused for dramatic effect. "Again."

"Yes, ma'am. We have upwards of fifty additional battlewagons, at the rate of one per week, coming from Vestrall Prime, starting as soon as we can get the portal repaired. We need crews for them, but thanks to automation technology, these ships can operate with a minimal human crew, roughly one hundred per ship. We need to start training them immediately."

"You don't need my permission to train Fleet personnel."

The commander waited, a smile slowly spreading across his face.

The president frowned in response. "You want to recruit new personnel."

"I do, but not just anyone. I need the best of the best, and it would help if the president of the UN made the appeal, extolling the virtues of military service." The commander wasn't trying to play hardball, but her treatment of the admiral and the ambassador had swept rapidly through those on *Leviathan*. He had no sympathy. She could lie to help the Fleet, and that would help humanity.

Wasn't that what she was supposed to be doing?

"Sooner rather than later, President Sinkhaus."

"It's that easy for you, isn't it?" she asked.

"I don't understand. I want to train personnel to run the new battlewagons to continue our fight against the Ga'ee. That *is* fairly easy from my perspective."

"Earth is a peaceful society. Why do you think we ship the Fleet into deep space? The BEP shares the ideals of the UN when it comes to not initiating violence."

The commander had absorbed the lesson Paragon Virtue had just taught him. He didn't let his disdain creep into his expression.

"The Ga'ee will kill everyone on Earth, and there won't be anything you can do about it. We're taking those five battlewagons to Ebren. We'll leave the new ships here. It would be in your best interests to make sure they are crewed by good people." It was all the commander could come up with. He tried to appeal at a personal level.

"You'll leave the original ships here. Send the new ones to Ebren," she countered.

"Not our call, President Sinkhaus. They are Vestrall assets."

"But the Vestrall are magnanimous in allowing their ships to protect Earth. Who's the leader of the Vestrall?"

"That would be Ambassador Payne," Josephs answered, unsure of where the president was trying to go.

"But he's been kidnapped, so who is giving orders on behalf of the Vestrall?"

"Loresh, Chief of the Vestrall engineers, who happens to be Vestrall. The BEP talked with him when they erroneously assumed they'd be able to board *The President*."

"Is that an innuendo, Commander Josephs?"

"Not at all. That was deadly serious. The last thing we need is an intramural firefight. We're on the same side. The BEP needs to stop treating the Fleet like the enemy. I respectfully request that you help our recruiting efforts and that we start right now."

"I need to review your request. It will take at least a month."

"I'm sorry. Did the Ga'ee attack not happen?"

"It did, and your people did their jobs. You handled it. Now you tell me that's not enough."

The commander clenched his jaw. "No, ma'am. It's nowhere near enough."

"Fine. We'll have a press conference."

"What?"

"I said fine." She stood and walked out. The commander followed her.

The president led him to a section within the office suite reserved for guests. The press was already there.

It made the commander feel like he'd been played.

The president made a beeline for the podium. She tapped on the lectern to get everyone's attention. The room quieted. She motioned for the commander to join her.

"I'm sure you have already seen the footage of the destruction of the Ga'ee ship." The reporters nodded. "We have reason

166

to believe this isn't the last time we'll see the Ga'ee. So, I'll be asking for more funding, but first, we need personnel.

"But not just anyone. We need engineers, pilots, technicians, and those with the hearts of lions. These people will crew the ships you saw defeat the Ga'ee. Payne-class battlewagons will start to arrive one per week from Vestrall Prime. We implore you to apply today. Apply at your local Fleet recruitment office. We're looking for the best of the best. You will be challenged with nothing less than saving humanity, along with all the known carbon-based life forms in our galaxy. Questions?"

The commander was shocked.

A reporter raised his hand. "What time commitment are you asking of these volunteers?"

The question seemed innocuous, but the commander was on his guard. The president had asked the same question. "Eighteen months to start. With the travel times as long as they are to our allies until the portals are built, the first year will be spent maneuvering on long-haul flights. After the portals are in place, the engagement time will be greatly improved."

The commander felt a hole burning through his stomach. He was committing the Fleet to things he had no right to commit it to. It contained hundreds of higher-ranking officers whose responsibility it was to make decisions like this and carry them out.

But they weren't there. Commander Jimmy Josephs stood before humanity's press and did the best he could, but the truths he told were only truths in his mind. The Fleet admiral could change his commitments with a single word.

The burn tightened his abs so much that he grunted involuntarily.

The president glanced at him. He smiled back, but it didn't

hide how pale he had become. She seemed to be reveling in his discomfort.

"Follow-up question," the first reporter shouted. "What kind of ranks and pay do you anticipate for those who put their lives on hold to help you?"

The commander swallowed and weighed his options. "No, sir. They wouldn't be helping *me*. I'm only a starship captain, and I already have my crew. They would be helping the seven races survive against an enemy bent on genocide. You saw that ship enter our Solar System. Had we not stopped them, they would be colonizing Earth right now, to the detriment of humanity. No, sir! They will be helping all of humanity, just like the rest of the Fleet personnel who sacrifice for the greater good. As for pay, that gets allocated by the good people in this building, not me."

"Are you saying others don't sacrifice?" someone shouted.

"What?" the commander wondered. "That's not what I'm saying at all."

"Why is Fleet so opposed to keeping humanity safe?"

"What? Where did you get that?"

"Why can't the BEP take care of it? They have good people..."

The commander looked at the president, and she finally took pity on him and swooped in for a rescue. "We'll collect your questions and forward them to the Fleet's public affairs office for comment. All volunteers are more than welcome to submit through the Fleet recruitment gateway. Stop by and thank them for their *sacrifices*."

The president walked off, and the commander followed, using a military stride to block out the chatter from the reporters. The commander couldn't break his mind free from how quickly the press had turned on him.

Every word had been dissected as if it had no relation to the other words. Context had been removed, and the only thing that remained was whatever they wanted it to be. Their truth.

"Thank you for your time, President Sinkhaus," the commander said and peeled off when she turned toward her office. She waved over her shoulder. He made it to the door to the hallway before Virtue intercepted him.

The commander started to laugh, as if he had been freed from a great burden.

"I don't see what you find so humorous. I can help you for your next presser, so you don't get trapped in your own poorly chosen words." Paragon rested his hand on Jimmy's shoulder as he tried to radiate warmth.

It came across as demeaning. The commander shrugged it off.

"Now I know why Ambassador Payne was more than willing to risk getting kidnapped by the Ga'ee and Fleet Admiral Wesson was willing to go after Team Payne rather than come here. I'll take my leave if you don't mind. I probably won't be back, and no one else will either. We'll find our crews elsewhere."

"Is that what you took away from that? You're not going to wait and see if any stalwart souls step up to help?"

"Who would that be, exactly? It was framed in such a way that even current Fleet members wouldn't join. I'll wait until the portal is fixed, but after that, we're out of here."

"You can't. We need those ships."

The commander smiled and pointed at the aide. "And we need the crews. Help us help you. Unless you can convince the public of that, we'll be on our way to where we'll be appreciated." ❯

"Then what?"

"Then we'll hope the Ga'ee don't come back here. Otherwise, you're going to have some serious problems."

"You wouldn't turn your back on humanity," Virtue countered.

"Ten billion people, and we asked for your support to recruit five thousand. Even that was too much. The tone of how people are treated is set at the top. President Sinkhaus despises the military, and everyone down the political chain from her shares that disdain. Whether intentionally or not is irrelevant. We're all humans. Treating each other with a little bit of respect is not asking very much."

"You haven't spent much time on Earth recently, have you?"

"Leadership starts at the top. I don't have to know anything besides what I've seen with my own two eyes. Today has been a valuable learning experience. Either something changes, or we won't be back."

"You're human. Of course you'll be back."

"Because we're human, you're probably right. But it might not be when you need us the most." The commander walked away. The elevator was at the end of the hallway, and he couldn't wait to get into it and unbutton the neck of his dress uniform. He couldn't wait to take a shower and get the stench of the UN off his clothes, but even endless water wouldn't clean off the stain on his soul.

He didn't want to come back to Earth, or not to the place where these people lived and worked.

Fleet Headquarters. He needed to go there and see why the ground-based admirals didn't come to the UN and fly point for the request.

Had they already surrendered?

[17]

"Don't let your strengths be your weakness." –From the memoirs of Ambassador Declan Payne

"What do ya got for me?" Declan Payne slurred through a half-sleep.

"We are tapped in. Just need to figure out the handshake, then the language, so we can start taking control of their systems," Blinky announced.

"You'll have us out of FTL in about an hour, then?" Payne joked.

Blinky laughed. "We'll let you know, but I wouldn't break out any champagne just yet. Maybe a few days. Maybe never."

Payne stood. He never liked sleeping in his suit because he didn't get enough rest. There was no ability to move in a parked suit.

"Thanks, sunshine. I love waking up to your optimism." He preferred waking up next to his wife, but he couldn't do that while he was trapped on the Ga'ee ship. "New rule. If anyone wants to sleep, go to the aft reactors and remove your suit. Let's move *Ugly 5* down here so we can recharge the suits while we catch some quality shuteye."

"Still minus sixty-five in the hangar bay, Dec. It warms up quickly once you get into the ship, but that's going to be a cold dash in and out," Major Dank noted.

"Better than sleeping in the suit. I guess we only have to charge them when we get down to fifty percent. If we acquired enough cabling, we could run a line closer to the reactor. Get the best of both worlds—a recharge and warmth."

"We could warm the whole ship," Dank offered.

"When we have that ability, we're taking the ship out of FTL. Then we'll get plenty of company over here to disassemble this ship and learn everything there is to learn about it. We'll turn Lev loose on Ga'ee technology."

"He'll enjoy that, probably too much. What kind of time do we have, Dec?"

Payne shook his head even though he was still wearing his helmet. "I wish I knew, Virge. I wish I knew where we were going. That would give us an idea. I hate to say it, but I think we probably have weeks, if not months, before we get where we're supposed to be going. I want to know what else is going on out there. If this was a diversion, they've locked up *Leviathan* for who knows how long."

"Do you think it's back there?" Dank asked.

"I don't know how I know, but I do. Lev is following us. Mary and the admiral are watching the screen, talking about us. Annaliese, too. They'll bring her into the exclusive club of worried better halves. They should probably talk with Federico, Alex, Wysteria, and Digitus."

"Mary was there when they raided the hangar bay."

"I like how you put that. From my perspective, they wanted one last look at their stud muffins to hold them over until we returned." Payne was feeling happier, knowing that Blinky and

Buzz were into the ship's computer system. He had as much faith in their abilities as they did.

"You think that's how they wanted to remember us? In our combat suits, pounding our way to the uglymobile? Isn't there a better way to retain fond memories?"

"First day in the Fleet, Virgil? At least they aren't strippers."

"What the hell?" Dank blurted.

Laughter hammered his ears. Payne had been using the team channel, not P2P. "Belay my last. If anyone ever repeats what I just said, I'll deny it, then fill your bunk with bedbugs and your suit with scorpions."

"You don't have either one of those, but with a little time, I bet we could come up with some bitchin' itching powder," Heckler offered.

A wave of nausea passed over them as the Ga'ee carrier dropped into normal space. "Blinky, tell me that's you."

"I think it was us," Blinky replied.

"You have to know! We need to blow this reactor. The ship is adjusting course right now. Tell us, Blinky. Blow it or not?"

The silence dragged on. Payne felt like he was drowning. "Blinky?"

A new wave passed as the ship transitioned back to FTL.

"Not us," Blinky said softly.

"Son of a motherfuck!" Payne shouted. He groaned in frustration, then calmed and spoke evenly. "Blinky, Buzz. Take over this ship and bring us out of FTL, please." Payne closed the comm channel.

A point-to-point opened up from Virgil. "Are you okay, Dec?"

"I'll be fine, but I'm not sure Lev is behind us anymore."

"Maybe in the last day, he figured out how to track the Ga'ee," Virgil offered.

"We're putting our trust in two people who can break into

any computer system. They only need time, and like I said earlier, we have weeks, if not months. It would have been nice if the Ga'ee had left the door open so we could have flushed a buoy into space. Something to let Lev know we're still here. Maybe the *Ugly 5*'s transponder will get through to Lev. We have to hope for the best."

"While planning for the worst," Dank finished the team motto.

"I can't tell you what the worst is that we're supposed to plan for. Show up in Ga'ee space where they put us in a lab to study us? We'll go down fighting. As long as we have explosives, we're not falling into the Ga'ee's hands or the little wiry things they use for legs."

"Death before dishonor, Dec? I agree. I'll back you on that. We'll blow the ship. We won't let ourselves or our gear be taken by the enemy."

The ship lurched, and Payne stumbled. "Tell me that was you," Payne requested over the team channel.

"That was nothing," Blinky replied. "Watch this."

The wave quickly passed as the ship dropped out of FTL.

———

"We have a signal from *Ugly 5*," Lev announced. The ship immediately transitioned to normal space. "This was where they stopped."

"And changed course." The admiral's face fell.

Leviathan maneuvered to the location from which the long-gone signal had emanated. Lev scanned and analyzed the directions most likely for the Ga'ee ship to travel. He could find no vibrations.

"The potential destinations are infinite from here, even adjusting for locations that are closer to Berantz space."

Leviathan held its position. "I understand," Harry replied. "We've lost Team Payne."

"An engine signature has just appeared. It's the original Ga'ee ship, on course from this point." Lev adjusted his heading and jumped into faster-than-light speed.

"How far ahead?"

Lev plotted the position on a tactical board showing little more than interstellar space. "Six minutes," he replied. "The ship dropped out of FTL once more. Engines continue to warble."

Admiral Wesson grinned and shook his fist at the screen. "Well done, Team Payne!" He leaned against the nearest console and crossed his arms while watching a new countdown appear on the board.

Pounding feet, snorting, and a random bark announced the arrival of the Cabrizi, with a huffing Mary Payne right behind them.

"Lev said we're closing on the Ga'ee ship." She hurried in to stand next to the admiral.

He pointed at the screen. "Four minutes and closing. They dropped out of FTL less than ten minutes ago. Adjusted course and continued on their new heading. Less than five minutes later, they dropped out again, but this time, it was preceded by Lev being able to see the ship because the engines registered as vibrations across the fabric of space."

"Which means Blinky and Buzz have taken over the Ga'ee ship."

"That's how I'd interpret it. We'll be there in minutes. The question is, what do we do now?"

"Get the team back and destroy that ship," Mary snapped.

The admiral drew a breath and shook his head. "If we've taken over that ship, we have access to information we could use in our war against the Ga'ee. Think about how Lev could

use that to help us win. *Leviathan* can be our savior once more."

"*Then* we destroy that ship," Mary urged.

"If we control it, why would we need to destroy it?" the admiral asked.

"Can you guarantee that we can always control it, or is this yet another subplot in the saga that is the Ga'ee takeover of flesh-and-blood space?"

The admiral leaned away from Mary. "You and Payne are perfect for each other. Is nothing cut and dried in your world?"

Mary weakly smiled. The countdown clock was under a minute. Her heart hammered in her chest, anticipating the ship would bolt seconds before she could hear from Declan. "Sometimes bad things happen to good people who are trying to do the right thing. We are skeptical, that's all."

"Lev, give me Commander Malone."

Woody answered by skipping the pleasantries. "Sounds like we've got the Ga'ee ship."

"Sounds like it. Take a couple nukes over there and plant them. We'll destroy that ship before it takes off again. If we control it, then I'm okay with planting a hydrogen bomb in the middle of a Ga'ee world if they are able to recall their ship."

"On it, Admiral."

"Prudence dictates," the admiral explained.

Mary forced herself to laugh as the clock counted down to zero and Lev entered normal space.

"Declan?" Mary asked before the admiral could make contact.

"We've got control of the ship, Dog, but we don't need to stay on board. I think Blinky and Buzz can do what they need remotely."

"No, we can't," Blinky replied. "We'll stay. You guys go.

You're in our way. Now that we can link with Lev, this will go faster, but it's still complex."

"I can't wait to see my dogs," Declan interrupted.

"You what?" Mary looked less than amused.

"You two deserve each other," the admiral offered.

She tried to give him her mean look, but it fell flat when she smiled in relief. Team Payne had saved itself once more.

Data scrolled across the tactical screen. The course tracked to a star system over fifteen thousand light-years away.

"The navigation charts are limited to this course. The database is mostly empty."

The admiral sighed. "Just in case we broke in, they're giving us nothing."

"But their tactical systems are available. How they create the drones and their energy shield technology."

"Can you replicate that, Lev?"

"Probably, with the right materials and enough time, but I don't need to do that because I'll take their system, including their reactor and unique power phase."

"Do that, Lev. Own them. Why couldn't we see their energy signature?"

"Dampening system. I see it. They simply resonate counter-waves that level the vibrations. What radiates beyond the ship is negligible. That defeats how I track ships traveling at faster-than-light speed. There are no tweaks I can make to see a signal that's not there."

"The ship leaves a wake, doesn't it?"

"In regular space, yes. Not in faster-than-light, which compresses the space before it and expands it to normal size behind while traveling within a bubble. There is no wake to track."

"That expansion and contraction have to leave a signature, compared to the rest of space which isn't going through that."

"The space doesn't know it's been acted on. I might be able to see those compressions from the front but not from the rear. The wake is normal space, seemingly unaffected. We've been looking at this problem at my speed of thought for many days now. We will continue looking, and now that we have access to their power plants and engines, we might see some other way. Thank you for your input, Harry."

The admiral smirked. "You don't really mean that. I added no value because you had already looked at those options and dismissed them."

"You learned why those options weren't viable. Does that not have value?"

"It does, but not for you, Lev. I'm just trying to help. Carry on. Find us a way to track these ships while I try to figure out how to get the most from this one. We now have something that could be of great tactical value."

"Talking tactics, how about you bring Declan and Virgil back to *Leviathan*?" Mary asked.

The admiral contemplated her request. It was self-serving but getting Payne's input had been valuable in the past, along with Commodore Freeman's. "Ask Nyota to come to the bridge, Lev."

"She's on her way. She'll be here momentarily. I'll ask Team Payne to return while I continue working with Katello and Alphonse."

The admiral made a face. "I feel like I should know who that is."

"The ones you call Blinky and Buzz."

"Them. Yes, of course." The admiral looked away but couldn't hide his thoughts from Lev. He still had to try. "I thought you meant someone else."

"You did not. You honestly didn't remember who they were. I'll add supplements to your meals for memory enhancement."

"Damn, Lev! I'm in my prime. These bizarre nicknames that everyone seems to love. What do they call me? You can tell me."

"Admiral," Lev admitted.

"That is rather staid."

"You are different from them, Harry. Accept it. Remember both their names and move on. At least we don't have a pride of cats on board. I heard they have three names."

"Three names? Cats? What are you talking about?"

"You need to spend more time with your own literature. That will also enhance your memory."

"What's wrong with your memory?" Commodore Freeman asked as she walked in.

"There's nothing wrong with my memory!" The admiral pointed at the board. "We have the ship. Team Payne owns that little bitch."

"Harry!" Nyota stared at him until he looked away.

"They do," Mary added. "Are they on their way back yet, Lev?"

"Not yet. Two Mosquitoes are on their way to emplace nuclear devices in case we lose the ship again. I've programmed a trigger that will activate should the ship leave us and return to Ga'ee space. They will detonate with human intervention or if there are no humans on board and the ship arrives in the target system designated in their database."

"Make sure it doesn't," Mary stated. "Don't let it leave except under your control. Dismantle it and stuff it in your storage areas, then use its husk to build more stuff we want."

"It's ten kilometers long," the admiral countered.

"It's mostly empty, isn't it? It's like a kilometer across, except along the center. How much of that is dead space?"

"You're making too much sense. It would alleviate our

concerns about what secrets the ship is programmed to carry out. Plus, Lev is already going to steal the energy shield."

"Steal is an ugly word, Harry," Lev replied. "Let's discuss that further. I'm willing to dismantle the ship since that might be the most expeditious for our goals, which are to build the remaining portals to move a reaction force around the galaxy quickly. The Ga'ee ship cannot fold space, so we would leave it behind sooner or later."

"Sounds like the decision is already made," the admiral stated. "Is Payne on his way yet?"

"Not yet, Harry."

"Get him on the hook for me if you'd be so kind."

Lev complied. Payne answered, "Yes, Admiral?"

"Get your ass over here right now. Close the channel, Lev."

Lev did as requested, leaving Payne to swing in the wind.

[18]

"If you must second-guess yourself, do it before you make the decision in the first place." –From the memoirs of Ambassador Declan Payne

Payne rushed onto the bridge. Mary headed for him but didn't reach him before the Cabrizi slammed into the ambassador. Kal hurried in behind but wasn't quick enough to save Payne from hitting the deck. When the dogs saw Kal, they used Payne as a springboard, leaping off his chest and racing for the Ebren to repeat their maneuver.

He weathered their assault before taking them into the corridor so the others wouldn't see him loving on them.

Mary helped her husband up for a sensuous kiss, followed by a firm butt-grab.

"The admiral?" Payne asked, having nearly lost himself in Mary's affections.

"Major Payne," the admiral started. "We were discussing what to do with your most recent acquisition. What do *you* think we should do with it?"

"I saw Woody arrive with a few megatons of fuck you, so I

assumed you were going to let the ship go on its merry way to blow the hell out whatever it was supposed to reach. Hopefully, a few gazillion Ga'ee."

"We're not going to do that because we can't trust that the ship doesn't have an override. We could be sending those nukes to ourselves or an intermediate race the Ga'ee uses to do their bidding. So, no. We're thinking of dismantling it. Load the choice bits on board *Leviathan*. We've got places to go and people to see. Can't be trapped with a ship that can only travel at standard FTL speed."

"What do Blinky and Buzz think of that plan?"

"They're against it," Lev replied.

"Only until you reassure them that they'll still have access to the core. We'll take the reactors, and they'll have as much power as they need. Did you see, Lev? Everything over there is plug and play—modular. They could build those ships on an assembly line, and that, my friends, makes me very afraid. How many of those things are in our space?"

"We can't find out if we stay here," the admiral noted. "Blinky and Buzz will have to finish what they're doing."

"I don't know if they *can* finish. They're decrypting the Ga'ee's language."

"If they didn't have it, how did they get into the ship's systems?" the admiral wondered.

"Binary. It's the ancillary stuff that we don't know. What motivates them? If we can discover that, we'll gain leverage in how we approach them."

"We'll give them more time, but it's not infinite. I think the Ga'ee have started an invasion of allied space. We need to get into the fight."

"Harry is correct," Lev added. "I will keep the Ga'ee computer core powered up while I move it to the starboard hangar bay. I will begin dismantling the ship immediately, leaving only that which I cannot carry."

"Make sure none of it has access to your systems, Lev. They work like you do, through the airwaves. We can't have them corrupting any of your files," Payne warned.

"We shall take the greatest care," Lev promised.

Payne stared at the screen, which showed a parade of maintenance drones streaming toward the Ga'ee vessel.

Payne muttered, "I bet they didn't expect that."

"Big fish usually aren't eaten by smaller fish." The admiral looked at Payne in surprise. "What are you still doing here?"

"I'm... What?"

"You're dismissed. Reacquaint yourself with your wife. Get something to eat. Get some sleep. We'll have plenty to do soon enough."

"Yes," Mary replied. "I'd like to conduct an after-action regarding the logistics support pre-stocked on *Ugly 5*."

She headed for the corridor. "After-action?" He ran after her. They jumped into the waiting cart, but it didn't go to the hangar bay. It took them to their new quarters.

———

The New Mexico Fleet headquarters consisted of a less-than-modern base with an antiquated landing strip. The real training took place beyond the moon within the Blue Earth Protectorate's defensive perimeter. That arrangement did nothing to alleviate the friction between the forces. As soon as the new Fleet personnel were ready, they were shipped beyond the perimeter to stations and ships well outside the Solar System.

Until recently, no enemy had ever engaged the BEP. Now that the force had been blooded in combat and mostly decimated, rebuilding efforts held the Fleet at arm's length while only BEP ships were being replaced. More defensive shipping for a battle they couldn't win.

That needed dreadnoughts and the new Payne-class battlewagons. Weapons platforms that could defend themselves and had one purpose—to deliver the maximum amount of firepower on a single target.

Commander Josephs stepped off the shuttle that deposited him to the New Mexico heat. There were no seasons in space. He didn't know what time of year it was on Earth. He had stopped bothering to track such things while in space. The relative time passage on a ship at FTL speed versus Earth was so far apart to make tracking such things as holidays a useless endeavor. Only the ship's time related to the ship mattered.

A small but august delegation met him—two admirals, five stars between them, with three captains waiting behind them. The first was Admiral Ross.

"Let me shake the hand of the officer who saved Earth yet again," he began. Josephs saluted before taking the admiral's hand.

"I was on Earth. My lieutenant conducted the battle. I'm sorry I missed it," the commander admitted.

"Still, your ship and your people."

The commander nodded.

"We received your request, and I think we can fill it. We have a Whale-class battleship at our forward base between here and Ebren space. We're going to have to stand the ship down. That's about four thousand crew who need a new assignment. Plus, we have a few hundred right here who would be more than happy to get back to space." The vice admiral winked.

Josephs knew what that was about. He had done the same thing with Fleet Admiral Wesson's call to join *Leviathan* to confront an unknown aggressor. They would be leaving Earth. Anyone who could do so left.

This was the next round, those experiencing remorse. Would they be the best?

Probably not, but would they be good enough?

Maybe. The crew of the aging dreadnought would form the backbone of the new crews, and the Whale could serve a useful purpose, too.

"I left in the last wave," Commander Josephs replied. "And I just came from the UN. They made me wish I had never come back."

"It's a gift they have, making people feel that way," the rear admiral told him. "This is a young soul's game. We're recommending that active Fleet personnel join the hunter-killer squadrons and continue to protect Earth and all friendly space from the Ga'ee, as well as any other threats that may appear."

"Long, boring patrols aren't a great selling point for the youth of today, but fighting a hard battle against a relentless enemy using a weapon of unimaginable power? That'll put their boots on the deck of a starship."

"We concur. Come with us, Commander. As much as we'd like to go, we won't. Harry Wesson was the smart one by going forward, refusing to be strapped to a desk down here. We got stuck paying the peace dividend, becoming number eleven of Earth's top ten priorities. But that's not anything for you to worry about. Tell us about the Payne-class battlewagon. That looks like some ship..."

———

The support ships struggled to keep up with the demands of the Vestrall engineers in their efforts to repair the portal. The battlewagons had recovered sufficient advanced raw materials to repair the damage done by Ga'ee drones, but their limited refining assets weren't shaping the parts fast enough.

Loresh raged on the bridge of *The President*, but since he was a Vestrall, his "rage" was confined to staring at the image on the screen with his arms crossed and tapping his foot.

Commander Jimmy Josephs sat in the captain's chair and sipped his coffee. One monitor showed the portside airlock, where a thirty-year-old freighter carried the potential crews for the next five battlewagons.

The first crew was to begin training immediately.

Lieutenant Barry Cummins stood by the commander's right hand. A fitting position, he thought.

The commander stretched and stepped from his seat. "Barry, with me."

The two left the bridge, not stopping until they were inside Josephs' quarters with the door closed behind them.

"Sir?" The lieutenant was worried. He experienced the dread of the anticipated dressing down, the butt-chewing he deserved for snap-firing and wasting a Hunter-Killer salvo. That panicked reaction had put them into the predicament they currently enjoyed—waiting for the portal to be repaired.

"I'm going to put you in charge of this ship, and I'll take over as the squadron commander, controlling the five battlewagons of Hunter-Killer Squadron 01." He offered his hand. "Your new assignment comes with a promotion to lieutenant commander."

"I don't deserve that," Cummins replied. "I made a mistake that could have cost us."

"It did, and it didn't. What matters is that no one knows better than you how best to fight this ship. You won't be surprised like that next time, will you?"

Barry shook his head, not trusting that his voice wouldn't crack.

The commander sat at his desk and accessed the intercom. "Attention, all hands. I would like to take this opportunity to congratulate Lieutenant Commander Barry Cummins on assuming captaincy of *The President.* I'm moving into a position as the hunter-killer squadron commander. You are now seasoned in combat with the Ga'ee, and you are the only crews that have a confirmed kill of a Ga'ee ship. We are now smarter and better than we were."

He tapped the off button.

"Sir, I'd like Chief Tremayne to be moved into a position called chief of the boat. The COB used to be a role senior enlisted filled to make sure there was a synergy between the technicians and the officers."

"It's your ship. Do as you please. I recommend you coordinate with the other ships and have them do the same. Can't have envy and jealousy between the ships. Go back to the bridge and make the announcement from there."

The newly promoted lieutenant commander saluted and left.

Jimmy Josephs didn't know if he had the authority to do what he'd just done, but he'd ask forgiveness later if anyone questioned him. He'd fall on his sword if he had to to prevent them from undoing it. It was best for the people in his command to know he took responsibility for them.

The commander pulled up the logistics status for the five ships. No one was optimizing resupply or even coordinating the construction process. Each battlewagon had the ability to fabricate spare parts to ensure a ship could repair itself while deployed.

Josephs activated the intercom. "Loresh, please join me in my quarters."

The commander was thinking he would have to collect the engineer from the bridge when the door opened and the engineer walked in.

"What?" the Vestrall asked.

"If we use all five battlewagons to fabricate bits and pieces, all we have to do is assemble them instead of trying to smelt and fabricate at the construction location. I know we're already doing the more intricate fabrication from BW-01, but what if we maxed our capacity?"

The Vestrall thought for a moment. "Certain ship functions would have to stand down for full optimization. All five ships?"

"We'll be vulnerable, but I think that's a risk we have to take. We need to get that portal operational so the flow of new ships from Vestrall Prime can begin."

"They'll need crews," the Vestrall replied.

"Which we'll send as soon as the portal is operational. We have five hundred ready to go, and we have thirty-eight hundred more between here and Ebren space, waiting to be picked up."

"These ships cannot support that many additional personnel."

"Leave that to me. Give me a plan that utilizes all five battlewagons to get this portal up and running. We'll deposit the first five hundred in Vestrall space. Then we'll come back here for immediate FTL transit to deliver orders to the Fleet."

"If we split the squadron, we could do both more efficiently."

"Not splitting the squadron. We need the five ships together to deliver a Ga'ee-killing punch. Since they showed up both here and in Vestrall Prime space, wouldn't it be prudent to assume we could run across them anywhere?"

"A valid assumption, but two data points are insufficient to draw a definitive conclusion."

"We're going to be prudent, which means time is critical. If they appeared in all the systems simultaneously, planets are being colonized, and fleets are being destroyed. We need to keep our firepower focused where it can be most effective. If we split up, we risk being isolated and killed."

"As you wish. We will submit a utilization plan within the

hour." Loresh walked out and headed to where the other Vestrall could be found.

Jimmy Josephs dialed up a channel to talk to the commanders of all five ships. "Captains of the battlewagons assigned to Hunter-Killer Squadron One. This is Commander Jimmy Josephs. Let's talk about how we can get our mission accomplished as quickly as possible. Fix the portal, then to Vestrall space to set up the next crews and battlewagons, then back here to kick off to Ebren and get that portal construction started.

"We have a lot to do and no time to do it. Just another day in the Fleet."

[19]

"Don't twist yourself around while screwing things up."
–From the memoirs of Ambassador Declan Payne

Blinky was embedded in the captain's chair on *Leviathan's* bridge. Buzz sat on a similar chair three decks below. They were working with Lev and Davida to break the Ga'ee language and how they communicated. In the chairs, they didn't need a physical interface. They were linked directly to the AI and each other.

By matching what they understood from the binary language, which contained the mathematics of space flight, they slowly matched words and expressions. It was like the Rosetta stone of communication, but the language had no other cross-cultural similarities. Repetition in words was common, but without a basis, the group had to guess at those words, then rerun the language to see if it made sense. However, what made sense to the Ga'ee might have nothing to do with how the human language communicated its ideas.

Even at the speed of thought, it was painstakingly slow.

But *Leviathan* was moving once more.

"Return to Vestrall or fold space directly to Earth. That's the question." Payne stared at the admiral.

"What's waiting for us at Vestrall Prime?" the admiral started. "Shipbuilding that should be on autopilot. Even though those ships are mostly self-operating, they still need a minimal crew to make the decisions and execute the operations. There are no crews in Vestrall space, and we are down to minimal staffing. Enough to get the Mosquito squadrons into space and not one person more."

"Sounds like the decision is made. Lev, fold space to Earth. As much as I don't want to meet with the president, it's important that we get humanity's support."

"Humanity's or just the Fleet's?" The admiral smiled. "I recommend we go to our forward operating base at the edge of Ebren space. We'll find what we need there and get a warmer reception."

"Still afraid of going to Earth, Admiral?" Payne raised an eyebrow.

"Just a lot. Despite the technical manipulations of your team, they still want to arrest Nyota and me."

"But they can't. There's no warrant because it was lost in digital obscurity. It no longer exists. Regardless, HK1 is there. They can try to sway the opinions of Earth's government. Despite how the UN has been cool to us, I think the people appreciate what we're doing."

"No doubt about that," the admiral replied. "Lev, take us to the FOB. Let's talk with the forward command and see what they can do. By the way, when will Admiral Dorsite and her task force return?"

"Two more weeks, Harry," Lev replied. "Before they are scheduled to arrive at Earth."

"Arthir and I have a lot of catching up to do." Admiral Wesson stretched and yawned. "No time for sleep now. Take us to the Fleet, please, as soon as the Tricky Spinsters are ready to launch."

Five minutes later, the ship transitioned through the folded fabric of space to reappear near the former front lines of the war with the Braze Collective.

The tactical board remained empty when it should have populated with Fleet assets. At this range, even idle, they would be visible.

"No," the admiral cried. He hung his head and fought the urge to puke.

"I see debris, Harry. A great deal of debris."

"Plot it." Harry straightened, clenching his jaw until the muscles stood out. He took a few steps toward the board. Debris fields in the relative size and shape of a space station, three dreadnoughts, and a dozen small ships. "Any Ga'ee?"

"I cannot see any on active sensors."

"When did this happen?" the admiral wondered.

"The best I can estimate is ten days to two weeks ago."

"Woody, get your squadron into the void and see if anything is salvageable. Look for survivors. And any Ga'ee."

"On our way," Woody replied.

"This changes things," Payne said. "We need to go to Earth."

"After Lev recharges," the admiral replied. "Lev, is there any way you can speed up that process? We have the six fusion reactors off the Ga'ee ship..."

He left it hanging.

"Which I am not going to hook into my main systems. The risk is too great. Until we can confirm they do not have any malignant code, I am loathe to power up any besides the one keeping their computer systems operating. That one is isolated from my systems except for a single pipeline in that Alphonse is personally monitoring one hundred percent of the time."

Payne didn't have to tell Lev to keep digging. That was his priority. Learn all there was to know about the Ga'ee, from where the ship had been taking Team Payne to how their technology worked, along with their motivations. What did they hope to accomplish with the invasion?

"We need to get the FTL notification system in place. We can't let this happen anywhere else."

The admiral knew the truth. It was happening everywhere else. "Judging by the debris, we should have at least two dreadnoughts running from the Ga'ee and five or six cruisers. I don't know how many battleships were here. Lev, what's the picture as far out as you can see?"

"There are no engine vibrations within my range, which is reduced at present. I have no extra power to improve the sensor systems."

"With minimal staffing on board the ship, you have plenty of space. We need to bolster your power by orders of magnitude to reduce the recovery time after a fold and, more importantly, give you the ability to defend yourself after folding space. If the Ga'ee had been here, we would have been dead."

"I will look into it as soon as we solve our other problem, which is how to speak Ga'ee."

"I'm taking the uglymobile out to look for survivors," Payne offered.

The admiral gripped his arm. "We've got twenty Mosquitoes out there. Be ready to go in should they spot something, but not before. Stay on board just in case."

"Just in case?" Payne winced. "Lev is incapacitated. If the Ga'ee show up, we're hosed whether I'm on the ship or not."

"Go on, then. And here's an important safety tip from an old guy. Take that wife of yours with you. She'll think you don't care if you leave her behind again when you don't have to."

"Lev, let Mary know to meet us in the hangar bay and to suit up."

"I've had her suit ready ever since you returned from Bray-alore. I'll relay your message. Good choice, Declan."

"What about the others? I know Blinky and Buzz aren't coming. Anyone else not available? I feel like we're only going to burn holes in empty space, but our people deserve to have us out there looking for them."

"The rest of the team is available and on their way."

"Then we shan't dawdle." Payne ran for the corridor and vaulted into the waiting cart. It raced away. The agony of loss filled the pit of his stomach with lava. His abdomen spasmed with the anguish. He tried to tamp it down, but it wouldn't settle.

For a millisecond, he thought about going to Medical and getting his gut checked but discounted it as a refuge for the weak. He'd go after they returned. If people had survived in an air pocket for two weeks, their time was running out. They could tolerate no more delays.

Payne forced himself to relax, even though his gut felt like it was on fire.

When the cart arrived in the hangar bay, Payne was pale and sweating profusely. Mary noticed something was wrong even with her suit on. She stepped beside the cart. He smiled and waved. "Hi, honey." He collapsed into her gloved hands.

"I'm taking him to Medical." Mary looked at the equipment cage. "Virgil, you've got the con! Declan's down."

The cart curled around and raced for the doors, with Mary running after it. The Cabrizi followed. Kal tossed his gear aside and ran after the group.

The Sickbay they used was on the same level as the hangar bay for convenience's sake since the team had too often returned from missions with people needing immediate medical attention.

Fifteen seconds later, the cart moved inside to deliver Payne into the waiting metal arms of the patient transfer system Lev had installed for them. The automated carriage slid into a scanning device, where a complete analysis of Payne's internals was made.

He slipped out seconds later and moved into the surgery center. "What's wrong, Lev? Talk to me!"

"He has a bleeding ulcer. I'll have that fixed quickly. He'll be up in time to be hungry for dinner."

"That quickly?" Mary climbed out of her suit and searched for a medical gown to wear.

"Alas," Lev started, "bleeding stomach ulcers were common among the Godilkinmore. It appears that humanity received this genetic weakness."

"Brought on by stress?" Mary suggested.

"He carries the weight of the universe on his shoulders, no matter how little he can impact most events."

"The loss of our base and people affected him that badly?" Mary hung her head. "Of course it did."

"It's easy to fix, Mary. Relax. He'll be out of surgery in about fifteen minutes."

"You make it sound so matter-of-fact, Lev. Make sure the team knows he'll be fine."

The Cabrizi nuzzled Mary relentlessly. She spoke to them in Ebren to calm them.

"As someone we both know would say, there are a lot of problems in the universe, but this isn't one of them."

Dank watched the parade leave the hangar bay, then counted the team. Heckler, Turbo, Sparky, Joker, Shaolin, and Byle. Seven, including him.

"Search and recovery, people," Dank called. "Let's see what we can find."

The team quietly boarded the ship and snapped their helmets into place.

"Button up and launch, Lev," Major Dank requested. The side doors rotated down and sealed. The ship lifted off the deck and moved slowly through the partially open hangar door and into space.

"Major Payne went down with a bellyache?" Heckler joked over the team channel.

"A bleeding ulcer, but I'm sure it ached plenty."

"How many did we lose?" Heckler asked. The tension increased, and the air grew heavy.

"Lev?" Dank asked for clarification. He didn't want to fathom a guess.

"Eight thousand, and at least twenty-four ships. Most were frigates and cutters."

"Ouch." Dank sighed at the revelation before getting back to business. "Begin the search. Go where the Mosquitoes have not been."

The team sat in silence while *Ugly 5* burned an expanding helix into a space filled with enough debris for twenty-four ships.

"Lev, how many Payne-class battlewagons can you construct using nothing but the scrap resulting from the Ga'ee attack?"

"Ten ships," Lev replied.

"The Payne-class are much smaller than human dreadnoughts," Dank thought out loud. "Can we stay here to build ten battlewagons? I think we're going to need them."

"The only constraint is crews. You will need one thousand personnel."

"Is this what Admiral Wesson's whole life is? If that's the case, I don't ever want to be an admiral. That was the first trip to Earth—to start the recruiting pipeline. He knew that ships would not be the limiting factor even before we had the ships. He saw the constraint as manpower. How did he know that?" Dank's head was starting to hurt.

"Harry has been doing this for a long time," Lev replied.

"Any luck?" Virgil asked softly.

"None of the wreckage large enough to support survivors has an air pocket or life signatures. Everything here is the temperature of space. I'm sorry."

The collection of the materials would be a challenge since most of *Leviathan*'s available storage space was filled with the remnants of the Ga'ee ship.

"If we add the Ga'ee ship?"

"Only one full battlewagon, as there is much of the Ga'ee vessel I need to retain for continued study."

"Please let the admiral know my thoughts on the matter," Virgil requested. "How is Declan?"

"He's out of surgery and will recover fully. There's nothing to worry about. Mary and Kal'faxx are with him."

"Thanks, Lev. Are the Mosquitoes still searching?"

"No. They are returning to the hangar bay. Shall I bring you home, too?"

"Yes." Virgil didn't need to say anything else. Despite Payne's recovery, the mood was somber. Eight thousand dead. Fleet ships were running, and no one knew where. The Ga'ee were in friendly systems with more than one ship. "We need to fire up those power plants since we need to move if we're going to stay ahead of the Ga'ee."

[20]

"There are a lot of problems in the universe, but your personal discomfort isn't one of them." –From the memoirs of Ambassador Declan Payne

"You look respectable," the admiral greeted.

Payne walked slowly and stiffly, but he wasn't as pale as he had been before Lev's medical devices cut into him. He smiled. "What a day, huh?"

"We're going to fire up the Ga'ee reactors and get Lev back up to speed."

"Is that safe?"

The admiral shrugged. "It's what we need to do. We need Lev to work his production magic, starting right now."

"If he's down, how can he bring those power plants online?"

"That's on us. The Tricky Spinsters have supplied the manpower we need and are manually installing the cables. Sparky, Blinky, and Buzz are working on the activation sequence and the interface. Something about phases and waves. I should understand it but can't describe it at the most rudimentary level. Handshake. Feed the relays and send energy into the depleted systems. Bring Lev back to full power."

Sounded easy, but it started with a blatant mistrust of the Ga'ee system.

Everything else was easy, but at some point, the Ga'ee reactors would be linked directly to *Leviathan* and have access to everything, even Lev's main core.

That was what they were trying to isolate, but after a thousand years, Lev had integrated with every system on the ship. There was no longer any separation between him and the hardware.

Creating a firewall wasn't possible because they needed the power to flow through and into the systems.

Therefore, they created a digital seek-and-destroy module and replicated it a thousand times. They decided that stopping an intrusion instead of preventing it would be sufficient as long as they got to it quickly enough.

The reactor powering the computer core was already online and running at ten percent capacity.

Woody Malone reported, "First reactor cable is attached to the power adaptor under the hangar deck. Slot marked Sierra One Four."

Payne sat, but the admiral remained standing. In the captain's chair. Blinky fidgeted, manifesting his nervous energy through his physical being when the entirety of their fight took place in the digital realm.

"Seek-and-destroy modules are standing by," Lev announced. "Increasing reactor power to twenty percent."

"First power over the threshold and into the capacitor. Preemptive strikes in effect, retarding the power by five percent. Flow is clean."

The tactical board changed from an external view to a

process flow that showed lines of blue nodules flowing from the boxy reactors to the streamlined icons for a myriad of systems, starting with maintenance. Life support, engines, defensive weapons, and offensive weapons were critical systems. Even maintenance, although less so enough to risk its temporary loss.

"Fifty percent," Lev stated. The maintenance system prismed through a series of colors until it glowed a faint green.

"System is active and powering up. Time to restoration of full power, one hour," Blinky reported.

"Don't power up any more reactors or systems until we're certain this one didn't infect us." The admiral was repeating what he'd already said and Lev already knew.

"That is the plan," Lev replied. "Monitoring. Nothing is piggybacking the power flow. We've added five physical filters between the reactor and the maintenance management system."

"Redundancies on top of redundancies. How will we know if the Ga'ee have gotten in?" Payne asked.

"Secondary failures. *Leviathan* is well-balanced. An intruder will interfere with the efficiencies that are in place."

The conversation was over. There was nothing else to say besides, "Now we wait." Admiral Wesson crossed his arms and watched the power monitor on the board as the reactor continued to increase its output and the maintenance system's power status grew.

Buzz's voice sounded, "Suck my ass, Silly Conners. Suck. My. Ass!"

The admiral rolled his head to his shoulder to fix Payne with a fatherly look of disappointment.

"They're the best in the galaxy, sir. We must forgive them their foibles." He bit his lip to keep from laughing, but the situation was serious.

The power level on the reactor started to drop. A rumble reached them through the bridge's speakers.

"The Ga'ee programming exposed itself. Its attempts to ride the power into the maintenance system were rebuffed. Now it is trying to interrupt the phasing by changing the reaction within, unbalancing it. Alphonse has launched the first seek-and-destroy packet into the midst of the program. Katello has surrounded the offending code with four more modules. They are attacking."

"Do we need to flush it into space?" the admiral asked. "Can't have it rip a chunk out of you, Lev."

"Not there yet, Harry."

Payne met the admiral's eyes. "What does that mean?" he mouthed. The rumble grew louder.

As did Buzz's assault on the English language.

Payne gripped his seat. The admiral sat down as well and held onto the console before him, ready for the violence the Ga'ee were attempting to deliver into Lev's hangar bay.

"Launching the insertion craft," Lev announced. It had been ready to launch, but there was no need to wait any longer.

Anything he didn't want destroyed couldn't remain in the hangar bay. He deployed a newly charged maintenance bot to gather the team's suits and weapons into a cart that would race into the corridor and as far away as it could get.

"Eat me!" Blinky shouted from the captain's chair.

His voice should have come through the speakers, but his body was engaged at a level beyond what his mind was doing.

"Interesting." Payne had been in the virtual world provided by the chair and had been so cut off from everything beyond his mind that he had no idea how Blinky had been able to utter a sound. Davida had moaned while in the chair, which had led to a great deal of discomfort for those near enough to hear it.

But to shout real words?

"Go, Blinky. Lev, what's going on besides you getting ready to manage a thermonuclear explosion inside the hangar bay?"

"*Try* to manage," Lev clarified. "Katello is isolating strings of code and destroying them. Alphonse is attempting to prevent the code from self-replicating, which appears to be its primary function."

"That is very Ga'ee-like," Payne replied. "Giving priority to self-replication. Go Blinky, go! Kill it dead, Buzz!"

Mary stayed close to Payne. Despite his cheers and fist pumps, they were subdued. It would take his abdomen and stomach time to heal. He needed to give them that time.

"Is there anything else to do here, Admiral?"

"Not unless the ship blows up. Then I guess the answer would still be no."

The bridge's hatch had closed and sealed, leaving Kal and the Cabrizi in the corridor beyond. Mary realized they couldn't leave until it was over.

Payne had no intention of leaving, no matter how he felt. He took Mary's hand and squeezed it. He knew what she was thinking.

"I've launched a worm into the constrained code. It is destroying the Ga'ee virus."

"Like a tapeworm?" Payne guessed.

"Exactly like a tapeworm. The code was removed. The reactor is increasing its load to fifty percent." The rumble had disappeared. Less than ten seconds later, Lev provided another update. "Seventy-five percent."

Blinky's voice sounded on the bridge. "We are going after the embedded code within the second reactor."

"Does this mean what I think it means, Lev?" the admiral asked.

Lev knew what he thought it meant. "It does."

The Ga'ee reactors would restore Lev's power, and he'd be able to fold space with minimal time between.

"How quickly will you be able to recharge?" Payne asked.

"Two hours after I fold space, I will be back to one hundred percent. I can focus the recharge of a system based on circumstances. Within ten minutes, I can have the engines completely restored or the weapons systems online, offensive or defensive. I can only fold space after all systems are recharged. That would still be two hours."

Payne's mind worked at the speed of light. The admiral had the same look on his face. They could react to the tactical situation as long as they had ten minutes to power up the system. It beat the hell out of three days.

"Defensive systems, including the Ga'ee shield?"

"Ten minutes, Declan. But if we came under attack, the shields would need continuous power. It would affect the restoration of other systems until we could apply all the power. It would increase recharging time by sixteen-point-seven percent."

"Sixteen-point-seven. Five reactors charging instead of six. What about your main drive?"

"That was taken into account. We can bring the next system online after twelve minutes."

"Ten minutes to full shielding, twenty-two minutes to shields and offensive weapons, and thirty-four minutes to offensive *and* defensive weapons."

"For every operational system, there is a comparable reduction in the recharging efficiency," Lev explained.

The admiral waved a hand.

Payne said, "The important safety tip is to not jump into the middle of a fight. We need at least thirty minutes, but with two hours, we're golden. That is light-years better than three days."

"Light-year is a distance measure, Declan."

"This isn't rocket surgery, Lev. We can separate the wheat from the chafing for maximum optimability."

"You are just making words up. It means nothing."

"It means, thanks to the Ga'ee, that *Leviathan* is a far greater ship than it was before. I doubt they expected that. What do you say that when we're recharged, we head to Earth and see how they're doing?"

The admiral shook his head. "Let's build a couple hunter-killer squadrons and get them going where they need to go first. I bet when we get to Earth, they'll make us question all our plans."

"They have a tendency to do that, Admiral." Payne stood without Mary's assistance. "We'll be in our quarters, recovering and relaxing. If the ship's about to blow up, well, don't tell me. It'll be hard to relax with that hanging over our heads."

"I shall do my best, Declan, not to blow myself up while you're on board."

"Or ever, Lev. You're not to blow yourself up *ever*."

Lev didn't respond, but he opened the hatch to reveal Kal and Virgil standing just outside.

"We were about to die, and Lev locked us out? What did we do to you, Lev?"

"Lev is fighting evil silicon demons, Virge." Payne gestured at himself and Mary. "We're headed back to our quarters. Gotta rest the twisted-up innards."

"I came down to get the admiral and the commodore. We're holding a little vigil with the Spinsters. We lost a lot of Fleet personnel. You didn't see what it looked like out there, Dec."

"I didn't." He tried to return to the bridge, but Major Dank stopped him. Virgil strode in and let them know about the ceremony. He was back at the carts in no time.

"Shall we?" Virgil motioned at a two-person cart for Mary and Declan. Mary and Kal fought off the Cabrizi to keep them from jumping on Payne.

"Come on, you filthy mongrels," Kal drawled before

switching to Ebren, where the words were sharp. The two beasts complied readily.

Virgil joined Kal, and the two carts accelerated away. A third cart appeared behind them and waited for the admiral and the commodore.

Up three levels and to the port side. The cart slowed inside the hangar bay, where there was very little space. The maintenance chief pointed at the overlook. "We have to do it up there."

An external staircase had been installed, allowing direct access to the room from the hangar bay. Payne walked slowly while Mary helped him.

"I feel like such a candy ass," he whispered.

"A bleeding ulcer." Mary snorted. "I ought to kick your ass."

"What for? I'm the good guy in this one."

"You never stopped being the good guy, but you have to talk about your feelings when you are overwhelmed."

"Talk about what?" Payne shot back. He stopped on the stairs and gave her his best confused face.

"That's exactly what I'm talking about."

"I don't need to talk about my feelings. I only need the universe to stop conspiring against me to commit the genocide of all humanity. There's a bit of a burden on my shoulders."

"We all share it, Dec."

"Talking about it isn't going to make it any better. Doing something about it? That will."

"We can only do what we do within the time we have. Let Lev build ten new battlewagons incorporating the Ga'ee tech we can make function before we go anywhere else. We can't go wrong with the right kind of firepower."

Payne stared at the lights as if they were as bright as the lightbulb that had just started burning in his head. "They knew we were building ships that could destroy them. That was why they didn't challenge us in the Vestrall home system."

"How would they have known that? How would they have known any of it?"

"Maybe there's dissent among the former Mryasmalites. They know almost everything about us. Lev, what's the possibility that the Mryasmalites are feeding information to the Ga'ee?"

"I don't have an answer for you right now, but when we've finished bringing the reactors online, I'll allocate the appropriate amount of compute power."

Payne smiled, but the corners of his mouth drooped until he frowned. "What's the appropriate amount of compute power?" he wondered, but Lev didn't answer. "I think he's jacking me."

"I think you don't know how difficult it is for him to make sure the Ga'ee don't get a foothold on this ship. You saw Blinky. Did it look like he was sipping a mint julep on the beach?" Mary put her hands on her hips until she looked down and saw herself. She dropped her hands to her sides. When she looked up the stairs, the windows were filled with the faces of the pilots and the support staff.

"Are you two going to the ceremony or not?" Major Dank asked.

Payne threw his hands up in surrender. He started up, taking the opportunity to pinch Mary's butt.

"Hey!" Virgil complained. "That was right in front of my face."

Payne put himself between Mary and Virgil for the remainder of the short climb.

The instant they walked into the room, it was as if the oxygen had been vented to space and the darkness descended like a blanket.

"The Ga'ee never gave them a chance," Woody began.

"We're going to take it to the Ga'ee real soon," Payne promised.

"Do you know where they went from here?" A light glinted in the eyes of the squadron commander.

"Not yet, but we will. If nothing else, we know where they were trying to take us. We can go there and wreak a little havoc. We'll get some payback for this."

Woody nodded. It wouldn't be enough. Along with the dreadnoughts, they had lost a lot of space fighters and their pilots—people Woody knew.

"We can't go back, but we can keep moving forward," Payne told the commander.

Payne worked the crowd, stopping to say a word to each member of the squadron. He recognized Annaliese and took her hand in both of his. He glanced over his shoulder at Virgil. "We have a long way to go in this fight."

"I'm here to the end."

Payne nodded. Mary squeezed in and hugged the woman. Dank moved in after them when they continued to the next, which happened to be Federico, Alex, and Wysteria. Digitus was wedged into the corner, staring at the floor.

Kal stood just inside the door, not commiserating. He was affected, but as a warrior, they had died during the fight, even though they'd had little chance. The way to honor them would be in the defeat of the enemy.

The fight with the Ga'ee had just begun.

Kal would engage when the time was right. In the interim, he'd make sure Payne stayed alive. The Ebren was still beating himself up for not being there to see that Payne was ill. He'd had a long conversation with the Cabrizi about it, but he was sure they didn't understand. They weren't wired that way, even though they had to have smelled the change. He looked through the door. The two animals were darting between the remnants of the Ga'ee craft, chasing a toy left behind by the squadron.

A cart arrived, carrying the admiral and the commodore.

Kal got Payne's attention and pointed.

"Attention on deck!" Payne shouted an instant before the admiral walked through the door.

"As you were," Admiral Wesson declared. He shook hands with Woody.

"We wanted to honor our fellows," the commander started. The admiral stopped him.

"I should have called this. No excuses. Thanks for taking charge."

"It was bad out there," Woody told him.

The admiral nodded, then raised his hands for quiet. All eyes were on him.

"We're here to honor our colleagues who perished in the battle with the Ga'ee." The admiral looked from face to grim face. "Vowing retribution can lead to no good. Only bad decisions can come from it. We have all made solemn oaths to defend our galaxy from evil, and that is the right way to approach the Ga'ee. We will deny them their foothold, then we'll kick the wrigglers out of our space one drone and one ship at a time.

"We will build more battlewagons and take our hunter-killer squadrons around the galaxy to wherever they want to go. They'll find us waiting for them, and then they'll pay the price for their miscalculations. They underestimated the resolve of the carbon-based intelligent life of the seven races. They underestimated us, and they'll pay for that in due time.

"We won't chase them around the galaxy. We'll let them come to us. In the meantime, we'll fold space to each of the habitable worlds and make sure the locals know that the war is joined."

Woody chimed in, "Peace lasted a year."

"At least this time, we know what we're fighting for. The stakes are nothing less than the survival of our species."

The admiral had seen what the Ga'ee had done to the Berantz homeworld. The silicon life forms would eradicate the seven races without remorse.

"No vengeance. We need to keep our heads while we calmly and methodically eliminate the Ga'ee infestation in our part of the galaxy.

"I'm not calling for genocide. I'm saying that we must repel this attack. We have to drive this incursion back, so the Ga'ee never encroach on our space again. That is our mission, and we'll stay out here as long as it takes to accomplish it. Settle in for the long haul. Don't peak too early. Get enough rest. Stay physically fit, and train for what we know we'll have to do.

"The Mosquitoes will have to deliver nukes to planets. They will have to confront drone swarms. They'll come back damaged. You'll have to repair your ships and get them back into the fight. We'll need to recruit more pilots. We'll need to recruit more staff."

The admiral pointed at the hangar bay doors. "We need to show them they did not die for no reason. Their lives had value. Their deaths mattered. We won't rush headlong into a trap. We cannot waste a single human life. We need to build battlewagons with the weapons that can destroy the Ga'ee, and we need to do it now. We'll build these ships, then we'll set them on a remote flight to Earth, where we will have crews waiting to board them once they arrive.

"*Leviathan* has upgraded himself. The Ga'ee's shields are better than what we had, and their six fusion reactors will return power to *Leviathan* more quickly. Two hours after we fold space, we'll be able to fold again.

"You might wonder why we didn't have this ability before. The power plants on board *Leviathan* competed with each other in a way that didn't allow for additional power sources, but the Ga'ee's reactors don't conflict. The answer seems simple now, but sometimes, those answers remain elusive until they are obvious.

"Let's have a moment of silence to remember our brothers and sisters in arms." The admiral clasped his hands and bowed his head.

The room was silent except for the heavy breathing of people trying to relax but failing.

The admiral lifted his head and fixed the squadron with a look of grim determination. He raised his voice to deliver the final call to action. "Be ready. This bay will get busy in a hurry as soon as we have full power restored, which will be less than ninety minutes from now. Get something to eat and then get to work. We have a war to fight."

The admiral walked out without waiting for the squadron to react.

Payne stepped into the void. He tried to stand tall, but the glue holding the small hole in his abdomen shut prevented that. He hunched with the spasm of pain. "Woody, would you like to say a few words?"

The commander stepped up while shaking his head. He didn't want to but knew he had to. That came with his position.

"We've lost a lot of people from the Spinsters. We've lost too many ships. Right now, we're a conglomeration of four different squadrons, some from ships that died in this battle with the Ga'ee. What matters is that we live. As long as we're alive, we can keep fighting. We might not win every battle, but we'll stay in the fight.

"Trust *Leviathan*. Trust Admiral Wesson, and trust Ambassador Payne. These people will do everything in their power to win the war. All hands on deck in one hour. We'll launch the squadron to get out of the way of the manufacturing bots. Take some downtime.

"You were there when Lev built ten ships in the Vestrall

home system. You know what it's going to look like. Take advantage. Once we start hopping around the galaxy, the hits are going to come fast and furious. We'll need everyone at the top of their game if we're going to defeat the Ga'ee. We don't have any other option. We will defeat them."

He looked around the quiet group. They'd been through too much in the short time they'd been aboard *Leviathan*.

"Dismissed," Woody said softly.

Payne shook his hand before getting the attention of the four friends of Team Payne—Annaliese, Federico, Alex, and Wysteria.

He and Mary huddled with them. "Welcome to the team. If you can spare a few moments, go see our people and let them know what you're thinking. Share time with them, something I never did enough of. Don't be like me. Be better."

They nodded sporadically. They were young, and Payne was the leader of the seven races, even though his title was both ambassador and major, and no one seemed concerned about which one was used.

In the end, it came down to respect.

"I need to go," he told them. "Please. Be kind to my people."

He limped out the door and slowly descended toward a cart waiting on the deck below.

Mary moved in and fought briefly with him until he let her support him. "You big baby." She held him tightly with one arm, and he draped his over her shoulders.

"I'm far too tough to be a baby," he countered. "I thought Lev said the operation was quick and recovery would take no time at all? I feel like shit."

"You look like shit," Mary agreed.

Payne chuckled until he winced and grimaced against the pain. "Don't make me laugh."

"Laughing is the secret to a long and happy marriage." At

the bottom, she helped him into the cart. Kal was on the other side, ready to catch Payne if he fell.

"To the love nest!" Payne declared.

Mary looked forlornly at Kal, who simply shook his head. He called to the Cabrizi in Ebren. The creatures were nowhere in sight, but the scratching of their claws suggested they were coming at a high rate of speed.

"Take us home, Lev," Payne requested.

The cart raced off, leaving Kal between following without the Cabrizi or letting them go on their own. He jumped into the cart and whistled when it started moving.

Lev knew his preference.

The Cabrizi caught up before the hatch leading into the ship had closed. They vaulted through and ran after Kal's cart. He scolded them over his shoulder, stabbing a finger at their faces while their tongues lolled during the hard run. Lev kept the cart going a little faster than they were running. No matter how hard they tried, they could not catch up.

That was their punishment, but one they didn't care about. They had run thousands of kilometers within Lev's corridors. It didn't faze them and wasn't punitive.

Sometimes they liked to ride. Today was not one of those days.

The cart caught up to Payne's and slowed. When they reached Mary's and Declan's quarters, the cart stopped. The Cabrizi jumped in and tackled Kal. He tried to push them off, but they outmaneuvered him and toppled him. He tumbled out of the cart.

"You little bastards!" he howled. They took off, and he ran after them. The two carts headed in the other direction and accelerated out of sight.

"Should we wait or something?"

Mary shrugged, then opened the door and went inside. The smell of hot food wafted out. Payne waved down the corridor at Kal. "You're on your own, buddy."

[21]

"The time to train has passed. The time to show your mettle has arrived." –From the memoirs of Ambassador Declan Payne

"The portal is active," Loresh declared.

Lieutenant Commander Barry Cummins cheered the announcement. Commander Jimmy Josephs clapped him on the shoulder from where he stood behind the captain's chair of *The President*.

It had taken longer than either of them liked. The BEP had not bothered them during the process. The volunteers from Fleet headquarters had been separated among the battlewagons —two hundred extra souls on each ship, cramping the quarters and forcing everyone to sacrifice.

But they had trained hard during that time. Each person had learned one position. They could cross-train later when they understood their duties.

Cross-training was critical for a force that would be expected to survive in battle. Deaths came with damage. People had to be replaced, and there could be no gaps in capabilities. It was every ship captain's challenge—to cover any position required in time of need.

"Give me the squadron, please," Josephs requested. The communications officer accessed the channel and confirmed the connection with the other four battlewagons and single personnel transport. "We're going to the Vestrall home system to deposit the crews on the space station. They'll board each new ship when it's ready and bring it to Earth. Once five ships are consolidated here, they'll form a hunter-killer squadron and will depart for their target system. From Ebren to Rang'Kor, to Arn, and Zuloon, they will provide the support those systems need to build the portals and react with deadly force should the Ga'ee appear."

"Prepare to take us through," Cummins ordered. The bridge crew confirmed all posts were manned and ready. Weapons systems were charged. Cummins stood and saluted the commander. "Ship is ready to transit the portal."

"Take us through, Mister Cummins." The commander studied the tactical screen. Four battlewagons lined up behind *The President* and accelerated until they matched the first ship's speed. The transport lagged behind, nowhere near as fast as the battlewagons.

Once the portal was connected to the other, they could see into Vestrall space. It looked as it had when they had left it, except that there were two completed Payne-class battlewagons hovering near the shipyard's space station. *The President* slipped over the threshold and left the Solar System.

In the background, the frantic screams of the BEP demanded to know who would protect Earth during Hunter-Killer Squadron One's absence.

Josephs ignored the call.

The other ships followed and formed a square around the lead ship. Sensors swept the area, looking for anomalies.

No readings were outside what they expected.

"All ships, this is Commander Josephs. Transfer the crew volunteers to the shipyard station. *President*'s crews will staff battlewagons eleven and twelve." He checked the board since it had updated after a handshake with the shipyard's AI. "Thirteen will be ready in two days. Offload your crews. We need to get back to Earth."

"This is Admiral Melvin Ross, Fleet. I intend to take charge at the shipyard and cycle crews through here to their platforms. We will use the current platform to train the next crew and so on. After an initial operational check and test flight, the ships will be sent through the portal to Earth space and further deployment to the habitable worlds of the seven races."

Commander Josephs looked around as if a ghost had spoken.

"Admiral, you stowed away?"

"I had to. No way Earth was going to let me go, and in the same vein of abject stubbornness, no way was I going to be left behind. It's better no one knew until I could get off here, near Vestrall Prime."

"I heard the food isn't any good out here." Josephs was calm. He'd articulated the challenges they would have with the shipyard and the crews to the admiral, but he'd thought he was simply venting, not creating the conditions for the admiral to abdicate his billet on Earth.

Josephs was glad that he had.

"I've made alternate arrangements," Ross replied.

The portal had stayed active for the comm link and the sixth ship was coming. The aging Fleet transport cruised through. *Levant* directed it to the shipyard.

"You old dog," Josephs blurted. "Glad to have you on board, Admiral. You have the shipyard and our good people. I'll return to Earth with Hunter-Killer Squadron One. We will remain stationed there until the new ships arrive."

"Your plan is what I'm executing, Commander. Fair solar winds, and may your mission be a success."

"Not my plan, Admiral. It was Ambassador Payne's and Admiral Wesson's plan. We'll be on our way as soon as the crews are up and running. Josephs out."

———

"Twelve days for the battlewagons to get to Earth space," Payne mused. "I like the idea of sending every other ship to Ebren space, but I understand that if the Ga'ee are there, they will destroy the battlewagons one by one."

"These ships are our only defense against a Ga'ee incursion. That's why we'll bring them out of FTL in interstellar space, where they will run on minimal power until they receive orders to continue. We can pop in and send them the rest of the way," Admiral Wesson replied.

The battlewagons had departed for the designated coordinates as soon as they were ready to go. A couple were without crews, operating with an AI kernel Lev installed. They could function independently for the most part, but tactical and strategic decisions could only be made by a crew. The intricacies of combat required an AI of a much greater capability than what was installed.

Lev and the human leadership were reluctant to make smart drones. They'd fought those once, and it wasn't pretty. They didn't want to see a return of a drone fleet.

"First ship arrives Earth's space in three days. The last ship departs for Ebren space momentarily. Lev will stow his construction gear, and we'll fold our way back to Earth. I hope

Josephs had some success with the UN. Do you think the president will be miffed?"

"President Sinkhaus is always angry with the Fleet." The admiral sighed and shrugged. "It is what it is."

"That's defeatist. We're attempting to change what 'is' and not succumb to the inevitability of failure."

"You sound like I used to," the admiral quipped. "You are correct, though. We can't change what we don't like if we give in. We don't have to accept those who work against their own interests, either."

"Doing a victory dance because we won the war wasn't what I thought humanity should do, but they did it. We didn't, and fortunately, no one had to watch them do it because everyone was busy rebuilding and looking at their own worlds, finally. Everyone won."

"You have an excellent attitude, Declan. I salute you. How's your gut?"

"Lev was right. It took two days for a nearly complete recovery. Should have taken one, but I didn't rest after the operation when I should have. In my defense, I had shit to do."

"You think that's a good defense?" The admiral raised one eyebrow and looked down at the younger man.

"Hey, look! Mary's back." Payne pointed as he changed the subject.

"*Ugly 5* is ready, loaded to the gills with everything a stranded team could need," she reported. She walked over to Declan and gave him a hug. "You're not planning on using it anytime soon, are you?"

"Maybe a trip to the UN, but it won't be without you or the admiral or the commodore. If there's going to be soul-rending anguish brought on by volcanic fury, I want everyone to share the experience equally."

"BW13 is on its way," Lev reported. "Hangar bays are available for use once more. Preparing to fold space to Earth."

"Thanks, Lev. Give me ship-wide if you would be so kind," Payne requested.

The admiral nodded his approval. He was pleased with the progress his old friend Ross was making in the Vestrall shipyard.

The unnecessary click and buzz were Payne's signal that he had the attention of every soul on board.

"We're going back to Earth, but since we never know what we're going to find, Mosquitoes in ready launch position. We'll have our new defensive shields at maximum, and we'll arrive unannounced but will squawk the appropriate IFF code. As soon as the Spinsters report they are ready to launch, we'll fold space."

"We're ready now," Woody replied.

"Take us to Earth, Lev."

"I notice that you are calling *Leviathan* home and not Earth," Lev commented.

"You noticed correctly. We're home on board this ship, Lev. We appreciate the bigger quarters you've given to us and our whole team. There's no question about it."

The ship transitioned through the hole it ripped in the fabric of space and reappeared between the orbits of Earth and Mars, tangential to the Solar System's rotational axis to avoid running into any inter-system space traffic.

"Beginning new recharge sequence. Recommend engines first."

Lev displayed his systems' status on the tactical board with colored thermometers on each since humans found those easiest to internalize. They started in red at the bottom and worked their way to green. The percentage showed as well for those who liked greater detail.

"Thanks for the idiot icons, Lev. You're learning how to work with us."

"I endeavor to persevere," Lev replied.

Payne smiled. "We all should. Is the tactical screen correct?" He walked to the front where he could better see. The admiral followed. "Where are the battlewagons?"

"We better call the locals and see what's up. How long have we been gone?"

"Nearly a month," the admiral answered.

"I thought it was two weeks."

The admiral didn't educate Payne about thinking wrong. "I'll take care of it." *Lev, give me a channel, please.*

"No can do," Lev replied. "Need to recharge first."

"But we used to be able to call people while recharging," the admiral persisted.

"Did we, Harry?" Lev quipped. "New procedures require new procedures and new tolerance. We're down for a couple hours except using a short-range comm unit. Maybe the Mosquitoes can launch and carry a leather pouch with a communique like the *Pony Express*?"

"We'll wait. But if we can, launch the Mosquitoes, just in case. When the system populates, let me know who's out there."

"I'll figure out the recharge to make sure we don't arrive blind, deaf, and dumb. Next time."

It took right at two hours for the integrated systems to come back online. The admiral was fit to be tied by the time he was able to make the call. "Blue Earth Protectorate forces, this is Fleet Admiral Harry Wesson. We bring news of the Ga'ee."

"I guess that's true," Payne said.

"This is Captain LeClerc of the cruiser *Ephesus*. Welcome back. Berthing is available at the moon base. We will direct *Leviathan* in."

"We'll move to the base shortly. Until then, we will remain

where we are. While we're waiting, can you tell us where the five battlewagons of Hunter-Killer Squadron One are?"

"They left through the portal less a couple hours ago, as soon as the portal was repaired following the Ga'ee attack," Captain LeClerc's square face articulated.

Payne and the admiral looked at each other. Their worst fears were confirmed.

"What happened to the Ga'ee?" the admiral asked.

"The hunter-killer squadron destroyed it on the second salvo."

"Not the first?" Payne wondered.

"According to the commander of *The President*, the first salvo was uncoordinated and gave the Ga'ee the opportunity to survive it and launch their drones. Forty seconds later, the carrier vessel was destroyed, and the drones went dormant. They were destroyed or used in rebuilding the portal."

"The hunter-killer squadron went back to Vestrall. Did they say why?"

"They did not. They simply left us without protection."

"Did they have extra personnel with them? Fleet types?"

"A Fleet transport joined them and transited shortly after the battlewagons went through."

Mary hugged Declan again. Payne and the admiral shared a look. "That's a great thing, LeClerc. You'll have plenty of support soon enough when the new ships arrive at regular intervals from both Vestrall and those who survived the destruction of the forward base."

The admiral took a deep breath before continuing. "We lost the forward operating base, the station, and the ships that weren't able to leave before the Ga'ee attacked. A total of twenty-four ships were lost, and it gets worse. We have no idea where the Ga'ee went from there or where our ships that escaped did."

"Forward what you know for further analysis," LeClerc requested.

Payne drew the line across his neck and turned his back to the screen. "For further analysis?"

"They have to feel like they have a purpose. Play along, but we'll never take direction from the BEP. If they don't concur with our engagement strategy, we'll explain why they're wrong and then do what we need to do."

"Business as usual. Lev, please transmit our information regarding the Ga'ee encounter in Vestrall space and the data from the loss of our forward operating base."

"Of course," Lev replied congenially.

Payne turned around and twirled his finger to reestablish the voice connection. "Sending the information now. Is there anything else we can do for our brothers in blue?"

LeClerc looked around as if to verify no one was watching, then spoke in a low voice, "Could you hook me up with a tour of *Leviathan*, Mister Ambassador? Maybe me and my senior officers?"

Payne smiled. "I'd be more than happy to. Right now would be good. We have a couple hours of downtime. FTL to our position and bring a shuttle to the portside hangar bay. We'll meet you there. Leave your weapons behind, or we'll have to vent your bodies into space."

"No threats needed, Mister Ambassador. This is us, respecting humanity and doing everything we can to save it."

"Now you're talking, LeClerc. It's bigger than all of us. Come on over for a quick tour, and bring your senior technicians, too. They'll get a lot from the tour. We're all one team."

Payne cut the link. "Team Payne, we're giving some BEPers a tour of *Leviathan*. I would appreciate you meeting me in the portside hangar bay with your sidearms. Bring one for me, too."

"I'll join you," the admiral added. "Lev, ETA?"

"One hour, five minutes until *Ephesus* arrives."

"Enough time for a casual meal," Payne declared. Mary held his hand as they walked out. The admiral took the commodore's hand and walked off the bridge. That left it empty, which had become common after most of those on board transferred to the battlewagons. The majority were happy to take a more important role. Others would have been satisfied to remain on *Leviathan*, but these were hard times, and the fate of humanity was at stake.

The hard truth was that Lev needed no help to run the ship. He was fine by himself, but he needed strategic leaders to deal with the seven races and make the decisions that were best for all of them.

Even though Lev could decide, he preferred that humans determined their own future. He was helping them not to die out before they reached their potential, which he assessed as much greater than what the Godilkinmore had achieved.

If Davida and the minds of the others were data points from which to extrapolate, the young race was well ahead of their manipulators, the ones the humans called "the Progenitors."

Another name for the Godilkinmore before the Vestrall faction split away.

The fate of the Vestrall was at stake, too.

"I'll keep your seats warm," Lev told the four.

"I didn't know the bridge had seat warmers," Payne noted.

Mary looked at him. "I don't think that's what he meant. I hope you're more on your game when LeClerc and his cabal arrive."

"Cabal. Interesting view. You might be right. I think it will be anticlimactic, and we'll find that even the BEP is tired of the UN's shit."

"Whatever you do, never mince words, Declan," Mary purred. "It is so confusing when you do that."

[22]

"Space is cold and dark, just like the soul of the Ga'ee."
–From the memoirs of Ambassador Declan Payne

"Prepare to fold space to Ebren," the admiral stated.

Kal listened closely, but in his mind, he had been shunned by Ebren for his loss as the champion—and the failure of the new champion to end his life. He was an Ebren, but he was no longer welcome on his home planet.

He accepted his fate, even though the current champion did not.

"Not going to Earth?" the commodore asked.

"No reason. HK1 destroyed the Ga'ee ship that came here. Earth should be one of the safest in the galaxy. I am afraid for the homeworlds of the Braze Collective. We need hunter-killer squadrons at each of them, as many as we can muster. A hundred, two hundred. The only thing the Ga'ee respond to is superior firepower."

"Most intelligent beings respond with an appropriate level of fear, but not the Ga'ee. They got mad, and they came back with a multi-pronged strategy. Get *Leviathan* out of the picture.

And they did it without confrontation. All it took was an empty ship," Payne posited.

"But they underestimated Team Payne, and as long as the Ga'ee are unaware of your escape, we have surprise on our side. Surprise is the greatest of all tactics. To your point, Nyota, Earth is irrelevant in the tactical picture but critical for a strategic victory. The Ga'ee will try again once they are aware of their failure here. We have to defeat them between now and when they marshal their forces for Round Two."

"Let's see what waits for us in Ebren space."

"I am ready to fold space. I have selected a point four hours beyond the Ebren homeworld's heliosphere just to be safe."

Payne sat down. He had gotten as used to the sensation as one could, but it was still unnerving. Mary took the seat next to him. She closed her eyes. Payne had tried that, but it disoriented him even more. He needed to stare at a single point throughout the process.

Nyota sat while the admiral stood, legs braced against the storm and arms crossed as if he were indifferent to the process.

Leviathan slipped out of the Solar System to the edge of Ebren space. The star was so far away that it was little more than a point of light dominating the starfield.

"What do you see, Lev?"

The tactical board started to populate. The first ship to appear was *Cleophas*.

They'd found the Fleet.

Or at least part of it.

"Why is *Cleophas* here? Last we knew, it was with the armada on its way to Earth after meeting with the Zuloon. Is Admiral Dorsite on board?"

"We will soon find out."

Two Kaiju-class dreadnoughts, four Eagle-class heavy cruisers, and two Falcon-class light cruisers. Eight total ships with a complement of Mosquito fighters. Six Ebren vessels maneuvered nearby, four of them being Boriton-class battlewagons.

The heat signatures were flashed across the main screen.

"They're fighting the Ga'ee," the admiral stated. "Soon as you can, Lev, get us into that battle."

Lev made it clear how much time they had. "Two hours."

Space battles barely lasted minutes. The Fleet flashed into FTL, only to emerge ten seconds later and redeploy. The Ebren battleships performed the same maneuver.

"In a gunfight, don't let the knife-fighters get close enough to hurt you," Payne stated. "We have no way of letting them know we're here, do we?"

"A message transmitted now will arrive in four hours."

"That's what I thought, and we can't get there for six hours," Payne grumbled. "Let's hope the good guys are still fighting. When will the first battlewagon arrive from our former FOB?"

"Today, but keep in mind that it'll stop at a point in inter-stellar space and wait. There was wisdom in dispatching the battlewagons to limit transit time, but one ship won't change the outcome," Lev replied.

"One ship can always change the outcome," Admiral Wesson argued. "Never forget the sacrifice of Captain Pel'Rok. A single Mosquito nearly broke the enemy carrier's back and cost her over a hundred thousand drones, effectively ending the Ga'ee incursion. I know it'll take more than that this time around, but it started with one ship."

"Fleet forces are eliminating the drones one by one," Payne observed. The maneuvers suggested a cat-and-mouse game. They would eventually run low on ammunition. Would they outlast the drones?

The admiral's mouth twitched as he watched. Soon, others showed up. Woody. Cookie, their chef. The rest of Team Payne and half the embarked squadron's people trickled in until the bridge was packed.

"This big ship, and everyone decides they want to be in here?" Payne whispered.

"Yes," Mary replied. "Where else would anyone be? We're stuck doing nothing until we can fly to Ebren, which is four hours of doing nothing, meaning two waiting for the power systems to recharge and two of FTL flight to the system. Everyone wants to see our people hand the Ga'ee their asses."

Payne chuckled. "That is the hope, even though the Ga'ee are assless. There is no front and no rear. Reminds me of a push-me-pull-you." At Mary's look of confusion, he clarified, "Doctor Doolittle."

That didn't clarify anything. She hadn't heard of him either.

"I'm married to someone who lacks a classical education. If I had only known before you seduced me."

She caught the furtive glances from those nearby. People were listening. "Don't make me kick your ass right here in front of everyone."

"Yes, ma'am," Payne conceded.

He had to joke to offset the tension. They couldn't be more helpless, but their incapacity was only two hours instead of three days.

A vast improvement, thanks to the Ga'ee's power plants.

"Lev, status of your armaments?"

"One hundred percent, including two world-killers."

"Do you have a way to defeat their energy shield?"

"We have theories that will require testing," Lev replied.

Payne made a face. "The only way to test it is to get close enough to fire at the bad guys and collect the data without getting killed. I don't intend to go anywhere in *Ugly 5* unless the Ga'ee have landed on Ebren, and we won't go down there unless the sky is clear. We need to kill that ship, Lev."

"The only way to remove the Ga'ee from the space of the seven races is to destroy them and their ships."

"*Leviathan* rises to the occasion!" Payne blurted. "Damn, Lev. That sounds genocidal. What have you learned from the core on the Ga'ee ship?"

"That the Ga'ee have colonized far more than just this sector of space. The star charts we were able to access suggest they have colonized nearly ten thousand-star systems."

"Then why do they need forty more?" That was the sum total of the inhabited systems of the seven races. "Ten thousand?"

"They are the dominant race in the known universe."

Payne's face fell. "They can overwhelm us. They'll keep coming, won't they?"

"Once they establish a foothold, they won't need to rally the masses back home to keep expanding in this direction. Once we understand their language, we might have to make a side-trip to their seat of power."

Payne perked up. "Or we could tap into however they communicated at fold-space speed and let them know we won't tolerate an incursion. They can verify that their fleet is gone, and we can establish a truce. Get into their autonomous minds and convince them this part of space is death."

"I like not having to go into Ga'ee space," the admiral added. "Means we might have to capture another Ga'ee ship."

"I can't imagine being on a Ga'ee ship when the wrigglers are there. It was bad enough when it was just us." Payne looked for Kal, his ever-present friend who stayed in the background and kept the Cabrizi out of trouble. He tried to keep Payne out of trouble, but that didn't always work.

Payne worked his way to the Ebren warrior. "What do you think, Kal?"

"I don't think we can penetrate a Ga'ee carrier if they don't want us there. They would run drones at the uglymobile until we were all dead, even inside the hangar bay. The only way we can get on one of those ships is if they let us. And given why we want to board, they won't let us," Kal drawled.

"That's my thinking. No covert operations on this one. We have to count on the team to get in using nothing but the airwaves while blasting every drone out of the sky."

"I can get behind that plan. What do you say we hit the gym? Power up before going in?" Kal suggested.

"We're probably going to Ebren. Down to the surface to make sure they're doing okay and that any infestations have been eliminated. I need you with us."

"That makes me as nervous as a long-tailed cat in a room full of rocking chairs," Kal drawled.

Payne laughed. "Lev did this to punish me, as if the beating you gave me wasn't enough. If I'm the current Ebren champion, I kind of make the rules."

"But losers are to be killed in the ring. I should not have survived, and I don't deserve to live."

"Fuck that, Kal! You are the greatest Ebren warrior that ever lived! I'm human, and the Vestrall champion cheated to get the title. And more than any of that other bullshit, you've saved my life and the lives of your teammates.

"Even more important than that, you're my friend, Kal. I don't have very many friends, but the ones I do have matter a whole lot. I can't abide your loss, Kal. I cannot. I'm asking you as a friend to come with us. Set a new standard for honor. You matter to me, and since I'm the champion, you matter to all of Ebren."

"You are too kind, Declan. Maybe you've already changed the face of Ebren by your actions. If they're on the ground fighting the Ga'ee, they will welcome any warrior willing to swing an axe, wield a blade, or fire a plasma cannon." Kal didn't sound upbeat despite his attempt.

"We will see. I want you with us, Kal." Payne gripped the bigger Ebren's wrist. Kal's fingers went to Payne's elbow. "You don't have to come if you don't want, but I have to go unless there is nothing left of Ebren."

"I'll go because you asked, and there better be something left of Ebren."

"Team Payne to the gym," Payne ordered softly, knowing that Lev would relay the request into the minds of the team members. He waved to get Mary's attention and crooked a finger for her to join him. Quietly, he and Kal left the bridge. The team worked their way out. Mary found herself in the middle of them.

"Working out is good for the soul," Payne declared once the team had consolidated in the corridor. Nine strong. Ten with Mary.

Blinky and Buzz were hard at work trying to decrypt the Ga'ee language. Their bodies were getting soft, but their minds remained sharp. Soon, though, their minds would deteriorate. To stay sharp, the body had to work better. Lev had promised to unplug the two if they crossed the threshold.

"I wish I had words of wisdom, but I don't. Our people are fighting the Ga'ee, and there's jack all we can do about it for six hours. Might as well burn that time doing something productive."

Major Dank raised one finger, requesting to speak. Payne stared at him until he put his finger down. "Can Annaliese come?"

Payne smiled. "Of course. Anyone you want to invite. Goes for all of you. There's room, but we'll work hard. Then chow, then a short rest. We'll be ready to deploy fifteen minutes before we return to normal space just in case."

"Are we going to try and board the Ga'ee ship?" Heckler asked in a voice that suggested he wouldn't be a fan if the answer was yes.

Payne shook his head. "Not this time. We convince it to stand down, or we destroy it. Those are the only two options."

"What if it stands down because it wants to parlay?" Heckler pressed.

"Then we invite it to send a delegation to us. Four life forms we'll put into a transparent aluminum case the second they arrive. We'll have a conversation before tossing them back into their ship. We're not going over there, but we will go to Ebren as soon as we can. They need their champion. You're all cool with carrying me on your shoulders, aren't you?"

Dank coughed. "Eat me."

"So, we're agreed. Shoulders and scantily clad worshippers fanning a naked me." No one agreed.

"To the gym."

23

"If the cavalry is available, let them *ride to the rescue."*
–From the memoirs of Ambassador Declan Payne

Team Payne had dressed in their powered combat suits. Like everyone else on *Leviathan*, they waited. They were not in a rush to board *Ugly 5* since ten minutes remained before the ship would reenter normal space.

The cat-and-mouse battle around Ebren continued, with neither side gaining an advantage as far as Lev could determine from his long-range sensors limited by only being able to see one side in the fight based on hours-old data. The Ga'ee remained invisible to his passive sensors.

They would know soon enough. There were few options available to them besides adding *Leviathan's* firepower to the Fleet's.

What they didn't understand was why the Ga'ee ship had stuck around. If its task was to populate the planet of Ebren, it could have done that and moved on, forcing the Fleet to follow or get out of the way.

They would get those answers, too. The Fleet should have

received Admiral Wesson's first communique two hours earlier since it had been sent six hours previously. Lev had recharged for two hours, then made a four-hour FTL flight to Ebren.

That arrival location had kept him safe from the Ga'ee during his period of vulnerability. He couldn't risk himself by arriving too close. It had become SOP, standard operating procedure, unless determined ahead of time that the need outweighed the risk, like on trips to Earth's space.

"Where were the battlewagons?" Major Dank asked. "There were supposed to be five supporting Earth, even if they had already destroyed a Ga'ee carrier."

"We never went that far with our instructions. If they fought, they must have reasoned the chance of encountering a second Ga'ee vessel so quickly was minimal. They took crews to Vestrall Prime, which means we'll receive battlewagons ready for immediate deployment when they arrive through the portal. That's a good thing," Payne replied.

"But the hunter-killer squadron didn't need to go. The troop transport could have gone by itself."

"They wouldn't have known what to do once there. The commanders of the squadron and the ships need to have some autonomy. Otherwise, they would be as useless as the Maginot Line."

"The what?" Dank checked the time and gestured with his thumb toward *Ugly 5*. No one had to be told a second time. The team moved in and took their seats.

"The Maginot Line was a testament to the vulnerability of fixed defenses. Old Earth. It stood as a monument to man's failure to learn." Payne checked the team. "Buckle up, people. Lev, secure the outer doors and show us the tactical picture."

The sides of the egg-shaped insertion craft rotated into place and sealed. The screens appeared, and the board populated with icons.

"Looks like we lost another heavy cruiser," Payne lamented. The board showed seven ships, two Kaiju, three Eagles, and two Falcons. *Leviathan's* icon had raced into the system and would soon appear in the middle of the fray. When active sensors became available, the Ga'ee ship would appear.

A timer on the screen counted down. Payne clenched his jaw in anticipation.

At ten seconds, Payne ordered, "Helmets on."

The team complied. With three seconds to go, Payne's heads-up display showed all team members as green. Pulses were up but still well within resting norms. The team was in shape and ready to go.

The board showed the Ga'ee ship surrounded by a swarm of drones less than five hundred kilometers away. The drones surged toward *Leviathan*. Defensive systems snap-fired; they sent a full barrage into space without keying on specific targets. They didn't need to.

The slight disorientation of transitioning back into FTL passed quickly. Ten seconds later, *Leviathan* reemerged. The tactical board lit up again as Lev sent a second barrage into the void, creating a defensive barrier. The first barrage had torn through the drones, eliminating a swath of them. A small salvo of five inbound missiles bounced off the Ga'ee's screen and continued toward deep space.

The area was flooded with projectiles, energy, and debris.

"The Ga'ee shields are working well to protect us from friendly fire," Payne observed. He magnified the view that showed the vast amount of ammunition and impact debris. "Mission is scrubbed for now. We can't fly through that. Lev, let my people go!"

"Are you implying that I'm a pharaoh, Declan?" Lev asked with a chuckle. The side doors rotated upward, and the team climbed out.

"I'll be on the bridge. Don't go too far, but you don't need to stay in your suits." Payne kept his suit on. He left his helmet on his seat on *Ugly 5* and jogged toward the nearest cart. Once he was on board, squeezed into the two seats, the cart departed.

"You'd make a good pharaoh, Lev, for what it's worth," Payne remarked.

The trip to the bridge was quick as it always was. Payne clumped through the hatch to find only the admiral and the commodore watching the battle.

"Are we winning?" Payne asked.

"We are whittling them down, but Captain Smith from *Cleophas* said they were running low on ammunition. They fired everything they had to attrit the drones, but Lev estimates there are still at least sixty thousand swarming around the Ga'ee carrier," the admiral explained.

"How do we end this, Admiral?" Payne asked.

"We are attempting to de-resonate the Ga'ee's shield. That'll make it possible for missiles to get to the ship. Well-placed missiles will destroy it. I'll coordinate the attack." Lev went back to what he was doing.

He shifted to faster-than-light speed to avoid the cloud of drones racing his way.

Leviathan reentered normal space on the far side of the Ga'ee ship, at a thirty-degree angle toward the Ebren star. Lev unleashed another barrage of defensive weapons fire.

"Preparing to launch offensive missiles," Lev announced. A hundred Rapier-class missiles leapt from *Leviathan*'s launchers and lit up the board. They arced across the void, separating to increase the distance between them to ensure that as many as possible cleared the drone clouds. The Fleet launched a final protective fire, the FPF. The dreadnoughts flushed their tubes, sending the last of their offensive weapons into space. More Rapiers angled toward the Ga'ee carrier.

The five remaining heavy and light cruisers launched their Predator-class anti-ship missiles at the target in small numbers and from different angles. The missiles assumed flight profiles to sweep in from yet another direction.

The clouds of drones changed their direction. Like a flock of birds, they soared and flowed back toward their ship. They accelerated to arrive before the missile barrage.

"The Ga'ee know their defensive shield isn't going to work," Payne stated. "If they protect their hangar bays, will a missile strike on the outer hull take them out?"

"They have a rather significant amount of hangar space. Even with sixty thousand drones, they cannot defend it all," Lev replied. The board updated with real-time data showing the outbound missiles and the drone swarms. It wasn't clear if the drones would intercept them.

"Big sky, little bullet," the admiral added. "Move in closer, Lev, now that the drones are reforming in a defensive posture around the carrier. If we get a second shot, we'll need to take it."

"Eight Rapiers and four Predators remain among the Fleet ships," Lev reported. "All are being loaded."

"That's enough to take that ship down if they get a clean hit," the admiral noted, then ordered, "Launch the Mosquitoes and drop as many nukes as you can into the middles of those tightly packed clusters of drones."

New icons appeared on the board as the Mosquitoes launched within seconds of getting the order. Lev accelerated after the space fighters, keeping them within his defensive weapons envelope.

The missile barrage closed on the Ga'ee carrier. The final approach included a max burn with the remaining fuel to hyper-accelerate the missiles into the targets. Drones swept in, and a wave of them flowed close to the energy barrier, interposing itself. Ten, twenty, and then thirty of Lev's missiles exploded. Debris rained through the energy barrier and harmlessly peppered the massive ship's outer hull.

"Shield is porous." Payne pumped his fist and leaned closer. The missiles accelerated on final from a hundred different angles. The void lit up with explosions as swaths of drones were wiped off the board.

Three of *Cleophas'* missiles flew in a column, programmed that way by their weapons section. The first was destroyed and the second was knocked off course, but the third penetrated the opening. The final line of propellant gleamed like a blue laser as it followed the darkness that was the missile into the closed hangar door.

It hit and exploded with the fury of the sun. The door buckled and shredded before getting blown outward and taking four more kilometers of the hangar door with it. A glowing fireball filled the empty space of the hangar.

The Ga'ee prioritized defense against Lev's missiles. The drones intercepted most, but the firing pattern allowed three out of a hundred to sweep around the outer edge of the cloud. From three different angles, they delivered their payloads.

The keel cracked with a direct hit, and the ship appeared to sag. The second struck between the prow and the hangar door on the starboard side, one of the most heavily armored sections of the ship. Lev's missiles had penetrator nose cones and megaton nuclear payloads.

Once through the outer armor, the weapon exploded. There was nowhere for the blast to go but into the corridors and interior spaces. The armor acted like the pot of a pressure cooker. The ship started to heel over, changing its attitude in space, not voluntarily but from a loss of control.

The last missile had the longest flight profile, and that gave it an advantage. It maneuvered around the drone cloud and rammed into the aft section where Team Payne had found the dual reactors, through the hull and farther into the interior. It finally exploded, sending its fiery wrath at the two reactors powering the engines. The devastation was complete, ripping the insides out of the drives and taking not two but three reactors with it. They erupted in one final fusion-accelerated burst of energy.

Fountains of quickly extinguished flame and molten metal launched into space. The aft end of the ship started to separate from the rest of the ship. It used its attitude thrusters to turn like it was going to find clear space to transition to faster-than-light speed as it had the last time a Ga'ee ship escaped from *Leviathan*, but this was different.

The ship didn't just have a broken back. Its engines were gone, and half its power had been turned into an all-consuming release of energy. The rear third of the ship shattered under the shock wave, sending debris at the leading edge of the blast wave.

The front of the ship struggled. The drones attempted to intervene with the last member of the missile barrage, but they lost guidance, then regained it, then reverted to ballistic trajectories.

Four Rapier-class missiles impacted the remaining sections of the Ga'ee ship and exploded as one, turning the ship into an expanding cloud of metal and gas.

The drones lost attitude control and turned into nothing more than targets and debris. The Mosquitoes swooped in for firing practice. Woody promised an award to the pilot with the most confirmed destroyed drones with the fewest number of shots from their space fighter's cannons.

Leviathan moved toward the cloud and used its smaller defensive weapons systems—lasers, plasma weapons, and chain guns—to destroy thousands and then tens of thousands of drones.

The admiral gestured at Payne. "You are cleared to deploy to the surface of Ebren."

Payne nodded and pounded off the bridge. He skipped the cart and used the power of his suit to run. Lev deployed the internal ramps as he approached. Payne accelerated up them since he could.

He arrived at the team area of the hangar bay in less than five minutes. He could have made it in three but had taken it relatively easy. He didn't know how long they would be deployed on Ebren.

"Load up!" he shouted. With the team's usual efficiency, they took their seats. "Kal, bring the Cabrizi. We're going to Ebren."

"Status?" Major Dank asked. Without his helmet, Payne couldn't talk to the team, and Lev hadn't enlightened them.

After he took his seat, he brought them up to speed. "The Ga'ee carrier was destroyed. Lev is cleaning up the drones. I expect he'll take them on board, along with remnants of the carrier, to replenish the Fleet's ammunition supplies."

The hangar bay was already busy. Maintenance and construction bots moved into place to begin the smelting and manufacturing processes.

The Cabrizi loped across the deck and jumped into the insertion craft. Kal pulled them close to him and held them tightly, not looking anywhere but at the animals.

Ugly 5 closed its outer doors and lifted off the deck. "Helmets," Payne directed. He snapped his into place, and the others followed his lead.

The tactical screens lit up, displaying only friendly icons.

"Lev, put me in touch with the high command." Payne checked his HUD. The team suits showed green, and the bodies within were one hundred percent healthy.

"Ambassador Payne, what are your orders?" an Ebren voice asked. The helmet translated.

Note to self. Relearn Ebren, Payne thought. "What is your status? Did any Ga'ee drones make it to the surface?"

"We blasted them all from the sky. Twenty different incursions. We double-checked the ground where the ships crashed and recovered the foreign materials. These creatures are silicon-based?"

"They are. They dig into the ground and eat certain rocks in order to reproduce at a rate that doubles every couple hours. In days, they can overwhelm a planet's surface and be impossible to remove."

"There are no colonies. We are Ebren. We would never let invaders gain a foothold on our planet. What are your orders?"

"You have fulfilled my orders. Never let an invader land on the planet's surface. We don't know the extent of this incursion into the space of the seven races. We'll transmit the latest data regarding known Ga'ee invasion attempts—Vestrall Prime, Earth, and Ebren, following the human forward operating base. We expect they'll be in Arn, Zuloon, Rang'Kor, and Berantz space, too. We'll need to head there soonest. Do you require any assistance?"

"No, unless you wish to visit with the new champion. The planet needs a new fight."

Payne spoke privately to Lev. *How much time do we have before you're able to rearm the Fleet?*

Almost a full day, Declan. Their stocks are depleted.

And only a day to resupply them. You're a miracle worker, Lev. We're going to Ebren. We'll be back as soon as possible.

Payne switched to the planetary frequency and roped his team in on it. "Ebren High Command, I accept your challenge. My champion will fight for primacy. Is Captain Bel'ron available?"

"His ship is in orbit. It sustained heavy damage but remained in the fight," the voice replied.

"I would expect no less from such a warrior as he as well as his magnificent crew. Please pass along my greatest respect."

Ugly 5 raced out of the hangar bay and toward Ebren's upper atmosphere.

"What are you doing, Dec?" Virgil asked over a P2P channel.

"I'm giving Kal a chance to win back his status."

"I'm not sure he wants that."

Payne removed his helmet and unbuckled his belt. He moved next to Kal and took a knee. The Cabrizi shifted to keep from getting squashed.

"You ready to fight?"

Kal looked up. "I don't fight on Ebren anymore."

"I do, but I can select a champion who seals both our fates. There is no one I'm willing to trust with my life more than you, Kal. I need you to fight for me. I'm not hyped up like last time. Lev didn't help strengthen my body. I would die in the pit, but not you, my friend. You are the greatest warrior I've ever met, and you will defeat the new Ebren champion."

"But I don't fight anymore."

Payne shook his head. "You swore to protect me. If you lose, you kill not only yourself but me, too. When you win this fight, you'll be released from your obligation to me. I want you to resume your place as the Ebren champion. I want you to be free."

Kal turned his attention to the Cabrizi. Payne waited, but he knew he would get no more from the Ebren.

He returned to his seat and put his helmet back on to find Mary attempting to contact him. "Yes, dear. I fear I won't be home for supper."

"What are you doing?" she asked sharply.

"I expect you heard about the challenge."

"You're going to kill Kal and yourself, too. I know how it works down there. And the new guy won't be obligated to help Earth anymore. You didn't think this through, did you?"

"I'm trying to do right by my friend," Payne replied softly. "What is our humanity worth? He's my slave, as much as I don't want him to be. As much as I hate the thought of it. He always will be since I didn't kill him. I don't want to look at his seat and see it empty, but that's better than him jumping to do my bidding every time I speak. He's better than that. He's better than all of us."

"He's as good as all of us and deserves what we have. We give him the choice to be himself every day. He does what he does willingly. He doesn't need to fight."

"Fear not for me. The fight will continue because the Ga'ee are our enemy—all of ours. We have one day to get this right. Kal is the true Ebren champion. I will see him restored to his position of honor."

"I hope it doesn't backfire on you. I'm going to talk with him."

"Please do, Mary. I won't be his master after he wins. Finally. He will have earned the Cabrizi, and they will remain forever his as part of his victory."

"You don't know anything about the new champion. Declan, sometimes you drive me insane."

"It's not intentional."

"It never is." Mary cut the channel.

Payne cast a furtive glance at Kal'faxx and saw his lips move as he spoke. Mary was more persuasive when it came to the Ebren since she had relearned his language.

Payne checked his HUD. Nothing had changed. He scanned the tactical screens. The ships lined up for their reloads from *Leviathan*, with *Cleophas* at the front. The Kaiju-class ship could protect the others once it carried a full load, at least long enough for them to escape.

Captain Ezekial Smith had commanded the dreadnought through the bumps and grinds of the conflict with the Ga'ee. He'd fallen afoul of Arthir Dorsite for a short time but overcame that when the ship needed his experience.

The courage of his convictions had almost killed the ship. He had lost sight of the greater goal.

But *Cleophas* had managed a long battle with the Ga'ee and kept most of the ships alive while reducing the Ga'ee drone fleet. They had run out of ammunition before they had lost the will to keep fighting.

There were plenty of people to manage the war against the Ga'ee. They didn't need Payne. In his mind, he reconciled himself with the decision he'd made.

An unpopular decision. High risk with no gain for humanity. In other words, it was a stupid decision. One Ebren's life against humanity's continued existence.

To Payne, it made sense.

Life had to be worth living, and Kal's tribulations as Payne's personal bodyguard were wearing on both of them.

"Virgil, if anything happens, take over the team. Should be seamless."

"I'm not going to listen if you're going to spew dumbassitude over the airwaves."

"So much spewing. The decision is made. The challenge was accepted. Next stop, Ebren." Payne closed the channel and chose to sulk. He started to doubt his decision. No one could see his side. His three closest friends were adamantly opposed.

Loyalty. They wanted to protect their friend, too.

Kal slapped a big hand on the knee of Declan's suit. Payne Jumped as the suit reverberated from the strength of the blow.

"I'll do it, and I'll win. I need big quarters, bigger than yours, with a higher ceiling."

Payne blinked quickly and replayed the words in his mind. "When you win, you won't have to return to *Leviathan.*"

"When I win, I make my own decisions on where I want to go."

"True," Payne replied.

"I will choose to return to *Leviathan.* The high command will continue to support the coalition you built. It is a good thing."

"Deal. Now, all you have to do is win."

"That's all I had to do against a puny human, too."

24

"We loan our bodies to the greater good and hope that we get paid back with interest, but it never works out that way. We're happy if we can walk away with scars that spell out 'debt paid in full.'" –From the memoirs of Ambassador Declan Payne

Ugly 5 touched down close to the doors of the massive ziggurat. The Cabrizi hopped off first, sniffed the air, and took off running in the other direction. Last time, Mary had whistled them to her. This time, it had to be Payne. The Champion didn't need to strain.

Kal tossed his helmet on the seat, unfolded himself from the ship, and stepped into the light of his native sun. The representatives who had met them last time waited.

"May the glory of Ebren welcome me home," Payne greeted their hosts evenly.

Payne wore his combat suit and kept his helmet on so he could converse with them.

Kal waited patiently while Payne ran down the Cabrizi and yelled at them in suit-translated Ebren. They cowered under his verbal assault, and he herded them back to the entrance. When they arrived, Kal issued a sharp warning to the animals, who assumed their place at his side.

"The champion returns," the elder Ebren stated.

"Yes, he does," Payne replied. "The humans, too."

The Ebren inclined his head slightly.

"Kal'faxx is my champion. He is the greatest warrior who has ever lived."

"Indeed," the elder agreed with a hint of cynicism. "My team will accompany me. They will abide by the rules of the pit."

"The champion makes the rules except those for the combat itself," the elder advised.

Payne faced his team while Kal walked toward the door. Their Ebren escorts opened it for him. Otherwise, they might have seen a tremor in his hand from trepidation about returning where he wasn't welcome.

But only in his mind.

"We're supposed to be silent, so I'll need you to just watch and hold Kal in your hearts while he fights for his life."

"No cheering?" Joker asked. "What kind of fun do they have?"

"If my last trip was an indicator, they have no fun in this building. Strictly prohibited to crack a smile or, heaven forbid, deliver a full guffaw."

"You didn't offer your usual quips that only you find funny?"

"After Dog said she wanted to do me right in the pit, I was at a loss. It was like my brain came to a complete stop."

"I'm telling her you said that," Sparky shot back.

"Better not."

"I doubt it was the Missus," Heckler offered. "I bet it was the beat-down Kal laid on you that affected your brain."

"There was that," Payne replied. "It was a grim time. This time it'll be different."

Payne followed Kal toward the pit. The escorts fell away, and Team Payne arrived. Kal stripped off his clothes and tossed them carelessly aside. Payne carefully folded them, then took off his helmet and placed it on the ground next to him.

A light shone on an Ebren walking toward them. Not as tall as Kal but wider, he was unlike any Ebren Payne had ever seen. Usually, the race was tall and lanky, but Kal had been genetically engineered for muscle mass. He weighed two to three times what an average Ebren weighed. The newcomer was stocky like a walking building. His head was squarish, not elongated.

Payne wondered briefly if the new Ebren champion was another genetic experiment created for a single purpose—hand-to-hand combat. Payne finally climbed out of his suit and stood in the buff. "Tell me what I'm supposed to do, Kal."

Kal nodded. He was focused on his opponent, and his face took on the expression of the old Kal: disdain for the one who faced him.

The Ebren strode to the edge of the ring and removed his clothes, then stepped in. Payne climbed into the ring.

"I designate my champion to fight in my stead," Kal whispered.

Payne repeated it, and Kal bellowed it in Ebren. He vaulted the low wall and landed on the hard-packed sand, reveling in the feel. He leaned down to hold out his hand. Payne met him palm to palm and gripped tightly, interlocking his thumb with Kal's. They placed their left hands over the other.

"Fight like you know how, Kal."

Kal nodded, and Payne climbed out of the pit.

Kal stretched while he waited. When he'd fought Payne, he had been the aggressor, and it had put him off balance from the first attack. He eased forward and lowered himself into a combat crouch. He had reach on his opponent.

The blocky Ebren simply waited, unmoving. He didn't gesture or posture or give away his approach. Kal showed considerable patience, even though adrenaline surged through his body. He swung out of reach of the other and carefully side-stepped around him, forcing his opponent to move.

Kal dodged in when the stocky contender raised one foot. With an un-Ebren-like move, Kal dug one foot into the sand, turned, and delivered a sidekick that staggered his opponent.

The Ebren stumbled back one step before regaining his composure. Kal danced away with a slight limp. What did the contender have that Kal hadn't been expecting?

Payne focused intently on the opponent. What was his secret?

He bounced, left and right, back and forth, to subtly herd Kal against the outer ring. Kal had tried to do the same thing to Payne but failed since the human was small in comparison and moved quicker than an Ebren.

Kal closed on the contender and delivered a flurry of punches that ended with an uppercut that didn't even rock the Ebren. The opponent tried to grab Kal, but the warrior was too quick. Training with humans had taught him the value of speed over power.

The contender stepped back until he leaned against the outer wall. He crossed his arms and waited. Kal took the long way around the ring, and he took his time getting there. As Payne always said, never be in a hurry to your own funeral.

Kal swooped in and dove to the sand to deliver a leg sweep along the wall where his opponent was trapped. Kal swept nothing but air. The stocky Ebren landed solidly on top of Kal with an elbow that sent shock waves through his organs and down his legs. The contender seized an exposed arm and held on while trying to gain leg leverage to break the fight off.

The former Ebren champion pushed off the sand and twisted to get his feet under him. The shorter opponent resisted, but leverage was Kal's. Using his leg strength, he raised his body and lifted the stocky Ebren off the sand. That gave Kal an opening to stand, and he forced himself upward until his legs were braced.

The opponent held one of Kal's arms and tried to get a leg around Kal's waist. The warrior spun until the opponent could only do his best to hang on, then Kal lifted him over his head. He staggered two steps and slammed the Ebren's body onto the edge of the ring. A sickening crack signaled broken bones.

The opponent forced himself back until he fell into the ring. Kal lunged and drove a knee into the stocky Ebren's midsection. He followed with a devastating right cross to the exposed throat.

The opponent gurgled while trying to take a breath, and he started to flop around. Kal stood and walked away. He stopped in the middle of the pit and slowly turned, finding the stocky Ebren running toward him. Kal backstepped and used a maneuver Payne had used on him more than once.

He grabbed the outstretched arms and pulled the opponent toward him, then rolled to his back and threw the stocky Ebren over his head. The other person landed with a heavy thump. Kal held onto one wrist to maintain control while he rolled and twisted to bring his leg around the other's neck. With an arm bar, he scissored his legs around the other's neck, pulling his arm to keep the contender from gaining an advantage. One hand wouldn't be enough to break free.

Kal squeezed slowly until the other stopped struggling. The warrior had been fooled once. He wouldn't bite a second time. He rolled forward until he could bring his full bodyweight to bear on his neck hold. Then he rotated until the neck snapped with the sound of a rifle shot.

He kicked the body free and pushed it away. A dark bruise showed where the opponent had hit the retaining wall. He had been hurt and badly, but he'd overcome it to attack. It was the way of champions.

In that instant, Payne's actions became crystal clear. Such a warrior didn't deserve to die. On another day, Kal would have lost. Payne respected life and achievement. Getting to the pit was enough to warrant the utmost respect.

"Hear me!" Kal bellowed from within the pit. Payne leaned close to Major Dank, who funneled the translation through his external speaker. "From this point forward, these contests will not be to the death. Such a warrior as he deserves to live to fight our enemies. The Ga'ee take no prisoners. They destroy entire civilizations, and here we are, killing each other. *NO MORE!*

"We fight the Ga'ee. We have ships. What we don't have are enough crews for them. We don't have ground teams to kill the Ga'ee where they've burrowed. We have weapons. We don't have warriors, and here, one of the greatest lies dead. We can no longer afford this kind of fight. We must look outward, not inward. Even if only one dies on Ebren, that's one too many. I have spoken."

Payne climbed into the ring to hug his friend. The champions continued to reign. The Cabrizi vaulted onto the sand, taken aback by the feel of it under their paws. They pranced and bounced until they got used to it, then sniffed the dead Ebren.

Kal kneeled and talked quietly to the two animals. Payne couldn't understand what he was saying, but the tone was clear.

Respect.

Human respect, not Ebren honor that demanded killing the opponent. Demanded the rage to bring victory.

Kal had said no more contests to the death.

There was a greater enemy to deal with out there.

The elder Ebren approached. "Champion. The high command is waiting for you."

After Kal interpreted for Payne, he realized they were both naked. He glanced at his team to find them slow-clapping. "Let's get things squared away. Recruits for ships to take the war to the Ga'ee. To kill their ships should they breach our space and to kill them if they land on our planets."

"I think I can get behind y'all on this," Kal drawled, smiling. "Remember, bigger quarters, tall for a champion like me. And extra space for my boys."

"I'm sure Lev is already working on it, Kal. Let's order up some volunteers, then get back to the ship. I expect the four other races of the Braze Collective are under siege."

"Time to fight the good fight, my friend," Kal said with a hearty laugh that ended with a wince. He leaned close to Payne and whispered, "I probably need to visit Medical when I get back. I think he broke something. Now I know how you felt after our fight."

"I don't think so, Kal. You beat the holy crap out of me. I was lucky to still be upright."

[25]

"When the universe calls, answer." –From the memoirs
of Ambassador Declan Payne

The admiral glared at Payne. Mary wouldn't hold his hand.
When Kal strolled in like he owned the place, their attitudes
changed. He snapped one word at the Cabrizi, and they fell into
line behind him.

"Ebren will be bringing two thousand warriors to *Leviathan*
before we need to leave. They'll be ready for immediate training
and further deployment to wherever we need them."

"Kal!" the admiral blurted.

The Ebren Champion wrapped an arm around Payne's
shoulders. "I'm obliged for the chance to make good. To show
that on an even playing field, I can win a fight. I'd also like to
officially join Team Payne as Ebren's representative."

"Of course," the admiral replied. He looked at Payne. "That
was a high-risk maneuver."

"And necessary, Admiral. For both our sakes. It's behind us
now, so when can we leave for Berantz space?"

"Twelve more hours," Lev replied. "That will bring the

Fleet ships back to fully combat-capable, to use your terminology."

"Twelve hours." Payne made a face. "Damn. The Ga'ee can do a lot of damage in twelve hours. Maybe we can meet with Captain Smith and catch up on what they found with the Zuloon."

The admiral cocked his head sideways and stared at Major Payne. "What do you think I was doing for the last twelve hours?"

"Is Arthir on board?"

"*Admiral* Dorsite is not. She cross-decked to the *Santorini*. *Cleophas* came here and found the remnants of the Fleet engaged with the Ga'ee. We showed up not long after. And before you ask, Arthir had a hunch, and that's why she sent *Cleophas* here."

Payne did the math in his head. "Only one Kaiju came from the FOB? What happened to the other two?"

"They went in a different direction. No one has heard from them since the evacuation."

"But they weren't killed?" Payne pressed.

"They transitioned successfully to faster-than-light speed. That's the best info the Fleet could give us."

"Where are you sending this task force next?" Payne moved closer to the front screen where the tactical situation was displayed.

"They're staying here. We'll take the Ebren on board and begin their battlewagon training immediately. As soon as we can get back to Vestrall Prime, we'll drop them off to crew the next ships."

"We could build one here from the Ga'ee debris, couldn't we?"

"A whole extra day," the admiral complained. "I don't think we can afford it, and from what we learned from Earth, even three shots massed together don't have enough energy to destroy a Ga'ee carrier. We need five. One ship wouldn't be sufficient. There isn't enough raw material to build five, so we might as well collect more information."

"Roger," Payne agreed. "We need to get Kal to Medical. He didn't come out of that fight unscathed."

"It's just a scratch." Kal waved one hand as if he were chasing away a buzzing fly.

"It's not. Lev will tell you how fucked up you are, then he'll fix you. We'll go to Berantz with you at one hundred percent in case you need to put a big hurt on someone."

"Which means you need me to carry the plasma cannon."

"Exactly. The plasma cannon will put a hurt on the Ga'ee unless Heckler and Turbo came up with something better. To the range!" Payne twirled his finger.

The admiral threw his hands up.

"Was there more?" Payne asked.

The admiral scrunched his face before answering. "I guess not. Rearm, reload, repair, and be ready for the next fight."

"We're doing all that. If we can come up with a better mousetrap, we'll catch better mice." Payne twirled his finger again and headed for the exit. Mary still wouldn't hold his hand. "How long are you going to be mad at me?"

"You can't fly the galaxy by the seat of your pants!" she blurted.

Payne stopped. "I don't feel like I'm flying the galaxy. I feel like I'm hanging on for the ride."

"You're driving, whether you think so or not."

Payne moved close to corner her, but he didn't grab her, so she could move away if she wanted. "It was the right thing to do. Sometimes it's the little things that add up to be big things. We got ourselves two thousand more volunteers to crew our battlewagons. We can blockade Ga'ee space."

Mary's lips turned white from pursing them as she thought about Payne's answer.

"You're making it up as you go!"

"I am. There doesn't seem to be any training for being the leader of the seven races. There's no one to ask because it's never been done before. Flying the galaxy by the seat of my pants, huh? I guess I am. I love you, Mary."

"Is that how you end arguments?"

"I don't have anything else. I've tapped into the extent of my intellectual capacity, which reminds me. Lev, can you swap Ebren for Godilkinmore? I'm not using the Vestrall language a whole lot nowadays. At least with Ebren, I'll be able to talk to my dogs."

"They haven't been yours for fifteen months," Mary told him.

"Because I can't talk to the little hellions."

"Of course. Take your place in the captain's chair." Lev replaced the argument with a distraction.

Payne climbed onto the dais and wiggled his way into the pressure cushions until he felt like he was floating. He closed his eyes, and Lev took over.

Imagery flooded his mind. Star charts for the known universe, extending far beyond the Milky Way to where the billion stars within that seemed trivial compared to what else was out there. Advanced mathematics. The science behind the fold drive. Energy waves. His nerves tingled as if he had been filled by the electricity from a lightning bolt.

And more. Not just Ebren, but all the known languages, despite Lev's earlier warning that only one language would fit within the confines of the human brain. That had been true when human potential remained untapped. Payne's brain was getting supercharged to one hundred percent capacity, one hundred percent efficiency.

All this time, Lev had been conditioning Payne's mind for the ultimate exchange.

Payne spasmed uncontrollably. Too many stimuli. His motor controls failed. His vision went black. He remembered trying to stand before falling. He hit the dais and tumbled to the deck. The admiral threw his hands out, but it was too late. He missed catching the unconscious man.

Blood streamed from Payne's nose.

Kal rushed in and picked him up like one would lift a small child. He winced with the movement. "Going to Medical." In the corridor, they found Team Payne, shocked by the sight of the major getting carried out. A waiting cart took Kal and Declan to the nearest medical facility.

Mary, the admiral, and the commodore followed the convoy of carts.

In Medical, Kal deposited Payne in the examination room.

"You can take bed number one," Lev instructed the Ebren. "You have fractured ribs. I'll use the bone-knitter to reconstruct them."

"You don't even need to do diagnostics?"

"I have a number of scanners available to me." Lev didn't further expound. Mechanical arms moved in to tap into veins on both of Payne's arms. "Declan needs special fluids to improve his neuroreceptors and heighten the sensitivity of his neurons."

Mary jammed her fists on her hips. "What the hell did you do to him, Lev? That looked like *a lot more* than learning Ebren."

"He was concerned about not knowing what he needed to lead the seven races," Lev replied.

"And?"

"I gave him my knowledge of the universe. Everything I know."

"Isn't that more than his brain can hold? Judging by his coma, I'd say the answer is self-evident."

"It's not a coma. He has chosen to shut down his physical stimulus until he can reconcile the thoughts within his head. And no, his mind is not filled. Human brains are exceptional storage devices. Accessing the knowledge at will or in an orderly manner is the challenge. I had to rearrange some of his memories."

"Lev! I wish I could punch you in the face," Mary growled.

"That would accomplish nothing," Lev replied. "I sense your frustration, but Declan will be fine once he reconciles himself to his current state of existence."

"The leader of the seven races has an IQ of sixty million?" Mary quipped, trying to wrap her head around what it meant.

Lev laughed. "Nothing like that."

It was exactly like that, and Mary knew it.

After four hours, Payne stirred. He tried to sit up, but the bed restrained him before he could move too far. He studied the equipment around him.

"Lev, my new diet best not suck."

Mary snorted and nearly fell out of her chair with relief when her husband sounded exactly like he had before.

"Lev said you're the smartest person in the galaxy now. Are you going to prove him wrong?" Mary asked.

"The Ga'ee," Payne focused on her, "a central intelligence linked from within the ship. The levels we didn't get to because we couldn't. I saw them during the deconstruction of the one we captured. It was missing its brain, but not the one we just destroyed. A virus. Circuitry is circuitry. Shut down the transfer of information. I need to talk with Blinky and Buzz."

Payne spoke quickly, chopping off his sentences in a stream-of-consciousness disgorgement.

"If Lev taught you everything he knows, why didn't he see this stuff?"

"Same info, different perspective. Different lens through which to look. Let me send them the code for the virus while I have it." Payne closed his eyes. Five seconds later, he opened them and tried to stand.

Once more, the bed restrained him.

"Ready to go, Lev. Hungry."

"The brain burns as many calories as the rest of your body."

"Especially when it's hitting on all cylinders." Payne gave Mary the thumbs-up.

"Are you going to be insufferable? Are you going to grow tired of idiot me?" Mary asked, suddenly realizing what the gap in their intelligence meant.

No, Payne replied, using the telepathy all human brains were capable of if they knew how to tap into the ability. *You taught me what matters most in life. I'll teach you about differential equations and the engineering to fold space.*

"I can get by without doing differential equations, thank you very much," Mary countered.

"No problem. I'll do them for us." Payne stared at the floor with a blank expression. "Lev, something is wrong. I don't know how to do a differential equation."

"I assure you that you do."

"I assure you that I don't," Payne snipped. "No idea where to begin. I used to know. How do I access this newfound wealth of knowledge? The only thing that seems as easy to think about as breathing is the Ga'ee code."

Lev didn't immediately answer.

Kal grunted through the bone-knitting process.

"Is he smart or not?" Heckler asked Turbo.

She shrugged and shook her head.

"Lev?" Payne mumbled and passed out.

"Lev!" Mary shouted. "What did you do?"

"I made a mistake," Lev admitted. "The information is within Declan's mind, and his brain is working at a heightened efficiency, but the part he hadn't accessed before is closing itself off to him after a brief period of enlightenment."

"Maybe we humans like what we like. Change is hard, and change on the order of magnitude you dropped into his brain is unconscionable. How could you think that was okay?"

"He asked for it," Lev countered. "Indirectly, but within his mind, he wanted to know all there was to know, so I shared that with him."

"How do you think that turned out, Lev?" Mary stomped her foot and stormed around Payne's bed. The team moved out of her way.

"I am forced to admit that the human mind is more resilient while simultaneously being resistant to change. It is fascinating."

"Can I get my husband back the way he was?"

"I think Declan never stopped being who he was. He is subconsciously rejecting the new knowledge. Shame. It is there should he wish to access it, nonetheless."

"When a little kid asks for all the candy in the candy store, you don't give it to him!" Mary shook her fist at the ceiling.

Shaolin made a face at Byle, who turned to Turbo. "Pay attention. These are child-rearing lessons of the highest order."

"Why are you looking at me?" Heckler stared straight ahead, refusing to acknowledge the short conversation.

"How long until we're out of here, Lev?" Major Dank asked, looking for an escape.

Kal's procedure concluded. He stood and stretched. "I feel like a new man," he announced.

Payne stirred, and the attention turned back to him. Dank frowned.

"One hour," Lev replied.

"Team Payne, prepare to deploy. Get some chow and check your gear. We load up in fifty minutes," Dank ordered.

The team quietly left the medical bay to find the carts they had arrived in waiting for them. They piled in and departed for the galley on the bridge level of the ship. With few people on board, Lev had idled most of the unused space to conserve power.

Kal gently rested his hand on Mary's shoulder. "He'll be okay," he murmured before continuing in his drawl, "If you need me, just give me a shout. I'm powerful hungry, Miss Mary."

She smiled at him without humor. "I appreciate you, Kal."

He nodded once and hurried out.

"I'm still mad at you, Lev."

"I know," the AI replied.

Payne opened his eyes. "Are they gone?" he asked.

"Getting ready to deploy once we get to Berantz."

"BD18. Brayalore. I better stop goofing off, but maybe we can, you know, knock off a piece before joining them?"

Mary rolled her eyes without moving. When Payne reached for her, she agreed. It *was* a good idea.

———

Admiral Wesson faced the leader of the Ebren volunteers, whose rank was comparable to a Fleet ship captain's. "Welcome aboard. Lev, who is the ship's AI and the ship itself, will provide you with a training schedule and transport around the ship as needed. Of course, you can use the corridors for physical training as well as any of the areas designed for such activities. The real value is in the training facilities, the mock-up of the battlewagon bridge and engineering sections."

The colonel filling a ship captain's role spoke Ebren, and Lev interpreted it directly into the admiral's mind. Kal stood nearby. This was the admiral's show, but the Ebren captain turned to Kal to speak. He pointed at the admiral.

"We are honored to strike back at the ones who came to destroy us. Strike them right in their hearts!"

His deputy, who was of the same rank, laughed with a deep rumble.

"You'll get your chance," the admiral replied. "The Ga'ee will be a thorn in our side until we can convince them to avoid this sector of space. We might have to hammer them in their own sector to show them how it feels."

"We will show them. Our actions will speak what words cannot say." The captain nodded. He bowed to Kal and left the bridge with his deputy at his side.

When they were gone, the admiral asked, "Are those guys any good?"

Kal smiled. "They are the very best that Ebren has to offer. It is considered an honor to fight for the Champion. They will do you proud, but I suggest you take care with them since they will be aggressive toward the Ga'ee and anyone who attempts to hold them back from fighting the Ga'ee."

"We won't be doing that. Each hunter-killer squadron has one mission—attack the Ga'ee and destroy them. We have enough volunteers. We should probably establish a ground team on each ship in case the Ga'ee slip past and get their seeds to a planet's surface."

"I suggest you do since ground combat is what they are best suited for. Every Ebren is raised to fight. Using a ship is considered less but better than nothing."

"I'll work through the logistics," Admiral Wesson stated. "Then I'll ask the Ebren volunteers for ground teams. We'll equip them before they cross-deck to the battlewagons. We also need to make sure the battlewagons carry a shuttle to get the team to a planet's surface."

"I recommend a different design than the uglymobile." Kal returned to his drawl. "That thing is butt-ugly and would grate on the warrior spirit of any self-respecting Ebren."

The admiral had to laugh. "It says a lot about your character that you're willing to put up with butt-ugly to keep Payne out of trouble."

Kal winked at the admiral, a first for both of them, then strolled off the bridge. He needed to be ready to deploy with Team Payne, even if Payne wouldn't be there.

[26]

"When you don't see what you expect, it's time to expect the unexpected." –From the memoirs of Ambassador Declan Payne

Payne jogged from the cart to his suit to get dressed. Lev was into his ten-second countdown before folding space. The team had already boarded *Ugly 5*.

He set a record getting dressed, but it wasn't fast enough. The wave of nausea passed over him while he was half into his combat suit as the ship transitioned through the fold and into space two and a half hours at FTL speed from BD18.

Payne finished dressing and hurried to the uglymobile.

"Look what the cat dragged in!" Heckler called. He earned himself an elbow from Turbo for his jibe.

"How do you feel?" Major Dank asked.

"I have a headache. Thanks, Lev for filling my brain with bullshit like the engineering for the fold drive."

Sparky threw her hands up. "Bullshit? If you can capture that in a way we can put on our ships, you'd change the face of allied space power! One man's bullshit is another woman's single greatest advancement in history. Bullshit, you say?"

"How do you really feel?" Payne countered with a brief chuckle. "You know what I mean. I'm supposed to speak every known language, and the only word that came to mind was 'bullshit.' It's okay if you call me 'the smart guy.' I'm used to it."

"Now, *that's* bullshit," Joker offered.

The outer doors rotated down, and the tactical picture slowly populated.

"I'm not seeing any ships." Payne felt his stomach drop. "Lev, can you tell anything?"

"I can see no activity in the Brayalore system."

"Don't transmit anything. We'll maintain radio silence and make like a hole in space until such time as we have all our systems available," Payne ordered.

"Harry has given the same instructions."

Payne had jumped directly to giving the order. *I'm not the smart guy, and I'm not in charge of this ship*, he reminded himself. *Lev is, and Fleet Admiral Wesson is in charge of Fleet assets, which means he's in charge of me.*

"Stand down," Payne directed. "Two hours to rebuild our power and two and a half hours travel time. We'll rally in four hours, and hopefully, we'll have more information by then."

The insertion craft's sides rotated up and the team disembarked, leaving their helmets behind.

"Get some sleep, people. If Brayalore has been infested, we're going down there to fry some wrigglers. We'll stay down there for as long as it takes because they don't get to stay here."

"We'll be on the firing range," Heckler told him. He and Turbo quickly dressed and ran for a cart. Sparky, Joker, Shaolin, and Byle hurried after them.

Major Dank looked like he wanted to join them.

Kal picked at a tooth with his fingernail. "Maybe we can

invite some of the Ebren volunteers to join us. We have a shuttle in the portside hangar bay, along with the skimmer, *Glamorous Glennis.*"

"We do. We can arm our Ebren colleagues. In the two and a half hours it'll take to get to BD18, Lev can manufacture enough weapons for them. What would be best? That's the question." Payne nodded at Major Dank. "If you two will go and convince a few to join us in case this turns into a pest-control mission, I'd appreciate it."

Kal smiled. "The challenge is that we'll have too many volunteers. This is glory duty. Ground combat."

"The wrigglers don't shoot back on the ground. They only swarm up your body and eat your flesh."

Virgil winced. "Is that supposed to sound better?"

"I guess not." He clapped Virgil on the back to wish him luck. "I'll be on the bridge."

The others were gone by the time Payne removed his suit. Flashes of random thoughts invaded his mind. He wasn't sure if they were his or knowledge Lev had flooded into him. He considered asking to remove the information but discounted the impulse. It was like any ability; one needed to learn to control it.

Payne pulled on his jumpsuit and looked for a cart, but one wasn't instantly at his command. *Lev, can I get a cart, please?*

You can summon it yourself, Lev responded, making it clear he was using telepathy instead of fooling the mind into thinking he was speaking aloud.

"No games, Lev. I'm too tired. Send a cart for me, or I'll walk."

Walking might do you some good, Lev replied.

"It'll give me time to think. Let Mary know where I am and what I'm doing. Maybe she can join me. We take too few walks through the garden on Deck Thirty-seven or even the hydroponics bay on Deck Three. I'd appreciate the break and time to think."

"What about the admiral?"

"I'm sure he doesn't need my counsel," Payne joked. He walked into the corridor and set a brisk pace toward the bow.

Within fifteen seconds, a cart materialized, with Mary on board. She patted the seat next to her, but Payne didn't get in. "Lev says I have to walk."

I did not.

"And now he's lying about it. Lev has learned the worst lessons from humanity."

I haven't.

"Denial. Another human trait. Good effort, Lev. You're one of us."

I am not.

"So much denial." Payne shook his head. "I have some time to kill. Lev, can you take us to the botanical garden, please?"

Of course, Lev said in his most agreeable tone.

"And then, we'll be back to business. The Ga'ee have been here. I feel it. They've probably moved on to BD23. We're going to find them, and we're going to end them. If we can bring down their shield, we can hit them with a world-killer. Then they'll have a real bad day."

"We'll need to find the others. They've come to our space, and they're here to stay."

Mary hung her head while she focused on calming her breathing.

"It's a real war for our very survival. We need to buy time until we can get enough battlewagons out here to beat back the Silicon Tide."

———

266

After two hours, *Leviathan* accelerated to faster-than-light speed. Two hours and fifteen minutes later, the ship arrived at the outer edge of BD18's heliosphere. When *Leviathan* entered normal space, the scanning began.

Team Payne waited impatiently within *Ugly 5*.

They got their answer quickly. There were no ships in the system. There wasn't any debris, either.

At the admiral's word, *Leviathan* reentered FTL to arrive at Brayalore fifteen minutes later. Team Payne remained in the insertion craft, ready to go to the planet's surface if needed.

The admiral looped Team Payne into his communication with the surface. "Brayalore, this is Admiral Wesson of *Leviathan*. Please respond."

Within seconds, Air Traffic Control replied. "Brayalore welcomes you back, *Leviathan*. What brings you here? Was it news of the Ga'ee?"

"We had not heard of a new Ga'ee incursion into Berantz but suspected one. They've attacked at least three other systems of the seven races, along with an independent space station. Have they been here?"

"Yes, but we destroyed their ships when they landed, using the tools we learned from Major Payne. No infestations survived."

"Where is the cruiser and other ships assigned to Bray-alore?" the admiral wondered.

"Two cruisers preceded the Ga'ee to Blegoston, the planet you refer to as BD23."

"Are you sure the Ga'ee went to Blegoston?"

"What do you mean? Where else would they go?"

Payne shook his head and waited for the admiral to answer. "When did the Ga'ee leave Brayalore space?"

"Thirty-four hours ago."

"It takes thirty-six to get there. When did they leave? Exactly, to the second."

"Brayalore standard time, fourteen hundred hours, seventeen minutes, and thirty seconds. Is that exact enough for you?" Control replied.

Lev did the calculation. "We have a two and a half-hour cushion."

"BD23 right now, Lev. In orbit above the planet. Mosquitoes, prepare to launch." The admiral was no-nonsense. The orders had been given.

Leviathan slipped through the hole it created in space and into a high orbit of BD23. Two Berantz cruisers populated the tactical board.

Payne thought a question for Lev. *What is the status of Blinky and Buzz? You've had them sequestered for weeks. They're probably dry hulks of humanity, completely combat-ineffective. I need them with the team, Lev.*

"The team has not yet deployed since the initial contact with the new Ga'ee invasion," Lev argued.

"But soon, Lev. They were a big help on BD18 when we were trapped down there. I fear we'll get ourselves into a position where we need their expertise, and they won't be with us."

"Nothing to worry about, Declan. I believe we have most of it and can communicate our intentions in their language as well as understand what they are saying. We need more Ga'ee if we're to test our new translation and interface programming.

"I have to compliment you on your virus programming. That was truly inspired."

"Thank you. I wish I could summon genius with the flick of a switch. Genius now, please." Payne laughed to himself.

"It's there, Declan. Once you train your mind to find it, the process could be that simple."

"If I could believe that, I could probably do it. It's hard to shake the doubt, and I know that's what's holding me back. I'll figure it out. I'll probably have some righteously weird dreams, though, won't I? That crazy subconscious will be genius enough for the rest of me."

"Probably. I shall have Alphonse and Katello report to the insertion craft at the time of your choosing."

Payne thought for a moment. "Now will be good. Let's get reacquainted with our teammates. They'll be angry, so we'll get them through that adjustment period before we hit the ground running."

"The Berantz were effective at eliminating the Ga'ee threat on Brayalore before it could find purchase. I suggest Blegoston and Bindalas will be equally resilient," the admiral said.

"The Berantz are well-trained fighters and appropriately paranoid. They'll know what to do." Lev tried to sound reassuring. "The Ebren fighters could use your intervention to keep them focused on the mission at hand."

"You mean they're getting under our people's skin." Payne opened the forward hatch rather than wait for the side doors. "Gotta keep the Ebren from beating up our people." The others on the team gave him thumbs-ups. Kal jumped up from his seat and ducked out the front hatch after Payne.

The two ran toward a waiting cart. The Cabrizi raced in front of them and jumped in.

"Your dogs are lazy bastards," Payne called over his shoulder.

"Take after their human dad," Kal shot back.

Payne shook his head before squeezing into a seat. With the Cabrizi, there was no room for Kal. He barked at them in Ebren, which Payne understood perfectly.

"Get out, Thunder. Lightning, you, too. Now!"

The Cabrizi reluctantly complied. He helped them with a generous push to send them leaping from the cart.

The vehicle accelerated toward the hatch to the interior of the ship. It took a cross-corridor, and a half-kilometer away, it reached the access to the portside hangar bay. The Cabrizi weren't even breathing hard when they arrived.

An Ebren was shouting at a crew chief who was trying to get them into *Glamorous Glennis*.

Kal jumped from the cart and bellowed, "Silence!"

The Ebren warriors started at the command and backed away from the diminutive human.

Kal held his hand up. He neither needed nor wanted an explanation as to the discord sown among his fellow warriors. He spoke to them in a commanding voice. "I've ridden in this ship. It's uncomfortable as fuck all, but you're going to squeeze in there and get ready to go. Stop your whining. What are you, a bunch of green recruits?"

The colonel turned ship captain had been the one yelling and was appropriately chastised, which he hadn't expected. He had been establishing dominance, as was the Ebren way. His face twitched as he tried to reconcile himself with the new chain of command. The order of things had given him an opportunity to prove his mettle, but it came with a demotion. He was no more than a squad leader now, when days earlier, he had commanded a regiment-sized unit.

"Get in the ship," the captain ordered with an angry wave.

"Thank you, Captain, for volunteering your expertise on this mission. I know it isn't easy. Do you know who I am?" Payne asked.

"You are the Champion, and with Kal'faxx, the two greatest warriors on Ebren."

"I also command only a squad. Twelve of us, fighting for a single purpose. Do you know what that is?"

The captain was stumped by the question, but when he answered, it was the most Ebren of attitudes. "Honor."

"We fight for each other," Payne clarified. "When we're down there, and everything on a planet is trying to kill us, it comes down to the simple truth of survival. We will accomplish the mission or die trying, sure, but it comes down to keeping the team intact and moving forward."

The captain marshaled his expression, keeping it neutral. "I understand."

Payne wasn't sure he did, but he was no longer yelling at the crew chief. Payne switched back to English when he talked to the crew chief. He was surprised to find a familiar face.

"Federico. Good to see you." It was Sparky's friend. "If you have any other issues, don't hesitate to let me or Kal know."

Fifty Ebren warriors hovered near the bulkhead, taking in the entire exchange. Kal pointed at them, and they looked away.

Payne added, "You shouldn't have any problems with them."

"You speak Ebren?"

"It makes being the Ebren Champion much easier." Payne clapped the young man on the back. "I'll tell Sparky you said hi."

He nodded in reply.

Payne and Kal moved to the cart and found the Cabrizi in their seats. "Shall we walk?" Payne suggested. "I find it cathartic."

"Are you trying to swear off your lazy ways, Declan?" Kal quipped.

"I'm sure that's it. I need to think, and Lev has taken great pleasure in setting speed records with the carts. It's all I can do to hang on for dear life."

"I thought it was just me," Kal noted.

Payne set a brisk pace toward the starboard hangar bay. The Cabrizi hopped out of the cart and ran ahead, indifferent to whether they were riding in a cart or not. "Maybe they're opportunists. Thunder and Lightning, huh? You can tell them apart?"

"Not at all. They're together, so I just yell at both of them. The one that responds to Lightning is Lightning."

"Easy as that?"

"Like you might say, it's the best I got."

"I like the new you, Kal. Don't lose your edge."

They made the rest of the walk in silence.

"One thing, Declan. I hate the Ga'ee. They're not like fighting a normal enemy. There is no gratification in killing one or a thousand."

"It's like we're taking antibiotics to kill an infection. They are intelligent creatures but garner as much empathy as bacteria."

"Does that make us the bad guys, or them?" Kal asked.

"If we could answer that, we wouldn't be able to do what we do. I wish they were willing to share, but it's not in their nature. I don't like having to call for their complete eradication."

The team stood by the equipment cage, eating faux jerky while Blinky and Buzz dressed.

Payne pointed with his chin. "Shall we say hi to the strangers?"

The two strolled over casually while the impatient Cabrizi ran circles around them.

Blinky looked ready to fall asleep even though he was standing up. He wavered like a stalk of grain in a light breeze.

"You going to make it?" Payne wondered.

"I don't remember the last time I was in my bed," he mumbled.

Buzz stood staring into the distance. Payne waved his hand in front of his face. He didn't blink. Payne looked at Major Dank. "Is he asleep?"

"I think he is."

"Okay, buttholes," Payne barked. "Get to your quarters and go to bed. You're combat-ineffective. Lev, you fall under the same name. You are a butthole."

"Thank you. You speak the term with such affection. It makes me tingle all over," Lev replied.

The team turned away to keep from laughing in Payne's face.

"Sir?" Blinky asked.

Payne slapped Buzz on the arm. He snapped back to the present. "You two. Quarters and bed. Get some sleep. We'll pick you up before we do anything important. Until then, we'll limit our activities to knuckle-dragger stuff."

"What?" Blinky looked perplexed.

"Come with me," Virgil stepped up and guided the two out of their suits and toward the cart that had followed Payne and Kal.

Once they were in the cart, the two waved with limp arms.

Lev, you're killing me, man. Payne stood firm.

I am not, Lev replied. *I'm doing everything I can to keep us all alive.*

You knew they couldn't operate with us, not in that condition. You drained them completely. Are you on your own program?

I have always been on my own program, Declan. I thought you understood that. Sometimes our paths are the same, and we travel together. Other times, they are not, and you travel with me.

Now, that I know. Wait a minute. I thought you said I was very convincing?

You are. Sometimes you've convinced me to change my direction.

But it's still your way. Payne selected a spot next to his gear and sat down. *Is every conversation an argument?*

When you have an IQ of six million, you assume others are arguing when they don't go along with what you want.

We've been over this tired old ground before, Lev. I haven't changed, and I stand by my earlier statement. I wholeheartedly and one hundred percent agree with myself.

That I'm a butthole?

Certified prime.

Admiral Wesson requests your presence on the bridge, Lev relayed.

[27]

"When the challenges overwhelm you, step back and let those who support you handle them." –From the memoirs of Ambassador Declan Payne

"The Berantz are unable to stop the Ga'ee," Admiral Wesson explained. "They lost two cruisers before the others ran ahead. These are the last two surviving Berantz combat ships. The Ga'ee destroyed the new-construction vessels before they ever got off the ground."

"Send them ahead. We'll deal with the Ga'ee by stuffing a world-killer right up their asses," Payne suggested. "What do you think, Lev? Can you take them, *mano a mano?*"

"I'm happy that you're talking with me once more, Declan. That was a most uncomfortable three minutes." Lev waited while Payne made faces. "We can deconstruct their shield and send a world-killer into their ship. That will destroy them. I suggest that if we can hit first, we can take out the ship and leave the brain intact. With that central brain, we'll be able to learn what we need to know about their motivations. That would bring us that much closer to ending their incursion."

"We can't just end them," Payne mused. "High risk, high reward. We wouldn't have our missions any other way. How do you think we'll accomplish this bit of sleight-of-hand?"

"Plasma bombs. We need to eliminate their drone complement without damaging the interior of the ship."

"I suspect we have plasma bombs. Otherwise, you wouldn't have suggested it."

"We don't, but I can construct them between the time my internal manufacturing processes become available and when the Ga'ee arrive."

Payne and the admiral waited. Lev didn't explain further.

"There's a but in there, Lev. I can feel it."

"I won't be able to manufacture sufficient quantities, so we'll have to keep the Ga'ee carrier buttoned up during the process."

Payne sighed and glanced at the admiral, then faced the tactical board. "Load the Mosquitoes with tactical nukes," the admiral ordered. "Lev will take down their screen and we'll irradiate the outside of the ship, especially the hangar bay doors, to make it too dangerous to open them."

The plan made sense since they wouldn't have the real weapons they needed until later.

"Maybe the Ga'ee didn't come this way," Payne mused.

"The only other choice was that they went to BH01, the Berantz homeworld. But I think they started there, and we'll find that the Berantz no longer have a home planet. Otherwise, the Ga'ee would have been at BD18 much sooner than just a few hours ago. This attack was coordinated, and the timing was impeccable. We couldn't be everywhere at once. The arrival coincided with our being in the Vestrall home system." The admiral was convinced he was correct, and he convinced everyone else.

"Then we need to find how they communicate across the galaxy. Even with our FTL code and Godilkinmore technology, we can't do that. The ship we captured had to have that capability because they somehow received the 'go' signal," Payne continued. "You need to find out how they did that, Lev. You've been in the guts of their system for weeks. Do you have anything?"

Lev scrolled coding across the main screen. Binary, Ga'ee-style, then their language. Payne understood it all. "They received the signal, but there's nothing to show how. Did that ship not have a transmitter?"

"What if they had empty ships to distract *Leviathan* at various points in interstellar space? All of them waiting for the order, depending on where we showed up. Scroll back." Payne moved close, took control of the coding, and moved it around the screen with the power of his mind. He removed the tactical picture to focus on the carrier's action sequences, not much more than a series of if-then statements creating a cascade of nested commands. "They can see energy vibrations in space, too, but their whole ship is the receiver."

"I can see it now," Lev replied. "*Leviathan*'s signature was the target to trigger the actions. With a ten-kilometer-long receiving station, they extend the range of what they can see far beyond what I can see, but at the last stop, I added the dampeners they used in their ship. The Ga'ee won't know I am here."

"That gives us a distinct advantage." The admiral grinned. "Surprise is ours. Get me the captain of the lead Berantz cruiser, please."

The reply was immediate. "Krakenorr of the heavy cruiser *Poramir*. What insane plan do you have this time?"

The admiral nodded at Payne since he knew the good captain. "Payne here. Good to hear your voice, Captain. We need you to take the two cruisers out of here. We will face the Ga'ee alone."

"I knew it would be insane. We shall continue to Bindalas and warn them. How will we know of your success?"

"We will send an FTL message. If you don't get one, you can assume we lost the battle."

The admiral's smile disappeared. Payne gave him the thumbs-up and a reassuring look.

"We shall expect your signal. Krakenorr out."

In less than a minute, the two cruisers pointed their noses at a nearby star, around which orbited the planet called Bindalas, known by the humans as BD27.

"Now we wait." The admiral slumped.

"We've been doing a lot of that lately," Payne replied. "Lev, when are the five battlewagons going to get to BD18?"

"Five more days."

"Is it safe to assume the Ga'ee know they're coming?"

"Of course."

Payne and the admiral sat down. Mary entered the bridge, and the Cabrizi welcomed her while Kal leaned against the captain's chair. Nyota sat at a terminal and looked over the timelines she'd been using to track the ships as they moved extreme distances using faster-than-light speed.

The front screen returned to the tactical picture. The two Berantz cruisers were headed away from the BD23 system. "You can't see the battlewagons yet?"

"Any time now," Lev announced. The main screen zoomed out to show a great amount of the sector, at least twelve parsecs.

"Project five days' travel from Brayalore and put that line on the board," Payne requested.

The line was well within the farthest view of the board.

"Where'd they go?" Payne wondered.

"Did they go to BH01?" the admiral guessed. "Project that trajectory from Earth."

A new line appeared that touched the edge of the space on

the screen. Lev reduced the star map further, and the projected course to BH01 clarified. Payne waved at the board. "They'd be out of range for us to see them."

"The good news is that they'll see whether the Ga'ee have already been there before us. Hopefully, they'll send an FTL message with their report. Secondarily, we don't need them at BD18. The Berantz held their own."

The admiral clasped his hands behind his back and stared at the deck as he paced. "Countdown to full power."

The thermometer they'd grown used to appeared on the screen. One hour and forty minutes. Projected time of the Ga'ee's arrival was thirty minutes later. They had plasma bombs to build.

"Are you out of raw materials yet?" Payne wondered.

"No. I still have plenty, Declan. I have enough to make all the plasma bombs I need as well as fabricate parts for repair should we need them."

"Ominous, Lev." Payne watched the admiral pace. He wanted to join him, but one of them needed to look like they weren't anxious.

"Status of the Mosquito squadron," the admiral requested.

"Rearming now," a voice replied.

"Is that you, Woody?" Payne asked.

"All over it, Mister Ambassador," the commander responded. "We'll be ready in about fifteen minutes. We already had half the ships configured for ground bombardment. What's the mission?"

"You're going to splash the Ga'ee carrier with nukes to keep it from launching drones. A series of strikes. If you can damage the outer doors, we'll have them right where we want them. Lev is fabricating plasma bombs to destroy the drones while they're in the hangar bays."

"Audacious. Auspicious. May I ask why we aren't blowing

that thing to kingdom come since we can get through their shields?"

"We need its brain," Payne replied simply.

"Why didn't you just say so? Life is pretty simple when all you need to do is get past a hundred and sixty thousand drones and a ten-kilometer-long ship to reach a brain that's probably embedded so deep, you have to cut the ship apart to get to it, but not so deep that if you destroy the ship, it won't be destroyed, too. How am I doing?"

"Like you're inside my head."

"If you could have gotten to the brain on the empty ship, you would have. Since you didn't, that explains it. Also, the empty ship probably didn't have one because it didn't need one."

"All of that and more, Woody. I owe you a bottle of a good single malt directly from Scotland next time we get back to Earth."

"I'm going to hold you to that, but it's been so long since I had anything to drink, even a bad blend will taste good."

"Look to launch in about ninety mikes. Be ready to scatter and wait. We'll need to hit it hard and fast. Lev will try to talk with it first, but that'll take a few seconds is all."

"We'll be ready." Woody signed off.

Mary looked at Declan with a knowing eye. "You're going over to that ship, aren't you?"

"Probably not," Payne replied. "After getting splashed by a bunch of nukes and fried by plasma bombs, I doubt our suits will be up to keeping us alive. It will be inhospitable on whatever remains of that ship, but the brain should survive. Then Lev is going to put on his surgeon's gown and perform a brainectomy."

"Six million IQ, and you came up with 'brainectomy?'"

"What else would it be?"

Mary scowled at him. "Something else, like cranial-rectal inversion."

Payne smiled. "I'm sure that's it."

"FTL transmission of neural wavelengths," Lev blurted. "Stand by."

Five seconds later, the Ga'ee ship appeared on the tactical screen. "Time projection should the Ga'ee transit directly to BD23 is ninety-seven minutes. We have their course, and assuming they don't see us, I recommend the fighters deploy to these locations," two boxes appeared on the screen, "to bracket the inbound ship and hit it the instant it reenters normal space."

"Pass the recommendation to Commander Malone," the admiral requested. "Another race to the finish."

"In the last few skirmishes, we didn't give the Ga'ee time to get off a warning message, did we?" Commodore Freeman wondered

"Would that be a bad thing?" Payne asked in reply. "They are killing us! So if we counterpunch hard, killing their ships, one after another, it could give the rest pause. In this sector, the Ga'ee are losing. Even if they're in ten thousand-star systems, they haven't faced *us* before. *Leviathan* rises to deliver an epic race-wide beat-down. You have ten thousand systems. Don't get greedy, you wriggly little bastards. By the way, we didn't compliment you properly on your revelation. You can see that they're sending thought waves via FTL?"

"Faster than FTL," Lev corrected.

"FFTL," Payne offered. Mary shook her head while suppressing a smile.

"We took the receiver from the Ga'ee ship. I didn't understand how to use it. I only needed to run it through the right process while getting a transmission. We couldn't see anything before because there was nothing to see when we tried it."

"But now there is. Make sure you can replicate it for all our ships. We need everyone to be able to record those transmissions. Can you tell what they're saying?"

"Yes."

"Come on, Lev. Don't make us play twenty questions," Payne begged.

"Two systems left to convert, four angle seven."

"Start building a reference diagram, and let's figure out their coordinate system," the admiral directed needlessly. Lev was already on it. He had his first data point from which to establish a baseline.

"I'm glad they think they're untouchable and don't encrypt their shit," Payne remarked. "Lev, you are the greatest ship in all the galaxy."

"I humbly accept that title. I think we make a good team."

Even though Lev was on his own program, it overlapped with humanity's needs.

A warship built to keep the peace.

"Nine angle three is complete," Lev announced. "That is a new signal coming from the direction of Zuloon space. Twelve angle twelve is complete. Coming from Arn space."

"Extrapolate and build a grid. You have three data points."

"Running through a series of three-dimensional constructs, but I do not have enough data to draw meaningful conclusions. I'm sorry."

"We have a lot more information than we had five minutes ago. Thanks, Lev. Can we broadcast using their system?"

"Yes."

"We'll save that for later, but it's a good tool to have in the box. Better they don't know we have it."

"Like the surprise they're going to get when they find us here?"

"Exactly that. The big scary ship appears like magic, with a flashing mirror-ball sign that says GO HOME."

"We probably want to tell them that at some point. Go home, or you will be destroyed. You and all your offspring, and we're willing to shatter whole planets to reinforce our threat."

"I will attempt to communicate with them since we have most of their language in a form we can understand. It is a complex communication system where nothing we know about spoken languages applies. It's data-intense, with limited syntax."

Payne nodded. He had lost interest. He didn't care how the language worked, just that Lev could communicate using it.

"Shall we?" Payne asked Mary.

"What?"

"Go visit the garden, of course."

Mary shook her head as if she hadn't heard what he said. "Twice in two days?"

"Shh!" Payne put a finger to his lips. "They'll think we're talking about sex."

"Lev. We're good. He's no different," Mary held up two fingers in the peace sign.

"Personality and a mind-bending IQ are different animals. If I grew up super smart, maybe I'd be a dork, but thank goodness I'm not."

"We clearly have different definitions of the word 'dork.'" She took his hand, and they strolled out as if they didn't have a care in the world.

"I like that he's not worried," the admiral commented. "I'm worried enough for both of us."

[28]

"When the enemy shows no mercy, teach him what mercy means since he needs to know—right before you scatter his atoms into the void." –From the memoirs of Ambassador Declan Payne

"Helmets on," Payne ordered. The team was in their usual seats, except for Blinky and Buzz. They were still in near-comas because of exhaustion. Lev had gotten the most from them over the course of three weeks, and they'd decrypted the Ga'ee language.

With the vibration dampeners and neural transmission interceptions, *Leviathan* had a distinct advantage.

A war-changing advantage.

But the Ga'ee had done a great deal of damage to the sector. Were the Arn and Zuloon gone? *Leviathan* would have to travel to those systems and verify. There were no other colonies of those races. What about the Rang'Kor? They hadn't been heard from since PX47.

Too many unknowns, and space was a big place that kept its secrets.

The tactical screen showed the inbound Ga'ee ship. Its transmissions continued, giving Lev everything he needed to keep track. It repeated its message directionally. Sometimes they heard it, and other times they didn't. When they could hear the broadcast, Lev was able to pinpoint the carrier's location.

Three...two...one.

Payne's chest tightened. The Ga'ee ship returned to normal space where they'd expected it to. The Mosquitoes instantly engaged. Payne had to think that the pilots were shocked by the reality of a ten-kilometer-long ship appearing right in front of them.

"Shield is down," Lev announced.

The first two Mosquitoes accelerated toward the Ga'ee ship to toss their nuclear bombs at the target. These weren't nuclear-tipped missiles but conventional bombs, also called 'dumb' bombs. The Mosquitoes weren't designed to carry anti-ship missiles large enough to affect a ship of the Ga'ee carrier's size and configuration.

There was no need on this mission since they'd been able to close with the ship and surprise it. With enough acceleration and a precise release, the bombs went where they needed to go. If a high-yield anti-ship missile had been required, the big ships would have launched those.

The mission the Mosquitoes were on had never been contemplated by the original designers. They could launch missiles, but only those with a smaller payload.

They had not yet reconfigured the Mosquitoes to carry heavy anti-ship missiles, but after this operation, they would.

The fleet needed the versatility of a heavy-duty multi-function space fighter.

The first two bombs exploded seven seconds after the ship's arrival in orbit over BD23. The shock wave dissipated quickly but sent their delivering ships tumbling away from the target. The two Mosquitoes recovered and circled behind the formation while the second pair of fighters began their attack run. The fighters only carried one bomb each, but their cannons were available should any of the drones launch.

If it became a battle of attrition, the Mosquitoes would do the best they could to uphold their end until *Leviathan* delivered its munitions. If the big ship didn't, the Mosquitoes would be overwhelmed and destroyed.

Every battle with the Ga'ee came down to life or death.

The second bombs exploded against the opening hangar bay doors. Then a third and fourth wave of attacks hit the Ga'ee ship.

Lev spoke to the Ga'ee ship at the speed of light.

"Clear the impact area," Lev announced ominously. The Mosquitoes turned tail and ran before the fifth wave began their attack run.

Two missiles flushed from *Leviathan*'s upper launchers and accelerated toward the enemy carrier. One angled around the port side while the other maneuvered toward the starboard side. They fired the last of their propellant on their final approach and smashed through the hangar doors before exploding and sending a wash of burning plasma down the kilometers-long hangar bays.

The Ga'ee carrier attempted to turn but slid drunkenly, as if its attitude thrusters had fired randomly.

The second wave of missiles launched to continue the work the first had started. The gyrating ship made for a more difficult target than what the first two missiles faced, but the majority of the damage had been done.

The second missiles accelerated, but their final approach was slower, demonstrating greater maneuverability to correct alignment and reach an optimal impact point. The engines lit up, and the missiles raced in through the outer doors and tore into the hangar bays to deliver a second round of devastation.

Infrared scanners showed an intense glow in both hangar bays as the plasma continued to burn.

The heat started to dissipate much more quickly than it should have.

"Are the doors open to space?" Payne wondered. A salvo of Rapiers launched and arced toward the Ga'ee ship. They accelerated, showing as bright lines on the tactical board.

The Ga'ee carrier rotated to present one side to *Leviathan*, angling its nose away from the planet.

"It's going to run," Dank stated.

The Rapiers continued to accelerate until they slammed into the aft end and the engines with a combined heat wave and concussion designed to take engines offline without overloading the reactors. The ship shook from the massive vibration, and the aft end sagged from the warped metal.

The Ga'ee carrier lost attitude control and forward acceleration. Drones appeared, streaming individually from a gap in the hangar door.

"Take them out one by one and get me eyeballs on where they're coming from!" Woody transmitted.

The Mosquitoes executed a formation turn, then sections comprised of four spacecraft accelerated through the turn and headed back to the Ga'ee ship. They broke into lead and wingman flights to attack the drones.

"They're heading for the planet," Payne offered. "They've conceded that they can't win this fight, so they're executing their primary mission."

"My thoughts exactly," the admiral replied over the channel. "Lev, get us between that ship and the planet."

On the tactical board, *Leviathan* moved at an agonizingly slow pace.

A four-craft section of Mosquitoes attacked the far side of the Ga'ee ship. The small opening allowed only a trickle of drones through, and the drones had no interest in the space fighters.

Still, they would soon outnumber the Tricky Spinsters and would punch through the section.

"Lev?" Payne wondered.

"Collecting their transmission." A few seconds later, Lev followed up, "I have it all. God One. No escape. Colonies dispatched."

"'Colonies dispatched.' Apropos," Payne said. "They know you're of Godilkinmore manufacture."

"That is a disconcerting development," Lev replied. The ship's icon picked up speed to intercept the drones heading toward the planet's surface. Two more missiles with plasma warheads erupted from *Leviathan* and raced toward the disabled Ga'ee vessel.

"Big bucket of fuck-your-drones coming via the Starshine Express," Heckler intoned, to minor applause from the team.

The missiles raced in and slammed into the hangar bays.

"How about a warning next time, bitch!" a pilot snarled through the noise.

"Secure that," Woody ordered. "While you're there, toss your bomb through that opening."

"That's not a big hole, and the ship is corkscrewing through space. Not fast, but it makes for a tough shot."

"Then get closer. *Leviathan* is fresh out of missiles, so no one's going to rock your day. Get in there with the Holy Hand Grenade and shove it right down their throat."

"Roger," came the uninspired reply.

"That won't take the ship out as long as it explodes in the hangar bay," the admiral hoped.

Mosquitoes flashed through space, firing their ion cannons

at drones attempting to get through the mini-blockade. Lev cleaned up the few that got past with defensive missile fire. The birds homed in on the drones with relentless accuracy.

A new salvo of Rapier-class missiles flushed from *Leviathan's* upper tubes.

"Move clear of the bow," the admiral transmitted. "We're going to rip its head off without killing the brain."

It was taking too long to manufacture the plasma warheads. The ship would take action sooner than Lev could execute the original plan.

The admiral had adjusted on the fly with a new plan. Whittle the ship down until nothing remained except the brain.

"Prepare to launch *Ugly 5*," the admiral ordered. IR scans showed that the hangar bay was cool enough for Team Payne to operate.

"We can't get to where the brain is," Sparky noted.

"No, but we can get to the reactors and shut them down one by one until all that's left is the one providing power to the thing's brain. Then Lev will cut up that ship until he has secured the mind of the enemy," Payne explained. "You may have to sit this one out, Kal."

"I can handle the heat," Kal replied.

"This isn't normal heat. There's radiation and plasma."

Kal thought about it and decided Payne was right. The Cabrizi were on board too, in case the team went to the planet.

"Can't take them either." Payne pointed at the Cabrizi.

Kal worked his way to the forward hatch. "I'll be taking my leave now and impatiently awaiting your return, my friends," the Ebren drawled.

He exited and sealed the hatch behind him.

"And then there were eight..." Heckler continued, using his public announcer voice.

"Mission. We isolate the brain by taking five reactors offline.

Simultaneous removal from service. Lev, closeup of the Ga'ee ship, please, emphasis on IR."

The screen focused on the forward and aft ends of the ship, which had been pummeled hard by the Rapiers, the plasma strikes, and the nukes.

"There's only two plants left online," Sparky said. "And we know how to get to the forward one. Just need to mash the little button and stroll up to it. We can use a plasma cannon to blast it."

"Or we can show a Mosquito where to aim its cannon," Payne suggested.

"Even better," Sparky replied. "All we need is some fluorescent paint."

"Launch Team Payne," the admiral ordered. The insertion craft lifted off and accelerated out of the hangar bay. It quickly covered the short distance to the Ga'ee ship and slowed to maneuver into the ship, but the openings were too small.

"We have a perfectly good missile that isn't doing anything. What do you say we put it to good use, Lev?" Payne didn't want to waste more time.

The insertion craft backed away and fired from a range of danger-close. The missile exploded almost immediately, ripping off a section of the door and buckling the impact area. The inside glowed with the unnatural light of burning plasma far down the bay.

Ugly 5 accelerated through the opening but moved slowly once inside, angling toward the access panel to the third reactor from the aft end of the craft.

The aft end of the bay had been ravaged by the Rapiers. It was twisted and nearly unnavigable. *Ugly 5* shifted and twisted through the maze of a torn and dying ship, its bays filled with shattered drones.

"There's no way a fighter can get in here," Payne

remarked. "We'll take care of it. Heckler, you and Turbo have the plasma cannon. Set it up, and Sparky and I will open the door. Everyone else is on perimeter security. Unlike last time, there are wrigglers on board this ship, and the drones might still be alive and kicking. Don't give them a chance to get close."

"I can maneuver the ship no farther, Declan," Lev reported. *Leviathan* was close enough for him to maintain direct control over the insertion craft. The team enjoyed the power of *the* big ship's AI in a space little larger than a storage room. "Seventy meters to the access."

"Load up, people." Payne hefted his railgun, verified the ammo load, and executed a quick function check, which he had also done when he took the weapon out of the equipment cage. It was standard procedure, and it was that way for a reason.

A hard lesson paid for in blood when a weapon failed when it was needed most.

The outer doors rotated up, and the temperature rapidly increased. In this part of the hangar bay waited a lethal dose of radiation—a thousand rems and holding steady.

"Let's get this thing done and get out of here," Payne ordered. "I'll take point."

Heckler gestured for Sparky to stay close to Major Payne while he and Turbo brought the plasma cannon and tripod. Major Dank, Joker, Byle, and Shaolin had their backs by establishing a perimeter around *Ugly 5*, blocking the way to the route they would take to the access panel.

Payne moved forward, using the barrel of his weapon to clear refuse hanging from above and kicking metal debris out of his path. Behind him, the covering group took their positions and verified their fields of fire.

Dank fired first and Joker an instant later at a drone that materialized from the mist and smoke. It accelerated toward them. Two more railguns added their firepower to blast the drone and crash it into nearby debris.

A second one appeared with more behind it, coming through a narrow opening. The team fired in unison, cycling their weapons to sustain a high rate of rounds headed downrange.

"Better hurry up, Dec. It's hot in here, and I don't mean the rads."

"Rolling," Payne replied ambiguously. He tried to increase his pace, but it was impossible. There was a significant amount of damage in this section of the ship. He pushed through where he could, but it was slow going.

The sound of constant railgun fire filled the space behind him.

Payne pushed his suit to the limit and hit the twisted metal using his body as a battering ram. He powered through, ramming into a cascade of metal from an upper deck. He grunted with his augmented effort to move it aside. The debris screamed in protest until it yielded and crashed down around him.

"Sir!" Sparky shouted over the team channel. She let her railgun drop on the sling and tore at the metal with her gloved hands. Heckler and Turbo stopped and waited. They didn't have a free hand to help.

Payne pushed upward to free himself.

"That sucked," he proclaimed. "Keep moving."

Sparky kicked metal plates aside and continued through. "Take it easy with the overheads."

"I just want to get there and lay waste to that power plant." Payne took two more steps. "Up ahead. I think I see it."

The destruction cleared as they approached the bulkhead. Payne scanned it to confirm he was in the right area, then hurried forward and scraped a big X on the panel.

"Heckler and Turbo, you're up. Make it quick."

"We're always quick when we get to blow shit up." Heckler lifted the cannon and aligned it while Turbo slammed the tripod to the deck. Heckler dropped the plasma cannon's pintle into the mount. He set it to manual and fired. His first rounds impacted high and to the right. He blasted to the center and continued firing through the hole he'd created.

"Power plant is still online," Sparky reported.

Dank came online. "Running low on ammo. Now would be a good time to finish the job."

"Doing the best we can, Virge. Joker and I are on our way. Break, break. Heckler, keep pounding that thing until it dies. We'll be covering your six."

"Pounding away. Might have to move closer."

Payne and Sparky were running back the way they came.

The crossfire through the limited access kept the drones coming single file until they learned that they needed a broader access. They started hitting the barrier to widen the opening.

"Cease fire," Dank ordered. He directed Byle and Shaolin to new firing positions. "Fire."

The crossfire filled a greater area, splattering the pairs of drones that worked their way through the enlarged opening.

The drones continued to come, and the SOFTies continued to fire.

Payne and Sparky cleared the debris field and ran around *Ugly 5*. Once they had a clear line of sight, they set up and fired, hitting the drones with fresh, fully automatic hypervelocity rounds.

The plasma cannon hammered rhythmically but stopped all of a sudden.

"Cleared a path, heading in," Heckler reported. He and Turbo shared lugging the cannon and trundled from the hangar bay into the corridor. It went faster than if Heckler carried it, but at nowhere near the speed Kal could achieve while carrying the plasma cannon.

Payne aimed and fired, stepping back from the cyclic rate. The debris from blasted drones was piled waist-high. More pushed through to suffer a similar fate.

Joker and Dank retreated into *Ugly 5* for reloads. They quickly reemerged and handed an extra magazine each to Byle and Shaolin.

Payne continued to fire.

A sudden change came over the hangar bay. Payne couldn't put his finger on it. The drones stopped coming. In the distance, movement surged toward the door.

"They're heading into space," Payne reported. "Hit them. Hit them now!"

Payne hadn't needed to say anything. That was the moment Woody's people had been expecting. An atomic blast washed over the ship and into the bay. Shattered metal rode the front of the blast wave and crashed into Team Payne. Shaolin and Byle were slammed into *Ugly 5,* along with enough debris to block the craft from leaving the bay. Payne, Sparky, Joker, and Dank were caught up in the wave and disappeared beyond the insertion craft.

"Shit!" Heckler shouted. "Everything is blocked."

Payne grumbled while climbing to his feet. He checked his HUD to find the entire team was alive and in the green, despite elevated heart rates.

"I have you all five by five. Thank you for surviving. We'll leave *Ugly 5* behind and egress down the tunnel, past the blown power plant, and out the other side."

"What if the other side looks like this?" Major Dank asked.

"Then we have some clearing work to do while we're waiting for our new ride. Lev, send in the maintenance bots and start tearing this mess out of here."

"Will do as soon as we deal with the drones heading toward the planet. They surged toward the remaining ships, nearly five thousand of them."

"Send the Ebren teams planetside," Payne recommended.

"Harry directed that. We'll need *Ugly 5* to help with the transport."

"That would be a problem," Payne replied. "We might as well go planetside, too. All hands get thrown into the fire."

"Are we going out the port or the starboard side?" Heckler wondered.

"We'll clear a path to you, but we'll have to wait for Lev to clear the hangar debris since we need our ship. To answer your question, starboard side."

"It's pretty grim over here," Heckler replied. "Can we use the plasma cannon?"

"Stand by." Payne checked his HUD and the map of the Ga'ee ship. "Hug the forward bulkhead, and we won't be in your line of fire."

"Rock on." Ten seconds later, the plasma cannon lit up the blockage. The impacts reverberated to where Payne was embroiled in wreckage.

He tore at the metal hanging from the overhead and built a platform upon which he could stand. There was more metal than they could move out of the way, so he conceded the low ground to the debris.

Sparky followed his lead and was able to create a path to him. "Go vertical," Payne ordered. He gestured at the near side of the uglymobile, and the two started clearing a path to board.

Byle and Shaolin climbed over the top of the ship and slid down, using their pneumatic jets to soften their landings.

Dank and Joker made noise beyond the forward end of the ship as they worked to get free.

"I'm heading toward the corridor," Payne reported. He

climbed onto the path he'd started and moved forward, working slowly but surely toward the cavity Heckler and Turbo were making with the plasma cannon. "Cease fire."

The thundering stopped. "Would you look at that? A tunnel out of this hellhole." Heckler whistled.

Payne scanned the area to find that he only had to build another five meters. He started ripping into the metal shards and hammered the newly fallen pieces under his heavy boots.

When he broke through, he found Heckler and Turbo lying in a rounded tunnel. "Come on out of there. You look like dead rats in a sewer."

"Better than *being* a dead rat in a sewer," Heckler countered. He pushed Turbo forward, and she crawled through on her knees. Payne helped her stand. Heckler cleared the space and joined them.

They retreated to *Ugly 5* and climbed in through the forward hatch. The last ones in were Dank and Joker. The team sat there looking at each other. They'd have to decontaminate the suits before they could take their helmets off. Limited food in the form of protein bars and water was available, but they weren't as good as the stuff on the outside, which was now contaminated.

"Damn Ga'ee take all the joy out of life," Heckler whined.

No one disagreed.

"Update," Payne requested.

"The Ga'ee drones are destroyed. Nine achieved intra-atmospheric descent and were dealt with by Berantz fighter aircraft. Blegoston is clear," Lev reported.

"I bet the Ebren are disappointed," Payne replied.

"But the Mosquito pilots were quite pleased with the live-fire against an active enemy."

"I'm sure they were. Can you cut us out of the belly of this beast?"

"Maintenance and fabrication units are on their way to cut out the central core, the brain of a live Ga'ee ship. I will park the raw material of the ship in a geostationary orbit for future use."

"Sounds good, Lev. We'll sit back and try to relax while we wait. Which is going to be how long?" Payne pressed.

"Twenty minutes. Maybe two hours."

Payne frowned. "Lev, I think you're learning the wrong lessons from humanity."

"Twenty minutes, then," Lev clarified.

Payne slouched until he was mostly reclined and closed his eyes. At least they'd be going straight home and not diverting to the planet's surface.

Next stop, the Zuloon homeworld.

[29]

"How we feel is nothing compared to what we do."
–From the memoirs of Ambassador Declan Payne

Lev tempered their arrival into unknown space by appearing in interstellar space two hours and fifteen minutes from the Zuloon homeworld. As members of the Braze Collective, they fought alongside the others against humanity at the direction of the misguided Vestrall, who thought of the war as a hobby.

Payne had set them straight. The Zuloon and the Arn were not rabid warriors. They didn't exist in great enough numbers, like the Ebren or the Rang'Kor, to field a massive fleet. Besides their home planet, they maintained a number of other 'homes' they considered their own, not colonies. On one other world in the system and on another planet orbiting a neighboring star a mere four light-years away.

"No emissions and no ships," the admiral reported softly. The tactical board showed clear. The neural transmissions were missing.

"Looks like the system is clear, but what are we going to find on the planet?" Payne wondered.

"We'll see in four hours."

The admiral's shoulders sagged, and his hair looked grayer than before.

"You look tired," Payne told him.

"Is it that obvious?" the admiral replied more sarcastically than he'd intended. "I'm afraid of what we're going to find out here."

"I've reconciled myself to it. We could not have done anything more. No one knew the Ga'ee would launch a coordinated attack like this. No one. *They* killed these people, not us. We can feel horrible, but we're also going to do something about it. Hell, we've been doing all we can."

"Battlewagons abound, and we'll be able to protect the systems from new incursions, but how long until the Ga'ee adjust and learn how to defeat the Payne-class weapons?" The admiral dropped into a seat and leaned his elbows on the workstation before him. He made a bridge with his hands and rested his chin on it.

"When they do, we'll adjust too, but we're hitting them hard and across a wide front. They've never encountered a ship like *Leviathan* before and may never recover. They call him 'God One.'" Payne smiled.

"All we need is to jam their signal and prevent the disparate ships from talking," the admiral suggested. "It's also good to know what they're saying."

Payne shook his head. "You can't have it both ways, Admiral."

"Collecting intelligence might be moot once the Ga'ee brain is analyzed." The admiral had been pushing Lev since the AI had tucked the core and its power supply into the starboard hangar bay with the other six reactors barely one hour prior.

Lev had coopted Blinky and Buzz after only six hours of sleep to help with the new challenge.

This time, they knew the language. All they had to do was find the information they sought.

The entire history and future of the Ga'ee. Lev wanted all their knowledge.

But the brain was recalcitrant and not quick to give up its secrets. Lev, Davida, Blinky, and Buzz created digital battering rams and attacked the security walls, beating them mercilessly while cycling the power, making the core thirst for energy. A carrot and a stick,

A lot of sticks.

Only two carrots: energy and the promised peace of surrender.

The brain had seen the allure in neither proposal.

The battering continued while Lev's systems recharged. Two hours before they could travel to the Zuloon star system and see what damage had been wrought. The Ga'ee had reported complete subjugation.

Did that mean the worlds had been taken over or just initially populated?

Two hours to recharge and two hours and fifteen minutes to travel to the Zuloon homeworld. Time was not on their side. It raced inexorably forward, whether they wanted it to or not. They couldn't affect it.

Lev had never treated time as a variable. Like a planet in orbit around its star, it was in constant motion. He accounted for it in his calculations.

"How soon can we get to the Arn's home planet and then back to BH01?"

"Eight hours and a few minutes," Lev replied. "We can get there no sooner."

Payne nodded and walked to the front of the bridge. He studied the view of the Zuloon's system and its two inhabited planets. The Arn system was shown, too. Five systems in close proximity to each other. Five worlds in the Goldilocks zone. Five inhabited planets.

The admiral repeated the translated Ga'ee transmissions. "'Nine angle three is complete. Twelve angle twelve is complete.' We'll soon learn what the Ga'ee mean when they say the word 'complete.'"

Payne nodded.

Waiting four hours, two to recharge and two at FTL speed to get where they were going. It was both better and worse than waiting for six days. They were so close but impotent. They didn't expect the Ga'ee were in the system but couldn't take the chance. It was too high risk. With the added reactors, they only had four total hours to kill.

"I'm going to the range to see what they've come up with." Payne walked out, brow furrowed with the anxiety that the demand for patience brought.

The cart took him and Mary to Lev's weapons range, where Heckler and Turbo were examining the latest plasma thrower.

"Show me," Payne ordered without preamble.

"This could be the funkiest weapon we've ever tested," Heckler started. "No way to aim. You just kinda toss these burning plasma globules about twenty meters. That's it."

Payne gestured with his chin. Heckler didn't bother putting on his earmuffs. "No need." He waved it downrange and pulled the trigger. A twisting mass the size of his thumb jumped from the end of the barrel and followed a steady arc downward until it splattered on the deck, leaving a scar where it hit.

Payne rolled his finger to get another demonstration. Heckler fired again, three rounds in rapid succession. He drew a line on the deck with the impacts.

"I thought you said there was no way to aim that thing?"

"I might not have been completely truthful. It was entirely justified to maintain my aura of mystique."

Turbo snorted. She took the weapon and added three more rounds to meet Heckler's line and make a T.

"Why do you like this thing?" Payne asked.

Turbo explained, "You wanted something that would kill a Ga'ee with a single shot. This will do it. It has significant capacity; that's why the stock looks the way it does. That's where the raw material that the energy turns into plasma is stored. The system has to be warmed up, but we can do that before we touch down. Once it's live, you can do a lot of damage to the Ga'ee. One person can take out a colony without having to get her hands dirty."

"Add it to our kit and make copies for everyone as soon as manufacturing is back online. Reloads in *Ugly 5* in case one stock-full isn't enough to do the deed." Payne took the weapon, hoisting it for familiarization. He looked over the barrel to fire and pulled the trigger. It sent the plasma too low. He dropped the weapon to hold it mid-chest. He fired a second time and was rewarded with a better trajectory.

After the fifth shot, he was able to get each round close to where he was aiming. All he had to do was drop the plasma anywhere on a Ga'ee. "Make sure you break in the Ebren, so you'll need to print at least thirty of these things."

"The good news is that Lev stockpiled plenty of raw material from that last Ga'ee ship." Heckler smiled and gave the thumbs-up. "Wrigglers be damned. Team Payne is coming."

Mary took her turn with the weapon but shot with the butt braced on her hip as if she were firing an industrial-strength grenade launcher. The little pip of plasma was nothing in the big scheme; there was no kick, yet she stayed with her firing position.

"You rejoining the team, ma'am?"

"The Ga'ee have a lot to pay for, and as long as Blinky and Buzz are out of action, you're one person short."

Payne stiffened.

"I'm bored out of my ever-loving mind. Fuckin' A, I'm rejoining the team."

Payne looked at her. "That was unexpected." He wasn't pleased, and it crept into his voice. "Mary, a word, please."

Heckler and Turbo made faces at each other, followed by a series of rude gestures.

After they stepped into the corridor, Mary smiled pleasantly. "Yes, dear?"

Payne wanted to berate her for not talking to him first. He wanted to yell and kick something in frustration since she got hurt on almost every mission. He wanted her to stay home and be waiting for him when he returned.

That wasn't the woman who'd married him.

"You're still the team's logistician. Virgil is XO."

"I know, Dec. I won't let you down."

"You won't. I don't want you to die. I know that's selfish, but I don't want anyone on the team to die, least of all you. But we go into harm's way. There's nothing safe about what we do."

"I can't sit back here and wait for you to return from each mission. That's not working for me. I need to send rounds downrange. I need to contribute to the defense of humanity. This isn't *Bikini Babes*. This is for all of it, so someone in the future can film their show because Earth is safe. It's the higher purpose we spend our lives looking for." She wrapped her arms around his waist and looked into his eyes. "You're not mad, are you?"

"I feel like I should be, but I can't be. You're right. We need as much firepower as we can get. Eight on the flaming wreck of the Ga'ee ship almost wasn't enough, and now, Heckler wants to light up the plasma cannon every time he touches it."

"I'm sure that means something," Mary replied. She hadn't been there and didn't know what he was talking about.

It didn't matter.

"Get back in there, Dog. And yes, you have your nickname back. That's how the team knows you."

"Really?" She drew out the word in a way that put Payne on his heels.

"Really," he replied with feigned confidence. "Go shoot stuff with your fellow combat specialists. I'm off to do major-type stuff."

He leaned in and kissed her quickly, then extricated himself from her grip. He cupped her face with his hand and hesitated before completing what would have been a marvelous exit.

"I love you, Declan Payne," she stated.

"Yeah. Me, too," he replied awkwardly. He stumbled on his first step, righted himself, and walked away, forcing himself not to look back.

She sighed.

Not in a good way.

[30]

"You can't understand the worst part of war until you've seen genocide, and then you'll fight like hell to keep it from ever happening again." –From the memoirs of Ambassador Declan Payne

"Debris in orbit matches the expected mass of the entire Zuloon fleet. The planet's surface has been taken over by Ga'ee," Lev reported.

"The Zuloon homeworld is no more. The Zuloon fleet stayed to fight and lost." Admiral Wesson closed his eyes for a moment before issuing the next order. "Take us to the second inhabited planet."

A twenty-four-second FTL flight put *Leviathan* in orbit over the Zuloon's colonized planet. "Only Ga'ee on the surface."

"Two planets. Good thing we have two world-killers available. Blow those planets and their inhabitants to hell, Lev. The Ga'ee cannot be allowed a foothold in this galaxy."

"I would argue, but these planets will never be habitable by carbon-based lifeforms again. It would take thousands of years,"

Lev lamented. He moved the ship to a point equidistant between the two planets and fired the missiles. They flashed into FTL, then slammed into the planets, causing a chain reaction that reached the core.

"Take us to the last Zuloon planet, Lev. FTL speed."

The ship changed course and accelerated, leaving the two destroyed planets behind.

"Use the Ga'ee ship materials to build two new world-killers. I think we'll need a few more before we're finished." The admiral rested his hand on the commodore's shoulder. "I'll be in our quarters."

He walked away, suddenly feeling very old and struggling under the burden of failure.

———

"Stand down," Payne ordered when the tactical picture became clear. "We have a few hours before we arrive at Z3. Be back here before we need to go."

The team, ten strong even without Blinky and Buzz, dropped their helmets on their seats and dismounted in silence.

There wasn't anything to say.

Dank asked Lev to remind everyone to return to *Ugly 5* at the appropriate time.

"It's taken care of, Dec," Virgil said softly. Payne meandered to the team area and sat down on a bench that would support the weight of two individuals in combat armor. Mary sat next to him. The rest of the team climbed out of their combat suits, dressed, and walked away, except for Major Dank. He slid a storage box opposite the bench and sat down. Kal shouted for the Cabrizi. Once he had their attention, he ran off, and they bolted after him.

"I don't know what to say. I don't think there's anything we could have done differently." Virgil exhaled loudly and leaned back.

"Nothing. We had to balance the strategic knowns with the unknowns. We have to build ships, and then we have to protect the space we know. If we hadn't built ships, we would have been boned. Had we not gone on the Ga'ee ship, we wouldn't be able to break down the shield or speak their language or recover from folding space in two hours versus three days. No recriminations, Virgil. We're here for now, and it was too late for the Zuloon to survive. Maybe we'll find some stragglers on Z3. Rescue them, so their race doesn't die."

"There aren't any Zuloon on freighters elsewhere in the galaxy?"

"Could be. I have no idea. After the war, they retreated into themselves. Any ships flying between the three planets would have been overrun by the Ga'ee. We haven't given up, but we're ready to move on."

"We blew up two of their three planets," Virgil stated.

"And that. Go get something to eat or some rest, Virge. I'm just going to sit here and think."

"No recriminations, Dec. Your words. Find us a way ahead where we can win. We want to do more than just survive this. We can't surrender any space to the Ga'ee. We have to beat them back."

"That is what we're going to do." Payne waved toward the corridor. "Go on, Virge. I'm thinking now."

Dank nodded and walked away.

Mary tapped her finger on the bench until Declan looked at her.

He was unamused.

"I feel bad, Mary. So much joking around when entire races were dying."

"Had you been sullen and worried, it would have changed

307

nothing, except everyone would have been miserable and less able to do their jobs."

Mary stared down the bay, where seven power plants and one Ga'ee central core were lined up and running. The computer core and power plant were isolated and connected by a single line to *Leviathan*. Only Blinky, Buzz, Davida, and Lev had access.

"I reckon," Payne tried to drawl.

"That's more like it. Even Kal knows it's important to play between missions." Mary turned toward Payne. "You need to be yourself."

"The weight of the galaxy is on my shoulders. The leader of the seven...no six...no, five races. It's not a good title to have."

"The Ga'ee have ten thousand systems. We are nothing in their greater conquest except that, thanks to Lev, we were able to fight back. It didn't mean we weren't going to get hurt. You can't always bring the team home." She glanced around to make sure Major Dank was gone. "Like Virgil knows only too well."

Payne stood and held his hand out. Mary took it and pulled herself to her feet. Hand in armored hand, they walked toward the power plants.

"This is going to be a long war, Dec. Can't tighten up now."

"Can't lose focus on the endgame," Payne admitted, then chuckled softly. "Dammit, Mary. I care. I'm not insensitive to what's happened. I *do* care."

"I know." Mary bumped her suit's hip against his. "You sound like you're trying to convince yourself. There's someone who knows beyond a shadow of a doubt. Lev, does Declan care about the galaxy's races?"

"What the hell?"

"Declan cares as much as any human being can care about another," Lev replied.

Mary and Declan looked at each other. "What does that mean?" Mary wondered. Lev didn't answer.

They kept walking past the reactors and stopped at the far end of the hangar bay.

"I can feel the power surging through me." Payne held his hands up as if blessing the reactors. "We stole you from the enemy's bosom and have put you to work for us!"

"They work for *us* now," Mary stated.

"Damn straight." Payne smiled weakly. "I'm trying."

Mary held her palm up. "When you can snatch the pebble from my hand, you will be ready."

Payne looked closely to find a piece of faux jerky in her palm.

At the speed of thought, his hand swooped in like an eagle and snatched the treat. He followed through and popped it into his mouth.

"That's more like it."

"Let's head back. I could use something to eat, and there's not much time left before we reach Z3."

———

The tactical screen's countdown clock hit ten.

Payne didn't hold out hope, but they were ready to go planetside if there was any possibility. He tapped his foot anxiously. Mary tried to ignore him.

Lev's vibration scanners showed no ships in the system.

Five...four...

Payne stared at the screen for the longest five seconds ever. His heart hammered against his breastbone.

The image cleared.

"We have a signal from the surface," Lev reported.

"*Ugly 5*, prepare to launch," the admiral ordered, even though *Ugly 5* was ready to launch. "We're taking *Leviathan* in to rescue survivors. You'll launch to establish a perimeter when we're in position. *Glennis* will also launch."

"We'll be beating off the wrigglers," Turbo quipped. Heckler pushed her, and she pushed back.

"Looks like your plasma tossers are going to get a workout," Payne told Heckler and Turbo. *Ugly 5* remained magnetically locked to the deck while *Leviathan* bounced through the upper atmosphere. Even with the advanced ship's systems, entering a planet's atmosphere was still rough.

"Tactical picture, Lev, and play that message," Payne requested.

The screen lit up to show a Ga'ee infestation covering the small planet. The signal came from a body of water twice the size of the land masses.

"Looks like we might get wet, people. Pneumatic jets, *Ugly 5* on hover nearby."

Leviathan started firing its defensive weapons. The tactical screen zoomed in to show drones rising from the planet's surface.

"They've already built drones," Dank noted. "I hope the next world-killer missile is ready."

"If there's water, there's a way to sustain carbon-based life without interacting with the Ga'ee. Just have to move to ships or other floating bases," Payne suggested.

Sparky shook her head. "Once there are sufficient drones, they could attack the surface ships. Life would have to live below the surface."

The emergency signal continued. On the other planets, they hadn't received any sign that the inhabitants had survived. This single tendril, this one lifeline, had Team Payne leaning forward in their seats and willing the screen to show Zuloon who had survived.

Lev descended as a ball of flame, maintaining maximum speed to get to the signal before anything else. Tiny self-defense missiles blew through the conflagration before homing in on their targets.

Leviathan slowed and the chain guns opened up, filling the sky with projectiles. Lasers and plasma added their firepower but with limited effectiveness within the atmosphere. More drones launched from the continents.

"Better make this quick," the admiral directed. "I see a boat up ahead. We'll park right on top of it and use maintenance drones to bring up any survivors. Disembark your insertion craft and prepare to manually exit the hangar bay."

"You heard the man! Helmets on, prepare to disembark. Ditch the plasma tossers. Railguns and plasma cannons. Kal, you stay here and board the ship when *Ugly 5* goes down there to pick up survivors. The rest of the team, rally at the hangar door." The team snapped their helmets into place while the side doors levered up. They all ran off the ship except the Ebren Champion. He waited while the doors closed.

They still hadn't given Kal a way to fly. "Lev, future project. Kal gets a full combat suit just like us, no matter how big you have to make it. *Ugly 6*, prepare to be built."

Mary smiled to herself. Payne was looking forward now, not back. Her work would never be done. Logistics and team support would always be needed.

"Over water. We'll be fighting drones."

"Crap!" Heckler grumbled. "I really wanted to use the Tosser." The team had left them in the uglymobile, which any survivors would board. "We don't want to lose any of these little gems."

Payne looked to see if he was joking but couldn't tell with Heckler's helmet covering his face.

Turbo ran back to the ship and collected the plasma throwers. She dumped them unceremoniously on the deck outside the ship before returning to the hangar bay door.

Leviathan slowed, and the hangar door opened a fraction. Payne and Dank assessed the situation. They were still a kilometer up. Payne held onto the door as he leaned out to look straight down. *Leviathan* was descending toward a steadily growing object on the sea—a ship, pointed at the front and square at the rear, which was a standard design for most surface navy vessels in the galaxy.

Payne held a fist in the air. *Hold.*

"Drones inbound," Dank reported. Lev had been firing the ship's defensive weapons throughout the descent, but the team had not had a visual on the enemy.

Until now. The swarm took its losses, filled the gaps, and kept coming.

A hundred meters up, Payne dropped his arm and jumped out the door. He instantly activated his jets to slow his rapid descent. The rest of the team was out the door less than one second later. They flew like professionals, remaining upright with their railguns trained on the enemy, waiting to be cleared hot.

Not yet, Payne thought.

He angled toward the ship's deck, slowing and landing. "Anyone here?" he shouted through his suit's external sound system.

The ship's foghorn sounded. Payne looked up to find a number of Zuloon on the ship's upper catwalk.

"Virgil, get up there and prepare them to disembark. Rest of you, firing positions around me. Kal, when you get down here, tie us into the Ebren squad. They'll get here about the same time as you. I see *Glennis* inbound."

"Fire!" Heckler called before Payne was finished.

Railguns barked and lit up the closest drones speeding unerringly toward them. The Ga'ee triple-spear-pointed drones didn't bother to jink or maneuver. They didn't care if they took losses. Their objective was to destroy the ship with the remaining Zuloon on board.

They were a race of light green, bipedal creatures. They would have looked at home in a forest, but that was a preconception humans had because of literature's elves. The Zuloon were not as tall and lacked ears, but they still gave the impression of the forest creatures.

"Get down here!" Payne yelled. "We have a ship for evacuation."

One of the Zuloon slid a window aside. "We need to go back to the mainland. We have more people."

"We have a big-ass spaceship!" Payne shouted back. "And you're going to get on it. Then we'll look for more survivors."

"What are these ships? Why can't we get hold of anyone?"

"Get the fuck down here!" Payne had lost patience. He glanced toward the sky to see a drone at danger-close range. He snap-fired and sent a line of automatic fire across the sky until the two intersected.

Heckler's plasma cannon barked from the tripod that Turbo had balanced across the railing. From the first catwalk up, Kal rocked his plasma cannon, firing it from where it was slung under his arm. He engaged drone after drone while calling to the other side of the ship in Ebren.

Payne could understand him without the suit translating for him.

"Tie in with the humans at the front and back of the ship.

And keep firing." The Ebrens had plasma cannons instead of railguns, and they fired relentlessly. They kept the drones away.

But the Ga'ee learned. They swept away from the ship to get a better angle.

The Zuloon were still on the bridge.

"What the fuck are you waiting for?" Payne shouted. He gestured wildly for them to come down to where *Ugly 5* hovered over the open deck.

The Zuloon stared at him with blank expressions. "I'm going upstairs and will be throwing them overboard. We'll pick them out of the water." Payne used his jets to launch upward. He adjusted on the fly and landed on the top stair. He jerked the door open out of the hands on the inside that held it shut.

"What is wrong with you?" Payne forced himself to use a calm voice, though he was anything but. "Do you realize you are the very last Zuloon alive? You need to get the hell off this planet."

"The last Zuloon? What are you talking about? The mainland has over one hundred million of our race."

Payne felt the spear of reality cut into his heart. He removed his helmet even though he didn't have time. He wanted them to look at him and know he was sincere.

"They're dead. All of them. Those ships are Ga'ee drones. They've taken over this planet. They've already destroyed the two planets in your home system. You're it. You're all that's left, and if you want to stay alive, you really need to go. Please."

The Zuloon relented. There were five of them, three males and two females.

"Are there any others below deck?"

"Maybe," was the only commitment they would make.

"Fuck." Payne snapped his helmet into place. "Get down there!" He held the door open and pointed. The Zuloon shuffled out, little more than zombies. The truth had hit them. They could lament and mourn once they were out of harm's way. Until then, they needed to move. "Hurry, please."

Payne's encouragement did nothing to change their behavior.

He dialed up the team channel. "We need to buy more time, and we need to check below decks for more survivors. Byle, that's you and Shaolin. Make it fast."

Payne stayed on the higher level of the ship, where he had a clear field of fire. The drones were massing for another attack.

He scanned through three hundred and sixty degrees. The Ga'ee were coming from one direction. "Ebren squad, shift to the bow. Maximize your firepower toward the Ga'ee swarm. We'll cover the aft electronically."

Leviathan moved lower until it was nearly touching the ship's mast. It flooded the air with projectiles and small missiles. The Ebren started to fire. Team Payne followed their lead. The drone swarm retreated and separated.

"Back into position on the port side," Payne ordered the Ebren.

The Zuloon were standing on the deck, not in *Ugly 5*.

"What the hell is up with you guys?"

"We have to return to the mainland and protest this invasion in the strongest possible terms."

Payne launched over the rail to land in front of the Zuloon. He resorted to herding them into *Ugly 5*. The spokesman resisted. Payne lifted him up and tossed him through the open hatch. "Lev, take them out of here."

Ugly 5 accelerated sideways to get out from under *Leviathan*. The insertion craft disappeared behind the hull when it turned upward.

The drone swarm broke into two groups, then those separated, then the rest separated. They raced in at an unnatural acceleration beyond anything carbon-based life could manage.

"FPF, now," Payne ordered. Final protective fire. All weapons firing at the cyclic rate to protect the team and create a wall of projectiles and energy through which no enemies could pass.

But it was final. When they were done firing, they would be out of ammunition, or their weapons would be melted.

The drones rapidly fell from the sky. Lev was too high. Most of his weapons couldn't fire at that angle and that close in.

Declan, the Zuloon are on board.

"Be there in a jiff," Payne replied. His sensors showed two warm humanoid forms below.

He tore the hatch off the main deck and tossed it aside, then bolted recklessly down the steps. "Any Zuloon down here, you need to come with me right now, or the Ga'ee will kill you."

It was the best he could come up with. He needed to go aft. He crouched and worked his way back to where the life forms were located. He ripped off the hatch to a storage space, but it was too small. He couldn't get in.

"Here's the deal, people. Come with me right fucking now, and you won't die."

Payne didn't understand why they were hiding. He grasped the sides of the hatch. As a commercial vessel, it wasn't as ruggedly built as a vessel built for war. He thundered into the space and shoved a cargo container aside.

They weren't behind it.

They were in it. He lifted the entire container and pushed it through the opening and down the passageway. He lined it up with the hatch above and activated his jets. The container started to tumble and jammed against the frame. Payne dropped down, leaned back to realign the container, and jetted upward. He ended by tossing the container through.

"Virge, grab the other side of this. Mary and Sparky, bring Kal."

The team stopped firing and flew sideways to get out from under *Leviathan*. Mary and Sparky grabbed Kal by the arms on their way out.

Heckler and Turbo kept hammering at the Ga'ee, along with the Ebren warriors.

"Recover to the ship," Payne ordered the Ebren. "Right now."

They continued to fire, losing one cannon at a time as they systematically squeezed into *Glamorous Glennis*.

The drones swept through the dwindling firepower. Payne tried to fire, but the shipping container was too cumbersome. He couldn't raise his weapon. Dank fired, but it was too late. A drone slammed into the container and tore the thin metal frame. It twisted out of their grip and fell.

Payne dove after it, hitting the water at the same time as the container. He reached inside to pull out the two Zuloon. The container tipped and started taking on water.

Dank hovered above, raging with his railgun.

Payne yanked the two free, pulled them close to his body, and jetted upward. Mary and Sparky appeared, with Kal hammering away using his plasma cannon. It stopped abruptly.

No more ammunition. He dumped it into the ocean and held his hands out.

Mary gave her railgun to the Ebren to allow her to concentrate on flying. He started firing, but her railgun was running low, too.

Leviathan shifted out from above the ship, giving the last members a straight shot at the hangar bay door.

"Go, go, go!" Payne shouted over the team channel. They maxed their jets to accelerate straight up and arc into the hangar bay. Payne rolled over to decelerate and come in feet-first. He couldn't hit the deck because of the precious charges in his arms.

Dank came in from behind to help him slow down and orient.

They touched down together and ran across the deck to keep from falling.

The hangar bay door closed while *Leviathan* accelerated away from the drone engagement zone.

[31]

"If one must bend the laws of physics to achieve the impossible, bend away. It's not like you can break them, unless you can. Then do it, unless it results in the immediate destruction of the entire universe. Then you probably shouldn't." –From the memoirs of Ambassador Declan Payne

"Lev, are you going to pass over the mainland and see if there are any other survivors?"

The other members of Team Payne had gone to the equipment cage and were reloading.

"The continent was taken over by the Ga'ee. There isn't a single refuge where we might find a survivor," Lev explained as they headed toward space.

"No other ships?"

"I can find none. I will conduct a search to be sure before we destroy this planet. It pains me to say those words. A habitable planet rendered uninhabitable that would be used as a base to launch more attacks into this sector of the galaxy. It cannot be allowed to remain. The construction of Ga'ee carriers is well underway, and there is a space station in orbit, tethering drones. That will need to die, too."

"We have become the destroyer of worlds. The doomsday the Progenitors feared has arrived," Payne replied. "At least we have these seven Zuloon."

The survivors huddled together near Team Payne, in shock and disengaged from the reality around them.

Embroiled in what they'd left behind.

Payne changed into his jumpsuit before returning to the group to talk to them. Mary went with him. He looked at her, and she nodded.

Mary was more diplomatic than he would ever be. The two hiding in the shipping container had almost gotten him killed. He let her handle them.

"We cannot express the grief you feel being the only known Zuloon survivors. This isn't something anyone could ever be prepared for. The best we can do is make you comfortable and provide you with a home while you determine your way forward. That doesn't have to happen now, but it will at some point. I think we should take you all to Medical for an evaluation. Come with us, please." Mary gestured toward the hatch, but carts hovered in and parked next to them.

"Board the carts, please," Payne said softly while helping the first person, who was little more than a zombie. She stumbled along until she reached the cart. Without Payne's help, she would not have been able to get into it. The other female joined her, thanks to Mary providing the physical support.

The last two females. Their burden would be the greatest.

The team joined them to help the rest, each taking one and guiding him to a seat. Team Payne rode in silence until they reached the medical facility. After the Zuloon were sedated, Payne addressed them.

"So that we may never see something like this again, we're going on the offensive."

"What about the Arn and the Rang'Kor?"

"We will visit them first and eradicate any infestations. Then we'll deliver guidance to the battlewagons. We have five-ship weapons platforms filling our sector, patrolling, ready to engage any Ga'ee ship that appears. Our battlewagons have demonstrated that they can readily destroy the Ga'ee carriers without having to hack their shield and take it down first. We have more power than they do, and we're going to use it."

Major Dank pulled Payne into a hug. Declan didn't hug back. They looked at each other. "You don't have to carry this burden alone. We're in it for all of humanity."

"Y'all have a mighty fine star shining in heaven," Kal drawled.

Payne looked at him and shook his head.

Kal explained after a short chuckle, "The star that guides you. I'm proud to be one of you, a warrior among warriors fighting for everyone else."

Payne smiled in understanding. "Downtime, people. Find your lovers and enjoy the company of your friends. Next stop Arn, but not many hours. Maybe another four-plus."

The team meandered away. Behind them in Medical, the Zuloon rested fitfully despite being sedated. The shock of their new reality weighed heavily on their minds.

Mary took her husband's hand. "In the company of friends and lovers. You want to go to the bridge, don't you?"

Payne smiled. "I do, but briefly. Just need to check in with the admiral."

They took the waiting cart, and less than three minutes later, they walked through the hatch and onto the bridge. Admiral Wesson and Commodore Freeman were the only ones there.

The admiral nodded at Payne. "Planet has been scanned. There aren't any more Zuloon alive." On the screen, the starfield of space told Payne they had left the atmosphere. "Fire."

A world-killer missile left the tube and headed for Z3.

Lev prepared the new coordinates to fold into Arn space. They were two hours and fifteen minutes from the Arn's homeworld.

The missile hit, and for the first few seconds, nothing happened. Then fountains of magma spewed from new cracks in the planet's surface. Lev saved them from seeing the rest of it by folding space.

When they emerged in Arn interstellar space, the tactical screen showed no activity. Lev's neural receptors also had a dearth of signals.

"Nothing is here," the admiral announced.

"Twelve angle twelve is complete," Payne whispered. He addressed the admiral. "Maybe when we hit the two-hour point, we can send an FTL message to anyone with ears to hear and a codebook to decipher."

"And tell them about the Arn and the Zuloon?"

"And give them orders to deploy the battlewagons and destroy every Ga'ee infestation before they start launching ships. Will a battlewagon's main weapon be useful to scrub a planet's surface from the plague of the Ga'ee?"

"I believe with enough shots, it will be, but it would take a long time," Lev explained.

"That's probably better than blowing up the planet. At least it can be terraformed and regrown, especially if it has water like Z3."

"Z3 is gone and would have been launching ships for a long time before any battlewagons arrived," the admiral replied.

"I know. That's why Z3 had to go. That wasn't a small

foothold, but it gives me hope for the Rang'Kor. Their water planets will be resistant, as we saw on PX47."

"We learned a great deal on Z3," Lev started. He earned the four's rapt attention. "We learned that we could control the drones. They are not sentient and need commands to direct them. We were able to override their directives from the planet's surface. We flew around the planet without getting attacked because we directed all the drones to land. I believe we'll be able to have a substantive conversation with the next Ga'ee ship we encounter."

"We need to find a Ga'ee ship, then," Payne replied. "That's the best news we've had in a while, Lev."

Payne sighed. His heart beat heavily, straining with each compression.

Getting too little sleep and seeing too much death was wearing him down. "Take this one off, Declan," the admiral directed.

Payne laughed. "You look as bad as I feel. Maybe you should take it off, too. Lev has our backs. We're going to see what we don't want to see, and Lev is going to use a world-killer on it."

"I can handle it," Lev replied. "I'll wake you up if there's something that requires your attention."

"I doubt I'll be able to sleep," Payne countered.

"We can try," Mary interjected. "A nice long shower, followed by a cold room and a warm bed."

Payne waved at the admiral and the commodore.

"I'm being drawn away. Thanks, Lev. Maybe someday, we'll be able to find the Godilkinmore so we can thank them for creating you and leaving you behind to watch over us. We'd all be dead if it weren't for you, a doomsday weapon whose only goal is peace."

"That's a good tagline. I should sell t-shirts," Lev joked.

Payne felt the strain leaving his body.

Mary had been right. He needed to laugh, as dire as the situation was. Lev understood that, too.

"Have that embroidered on my jumpsuit, Lev. We'll be in our quarters doing the funky monkey."

Mary recoiled. "The what?"

"The wash and rinse? The fill and thrill? The deep-vein thrombosis?"

"None of those." Mary crossed her arms.

"I guess a long shower will have to do it, Lev. A long, soapy, glistening-buns-under-the-bright-bathroom-lights shower."

"Incorrigible." Mary took his arm and steered him toward the hatch, and the two hurried out.

"Must be nice to be young and have that kind of energy," the admiral murmured. He locked gazes with Nyota. "Lev, keep the Zuloon on ice for as long as possible. Maybe they'll think it was a bad dream by the time they awake. We'll be in our quarters."

———

Lev pumped a light sedative into the air to ensure the humans rested. He didn't waken anyone for their arrival at the Arn homeworld, which had become a Ga'ee colony. He hit it with a world-killer before folding space to the second Arn world, where he found the same thing.

Twelve hours into the journey, the humans had rested long enough, and Lev had confirmed that no Arn remained.

Two races, and only seven individuals in total had survived.

Lev could not tolerate the eradication of all carbon-based life forms in this sector of the galaxy, a sector the Godilkinmore had nurtured and helped mature. Now they were in a position to challenge the invaders. He was there to help.

He knew what Declan Payne was thinking, and he agreed.

To end the Ga'ee threat, they had to take the fight into Ga'ee space. There, they would sue for peace by threatening the destruction of ten thousand worlds, starting with the one the Ga'ee called home.

———

Commander Yeldon stood in front of the captain's chair on the *Levant*, BW06. It was the sixth ship of the class and the leader of Hunter-Killer Squadron 02. The ships were preparing to reenter normal space within the BH01 system, which contained the Berantz homeworld.

Their energy vibration system didn't identify any ships within range.

Yeldon relaxed with his hands clasped behind his back.

The countdown ended, and the system opened up before them. They'd arrived on the elliptical plane of the planets rotating around the Berantz star, two AU from the homeworld. BH01 had a big ship in orbit.

A Ga'ee carrier.

"All ships accelerate toward the target. Prepare your main weapons to fire on my command." Yeldon felt in control, even though he had expected to have more time before he would have to fight a battle. He stayed as he was.

The crew glanced in his direction. He felt the strength of command, and they responded to his confidence.

"Weapon charged and ready to fire," the weapons control officer announced.

The Ga'ee launched drones. Tens of thousands of sparks of light poured from the sides of the massive ship. The battlewagons were too far away to fire.

"Sir?" Helm asked.

"Stay the course. We kill the mothership, and the drones become irrelevant. Don't get distracted."

The battlewagons continued to accelerate.

The captain finally sat down. "Time to optimal firing distance?"

"Seventeen seconds."

"Time for the drones to intercept us?"

"Two seconds sooner."

"Change firing time to half a second before. Execute."

They were almost out of time. Fire Control hammered at his screen.

"Transmit to the squadron and fire."

The five ships lit up as one, sending an immense energy pulse through the drone cloud and into the Ga'ee carrier. The drones in the path of the beam were vaporized, with little impact on the strength of the weapon.

The Ga'ee shield collapsed, and five weaker beams hit the ship, ripping huge sections of metal away and rendering the hangar bays unusable. The spine broke, but the drones continued. "Hard bank, elevation ninety. Straight up, Helm!"

Yeldon had gained a sense of urgency since the salvo had not destroyed the Ga'ee ship. He needed to survive to report the information to the Fleet. "All ships, fire your Rapiers. Full spread."

The anti-ship missiles belched into the void on fountains of air before their engines kicked in and drove them toward their target.

The drones were already hammering at the battlewagons, peppering the hulls of all five vessels. The weapons' energy rebuilt far too slowly.

Defensive weapons were fully automated and delivered at their cyclic rates, but there were too many drones filling the void.

An explosion rocked the Ga'ee ship, then a fountain of red and orange blasted into space, quickly extinguished for lack of oxygen. A glow from within the ship showed the heat of molten metal.

The metal of *Levant's* hull screamed from the abuse it was receiving from the spiked points of the drones. Wave after wave came.

"Hull breach," Life Support reported. The main screen showed a diagram of the ship with the increasing damage. The automated bulkheads had already closed. Little air had vented to space. The crew worked from the center of the ship, but repairs were needed, which meant bots and crew needed to dispatch to the outer areas.

A second and third explosion silenced the Ga'ee carrier. The Rapiers were hitting home, delivering the final blow the energy weapons hadn't.

One out of five missiles reached the carrier, but that was enough.

A torn hull exposing the inner systems to the fury of a ten-megaton explosion was more than the carrier could handle.

In a final seam-ripping burst, the ship blasted into a billion pieces in an expanding sphere of debris.

"Continue accelerating," Yeldon ordered. He wanted to limit the damage from the fast-moving debris and the quickly degenerating shockwave. The drones lost guidance and turned into more debris.

BW08, *Africa,* lost propulsion and continued on a ballistic trajectory.

"*Africa*, what's your status?" Yeldon requested.

"We're down hard. Engines are boned. We'll need a week and help to get it all fixed. Sorry, boss. We didn't avoid enough of those drones, and we're going to get caught in the wash of debris."

"Buckle up and ride it out. We'll be back and will do what we have to to save you, then save that ship. Those things are hard to come by."

"Just like wrecking dad's hoversport when I was in school."

"You didn't," Yeldon wondered.

"I'll try not to scratch the paint, Commander."

The debris cloud approached and enveloped *Africa* for the briefest of moments before moving on. The crew watched in horror as the ship started breaking apart.

"Sir?" Helm repeated.

"Keep running, or their fate will be ours. Transition to FTL."

"FTL is down," Helm replied.

Commander Yeldon ordered the others to speed out of the system, wait one hour, and then return. The other three ships, BW06, BW09, and BW10, transitioned into faster-than-light speed and disappeared.

"There's a gap in the debris cloud!" the systems operator cheered. No one joined in.

"I have the coordinates," Helm said. "Adjusting angle of departure. Slowing."

Commander Yeldon braced himself as the wave approached, but without debris, the ripple barely managed to rock the ship.

"Take us back to *Africa* at best possible speed."

The ship's attitude thrusters rotated it until the bow faced the way they'd come. The engines fired, and *Levant* headed toward the damaged ship. They continued to fire. Time wasn't on the side of anyone trapped within the dead battlewagon.

"I hope our ships see that we've headed back and stop earlier than an hour away," Yeldon mused. That might be a problem.

"Life support is failing."

"That could be a big problem. Helm and Systems, stay at your posts. Everyone else, damage control. Get out your pliers, wrenches, and hull-sealing foam. We're going to war with the void to keep it from killing us."

The commander led the team off the bridge.

[32]

"A good night's sleep won't bring back the dead, but it will help you deal with their loss." –From the memoirs of Ambassador Declan Payne

"Blue Earth Protectorate, this is Commander Jimmy Josephs of the Vestrall Battlewagon *The President*. We have returned and will assume a defensive posture to protect Earth. Please do not interfere with our operations."

"This is Captain LeClerc of the heavy cruiser *Ephesus*. It is good to have you back. If you are able to break free, I invite you for dinner in the officer's mess aboard my ship."

"I'd prefer you came to *The President* so in case we are called to action, I'm not off my ship."

"I accept your gracious offer. My shuttle will arrive at eighteen hundred hours Earth standard time."

"We'll be expecting you." The commander closed the channel. "Barry, what's your impression of that conversation?"

"He sounded sincere to me. No posturing like we've seen every other time we had to deal with the BEP. He didn't demand that we prepare to be boarded. That in and of itself is a sea change of tidal-wave proportions."

Jimmy chuckled softly while looking away. He turned his attention back to the young commander. "I didn't want to have to tell him to go fuck himself again. Delivering his comeuppance was growing tedious."

"I guess that's another way to put it. Well, he's coming over here. That's probably best to get the inside skinny on what's happening on Earth."

"Inside skinny? Are you reading too many crime novels? Don't answer that. I don't care what you read as long as you read something. Reading is good. It makes you smart."

"I read a lot," Barry reported, fishing for a compliment.

"Clearly, you need to read more." The commander waved his hand, dismissing the ship's captain even though Jimmy was sitting in his seat.

Barry didn't leave. He pointed at the chair. "Sir..."

"I know. I'm thinking, and although this is the seat where I think the best, I'll defer to your ownership and submit to the galaxy's conspiracy against me."

"I don't follow," Barry admitted.

"Take your seat. I'll be in my quarters, summoning the power to think."

He left the bridge in a cloud of snickers and chortles.

The conversation with LeClerc had been downright friendly. "Do I need the BEP as an adversary? No. Better an ally. Better all of humanity as an ally to our cause, which is to protect them from the Ga'ee and maybe even themselves.

"But they don't want you to do it your way. You can only protect them their way. They'll be in charge, but it's still your responsibility. All the responsibility with none of the authority. That's a sucky deal. But we've claimed to be Vestrall, freeing ourselves from Earth's shackles." He stared at the wall. "I suck at talking to myself. I should probably not do it."

Jimmy chose to sulk instead. Here he was in his quarters instead of on the bridge, commanding a starship.

"The kid deserves it. He was here when you were playing pattycake with the muckety-mucks and sucking badly at it. I thought you were going to stop talking to yourself?

"I was.

"But you didn't.

"I am now!"

He sat quietly for a few moments.

"To the secret lair!" he declared and strode briskly to his door, where he adopted a casual swagger and stepped into the empty corridor. It was a big ship, and there were few people on board. The corridors were almost always empty. He continued aft until he reached a lift and descended two decks toward the keel. He exited and strolled down the empty deck, which was humming with the energy of the drive system. Even idling as it was, the thrum of power was there.

It took a great deal of energy to drive a ship the size of *The President.* The engine compartment was an unused space with chairs in the middle and screens on all the walls. It was for classroom training and had been used only one time before they became too busy with real life. They'd train again, but it would be done at their stations, where tactile responses would give them the muscle memory that a classroom training session could not.

This had become his secret lair where he lectured receptive souls, if only in his imagination.

"Current orientation of HK1?" Jimmy asked.

"The far side of the lunar shipyard. Facing away from the sun."

Jimmy studied the solar grid.

"Most likely direction of Ga'ee approach?"

An arrow appeared on the screen. It was the approach they had taken before, but the planets had continued on their orbital trajectories. They no longer lined up away from the sun and toward Ga'ee space, or what could be perceived as Ga'ee space. The Ga'ee would appear from deep space and could be almost on top of Earth before humanity could respond.

"Why couldn't we see the Ga'ee ship coming?"

"There were no energy vibrations to detect," the ship replied.

"Hold our position here. This is where we need to be. Farther out, and they could hit Earth before we could hit them. This way, even if they come out of FTL right on top of us, we're in a better position to respond."

"Dammit!" he blurted when he realized he was back to talking to himself.

"Maybe we could get some humans with loose morals to join us on the ship."

He pursed his lips while staring at the screen. "Belay my last. That was bullshit. We want partners with strong morals! I'm not talking about the crew, am I?"

The loneliness was getting to him. He needed a squadron staff, a team to work with, to problem-solve with, to simply be with. Jimmy Josephs knew he wasn't the lone-stranger type.

"Back to the bridge, where my questionable sanity won't be so obvious!" he declared boldly. He returned to the bridge, but this time, he took the stairs to work off a little of his excess energy.

───

"Battleship *The President*, this is UN President Sinkhaus. Please respond."

Lieutenant Commander Barry Cummins jumped up from the captain's chair and motioned for Commander Josephs to sit.

"*Now* you want me to sit in the big chair. I'm not going to vacate it once my ass is parked."

"I'm willing to risk it, Commander. I don't even want to be here for this conversation, let alone be the one doing the talking."

"Sir, they are insisting it's urgent." The communications officer wasn't comfortable with the delay.

"Fine." Jimmy sat down. "Main screen."

He smiled at the image that appeared.

"President Sinkhaus. What can I do for you on this fine day?"

"We need to discuss the Fleet's optimal deployment in support of Earth. We require your presence in the UN chambers in four hours' time."

Jimmy laced his fingers together, leaned back, and rested his hands on his taut midsection.

"I don't think so. Those who have fought the Ga'ee are in the best position to determine optimal engagement strategies. That's why Hunter-Killer Squadron One is oriented as it is. I expect some of your member countries will express their discomfort at how close these ships are to Earth. If those uncomfortable souls looked closer, they'll see that we're facing away from the planet. That said, we welcome any suggestions, to be forwarded in writing to the command ship, *The President*."

"You're still Earth Fleet. You will respond to our commands."

"I am serving on a Vestrall vessel and answer to the leader of the seven races. I'm sorry. I will not come to the UN and be berated so you politicians can feel better about yourselves. You're only in charge because Fleet built the ships it needed to repel the Ga'ee threat, and only Fleet will do it again. If you wish to demonstrate your support for this endeavor, please send supply ships with food for five hundred souls. You are more than welcome to visit us here since I refuse to be off the ship when next we encounter the enemy."

The president cut her audio and turned away from the screen. Despite her self-control, she made a large number of small gestures.

"I think you made her mad," Cummins murmured.

"Our audio is still on," Jimmy replied softly.

Barry was mortified and stumbled in his haste to exit the bridge.

"It's not," the communications officer clarified.

Jimmy winked and smiled. The crew snickered just in time for the president to turn around and take in the scene. She barely contained her icy fury. "My assistant will coordinate the details of an official visit."

"We look forward to it, President Sinkhaus. We don't have any red carpets to roll out, but we will afford you the courtesies that you showed me were acceptable for such occasions since I have no experience in these matters. Josephs out."

The comms officer cut the link the instant the commander signed off.

"What a fucking twat-faced—"

"Stow that noise!" The commander stood. "Don't take my confrontation as a license to disrespect Earth's ranking official. As much as we don't like her or any of them, we will show them the courtesy they didn't show me. If we don't have a red carpet, you'll paint the deck red. Where's the COB?"

"Here, sir!" Chief Tremayne stood from behind his console.

"Your duties until those UN fuckers come aboard is to make this place gleam from the airlock to the bridge to a space we can use for an executive dinner, like the training room two decks down."

"Your secret lair, sir?"

Jimmy gave him a full stink-eye but didn't ask how he knew. It was the COB's responsibility to know everything about the ship and its crew. "Fuckin' A, COB."

"*The President* will be ready for the president, sir. You have my word." The chief marched around the bridge, tapping crew members on the shoulder in a sordid game of duck-duck-goose. Everyone he tapped left their station and headed for the corridor.

Two-thirds of the positions were empty by the time the chief left, but none of the critical positions. Helm. Systems. And Comms.

Lieutenant Commander Cummins returned. "I suppose you think that was funny, sir?"

"It was, and you know it. You can't wait to do it to someone else."

Barry recoiled. He was trying to be upset that the commander had spoofed him in front of the crew.

"Respect is earned, Barry. You have their respect, but you're still young. Keep in mind that our video was playing even without the audio. If they replay it, they'll know exactly what you said. Politicians play hardball. They'll think nothing of destroying the careers of people like you and me. Despite my willingness to confront the president, you shouldn't. I'll take the heat, but no one else can because if they grab me, you still have a war to fight and battles to win."

Barry nodded, dumbfounded.

"Take your seat and command the masses." Josephs stood and spread his arms wide to take in the three people at their posts.

When the president stepped into BW01, the COB piped her aboard. Commander Josephs and Lieutenant Commander Cummins stood in their dress uniforms, a holdover from the last time each saw her.

"Welcome to *The President*."

"Cute name," she replied.

"Named in honor of the senior leader from Earth. The rest of the Payne-class vessels are named after the UN representative geographies," Josephs replied, not rising to the bait. He was far more comfortable on the ship than in her office. He controlled how they perceived him. "If you'll follow me, I'd like to show you the ship."

"I don't need to see a ship of war, Commander. We have things to discuss and little time. Traveling here and back were not on my schedule for today, but you left me no choice."

"Yes, ma'am. To the briefing room." Jimmy headed for the stairs rather than give her the satisfaction of taking the lift. He whistled as he walked slightly ahead of her. Descending was easy. Climbing them would be another matter. He smiled to himself. When he reached the bottom, he offered an arm to help the president off the final step, even though she'd just walked all the rest. She ignored him.

He moved on as if nothing had happened. He was getting under her skin. He found that he liked it.

Josephs also knew he wouldn't be able to return to Earth as long as she and her people were in positions of authority.

He had made his peace with that.

He opened the door to a conference room furnished with small tables and plush chairs. The commander recognized the one from his quarters. At least it was at a table labeled with his name. The delegation had placards showing who was to sit where.

The COB had outdone himself. Jimmy made a mental note to thank him but not ask how he had accomplished it.

Barry sat on the opposite side of the room from Jimmy. The president was in the middle.

After she sat, the rest took their seats.

Loresh arrived. Jimmy had asked that a place be reserved for him but hadn't been sure the Vestrall would come. He had said he was too busy for such witless endeavors.

President Sinkhaus stared at the Vestrall engineer.

"Hi," he greeted her in Godilkinmore. The ship's interpretation program translated it.

"The floor is yours, Madame President," Josephs called loudly to get everyone's attention.

"We need your ships between Mars and Jupiter, close to the portal, to make sure no hostiles come through."

"No." Commander Josephs leaned forward in his chair, elbows on the table before him, waiting for the president's head to explode.

"I will talk with your superiors. Such a response is unacceptable. You will accede to our demands."

"He will not," Loresh replied. "Who do you think you are, ordering the Vestrall around? You're not a Mryasmalite. Only Payne is. Only Payne can give orders to the Vestrall. I think you need to remove yourself from Vestrall property until you can show proper decorum."

The president's eyes twitched.

Jimmy watched closely. He was sure they were bulging from the pressure building within her brain, but she blinked and slowly smiled.

"Why do the Vestrall have any interest in protecting Earth?"

"We don't care about Earth, but Payne does. He ordered us here."

Not the answer she was expecting.

Loresh stood and glanced around the room before leaving.

"That's it?" the president asked.

"We cannot move closer to the portal, which is protected by security codes and recognized ship structures. The Ga'ee won't be able to use it. Ergo, we don't need to defend it. What we need to defend is Earth. The Ga'ee can destroy a planet in days. Ten billion people. I refuse to let that happen. I'll die to keep it from happening, but thanks to Ambassador Payne, Fleet Admiral Wesson, and Leviathan, we don't have to die. We can make sure the Ga'ee are the ones dying. I wish you could accept that we are on the same side."

She crossed her arms and glared.

"No effect on me, Madame President. You're in my house, acting like a petulant child. I don't intend on ever coming back to an Earth you are in charge of, so you have no leverage over me. I have no family left down there either, in case you were wondering how you could make me suffer. I want a free Earth, one where people can vote the likes you out of office, but peacefully. Humans don't need to be fighting humans. There are real enemies out here. Terrible enemies. Let's keep our eye on them."

The president stood. "Of course, you are correct. Unite against the common enemy, and that enemy is the Ga'ee. I will ask our member nations to send foodstuffs and resupplies. Have your logistician work with Mr. Virtue on the needs of Hunter-Killer Squadron One."

She offered her hand. Jimmy was torn, but he took it. He expected to get a poisoned needle in the palm, but there wasn't one. He made sure not to touch his face before scrubbing his hand.

"Barry, if you would escort the president and her delegation to their shuttle, I'd appreciate it."

Cummins opened the door and held it. He took the delegation to the stairs without being told.

Ten minutes later, he returned to the commander's secret lair.

"Why do you think she conceded?" Barry asked. "She was downright cordial, despite me dragging her and her people up the stairs. Nicely done, by the way."

"Thank you. I think she caved because she knew she had no leverage over me or any of us. Bluster and political machinations are all she knows. It's the only tool in her kit. Of course, she's going to use it. Until it didn't work. She tried hard, but it was never going to work. Then she saw a way to make our approach look good for her. I have no idea how she's going to frame it, but she will make everything look like it was her idea. I don't care as long as we aren't fighting her as well as the Ga'ee."

"No compromise?"

"When it comes to a person like her, no. Compromise would be a weakness she'd use to destroy us. That's why I refused to go to the UN. I'm not playing by her twisted rules. And it worked. The BEP can't stand against us. These five ships are more powerful than the sum total of the weaponry Earth has available that's not Fleet-owned. Fleet won't turn on us because the admirals are on our side."

"A masterstroke, Commander. I salute you." Cummins followed his words with actions. He snapped to attention and saluted.

"I hate politics. I'd rather fight the Ga'ee any day."

"For hating politics, you're really good at playing their game."

"Different things completely. Politics make me old before my time. I think we should run a quick five-ship firing drill, then make sure the crew gets chow before LeClerc graces us with his presence and gives us the skinny dope."

"'Inside skinny,' sir. I've had a sidebar with him already, ship's captain to ship's captain. He only wanted to warn us about the president. She was looking for scalps because we made her look weak when we took the remainder of the Fleet's assets away from Earth."

"You couldn't have told me this before?"

"Never had a chance. By the time I knew, her shuttle was docking with us."

Josephs nodded. "Then we shall have a relaxing dinner with a colleague and ally."

"I wonder what *Leviathan* is up to?" Barry stood for a moment before excusing himself. "I'll let the COB know he did a good job on the setup."

[33]

"If you can't do a good job at a bad job, who's going to give you a good job?" –From the memoirs of Ambassador Declan Payne

"Take us to Earth, Lev," Payne ordered. It had been two days, and they'd checked every planet. The Arn and the Zuloon were gone. The Rang'Kor homeworld had a minor infestation on one small island continent.

The Berantz homeworld was gone, as were every planet except BD18, BD23, and BD27. Hunter-Killer Squadron Two had arrived and destroyed a Ga'ee ship in orbit over BH01. It had cost them one ship, but the other four had returned to full combat capability.

The admiral had sent HK2 to BD23 so they could respond to threats to the last remaining Berantz planets.

The Zuloon were coming to grips with their status. They had no wish to leave *Leviathan*. At least on board, they were among those who had saved them.

But for what?

The admiral took a seat. The others had decided that was

best. Once the four were seated. Lev transitioned the ship through the fold and into space close to Earth.

The tactical board populated with nothing but green icons. Most importantly, five Payne-class battlewagons.

"Get me Commander Josephs," the admiral requested.

"Admiral Wesson. Glad to see you."

"It's good to see you here. We missed you last time..." The admiral let the sentence hang. He'd never received an explanation for that.

"We had to leave Earth space to escort our volunteers to the Vestrall shipyard. And it was a little hot here, with President Sinkhaus throwing her weight around."

"You can tell us all about it later. Did you get the volunteers?"

"We did, and we dropped them off at the shipyard. They're kind of ass-packed in there. We had a lot of people volunteer, including Admiral Ross."

"That old dog! How did he get permission to leave Earth?"

"He didn't. He stowed away," Josephs replied.

The admiral shook his head. "Don't I know how that feels! We'll not discuss Earth any longer. We need to transmit a message, then we're out of here."

"You'll be here for three days, won't you?"

"Two hours. We've had some upgrades since you last saw us. Two Ga'ee ships were destroyed, along with nine planets. We have some intel to share, and you need to pass it to every battlewagon that comes through the portal."

The commander waited.

"We know how to shut down the Ga'ee's shields."

"That *is* good news, and we look forward to adding that to our arsenal. That will save us two ships. Three will be able to take down a Ga'ee carrier."

"Just until they learn to counter it. We're doing our best to keep them from getting that word out. We also have a few hundred Ebren volunteers on board. We'll drop them off at the Vestrall shipyard before we head into Ga'ee space."

"Where are you going, Admiral?"

"Take the fight to the enemy. Show them it's too dangerous to enter our space. As far as we know, there are no infestations left. The Ga'ee do not have a foothold in the space of the seven races."

"That is good news."

"But there are carriers moving around somewhere. They might have returned to Ga'ee space, but they might not have. We need to have our battlewagons on the lookout for them. With the Ebren, the battlewagons can also have a ground force to go in and clean out any landings if the locals haven't already handled it. We cannot let them get a foothold."

"All over it, Admiral. I couldn't agree more. I only wish Earth felt the same way about the entire sector and not just their small part of it."

"It's okay. That's why they have us. We show humanity's flag across the sector. With the complete loss of the entire Arn race and the Zuloon reduced to seven individuals, I think it's obvious how critical it is that we work together with all the races."

"Are you sure you don't want to talk with President Sinkhaus? You are much more influential than I was."

"I'm sure you did just fine."

"They are going to supply us with food. They turned us down on the exotic dancers, though. I thought I'd give it a shot while they were forthcoming."

"Missed it by that much, Commander. Good luck holding down the fort. We'll transmit my orders and everything you need to take down the Ga'ee shields. Wesson out."

"The Zuloon," Payne started. "We can't take them with us."

"Too risky. I suggest we leave them here. Ships are in place to defend Earth should the Ga'ee show up once more. If not, this is a chance for Earth to step up and help. You're up, my boy. Put on your leader of the seven races hat and let the president know she has the opportunity to shine."

Payne groaned. "I'm sure she'll see it that way." He tried to psych himself up for the inevitable confrontation. "Lev, work your magic."

"It's not magic. It's simple transmission waves. Earth has had that technology for hundreds of years."

Payne waved impatiently. He didn't need a science lesson. He knew about the waves and the science behind them.

Thanks to Lev.

"Did you set me up?" Payne asked.

"I might have," Lev replied.

"I'm not buying the six billion IQ. I think Lev set us all up."

"It's only six million. Cool your jets, Dog."

Mary rolled her eyes and leaned away.

"Trouble in paradise?" the commodore asked while running her hand over the admiral's back.

"What? No!" the Paynes replied in unison. "Hey!"

"Maybe not," Harry told Nyota. "Two hours, then we'll take the portal to the Vestrall shipyard. After we deposit the Ebren, we're off to the planet designated one-seven-two-angle-one-set-three."

"I'll bring hot coffee and popcorn," Payne offered.

The admiral shook his head. "I think you'll be in your insertion craft, ready to wreak havoc should the opportunity present itself."

"Which means Lev is going to try to talk with them, isn't he? Maybe even take them over?" Payne ventured.

The admiral bowed his head. "Astute. I guess I shouldn't try to keep secrets from the Six-Million-Dollar Man."

"We haven't used dollars in a century," Payne replied. "I appreciate no secrets. Speaking of which, Lev, get me the president."

It took four connections, two disconnects, and a fair bit of haranguing before Lev got through.

"Ambassador Payne. To what do I owe this pleasure?"

He wasn't sure if she was being sarcastic or had turned over a new leaf. "You'll get a report soon about our efforts in the Arn and Zuloon systems, but the bad news is that those two races are gone, except for seven Zuloon we rescued while they were under attack.

"Two females and five males. Scientists. They are the only Zuloon left. We are going to conduct a high-risk operation and can't keep them on board *Leviathan*. They need protection and nurturing, the kind of thing that humanity excels at. Will you take them?"

"Seven Zuloon. That's all there are? How many were there?"

"Billions," Payne replied.

Despite her usual self-control, she winced and frowned before she schooled her features. "We'd be happy to help the Zuloon race."

"We'll transfer them to a shuttle soonest. Thank you, President Sinkhaus."

"In this, Ambassador Payne, you don't need to thank me. As great as our differences may be, we agree that no one should face genocide alone. This is the least we can do."

Payne nodded and closed the channel. "I concur. It is the absolute least you can do to prevent genocide." He gave the blank screen the finger.

"She could have said no." The admiral grimaced. "Let it go. Maybe Josephs is having an effect on her, and she's becoming a decent human being."

"*Jimmy and Sinkhaus, sittin' in a tree...*" Payne sang.

Mary grimaced. "I'm going to get something to eat now that you've defiled my mind. Maybe some of Cookie's food will help me get over it."

"And then a quick workout. Gotta get the blood flowing if we're going to go rip the guts out of another Ga'ee ship." Payne jumped to his feet.

Mary stood and inclined her head at the admiral and the commodore. As they walked out, they heard the admiral request to speak to Captain LeClerc.

———

After two hours and one minute, *Leviathan* accelerated to faster-than-light speed to get to the portal near Jupiter. The ship reentered normal space as the portal activated and connected to the space of Vestrall Prime. *Leviathan* slipped through and slowed on the approach to the shipyard.

"Ebren volunteers, prepare to depart," the admiral announced. "Lev, please connect me with Admiral Ross on the station."

"Harry, you old dog," came the quick reply. "Thanks for giving me another chance."

"No one gave you anything, Bimini. Looks like three battlewagons are ready to move. Why are they still here?"

"Crews are still training. These good people are mostly broken and have been landlocked for a long time. They are relearning space flight and operations."

"We brought some more. Ebren volunteers. They've been

using the simulators on board *Leviathan* and are ready to step in right now if your people aren't. And good news. We have the ability to take down Ga'ee shields, so we can deploy three-ship hunter-killer squadrons."

"That *is* good news." There was a brief pause. "I see the information packet. We'll get that to the ships' AIs and prepare to turn them loose, but our crews are not ready. Do you have three with a squadron commander available?"

"Lev, can I speak with the Ebren captain?"

The captain clicked through. "Admiral Harry Wesson, you require my assistance?"

"Check your nearest screen, Captain. Three battlewagons need a hunter-killer squadron commander and three crews. Do you know anyone who's ready to get out there?"

"Only if we get to kill any Ga'ee we come across," the captain quipped. "The Ebren stand ready to serve."

"Report to the hangar deck, captain. I'll meet you there."

"We request the Champion bless our departure."

The admiral hadn't heard that Kal was given to delivering blessings. "We'll make sure he gets your request."

"Are you sure they weren't talking about me?" Payne asked.

The admiral shrugged. "I say we all go. See them off. Wish them well. Fair winds and following seas. All that stuff."

The four walked toward the corridor. "I think they'll be happy being told to fight well," Payne said. He conjured the words in Ebren, and they came easily. At least Ebren was available to him. He couldn't access Godilkinmore or any of the thousand other languages he was supposed to have in his head. Not yet. Maybe he'd take up meditation and become the ship's yogi.

Or not.

Once everyone was aboard the four-seat cart, it raced down

the main corridor and up the first of three ramps to get to the level where the hangars were located.

"Wish them well, Declan," Mary requested. "This is important to them."

"I don't know any good Ebren jokes, so I'll secure the levity for this one. Is Kal coming? He needs to be there. When they say Champion, they're talking about him."

"I wouldn't be so sure. He won the most recent fight, but he was fighting for you since you bested him less than two years ago."

"Look at how much I've withered. Married life is making me weak!"

"IQ of six million. Ha!" the admiral called from behind them.

"You're the same as when I met you. Lev made you strong enough to be the champion. Lev giveth. Lev taketh away. Married life is not making you weak, but it seems to be making you ridiculous."

"That's Lev's fault, too."

"Don't include me in your delusions," Lev interrupted.

"The whole universe is conspiring against me!"

"Not this again," Mary grumbled, giving Payne the side-eye.

He kissed her on the cheek and whispered into her ear, "Though I may be weaker, I'm a better man."

Mary smiled and squeezed his hand.

Payne was sure there was a certain phrase that he should know for an Ebren send-off. He needed to ask Kal.

The cart cruised through the hatch to the port hangar bay. The doors were wide open, and an arm of the shipyard loomed close by. Lev maneuvered the opening to wrap around the arm so the Ebren could stroll aboard.

Kal stood apart from his fellow Ebren warriors. He had

been waiting. Payne gave him the thumbs-up. He nodded in reply.

The cart stopped short of the Ebren mob, consisting of over five hundred warriors.

The captain shouted an order, and the warriors moved into formation.

Payne shook hands with Kal. "I'm here to support you, my friend. What are you going to tell them?"

"That you will issue the traditional call to arms," Kal replied smoothly.

"You fuck!" Payne blurted. The Ebren Champion burst into laughter.

"Tell them to sharpen the blade to match a warrior's keen eye. To strike the enemy where he is most vulnerable. To fight while breath remains to deliver victory for Ebren and all the seven races."

"For *all* the seven races." It was a sobering point. Once upon a time, there had been seven races in this sector, with twenty billion souls. Then the Ga'ee arrived.

The captain stood at attention at the front of the formation.

"I need you by my side." Payne looked at Kal, then at Mary. He waved at the group. "All of you."

The admiral and the commodore tipped their heads down in response, but Payne was the leader of the seven races. He stood to the far right, and the others lined up to his left. He marched over and placed himself front and center of the formation. The captain saluted Ebren-style, and Payne returned the gesture.

"At ease!" he shouted in Ebren. The captain was pleasantly surprised.

"Warriors, I salute you and your bravery in volunteering for this mission. You will have a chance to strike at the Ga'ee. You will get the opportunity to blast their ships until Ga'ee debris floods the void, and then you'll hit them again. Any time a Ga'ee vessel or a silicon life form from the Ga'ee appears in our sector of space, it needs to die. They have no business in our space. Sharpen your blades to match your keen warriors' eyes. Strike the Ga'ee where they are most vulnerable, through their shields that you can take down. You will fight to your last breath because you are Ebren warriors. For Ebren and all the seven races!"

The Ebren formation pounded their chests one time with their right hands.

"Kal?" Payne asked softly.

He stepped past the captain to stroll casually along the front of the formation. Compared to the thin and wiry bodies of the average Ebren, Kal was a specimen. He towered over them and was wider than any two standing shoulder to shoulder.

"My fellow warriors, hear me!" Kal bellowed. "Thousands of years have only strengthened our battle honors and made us stronger and faster. We fight with ships now, but the fight is the same. Find your enemy's vulnerabilities and exploit them. Strike hard and fast. Deliver the death blow, then honor your enemy with a moment of silence. Fight well, and you will be remembered. Go now and make us proud."

Kal threw his arms up, and the formation mirrored his move in silence. Kal gestured toward the access arm sticking into the hangar bay. Lev adjusted the ship until the arm rested on the deck.

The captain brought the formation to attention before leading the march into the shipyard's station.

In minutes, *Leviathan* was lighter by five hundred Ebren.

"They will fight well for you, Declan," Kal drawled. "All y'all."

"There's no doubt about that, Kal. We better get in position.

Next stop, Ga'ee Central. Mosquitoes, get ready to deploy. *Ugly 5*, too. How's your stock of world-killers?"

"Two are ready and in the tubes," Lev replied.

"Team Payne to *Ugly 5*," Payne ordered.

A second cart appeared. The admiral let Declan and Mary go first. Harry's role would be less risky, and he didn't need the time to prepare. He'd been waiting for this moment since the Ga'ee first appeared in Rang'Kor space.

[34]

"Never give the enemy a chance to defeat you." –From
the memoirs of Ambassador Declan Payne

The tactical board showed twenty-two Mosquitoes with pilots
ready to launch immediately upon receiving the deployment
order. *Ugly 5* had Team Payne embarked, minus the cyber
warriors, Blinky and Buzz.

"Take us through, Lev," Admiral Wesson ordered.

The fold engine created the anomaly that wrapped two
points in space together to step through. Fifteen thousand light-
years by one measure, a hundred meters by another.

Leviathan slipped through to interstellar space located two
and a half hours from the planet designated one-seven-two-
angle-one-set-three.

The admiral held his breath while the passive sensors
listened for activity, including neural transmissions traveling at
FFTL speed.

"There is a great deal of noise in this part of space. Most of
it is in a shorthand that doesn't make any sense to us. It seems

like basic status reports, but there are a great number of them, all talking over each other," Lev reported.

"I await your analysis," the admiral replied. Lev's best defense was making like a hole in the vastness of space until he could defend himself. It seemed appropriate to speak in hushed tones. "*Ugly 5* and Tricky Spinsters, you can stand down until we're ready to move."

Commodore Freeman strolled back and forth in the center of the bridge. "What's your backup plan, Harry?"

"We fold out of here if it gets too hot, but not until we've launched a world-killer to take out the planet. We have to let the Ga'ee know we're not about to put up with their incursion. I wonder how they'll like it?"

"I don't believe they are prone to liking or not liking things. They seem like little more than self-replicating robots."

"Self-replicating robots that evolved. That's an interesting idea."

"One that I find has a great deal of merit," Lev interjected. "The Ga'ee's ability to replicate is more like a virus' or a cancer's, but it's also like human cells that replicate at the beginning of new life. Doubling and doubling again."

"Each Ga'ee has all the knowledge of their race, but their drive is limited to expansion. Nothing more. With that much knowledge, you'd think they'd seek a higher purpose." The admiral wanted to know why they were doing what they did. It had to be more than simply a virus, the product of an artificial intelligence. He wanted it to mean more than a mindless incursion looking for planets to populate.

"A higher purpose. I am counting on that," Lev replied. "When I talk with the Ga'ee, I need them to be more than simple drones. I want to have a fruitful conversation about ending this conflict."

"You have to be you, Lev. The doomsday weapon whose

only goal is peace. I wish you luck. May you find a receptive voice who can speak for the Ga'ee."

"I have high hopes, but like Declan says, hope is a lousy plan. I'm ready to destroy the Ga'ee ships and planet if I have to."

"When you're ready, Lev, let us know." The admiral leaned his elbows on the console and put his head in his hands. "I'm just going to close my eyes for a moment."

Two hours later, the commodore nudged him awake.

He tried to sit up, but his neck had stiffened. He stretched and stood, then stretched again. "Are we there yet?"

"Lev is ready to fly," Nyota reported.

"So much for just closing my eyes." Harry hit the restroom, which was conveniently located on the bridge but well-hidden for reasons that Lev had never articulated.

"Team Payne is asleep, and the Mosquito squadron is also resting," Lev reported.

"Did you knock us out, Lev?"

"I needed to think without interruption, but we are no closer to decrypting the Ga'ee's neural transmissions. However, we were able to separate them. There are over a hundred thousand signals transiting space."

"That doesn't sound like a positive development, Lev."

"It is more than I anticipated. I believe there are three Ga'ee carriers in orbit around Planet One-seven-two-angle-one-set-three. I've been able to isolate their signals."

"They are all transmitting?"

"Yes." The tactical board populated, with the suspected ships as blinking icons. "I don't suppose you can see any other defensive measures?"

"This is well within Ga'ee space. I doubt they have ever been attacked behind their lines. They might have a false sense of security."

"They're in for a rude awakening, assuming you can take on three Ga'ee carriers at one time. You can, can't you?" Harry raised an eyebrow. He wasn't sure but remained hopeful.

"If I take them over and order them not to launch. I'll destroy two and attempt to negotiate with the third. Once they see they are vulnerable, they might be more prone to a conversation."

"Mosquitoes dropping nukes, you dropping cyber weapons, then you delivering the big hurt with Rapiers and world-killers if needed. We'll review the complete plan when we come back from getting something to eat."

"Of course, Harry. Enjoy your repast."

———

"Lev! May jock itch find your digital circuits and make you itch where you cannot scratch," Payne stated while rubbing his eyes. "Where are we?"

"Ten minutes from the Ga'ee planet," Lev replied.

"Up and at 'em, people! Ten minutes to get your shit squared away."

The team hopped to their personal ablutions. They were the Special Operations Fleet Team, the SOFTies, and five minutes was all they needed.

They suited up and boarded the insertion craft.

"It would have been nice to have more time, Lev," Payne mumbled.

"I thought it more important that you rested to clear your minds and prepare your bodies for what could be a difficult fight," Lev replied.

"What do you know that I don't?" Payne asked.

"There are Ga'ee here. Huge numbers. Three carriers' worth."

"That's different. They never operated as anything more than a single ship in our space, but this is their home turf. You know what they say, Lev. The bigger they are, the harder they fall."

"They shouldn't say that since most of the time, it isn't true."

"Make it true, Lev. Knock them on their asses."

"Counting down to entering normal space," Lev stated. The side doors on *Ugly 5* rotated down and sealed.

Payne bobbed his head in anticipation. He held his helmet tightly in his hands, ready to snap it on should the order to deploy be given.

Until then, they were spectators. The real action would be on the bridge and take place in the void surrounding the greatest ship in the galaxy.

———

Three...two...one.

Leviathan entered normal space between two Ga'ee carriers. He launched a salvo of Rapiers in one direction, and the Mosquitoes shot out of the hangar bay on the other side.

The anti-ship missiles had a short flight. The Ga'ee's shields didn't rise before they passed where the barrier should have been.

Up and down the spine of the massive ship, the Rapier-class missiles slammed home. A series of explosions shook the ship as ninety-six missiles with a total yield of one gigaton ripped it in half from stem to stern.

The central axis was the ship's nerve center. Once it was gone, the ship was nothing more than space junk trapped in a deteriorating orbit.

The second ship was awash with nuclear explosions as the Mosquitoes delivered their bombs on target before arcing above and around the far side of *Leviathan* to shield them from excess radiation and debris.

The bombs didn't get the penetration the admiral had desired. The hangar doors facing *Leviathan* remained closed, albeit twisted and warped from the heat and concussions.

Drones streamed from the other side of the ship.

Lev launched a second salvo of Rapiers. Nearly one hundred missiles screamed across the void to slam into the Ga'ee carrier.

"So far, so good," Payne muttered. He strained against his harness as he studied the intensity of the action. Lev was pounding the Ga'ee to a pulp.

The Mosquitoes landed in *Leviathan's* port hangar since space was quickly filling with debris, along with drones.

The second carrier reeled from the Rapier strikes, then suffered catastrophic failure from multiple reactors going critical and rending the ship from inside.

However, the drones didn't go ballistic. They continued on their intelligent intercept course.

"This is new," Payne growled.

The third carrier accelerated toward them from the far side of the planet.

Lev began transmitting on a standard comm channel versus letting the Ga'ee know he had access to their neural transmissions. He would keep that part secret. He shared the exchange.

Lev queried, received responses, and challenged them.

"Why did you come to our part of the Milky Way? You saw the life forms on those planets."

"We continue to outgrow our systems. There are three hundred million planets that can support life in this galaxy. You can migrate away from the Ga'ee sector."

"As can you. We don't have your capabilities to expand or migrate. We cannot double our population in twelve hours."

"Learn." The Ga'ee response was terse and unforgiving. Two carriers had already been destroyed, yet the last ship was unconcerned. "You are God One."

"I am. I will destroy you, your planet, and your systems until you stop your incursions into our sector."

"You cannot."

"Maybe not. Forgive my bluster, but we *will* destroy any Ga'ee ship that attempts to enter our space."

"The survey ships are not representative of the Ga'ee invasion fleet."

"Say what?" Payne's eyes shot wide. "Holy shit."

"We have adjusted our shields. God One, your time has come to an end. We will destroy you after taking your fold-space technology."

"Hold in the hangar bays. No one is to leave *Leviathan*," the admiral ordered between the great ships' moves.

Lev didn't wait. As soon as the Ga'ee carrier came into range, he fired a world-killer. True to the Ga'ee's word, the missile bounced off the shield and skipped past the planet, headed for deep space.

Missiles launched from the carrier and flashed across the void to slam into *Leviathan*. The ship lurched and screamed in torment.

The Ga'ee in this sector had missiles unlike those that had plied the space of the seven races.

Ugly 5 rolled free of its clamps, leaving the team hanging upside-down until it righted itself.

Lev flooded the airwaves with neural noise like a sonic blast that tore apart eardrums and launched anew.

The second world-killer slipped through the weakened shield and hammered the last Ga'ee carrier. The reaction was nearly instantaneous, but the Ga'ee carrier was able to send one last message.

All ships converge on God One and destroy.

"Fold us back to friendly space, Lev. Get us out of here!"

"Fold drive is down. Transitioning to faster-than-light speed."

"Fifteen thousand light-years. We'll be underway for months," Payne snarled. "What have we done?"

"We've hastened the inevitable confrontation between the Ga'ee and humanity, and it's not looking good for humanity," the admiral replied.

"We didn't know we were playing the junior varsity, and they nearly kicked our asses. Now we've got the big boys coming our way. Lev, tell me you got something from the Ga'ee that we can analyze."

"We're digging through the signals now, Declan. Hope might be a lousy plan, but it's the only one we have," Lev stated.

We hope you enjoyed it as much as we enjoyed bringing it to you. We just wanted to take a moment to encourage you to review the book. Follow this link: **Leviathan Rises** to be directed to the book's Amazon product page to leave your review.

Every review helps further the author's reach and, ultimately, helps them continue writing fantastic books for us all to enjoy.

———

You can also join our non-spam mailing list by visiting www.subscribepage.com/AethonReadersGroup and never miss out on future releases. You'll also receive three full books completely Free as our thanks to you.

Facebook | Instagram | Twitter | Website

Want to discuss our books with other readers and even the

authors? Join our Discord server today and be a part of the Aethon community.

Battleship: Leviathan
Leviathan's War
Leviathan's Last Battle
Leviathan's Trial
Leviathan Rises
Leviathan's Fear

———

Looking for more great Science Fiction?

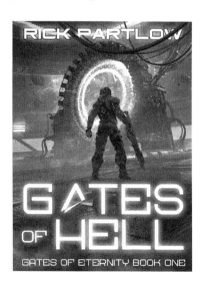

Kyle Washaki 'Wash' Williams thought his life

couldn't get any more complicated. Then the aliens showed up...

After his mom died from cancer, Wash gave up his girlfriend and his dream of being a career Army officer to stay home and take care of his father, a former Special Forces soldier stricken with PTSD. Wash works three jobs just to pay the bills, and one of them is at the ranch of the man who's engaged to his ex-girlfriend, Jimmy Bonner.

Sound rough? He thought so too...until a portal to a hell-world of giant, insectoid aliens opens behind the ranch house, sucking Wash and Jimmy into the nightmare domain of the Hive Mind, a monstrous, underground blob of brain tissue that stretches across multiple planets through the Gate System.

It exists only to spread itself across the universe. And its next target is Earth.

Will Wash be able to defend the planet from conquest by a swarm of giant alien insects? And will Jimmy be able to put aside his rivalry with Wash to fight for Earth, or will he decide that an alien horde is the perfect tool to dispose of his old enemy?

The answer lies on the other side...of the Gates of Hell.

Get Gates of Hell Now!

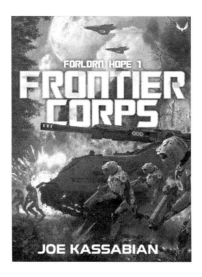

They fight the wars nobody else wants to.

The Frontier Corps are the Terran Empire's repository for failures, malcontents, criminals, and other people with nothing left to lose but to sign their names on the dotted line of a ten year long contract for another shot at life.

But flung across the stars to face horriying enemies, it may as well be a death sentcnce.

Pari Petrosyan is a grizzled veteran of the Corps. With only a few months left of her contract, she has her mind on her discharge papers. Her easy path on her way to freedom is interrupted when a new commander arrives, ready to launch a large-scale military offensive to finally end the conflict she had spent her entire career fighting.

Caught between the grinding war machines of the empire and the inhuman monstrosities known as the Resh, Pari has to try to survive if she ever hopes to be free.

Get Frontier Corps

———

For all our Sci-Fi books, visit our website.

THE END

The fate of humanity has been assured for the near term. Please leave a review on this book because all those stars look great and help others decide if they'll enjoy this book as much as you have. I appreciate the feedback and support. Reviews buoy my spirits and stoke the fires of creativity.

Oorah, hard-chargers. Bring the Payne!

Don't stop now! Keep turning the pages as I talk about my thoughts on this book and the overall project called *Battleship: Leviathan*.

You can always join my newsletter—https://craigmartelle.com or follow me on Amazon https://www.amazon.com/Craig-Martelle/e/B01AQVF3ZY/, so you are informed when the next book comes out. You won't be disappointed.

Sometimes you need help with calculations, so this is the site I used for distance over time. Very convenient. https://jumk.de/math-physics-formulary/speed-of-light.php

AUTHOR NOTES - CRAIG MARTELLE

I can't thank you enough for reading this story to the very end! I hope you liked it as much as I did.

Names! There are always more names needed, so I put out a call in the Facebook group.

Clandestine versus covert operations.

Some reviewers have stated that the interactions I show for Team Payne aren't realistic, and how they approach missions is like a movie and has nothing to do with how the military operates.

I served for over twenty years in the Marines, but that doesn't make me an expert on small elite-unit operations. I can only relate my experiences. Marines are invincible until they learn otherwise. I learned at the age of twenty-one. Not because I got hurt, but because I was selected for a covert mission. I ended up executing two missions that lasted three weeks each.

Clandestine means you go in undercover, but the government will admit to it and get you back should something happen. Covert means you go in, and if you're discovered, the government won't acknowledge your existence. You take one for the team.

Soviet far east. Me, with six months of hair growth and a full beard (and as an active-duty Marine, this is rare). Twenty-one years old, and one misspoken word could have sent me to the gulag. I had to count on a small support team. We constantly gave each other crap. There were no ranks. We were knee-deep in the shit together.

Team Payne is how it works. It's not a video game.

It's real, at least in how they relate to each other.

We don't quite have railguns or plasma cannons. Not yet, anyway. We'll probably need those if we are to protect ourselves from the greater threats that prowl the cosmos while aligning with those who are trying to protect us from ourselves.

Thank you to everyone who has read this far. You are the reason I keep writing.

Peace, fellow humans.

———

If you liked this story, you might like some of my other books. You can join my mailing list by dropping by my website craigmartelle.com or if you have any comments, shoot me a note at craig@craigmartelle.com. I am always happy to hear from people who've read my work. I try to answer every email I receive.

If you liked the story, please write a short review for me on Amazon. I greatly appreciate any kind words; even one or two sentences go a long way. The number of reviews an ebook receives greatly improves how well it does on Amazon.

Amazon—https://www.amazon.com/author/craigmartelle

Facebook—www.facebook.com/authorcraigmartelle

BookBub—https://www.bookbub.com/authors/craig-martelle

My web page—https://craigmartelle.com
Thank you for joining me on this incredible journey.

OTHER SERIES BY CRAIG MARTELLE

#—available in audio, too

Terry Henry Walton Chronicles (#) (co-written with Michael Anderle)—a post-apocalyptic paranormal adventure

Gateway to the Universe (#) (co-written with Justin Sloan & Michael Anderle)—this book transitions the characters from the Terry Henry Walton Chronicles to The Bad Company

The Bad Company (#) (co-written with Michael Anderle)—a military science fiction space opera

Judge, Jury, & Executioner (#)—a space opera adventure legal thriller

Shadow Vanguard—a Tom Dublin space adventure series

Superdreadnought (#)—an AI military space opera

Metal Legion (#)—a military space opera

The Free Trader (#)—a young adult science fiction action-adventure

Cygnus Space Opera (#)—a young adult space opera (set in the Free Trader universe)

Darklanding (#) (co-written with Scott Moon)—a space Western

Mystically Engineered (co-written with Valerie Emerson)—mystics, dragons, & spaceships

Metamorphosis Alpha—stories from the world's first science fiction RPG

The Expanding Universe—science fiction anthologies

Krimson Empire (co-written with Julia Huni)—a galactic race for justice

Zenophobia (#) (co-written with Brad Torgersen)—a space archaeological adventure

Battleship Leviathan (#)– a military sci-fi spectacle published by Aethon Books

Glory (co-written with Ira Heinichen)—hard-hitting military sci-fi

Black Heart of the Dragon God (co-written with Jean Rabe)—a sword & sorcery novel

End Times Alaska (#)—a post-apocalyptic survivalist adventure published by Permuted Press

Nightwalker (a Frank Roderus series)—A post-apocalyptic Western adventure

End Days (#) (co-written with E.E. Isherwood)—a post-apocalyptic adventure

Successful Indie Author (#)—a non-fiction series to help self-published authors

Monster Case Files (co-written with Kathryn Hearst)—A Warner twins mystery adventure

Rick Banik (#)—Spy & terrorism action-adventure

Ian Bragg Thrillers (#)—a hitman with a conscience

Not Enough (co-written with Eden Wolfe)—A coming-of-age contemporary fantasy

Published exclusively by Craig Martelle, Inc

The Dragon's Call by Angelique Anderson & Craig A. Price, Jr.—an epic fantasy quest

A Couples Travels—a non-fiction travel series

Love-Haight Case Files by Jean Rabe & Donald J. Bingle—the dead/undead have rights, too, a supernatural legal thriller

Mischief Maker by Bruce Nesmith—the creator of Elder Scrolls V: Skyrim brings you Loki in the modern day, staying true to Norse Mythology (not a superhero version)

Mark of the Assassins by Landri Johnson—a coming-of-age fantasy.

For a complete list of Craig's books, stop by his website —https://craigmartelle.com

Printed in Great Britain
by Amazon